PAUL SLAVONIK

Though I Fall

(Book II: Legacy Drive series)

DMG/UNITED

First edition

ISBN: 978-1-7330253-4-8

Editing by Tom Witcomb
Proofreading by Michael McConnell
Cover art by DMG United

This book was professionally typeset on Reedsy.
Find out more at reedsy.com

Foreword

Like many other great sports, motor racing brings people together. It is a sport that is passed down through the generations, and it forces those who pursue it to face their weaknesses in order to improve.

However, motor racing also has traits that are truly unique.

Unlike traditional stick and ball sports, racing doesn't just pit two teams against each other for a win. Rather, it throws in many teams that compete against one another in a heated battle where only one will achieve victory.

Added to this is the driver's need to risk serious injury and death to find speed and make passes. Crew members also risk getting hurt every time they step over the wall on pit lane as the cars speed by.

The best way I can describe how racing unites a team is that you are in the trenches together where the consequences are real. You're fighting the world around you for a common goal...*to WIN*.

During these battles, however, you soon find that you all become more than just a team.

You become a family.

I'd like to share with you a real story that very much resonates with Paul Slavonik's motorsports novel *Legacy Drive* and now its sequel, which you hold in your hands, *Though I Fall*.

Much like the Watson family, whom we were introduced to in the first book, I am part of a multigenerational racing family. If you're into racing, you might know my name—Jack Roush Jr., son of NASCAR team owner Jack Roush.

People often ask me what it was like growing up as the son of Jack Roush. On the one hand, I haven't known anything else, as I've been steeped in racing my whole life. It's strange to think about what it would have been like to *NOT* have grown up in a racing family.

On the other hand, I do understand and appreciate how truly lucky I am. Having grown up seeing my father's unstoppable spirit has been a great inspiration and model for me in achieving my own success—whether in racing, business, or other interests.

My Father's Story

Given my father's iconic status in racing, you might think that he was born into it or that it is was handed to him.

This is far from the case.

He came from humble beginnings where not only was his future in racing a longshot at best, but just succeeding on any level was far from guaranteed. It was only through a lifetime of hard work and a relentless will that he prevailed.

My father, Jack, was born in 1942 in the river town of Covington, Kentucky. He grew up just across the river, in Manchester, Ohio. In the first half of the twentieth century, Manchester was a thriving river shipping port town. However, this changed dramatically by the time my father arrived on the scene.

The growing trucking industry and the railway freight delivery system took away much of the town's business and its vitality by the middle of the twentieth century. Although my father's family was all right financially, many in the town were not.

Young Jack saw people struggle even just to feed themselves. Facing this harsh reality caused a fire to light inside him to work as hard as necessary to overcome hardship.

He still has this iron will to this day.

You might expect that my father got his entrepreneurial spirit and racing experience with the help and inspiration of *his* father, Charlie, but that was not the case.

It was his mother, Georgetta, who guided him in both.

She set him up to participate in the local soap box derby races. At the same time, she started multiple small businesses, including a local ice cream company, to help her struggling husband.

Due to the lack of affluence in the town, these family businesses never got traction. However, seeing her start them inspired my father to start a business of his own at just ten years of age.

He began mowing lawns for townspeople with his younger brother, Frank, to earn money. He was able to make this business viable financially by using old, discarded lawn mowers. He repaired several by taking parts from one old mower to fix another, thus returning one mower to service without incurring the cost of a new part.

If one were to say that he stuck the tired old engines together with chewing gum and baling wire, this would not be far from the truth.

One of his father's cousins owned an auto repair shop, where young Jack was allowed to borrow tools. It was also where he began to receive the sage advice he needed to make the necessary repairs. Due to his inherent curiosity as well as the new opportunities that were presented to him, this proved to be the beginning of a life-long passion for the internal combustion engine.

After he mastered the repair methods and techniques for keeping his lawn mowers running, he had an excellent idea.

Why don't I take one of the spare engines from my lawn mowers and build a go-kart that I can drive?

He was sure he could outrun anything that others might come up with, even though he wasn't really certain what a *go-kart* was. He had read about how fast these little machines could go, which spawned dreams in his head of challenging bicycle riders and unleashed pets.

He wasted no time figuring out a way to secure one of his spare lawn mower engines to an old soap box derby car. He immediately became the fastest kid in town. From that moment on, Jack never missed an opportunity to place one of his creations into competition.

In his high school years, he worked at a local new car dealership and a collision shop to gain experience with auto repair and servicing challenges. These both played a critical part in his background, both for his career in business as well as in his understanding of motor vehicles.

After high school, he went to Berea College in Kentucky. While there, he met and married my mother, Pauline. They had their first child—my older sister Susan—two days before his graduation in 1964.

Soon after, he moved his young family to Detroit—the Automotive Capital of the World—to seek his fame and fortune. His first job was at the Ford Motor Company as a Quality Control Engineer, and his first assignment there was at the Rouge Assembly Plant, where he participated in the initial launch of the Ford Mustang.

Very soon after arriving at Ford, he became acquainted with and joined a ten-member Ford employee drag racing club called The Fastbacks. It was through The Fastbacks' activities that Jack became acquainted with a Pro Stock drag racer named Wayne Gapp. The two shared an interest not only in racing but also in finding innovative ways to earn money from it.

The duo would ultimately form their own drag racing team, Gapp & Roush. They earned a number of prestigious drag racing titles in the early '70s, including three national championships.

In 1976, my dad split off from Gapp and started his own company, Jack Roush Performance Engineering. Although the name has since changed twice, this was the beginning of the same Roush company that lives on today.

While the company has been involved in developing the combustion engine for a myriad of racing applications, this has not been the company's primary purpose, which is to develop and produce engines for mainstream applications, well beyond those of racing.

Many don't know this about my father, but he was a driver himself at one time, and an excellent one at that. What he discovered, however, was that he could find other drivers that were good enough to win, given the potential built into his cars and engines. What he couldn't easily find, though, was a replacement for himself as an engineer and team leader.

Not long after the company was formed, my father made a big investment (given the size of the company at that time) in building an NHRA Pro Stock race car. The purpose of this was to demonstrate that Jack, by himself, could be just as competitive as he had been with Gapp involved.

He subsequently hired a respected and accomplished driver from an underfunded team to drive his new car at the 1977 NHRA Gatornationals event. He stood by and watched helplessly as it all went terribly wrong.

On the very first pass on the first day of time trials, the driver lost control and crashed the car, resulting in a total loss of the vehicle.

Jack later learned that the driver had taken some street drugs earlier that day and was likely still under their influence.

Disheartened, Jack gave up on the idea of running his own team for the time being. He instead focused on building and selling the best race engines available.

In 1984, the Ford Motor Company came to my father and encouraged him to form another team of his own. This time, however, it was not in drag racing; it was in road racing.

You might not be familiar with this part of our racing history, but it is one that we are very proud of. For the better part of two decades, my father built a legacy in road racing that is unmatched today, and includes:

- 10 victories at the prestigious 24 Hours of Daytona (we won each of the 10 times that we entered the event)
- 24 national championships
- 12 manufacturers championships
- 119 individual event titles
- Working with many highly acclaimed drivers, including Tommy Kendall, Scott Pruett, Carl Edwards, Wally Race, Willy T. Ribbs, Wally Dallenbach Jr., Mark Martin, Bill Elliott, Ricky Rudd, Kyle Petty, Dorsey Schroeder, as well as actor Paul Newman.

Due to my father's success in road racing, Ford later encouraged Jack to start a NASCAR team as well. He eventually did so in 1988 with Mark Martin.

The partnership with Mark yielded great success in the first seventeen years of our NASCAR program. Down through the years, many new drivers carried the Roush banner to victory. They include Matt Kenseth and Kurt Busch, both winning NASCAR Cup Championships. Also, Greg Biffle and Carl Edwards, along with Mark, are recognized as some of the greatest NASCAR drivers of all time, despite never winning a NASCAR Cup Championship.

The Roush driving ranks have included many other greats as well, including Ricky Stenhouse Jr., Ryan Newman, Bubba Wallace, Robby Gordon, and Trevor Bayne, to name just a few.

My father's total number of victories in professional racing events now exceeds 450, making his team one of the most successful of all time.

My Story

I was born in 1973. At the time, my father was heavily involved in drag racing, eventually winning championships in AHRA, NHRA, and IHRA Pro Stock. I have vague memories of being a toddler on a blanket with my mother next to the drag racing hauler and seeing the cars scream down the track.

In 1979, when I was just six years old, my father took on a new endeavor in racing, and a new driver.

This time it was in karting…

…and *I* was the driver.

For the next five years, my father was my crew chief. We won each of the five season championships that we participated in at our local track in Flat Rock, Michigan.

When I turned eleven in 1984, my father turned his focus towards the company's sportscar racing efforts. At this point, I backed off on my karting, at least for the time being.

During this time, however, I got to witness the amazing success that my father and his team achieved in road racing. I also went on to pursue other interests in technology, music, and business.

In college, I began getting back in local karting events and found that I still had it. I felt like I was hardwired to race, and I soon got the urge to get back in. After more karting, I got the itch to get into a full-sized car, this time in drag racing in the NMRA series.

In 2006, everything changed. Through a connection between Roush Performance and Dean Martin of KohR Motorsports, I was given the chance to hop in a sportscar and face some of the best racers in the world.

To me, this was simply impossible to turn down.

It was déjà vu. I felt like I'd been shot back in time to being that eleven-year-old kid fresh out of karting, as I was thrust into the road racing that my father competed in all those years ago.

The learning curve was incredibly steep, but I did find my own success in road racing as well. Currently, in professional sportscar racing, I have earned fourteen victories, thirty-seven podiums, and four pole positions.

The racing victory that has the most meaning to me personally took place in 2010. Competing in the IMSA GS class at Homestead Miami Speedway, I earned pole for the race.

Following qualifying, however, the tech inspectors didn't like the splitter on our car and bumped us to the back of the field for the beginning of the race.

Apparently, the splitter wasn't what made us so fast.

Within thirty minutes, I was able to claw my way up to the lead position, and my co-driver, Billy Johnson, was also able to capture the lead and bring it home in the top spot.

As it turns out, that victory marked the 400th professional racing win for Roush Racing. Through my entire racing career, my father has always looked out for me, despite also running multiple NASCAR programs.

Future Generations

Around the time that I began racing full-sized cars in road and drag racing events, I got married to my beautiful wife, Laura. We now have four children.

I have tried to expose them to racing without pressuring them into it. All of my children have experienced racing to some extent. Given the importance of racing in our family history, I feel that it's important to have given them a taste of it but not to force them to do it. Racing is a sport that you can get hurt in, and I don't believe that it's right to pressure anyone to get into the driver's seat.

It has to be *their* desire to do so.

My children all have their own unique talents and interests, which don't need to be in racing. They are all just as valid.

One of my children, JP, is very much into racing. He started karting even younger than I did, at the age of five. JP is now fourteen and is a very fast driver in his own right. He is now more experienced in racing than I was at fourteen, and he's hungry to keep going from here.

I feel quite confident that the Roush name will be in racing for many years to come.

My father also shared the tradition of racing with both of my sisters. My sister Tricia raced go-karts while I did growing up, and my sister Susan is an accomplished drag racer in the NMRA and NMCA series. Susan has now passed this on to her daughter, Josie, as well.

The Legacy Drive Saga

I have seen many examples of how racing is passed within families through the generations, just as it has in mine. From the outside, it's easy for racing to seem bigger than life, and in many ways, it is. In reality, though, racers find themselves fighting to overcome challenges just like everyone else.

While reading Paul Slavonik's *Legacy Drive*, I felt like I could have been reading one of the stories that I lived myself. From the action on the track, to the team, to personal life that surrounds racing as well.

Bill Watson's story in particular feels strangely familiar to me, given my own experience—in following in the footsteps of his legendary father, in having a son, Chad, with whom he shares a passion for motorsports, and in fighting adversity on multiple fronts to find success.

As for the action, I have never read a story or watched a film on racing that depicts racecraft in a way that is at this level of realism and excitement.

Now with the release of *Though I Fall*, it's my hope that the series will live on to be one of the great stories celebrating motorsports.

Sit back, relax, and enjoy this next installment of the *Legacy Drive* saga.

—Jack Roush Jr.

Acknowledgments

A special thank you to those who helped make this book possible. Whether it be through simple encouragement along the way, proofreading, technical guidance on racing lingo or just providing feedback, your words and actions helped to shape this story into what it is.

A massive thank you to my wife, Christina. Your love and support on a daily basis are what keeps me encouraged. Thank you for always dreaming with me.

To my racing buddies Daniel Johnson, Chris Coffey, Joey Atterbury and Douglas Vaughan. You guys always set me straight and were never afraid to share your opinion. I appreciate your honest feedback and your willingness to answer my seemingly endless questions.

A.J. Baime, thank you for your words that helped me to push forward. I took "write another one" quite literally.

To my Aunt Carolyn for your willingness (and eagerness!) to read my work and provide feedback.

To my developmental editor, Tom Witcomb. Thank you for your honest feedback, constructive criticism, your willingness to dive headfirst into this world with me and for taking the time to go through the various drafts. This story would not be what it is today without you.

To my copy editor, Michael McConnell. Thank you for your incredible help in putting the finishing touches on this story.

I would also like to thank all of my original readers who joined me on this journey when *Legacy Drive* first released back in May 2019. Your dedication to the story, your willingness to share it with others, the encouraging messages you sent me, the stories you shared about your own legacies… these are what kept me going in those early days when I wondered if I would continue writing or not.

And finally, I would like to dedicate this story to those of you who are in life's trenches. Through the struggles you face on a daily basis, the heartaches you continue to endure and the battles you fight, remember the words of our mutual friend, Bill Watson:

"Always keep fighting and never quit. Even when you fall down and even when the odds are stacked against you, fight to stand back up. Because you never know where you'll end up if you keep moving forward."

From my heart to yours, this novel is for you.

Prologue

I remember.

Each and every time I close my eyes, I remember the sights, the sounds and the horror of watching both of them die before my eyes.

Memories begin to sweep over me like a raging flood as my body trembles in the cold.

My mother, her body twisted and bent into an unnatural and terrifying figure. I'd never even had the chance to say goodbye.

My father, who'd hidden his own darkness from me and, with time, forgot my name and the names of everyone he'd ever loved. I sat by helplessly while he slowly faded away.

He was my champion.

My hero.

But just like everyone else, he was gone—existing as nothing more than a memory.

A cold chill shoots down my spine and sends shivers through my hands and into my fingers, which run over the smooth, cold steel of the gun.

In the years that followed my father's death, I learned that one thing is for certain: nothing is as it seems.

I've been to races, smiled for crowds, waved at strangers, shaken hands and even signed autographs. Everyone I meet seems to think that I'm living some high life because of my last name—my legacy. Inside, however, I feel as if I've been dead for years—a breathing body on the outside with a dead and rotting soul lying within. Now, these two worlds will meet upon the tip of a bullet.

Standing before them both, I slowly read their names over and over again, each time recalling a memory that began in my childhood but ended as a deadbeat failure of what is now a fallen legacy.

I slowly raise the gun and close my eyes as I feel a warm tear fall across my cheek. My lips begin to quiver. I adjust my stance for balance and let my walking cane fall to the ground beside me.

Pressing the muzzle of the gun to the side of my head, I impulsively flinch at the touch of it. Opening my eyes, I look upon their graves for the final time.

There is so much I could say but, in the end, it would mean nothing. I failed them in so many ways and simply ran out of things to say. These words will have to be enough as I whisper them into the cold and lonely dark.

"I'm so sorry."

I close my eyes and pull the trigger...

I

Part One

"Love what you do. Believe in your instincts. And you'd better be able to pick yourself up and brush yourself off every day. While life is not always fair, it is manageable. It is a matter of attitude and confidence."

—Mario Andretti

1

On This Day

I shifted my weight to the left, leaning into the turn as I rolled over the rumble strip and felt the series of small but thunderous vibrations surge up my spine.

Unwinding the steering wheel as I tracked out to the right side of the long straight, I checked my grip to ensure I wasn't wasting energy by clenching my hands tightly on the wheel. I took a deep breath as I crossed the line to start another lap at the Dallas Karting Complex located in Caddo Mills, Texas. I held a marginal lead as a train of six karts trailed directly behind me. Any mistake on my part would be costly.

Although I was driving a modified VLR kart that used hand controls for the gas and brake instead of pedals, the effect of having your ass two inches off the ground still amplified the sensation of racing at speeds of close to 65 mph. It was by no means a shifter kart, but I might as well have been a Formula 1 driver as I turned into the left-hand first corner.

My spine was essentially a giant shock absorber as I grabbed some of the inside curbing. I guess one of the benefits of having existing spinal damage from a previous car accident was that I could hardly feel a damn thing, and I'll take any advantage I could get.

I exited the corner and glanced over my left shoulder to see the train still behind me. Getting away from the mid-field drivers was one thing, but being able to drive away from the front runners who were all seemingly matched on power, skill and dedication was next to impossible.

Pascal Alexander's bright yellow helmet made him easy to spot—doubly so when he was riding on your back bumper like he was now.

I continued to lead the field single file through the various corners, but as the race was winding down, I could tell Pascal was getting antsy. I took another quick peek and noticed him beginning to go on the attack.

Pascal was no dummy. Unlike the rest of the field, full of people who thought they were Ayrton Senna incarnate and started battling the moment the race began, the leaders were content to settle in and—barring any mistake from the driver they were following—run away from the rest of the field. That way we could fight it out at the end of the race without any interference from the slower drivers. This also resulted in a good show for those in attendance, and we were all keen on that.

After negotiating a double-apex left-hander, I tracked out but swept back over to the left to prepare for the esses—a quick right-left turn section that only the brave took flat out.

Just before turn-in, Pascal showed his nose on my inside, no doubt an effort to throw me off. I ignored it and pressed on, taking the turn at full squeeze on my hand throttle, followed by another glance over my shoulder. I was doing a piss poor job of hiding the fact that I was beginning to stress out.

I led the field into the braking zone just in front of pit out. It was an ideal passing opportunity but also a risky one. I'd made double passes for position here several times due to low-percentage moves by one driver trying to dive-bomb another in front of me.

Again, Pascal was no dummy. He wasn't about to throw his own race away in a move that had a high probability of failure. He was nothing if not patient.

The 0.8-mile track went by quickly as we started another lap, traversing through the seventeen various turns. There had to be just a few laps left at that point.

I really wanted it to be over.

As the lead pack raced down the front straight, I glanced over my left shoulder again to see that Pascal had gotten a run out of the final corner. His momentum carried him up along my left side, and as we braked for the first corner and turned in to the left, I squeezed him as tightly as I could against the curbing on the left in an attempt to rob him of his momentum.

Despite my best efforts, we still came out side by side. However, the next right turn was favorable to me and hanging on the outside would put Pascal at risk of being passed by the kart in third. As I turned in, he lifted slightly off the gas and slotted back in directly behind me.

I was beginning to feel his aggression, or maybe it was my own anxiety. *Shut up. Press on.*

Pascal began tapping my back bumper every chance he could, no doubt trying to unnerve me.

As we approached the line, I saw the white flag waving.

Just one more lap.

The gloves came off as Pascal harnessed his European racing heritage and went on full attack.

Approaching the braking zone for the first corner, Pascal dived down the inside but out-braked himself. This resulted in backing up the field behind him but also caused me to have to run wide to avoid him. I could instantly hear and feel the loss of momentum in my kart.

In a moment of clarity, I noticed my hands were hurting. My grip on the wheel was tight and if I wasn't careful, I could compromise my hand control inputs. I took a short breath and looked over my shoulder to notice Pascal and friends were still directly behind me. But it was the final lap, and I was still leading.

I breathed, allowing myself to focus on what was in front instead of being distracted by what was behind.

I led them into the esses, and I noticed Pascal was now physically touching my bumper. He was pushing me ever so slightly, and I knew exactly why. Should he help me carry just a little more speed going into the approaching braking zone, I could compromise it and blow the lead.

I released the gas just a hair, which was followed by a heavy push from behind.

Message received, Pascal?

Entering the braking zone, I noticed the nose of his kart peeking towards my inside, right up to about my left rear tire. The corner was mine, but he may have decided to risk it, thinking I wouldn't be willing to turn in on him.

He would be wrong.

Just at turn-in, I noticed him back off at the last possible moment. Had I not gone on the attack, he would have been alongside me, but that wasn't the case.

I grabbed too much curbing at the next corner and gave my spine a flexibility exam as my kart bounced for a brief moment. The loss of momentum was immediate. Whatever ground Pascal had lost in his ill-fated attempt at a pass had just been given back to him on a golden platter.

I glanced over my shoulder to see that bright yellow helmet bearing down on me as I struggled to get my speed back up. I blocked the inside of the subsequent corners, but that wasn't enough. I was off my groove and was still trying to pick up my momentum. With only a few corners remaining, I made the right-hand sweeper, which was followed by two lefts and a slight dogleg left that spilled you out onto the front straight to the finish.

As I approached the final left before the dogleg, I saw Pascal swerve to the inside. He didn't have room for the pass, he was just trying to get me to turn my head the moment before turn-in—a ploy to get me to take my eyes away from my braking zone.

I was immediately taken back almost a decade. A bright yellow Chevrolet Camaro pulled a similar stunt on my dad at Road Atlanta during a Trans Am TA2 race. The maneuver had worked, and he never stopped kicking himself for it.

"Apexes and exits, apexes and exits."

His words echoed through my mind in that instant as I ignored Pascal's attempt at a distraction and made the corner.

The euphoria welled up inside of me even before I took the checkered flag.

As I crossed the line for the win, I suddenly felt the pressure lift as I screamed into my helmet.

Letting my hands drop off the wheel, I threw my arms into the air in victory as my head sank back.

One by one, my fellow competitors drove by giving me a thumbs up. Pascal took the cake, however. As he drove up alongside me, he reached over as far as he could and tried to shut my kart's engine off. I swatted his hand away and gave him the finger. Although he was wearing a full-face helmet, I could tell that he was laughing under there just as I was.

As we pulled into the pits, I found my spot and brought the kart to a stop. He was already there waiting for me, like always.

"Awesome job, Chad!" It was my grandad, his thick Australian accent unmistakable. "Way to hold them off! You drove smart and you kept your cool. I couldn't have done it better myself." He gave a smug grin as I removed my helmet.

"Thanks, Grandad."

I could've said something more but I didn't.

With a slight shake of his head, he chuckled as he took my helmet and set it aside.

"Up you go."

I extended my arms as he grabbed them and hoisted me up. I wrapped my right arm around his shoulders as he handed me my cane. Before I let go, I gave my legs a bit of a flex to make sure all of my pieces were still working. Once confident, I relaxed my grip on Grandad and adjusted my stance for balance.

"So... your first win..." He dabbed at his eyes and paused for a moment. "He'd be so proud of you, Chad. Just like I am."

There it was—the constant reminder of my past. It was like a shadow I could never escape from, no matter how fast I drove. Grandad looked past me over my shoulder.

"Looks like you've got company."

I quickly donned my sunglasses and turned around to see Pascal and Kate running towards me.

"I was just waiting for you two bozos to crash so I could take the win," said Kate as both she and Pascal stopped in front of me, her long blond hair flowing in the slight breeze.

"Yes, who would've thought," said Pascal in his heavy French accent. "A cripple, a Frenchman and a woman on the podium of a motor race in Texas. The world is changing, my friends."

If it had been anyone other than Pascal, I would've wacked them upside their head with my cane. But Pascal was my friend—born of rivalry but molded by mutual respect—and this wasn't the first time we'd traded banter.

"I could almost hear you screaming in French while we were battling," I joked. "You made me work for this one, buddy."

Pascal smiled, his tan face still glistening with sweat from the race.

"And what service would I have been had I made it easy for you, my very American friend? I needed to test your mettle. And maybe you did too. Plus, victory always tastes better when you have to fight hard for it."

I smiled.

"That's nice of you to say, mister *track record holder.*"

"Hey, my days of walking away from the field are over. You young kids are getting too fast for me."

* * *

The drive home to Austin was several hours. Given the company, though, the time would inevitably drag on forever.

Grandad had been fun to ride with when I was younger. Even more so after a race. He was always sharing stories about his racing days and he never seemed to run out of fresh ones.

And he always asked me questions. He'd wanted to know what I was thinking about before, during and after the race. Not to be critical, but more from a situational perspective.

"Your mind is your greatest ally," he would say to me. "But it can also be your greatest threat. You've got to have control over what you're thinking because what you're thinking ultimately controls you."

This was the Grandad I enjoyed; the one I could learn from and the one whose own wisdom and experience behind the wheel made my foray into racing a much smoother process than it could've been.

With my first win notched on my belt and the winner's trophy still in my hands, I sat in the passenger seat of the SUV in a contemplative mood. I looked down and smiled.

Of all the days to win.

I'd been racing karts for five years and, given that I was only a few months past my sixteenth birthday, my first win was something to be proud of.

Even so, I couldn't shake that feeling of hearing my dad's words in my head during the race. As I turned my attention to the scenery passing by on the other side of the window, my mind wandered to a place that now seemed like it was only yesterday...

We sat together in the nursing facility in Sydney, Australia. I had hated it there every time I'd ever been.

My dad lay in bed, staring blankly up at the television.

It was always cold in there. One of the many reasons I'd never liked going. Even as I sat next to his bed and we both watched the race that was on the TV, I couldn't help but realize just how much I'd wanted to leave.

His mind was nearly gone. He had trouble remembering the most basic things, like names and events. He would be confused and oftentimes scared when his friends would visit him—friends he confused as strangers he'd never seen before.

Conversations were nonexistent. The brain cancer had robbed him of his ability to remember things he'd heard only moments before. Something told me it was only a matter of time, but I guess I didn't want to believe it.

I hated seeing him like that, and I tried to get out of visiting him as often as I could. My speech had only returned to me about two years earlier, but I had few words to say in that place.

As we both sat and watched the race in silence, I often wondered if he even had any recollection as to what he was watching. I would look over to see him completely fixated on what was happening on the screen. He should be, given that it was the very race he had run in two years prior—the Bathurst 1000 at Mount Panorama Motor Racing Circuit.

The noise of the TV filled the screaming silence of that place. I couldn't take it any longer.

I turned my wheelchair towards the door and headed that way.

"That was one helluva race, Chad."

I turned suddenly to see my dad looking at me with a clarity and sound mind I hadn't seen in some time. I was completely taken by surprise.

"Dad?"

He exhaled and turned back towards the race, his eyes beginning to close ever so slightly.

"It's hard to remember having the energy to sit through a race like that," he said, noticeably weary.

I wheeled myself back and stopped alongside him. I still couldn't believe he was talking like that.

"You did so well, Dad," I said even as I tried to fight back tears.

He smiled at the comment as he closed his eyes and leaned his head back.

"Chad…"

I waited, my eyes fixated on his every move.

"I'm sorry it has to end this way. I did my best to make sure you have everything you need to succeed in life. The rest is up to you."

My words were gone as time seemed to stand still at that moment.

He took a series of deep breaths.

"I would've loved to have seen you race, Chad. Maybe one day."

I should've said something. I wished I'd told him I loved him and his life had served as an inspiration for me. I longed to tell him that he'd taught me how to live, even when life and circumstances weighed me down.

I wanted to tell him he was my hero.

As I sat there, however, I was speechless.

He reached over and took my hand as he smiled.

"How about you let your old man get some rest and we'll finish up the race tomorrow."

10

I put my other hand on top of his.

"Okay, Dad," I said, tears beginning to fall from my eyes.

He lifted his hand and placed it back on the bed as I slowly backed away.

He smiled again as he turned to look at me.

"See you tomorrow, Chad."

I didn't want to leave, but as he turned away and closed his eyes, I slowly wheeled myself towards the door. Before I could reach for the handle, however, I turned towards him again.

"I love you, Dad."

His eyes opened as he looked directly at me.

"I love you too, Chad."

"Chad..."

"Chad?"

I turned with a startle to find myself back in the passenger seat of the SUV with Grandad nudging my arm as he drove.

"We're here."

I turned back towards the window to see the all-too-familiar landscape.

We turned onto Legacy Drive, and the vehicle came to a stop moments later.

"Take as much time as you need," he said to me.

I nodded, reached for my cane and pulled the handle to open the door.

After I'd been sitting for an extended period of time, my first few steps were always a bit shaky but I soon found my footing. I carried my trophy in one hand and balanced my weight on the cane with the other, taking slow but gradual steps.

I counted rows as I walked even though I'd been here so many times that I no longer needed to. As I continued, my mind went back to my dream—a memory of the last time I saw my father alive.

See you tomorrow, Chad.

I sighed deeply.

Unfortunately, tomorrow never happened. Instead, on this very day six years ago, my father died.

I stopped in front of their graves. Both of my parents lay side by side in eternal rest.

Despite being here countless times, there was never a moment where my emotions didn't get the better of me.

"Hey, Dad," I said. "Hi, Mom."

I looked up, more so to stop the flow of tears.

"I, uh, I won my first race today," I said as I looked down at the trophy in my hands.

I paused for a moment, listening to the birds chirping in the background— the only sounds in this place aside from the rustling of the leaves in the trees.

"I really wish you could've been there, but deep down, I like to think you were."

I wiped my eyes and continued.

"Dad, thanks for the advice today. Looks like that yellow Camaro story you and Grandad beat into my head came to use. I dedicated the win to you. Who would've thought that the day you..."

My mind drifted back to the very moment I got the news from Grandad that he'd died followed by images of the funeral.

"...the day you died, I would win my first race."

Turning towards my mom, I said, "Mom, Grandad is always reminding me to use my rib protector when I'm racing. He's taking good care of me and making sure I'm safe out there so I know you'd be happy with him... You both would."

I paused again as my mind began to wander.

"I just, I don't understand why this had to happen..."

I could instantly feel it rising up inside of me again. I had been battling it for as long as I can remember so I knew its touch the moment it set in.

The anger was one thing. It would eventually subside but what would never seem to go away was the grief. The constant reminder that they were gone.

I couldn't remember the sounds of their voices but I could sure as hell hear Grandad's. Every day he would remind me of them. My parents; the ones who were both in wooden boxes under six feet of dirt beneath my feet. The ones I would never see or hear from again. The ones whose life lessons I'd since forgotten. The ones...

A strong gust of wind blew across the ground. It pulled me from my stupor, and I took the moment to shake my head free from the thought.

This wasn't the time or the place to be going down this path again.

Plus, I knew of other ways to escape when I needed to.

"I..."

Losing my words, I turned to walk away but stopped as I choked up and closed my eyes.

I took a deep breath.

"I miss you both so much."

Wiping my eyes again, I headed back towards Grandad so we could go home.

2

Temptation

The best part about school was leaving at the end of the day, doubly so on a Friday. Sure, I had a few classes that I enjoy but for the most part, everything else just seemed like a waste of time.

I slammed my locker shut and headed for the main entrance, where Grandad would usually be waiting to pick me up. Despite being a junior in high school and having my condition since I'd started attending here, I still got a few odd looks while I walked down the hallway. I guess being the only kid walking around with a cane would make anyone stand out.

"Chad, wait up!"

I stopped and turned to see Steve Nielsen hobbling towards me.

"The hell happened to you?" I asked.

"Football practice," he grunted. "My body went one way, and my leg went the other."

I chuckled. "I know what you mean."

"Maybe this means I can get a pimp cane like you," he joked as he slapped my arm. We both turned and continued towards the door.

"Don't get your hopes up. It takes a special kind of stupid to actually *want* this for yourself."

"It ain't for me," he said with a ridiculous smile. "It's all for the ladies."

"Like I said, a special kind of stupid," I muttered, shaking my head.

We arrived at the main entrance to the school and passed through the doors to head outside. The scenery was everything you'd expect from a high school with small groups of kids scattered here and there, segregated by their own personal interests. Steve and I continued down the covered walkway towards the curb, where our rides were typically waiting. No such luck today, though. We both arrived and shrugged our shoulders, content to wait and just hang out.

Steve was an idiot. He was the kind of guy who used his dick as a brain and his head as a brick. If he wasn't talking about his nonexistent sex life, he was telling everyone about how he liked to use his head to smash things, like other players on the football field...or beer cans.

We had absolutely nothing in common, but for some reason it just worked. We were both the kind of people who could stand along the side of the road waiting for our rides and not say a single word to each other. It was just my kind of friendship.

"Dude, I think Claire just winked at me!"

Then there was *that* side of Steve.

He turned to me with a look of shock on his face, frantically thinking that the hottest girl in school had just given him the time of day.

"Look!" he said to me in hushed excitement.

I turned towards her to see that she was in fact winking...very rapidly.

"Yeah, I'm pretty sure she's got something in her eye."

"Don't be so cynical. It could work you know," he rebutted.

"Hey, you used a big word," I said with a smile. "Were you paying attention in English class or..."

"Hey, Chad."

I turned to see where the voice had come from. It was Nora. As always, she had trouble written all over her face, and for some reason, I was drawn to it.

"Hey, yourself," I replied.

"I heard you won a race last weekend," she said, her dark lipstick giving a tempting smile.

"I did. Many dangers. Much excite," I said jokingly.

She raised her right eyebrow at me, which sent shivers down the parts of my spine I could actually feel.

How the hell does she do that?

"You gonna come out and party with us again tonight? You know, now that you've got a reason to celebrate."

"The thought crossed my mind, but I've gotta prepare for the next race," I replied.

It was true but also a lie.

"Oh c'mon, you know how much fun we have," she said, taking a step closer to me. "It's not like you ever get in trouble or anything."

She was inside my bubble, and it put me on the defensive. But the more I looked into her eyes, the more my guard lowered. There was just something so seductive about her that I couldn't resist.

"I'm gonna go ahead and assume this is an invitation for me as well, right?" Steve blurted out. It was a good break in the moment.

Nora noticeably cleared her throat, and she raised her eyebrows in a look that showed that Steve was completely beneath her notice.

Reaching into the pocket of her tight black jeans, she retrieved a scrap piece of paper, grabbed my hand and placed it in my palm. She closed my fingers around it and held on for far too long.

"Just in case you change your mind."

She released my hand, turned and walked away. She had to know that we were both watching as she did so.

As usual, Steve's mind nose-dived straight into the gutter.

"You're gonna get laid!"

"Shut up…" I said, as I heard a horn honk behind me. Before I could turn, Steve spoke.

"Looks like your da…I mean…grandad is here. Ahh, I'm sorry."

Steve—knowing what he had done—threw both of his hands over his face in shame. It wasn't the first time, but even so, his words threw me off balance. I had to physically shake my head to remember where I was. As innocent of a mistake as it was, I noticed my entire demeanor change at that instant. I don't know why, but something inside me felt different all of a sudden.

"See ya, Chad," said a defeated Steve as I headed towards Grandad's red Mustang.

I didn't acknowledge Steve. I just kept walking until I climbed into the car and closed the door.

"G'day, Chad," said Grandad. "Fine day for curbside service."

It was his customary greeting when I climbed into the car after school. However, I really wasn't in the mood for it.

"Yep," is all I could say.

I think he took the hint.

As he pulled out of the school parking lot, he spoke up again.

"I saw you were talking with that *Nora* girl back there," he said with an obvious disdain in his voice. "I thought you told me she was crazy?"

"We were just talking, Grandad," I said flatly.

"You've gotta be careful with girls like that. They'll latch on to good souls like you and pull you down to their level. We didn't have to worry about crazy women to that degree when I was your age."

I huffed. "Okay, boomer."

Although I was looking straight ahead, I could see out of the corner of my eye that he'd turned suddenly towards me after the comment.

"Hey, you watch who you're talking to," he said sternly. "I may not be your dad, but I'm the closest thing you've got to one. So you just watch it."

There it was again: The reminder of my past, which gave rise to a fountain of anger that was beginning to run once again. I'd learned over the years that the best way to prevent going overboard with it was to just use as few words as possible. Too bad that it usually felt like hot coals on the head of whoever I was talking to.

"Yeah. You're definitely not my dad."

"What the hell's gotten into you?"

"I don't wanna talk about it."

"Look, don't try this *'rebellious teenager'* bullshit again with me," said Grandad. "We've been through this before, and I'm not going through it again."

"Sorry to be such a burden," I said plainly, still staring aimlessly through the front windshield.

"Will you shut it with this sarcasm shitshow you do? When are you gonna grow the hell up?"

"I'm just an adolescent. What do I know?"

I saw him throw his hand up in frustration.

The gesture seemed to hang in the air for the rest of the ride home. Something told me that if we decided to keep firing shots back and forth, it wouldn't accomplish anything. That and I really just wanted to be left alone.

As we pulled up to the house, I got out of the car and immediately headed inside.

"Hey."

I stopped and turned to see Grandad standing in the driveway—arms crossed and looking straight at me.

"You know that if you ever have anything you wanna talk about, you can come to me anytime, right?"

Like you'd understand.

I didn't respond. Instead, I turned back towards the front door and went inside.

Heading down the hall of the place I'd called home ever since we'd moved back to Austin shortly after Dad died, I turned into my room and closed the door behind me. I stood there for a moment and listened to the silence.

As much as I loved things like screaming engines and loud music, there was something I always found soothing about complete silence. Odd, I know, but there was something familiar about it to me that seemed to help me calm down.

There were no memories in silence. Only the ones you carried with you.

The sound of the front door closing as Grandad finally came inside snapped me back to reality. Dropping my backpack on the ground, I reached into my pocket and retrieved the small slip of paper that Nora had given me.

Unfolding it, I saw the words "see you tonight" written on it.

Even in the safety of my room, I could still feel the pull towards her. Logic told me that—given my fascination with racing—I was drawn towards danger. I liked the risk and more importantly, the reward.

It was addicting.

Not just the material aspect but also the attention, something I feel that my seventy-three-year-old grandad couldn't relate to.

I saw that in Nora—the danger, the attention. Maybe she saw that in me too, which is why she even gave me the time of day. But more than that, I found in her a means to forget who I was even if it was just for a brief moment in time.

I'm not a party guy by any stretch of the imagination. I typically prefer to either hang around my close friends or no one at all. As I held Nora's note in my hand, however, I couldn't help but feel the pull towards my *other* addiction.

I began planning my evening.

* * *

I had dinner with Grandad and played nice, telling him that I'd had a rough day at school. I fell short of apologizing, though, but he offered one to me.

"I'm sorry if I was a bit harsh with you on the way home, Chaddy," he said, still referring to me by an old childhood nickname. "I'm just a cranky old man, I guess."

I just smiled as I ate, formulating my plan in my head as I did so. I did my best to play nice for the rest of the evening, if only to put his mind at ease.

Grandad typically settled down early every evening. Before doing so, however, he would always set the house alarm. There was a sensor on my bedroom window, which was my only real obstacle.

It was a delicate matter. The sensor had two parts, one on the window trim, the other on the window itself. Using a heat gun from the garage, I heated the adhesive tape to remove the sensor from the window. However, I only had two inches of leeway. If the two sensors got more than two

19

inches apart from each other, the alarm would detect the window was opening and go off. I carefully removed the first piece of the sensor from the window and, without moving it too far, taped it around the second piece on the trim. I could now open the window and make my escape.

At around 10 p.m., I opened the window and slid out feet-first. Despite being nimble-minded, my physical agility was lacking. I had about as much grace as a gorilla trying to ice skate. I held on to my cane during my egress and made ever so sure that it didn't hit against the house on my way out. A steel cane bouncing against the house would be a quick way to alert the older inhabitant.

Turns out, the cane did fine, but I wasn't so lucky.

I landed on my feet but the sudden need to balance backfired on me, as I was unable to do so. Despite the number of times I'd done this, I fell backwards and landed on my ass with a thud, albeit a *quiet* thud.

I slowly stood, brushed off any dirt and headed back over to close the window.

So far, so good.

As instructed by Nora when I'd called her earlier in the evening, I walked down the street to the end of the block where her ride would pick me up at our usual spot.

Even as I walked, I couldn't help but feel a slight pang of guilt over what I was doing. It felt wrong. Being a jerk to Grandad and then sneaking out of the house in the middle of the night to go party with a girl I knew was trouble, all the while knowing I had an important race tomorrow— something wasn't adding up.

Maybe there was still a good person buried inside me somewhere.

My feelings changed when I saw the white SUV waiting for me.

As I approached the beat-up vehicle, a backseat window slowly rolled down with the uneven motion of an old hand crank. Nora appeared within.

"Hey there, Chad Watson," she said with her devious smile.

Reaching out the window for the door handle on the exterior of the vehicle, she popped the door open and slid over. I jumped in and closed the door behind me. I could smell weed instantly.

I noticed the slightly older guy in the driver's seat; His unkept dark shaggy hair blowing in the wind from his open window as he started to drive.

"You remember my older brother, Davison," said Nora.

"How could I forget someone with a first name of Davison?" I may have laughed a bit too loud.

Maybe he heard me but chose to ignore the comment. I couldn't tell but he offered no response.

Turning my attention back to Nora, I finally got a good look at her. She'd changed her outfit and was now wearing a low-cut black tank top that left little to the imagination, along with black shorts that barely classified as clothing. There was also something different about her. Her eyes seemed glazed over. I started putting the smell in the car and the image of Nora together.

An image of Grandad shaking his head at me popped into my head, but as I returned to reality, the image I saw was Nora looking deep into my eyes. She leaned in close and whispered into my ear.

"We're gonna have some fun tonight."

3

I Know You

The last time we'd done that drive, I found out that Davison didn't actually have a driver's license and we'd had to evade a police car. We had no such trouble this night as we eventually arrived at our destination. Even though I'd been there a number of times already, I still couldn't convince myself that it was a place I actually wanted to be.

The trailer, parked in the middle of a wooded area just outside of town, had seen better days. It was covered with smatterings of dirt on the outside with at least one broken window. Lights followed by the dull roar of music emanated from within, where there looked to be a small crowd.

As the SUV came to a stop, we all climbed out and headed towards the front door.

Davison led the way in, followed by Nora and me. The smell of weed, alcohol and various other foul scents almost made me gag.

The moment I entered, Nora reached into a nearby cooler and grabbed two beers, handing one to me, which I immediately opened.

"C'mon," she said as she led me farther in.

"Hey, who's the cripple?"

The voice caused me to stop in my tracks. A few chuckles followed, but I was soon able to pinpoint where the comment came from.

The guy could've been in his thirties for all I knew. He looked stoned or drunk, maybe both. His clothes were about as trashed as his appearance, and it very well could've been his foul stench alone that was stinking the place up.

I knew most of the people there by sight, but there always seemed to be someone new every time I came. Even so, I wasn't about to let some clown get away with those words. I fixed my eyes on him and lowered my brow.

"This cripple's about to kick your ass if you ever make a comment like that again."

"What'd you say, kid?"

At that, the walking pile of trash made its way towards me in an expedited fashion. I wasn't about to wait around to see what would happen once he arrived.

With a quick thrust, I stuck my cane directly into his gut. He folded in two and with a swift motion—which I admit I'd practiced in my room hundreds of times—I did a full 360-degree spin and brought the steel cane around to finish him off.

There was a brief pause as I debated hitting him in the head with it, but I did a course correction midflight and aimed for his exposed ribs.

The crack to his side toppled him over.

Didn't even spill my beer.

Like a noble knight of old, I stood over my defeated foe and looked around the room.

"Anyone else?"

I got a few stares, but it wasn't long before the dozen or so people went back to whatever they were doing.

I randomly recalled Grandad's words from when I first received my cane. It was a gift from Dad's old business partner, Pat Henderson, who'd called in a favor from a local machine shop they did business with. When I got it, I think Grandad was more excited than I was.

"Learn how to use this thing, Chad. You never know when you might need it!"

Nora grabbed my hand, which brought me back to reality while also sending shock waves up my spine.

"All right, hero."

She gave me a smile and whisked me away towards one of the back rooms.

The deep beat of the music in the background seemed endless. We entered the old bedroom we'd been in many times before. Most of the furniture was destroyed and lay in several pieces, save the bed.

"I still can't believe you live here."

"Me either," she replied. "I've been in and out of homes since I was about twelve, but Davison got this place a while back. Our haven in the woods."

Haven isn't how I would describe it.

She sat me down on the bed and reached for one of the nearby drawers that was still in one piece. Pulling a small bag out, she reached in and pulled out two joints and handed one to me.

I recalled hesitating the first time I was here but now, it was pretty much the reason I came out.

She placed her hand on my shoulder as she used her other hand to put the joint between my lips.

"You've got a lot of tension, Chad," she commented as she did a quick squeeze of my shoulder. "Even I can pick up on it."

Exhaling deeply, I recalled how I felt like I could never escape from my past. I lived with it, was reminded of it on a daily basis, and even when I was doing what I loved, my mind would betray me with memories I thought I'd long since forgotten.

Despite my best efforts, I felt like I carried this all with me wherever I went. And on the rare occasion that I did actually forget, I was quickly reminded of who I was by my grandad.

"He'd be so proud of you," Grandad would say to me. *"I can tell they're watching down. Never forget your lineage, Chad."*

I physically shook my head to free myself from my own thoughts. Slowly turning, I looked deep into Nora's eyes.

"I just…need to forget."

Giving me a seductive smile, Nora leaned in close and produced a lighter. With a flip of her thumb, the flame ignited and made way for a path to the escape I so desperately wanted.

"Just breathe."

As I did so, the sensation slowly took hold of me.

I'd be lying if I said it was peace, but whatever it was, it offered a temporary respite from the life I was struggling my way through.

Nora leaned into my ear again as she spoke softly.

"Don't worry. I'll take care of you."

I felt weightless at moments and burdened in others as I began to inhale. Time seemed to become a thing of the past as I sat next to Nora. I turned to look at her and suddenly started laughing. She laughed as well as she lit her joint and put it to her lips.

She leaned her head against my shoulder. I have no idea how long we were sitting there, as I lost all track of time.

Nuzzling the side of her head against my shoulder, she then asked, "Why do you like racing?"

"Speed, danger," I immediately replied. "Or maybe just the rush of how it all makes me feel. Despite my injury—" I held up my cane for effect "—racing makes me feel like I'm just a normal person. That and sometimes I feel like I don't have anything to lose. Other times, I feel like I *want* to lose everything. It all helps me to push a little harder."

She lifted her head and looked at me.

"I know who you are, Chad Watson. You're just like me."

Pulling the joint from her lips and exhaling a cloud of smoke, she leaned her head back and closed her eyes.

"We like the unknown and we both know what it's like to live on our own."

I laughed, although I'm not sure why.

"But I'm not on my own. I've got my grandad."

"It's probably more like he's got *you* instead of the other way around."

Despite the floating feeling, I felt anger at her words.

"You're wrong," I said, suddenly defensive. "He's a good guy."

"I'm sure, but if he's as old as you've told me he is, do you really think he wants to be burdened by you?"

Her words stung. What's worse is that I couldn't help but feel like there was a grain of truth to them.

25

Am I really a burden?

I looked over at Nora, who'd opened her beer and began drinking.

"You've gotta be careful with girls like that. They'll latch on to good souls like you and pull you down to their level."

Grandad's words rang in my ears. I also began to wonder if I truly was a *burden*. He'd invested so much of his life into me. Even though I now despised the past that he reminded me of, he was still my grandad.

He was all the family I had left.

The thought of Grandad combined with Nora's question about racing suddenly reminded me of the race I had tomorrow morning.

More than smoking pot or hanging out with Nora, racing was the great escape. When that helmet was on, it was just me. When I was on the track, there was no past and no future.

There was only the moment.

Right then, however, I had a sudden sensation in my gut that I was squandering that.

"Look, Nora. I've really gotta get…"

Her lips on mine was a sensation I'll never forget. The kiss lasted longer than expected, even if it tasted like I was kissing an ashtray. She stopped and looked me in the eyes, giving me her tempting smile as she did so.

"Why do you look at me like that?" I asked.

"Because I know what I want," she replied as she kissed me again, this time leaning me back so I was lying down on the bed.

As my head hit the mattress, I was met with a spinning feeling followed by another foul smell, which came from the bed. Nora rolled on top of me, and I suddenly didn't want to leave anymore.

After a moment, she stopped and sat up—an intrigued look upon her face.

"You wanna ride this wave even higher with me?"

I lay there for a moment, unsure of what she meant.

"What do you mean by that?"

Rolling off me, Nora gave me her seductive smile as she quickly stepped out of the room.

The bass was still humming in the background, but I didn't seem to hear as many people as there were before.

How much time has passed?

There was a split second where I contemplated getting up and leaving just as Nora eventually returned. This time, she carried a small black backpack with her.

"This is Davison's stash," she quietly spoke as she sat on the bed beside me. Reaching in, she produced a small clear plastic bag that contained a white powder.

I'd seen enough movies and TV shows to know it was cocaine.

"C'mon, Chad," she said.

I had no problem smoking weed to escape, but something inside me immediately pushed back.

"You're always talking about forgetting and wanting to escape," she reminded me. "We'll do it together. Just once."

There was an initial hesitation, but just like my first-time smoking pot, I decided to simply give myself over to it.

As if she'd done this a hundred times before, Nora racked up two white lines on an old CD case and led the way.

* * *

I sat up suddenly, awakening after God knows how long. I was still on that smelly bed but my shirt was off. I had no memory of how I'd gotten there, what had transpired or how much time had passed. The world around me was spinning, and I had the sudden sensation that I was floating.

My arms came into view as my head hovered just above my body. I took note of the time on my watch.

3:05 a.m.

I recalled that I had somewhere I needed to be in the morning.

Home. And then…somewhere else.

Shit.

I need to get out of here.

Unsure if I'd said that out loud, I found my shirt on the bed next to me and noticed Nora passed out beside me. Fully dressed, her arms and legs were splayed in various directions. I nudged her, but she didn't respond.

After getting dressed, I located my cane and stood.

That weightless sensation was soon mixed with a new level of anxiety I'd never experienced before. With the sudden sense that I was now being chased by something, I put one foot in front of the other and made for the door. My feet were cold, and I realized I didn't have my shoes on.

I didn't care. Whatever was chasing me couldn't catch me. I needed to get back home to safety.

A sudden fear gripped my heart as I raced for the door—keenly aware that if whatever was chasing me actually caught me, my life would be over. Barreling past the roughly half dozen people passed out on the floor of that shithole, I burst out the front door and headed off into the night.

* * *

After walking for what felt like several miles, I finally got to a small market that had a decent cell signal. Using a mobile app on my phone to get a ride, it was another thirty minutes or so before it finally arrived.

I climbed into the back seat of the small sedan and laid my head against the headrest. Classic rock music played from the radio, and it wasn't ten seconds before I started getting a headache.

As I replayed the night's events in my head, I knew I was screwed. The credit card used to pay for this ride-share service—which he'd set up in case of an emergency—belonged to Grandad. He'd soon find out, and I'd have a lot of explaining to do.

As the car drove along, the driver said very little to me. I assumed this person had done this before. Driving while trying to carry on a conversation with someone who was high in the back seat of your car probably didn't end well.

I felt ashamed but also numb. It was almost as if my heart knew I'd done something terrible, but it was so disconnected from the rest of my body that I didn't feel any guilt.

Well, not at first anyways. At that moment, I could almost see the images of my mom and dad, who were both looking down on me from above— watching their sixteen-year-old son who was high and nearly passed out in the back of a stranger's car on his way home after sneaking out on a Friday night and now being a cocaine user. As much as I wanted to, I couldn't get away from that feeling.

I *needed* to.

I didn't belong to my parents anymore, and they were no longer a part of my life.

Where is the escape I want so bad?

I looked at the clock inside the car and it read nearly 4 a.m. I suddenly remembered that I needed to be awake in a few hours to prepare for the drive with Grandad for the race tomorrow morning.

As the driver approached the house, I asked him to drop me off at the end of the block.

When I finally climbed out, I stood there for a few moments as I listened to the sound of the car fade into the quiet of the night.

Silence.

It was the first moment of peace I'd felt all night, calming me as I collected myself before proceeding.

I took a few stumbling steps towards home. My mind seemed to race as I began thinking about all that still needed to be done to prepare for tomorrow. My steps were slow and clumsy and every second or so, I would feel like I was merely floating across the sidewalk. Aside from being thoroughly high, to say I was tired wouldn't do me justice.

After a few minutes, I was standing in front of the house with the now difficult task of climbing in through the window—the only thing separating me from much needed sleep.

I took a deep breath and made my way to the window. As I reached up and slid it open with my cane, I was just about to attempt to haul myself up when I heard a car drive by and suddenly stop. I turned to see who it was just as a bright light was shone in my face. This was followed by the unmistakable blue and red flashing lights of a police car.

Shit.

4

Sunset

It was a quiet ride.

I could sense Grandad's disappointment. If there's one thing I hated, it was knowing that I'd let someone down. I felt like a failure, too ashamed to say anything as I rode along beside him.

Even so, I was thankful that Grandad was good with his words.

A few moments after a heavy knock on the door, Grandad had emerged to see me standing alongside a police officer on the front porch. As he made eye contact with me, I felt the shame just as much as I could see the sadness in his eyes.

"I'm sorry to bother you at this hour, sir," said the officer. "We caught this kid trying to slip into a window. He said he lives here but we needed to be sure."

Grandad looked at me again but I couldn't meet his eyes. I lowered my head and stared at the ground.

"Yeah," said Grandad. "He's my grandson."

"All right but he smells of marijuana," the officer said. "Your grandson said he didn't smoke but I need to search him just the same."

Grandad paused a moment and then turned his full attention to the officer.

"There's really no need for that, sir," said Grandad. "He's just a kid who may have done something stupid. I've had my share of these moments and

I'm willing to bet you have too. I don't condone his actions but I'd imagine this will serve as a lesson to him."

The officer turned and looked at me. I met his stare but then instinctively looked away. I honestly thought he was about to reach back for his handcuffs any second.

"Let me take care of him, Officer," said Grandad. I could hear the sincerity in his words, and I think the officer did too.

"I'll turn him over to you if I can do a quick search to see if he's carrying anything. If he comes up clean, he's all yours."

After a few seconds, he nodded his head. "Fair enough."

The search was quick but efficient. My pockets, waistline, legs and the tops of my socks were checked. I knew I wasn't carrying anything, but I had a moment of fear at the thought that maybe someone had slipped something into my possession. Luckily that wasn't the case.

"He's clean."

The officer stepped in front of me and looked me in the eyes. His look was stern.

"Take this as a warning," he said. "I don't want to see you sneaking around in the dark again. Get things back on track and listen to your grandad. If we have this conversation again, the outcome will be very different."

He took a step away from the front porch towards his car.

"Be safe," he said as he turned to walk away.

Grandad and I both stood on the porch as the car drove off into the night. The silence that ensued was torture. I thought for sure that he would turn towards me and tell me to forget about the race this weekend. Maybe he'd give up on me altogether. Instead, he simply turned and walked back into the house. He held the door open behind him, which was all the cue I needed to follow him.

I half expected him to simply turn towards his bedroom and go back to sleep. Instead, he walked down the hall and turned into *my* room. Following, I saw him walk directly to the window as he knelt down to look at the alarm sensor I'd rigged to not go off when I opened it. He analyzed it for a few moments, taking notice of my earlier handiwork that had aided in my escape.

"Clever," was all he said.

I remained silent.

He turned—his gaze fixed on me—and then stood up. Much to my surprise, he walked out of my room.

He was halfway down the hall when I heard him say, "Get some sleep. We'll talk later."

It was like waiting for a shoe to drop. Even as we drove along, it felt wrong.

I felt wrong.

"I'm sorry, Grandad."

I heard him exhale sharply.

"Sorry for what?"

He knew the answer, he just wanted me to admit it.

"For sneaking out. For being stupid...again. For trying to slip back inside and..."

I paused.

"For not respecting you."

There was a long pause as I waited for his response. Even though my head was still a cloudy mess, I could tell he was gathering his thoughts.

"Chad, I don't ever want you to think you're oppressed and that you live in some dungeon with an old man. If you ever want to go out with your friends, just tell me. You're old enough now to make your own decisions but each of those comes with its share of consequences."

"I know, Grandad. I just—"

"I'm not done," he said, stopping me midsentence.

"Look, I get it. You're sixteen, I'm seventy-three. I don't expect to connect with you on everything and vice versa. But you do have to realize that you're my responsibility. If something happens to you, like, say, while you're off smoking pot with that Nora character..."

"How'd you know?" I asked, more shocked than anything.

"I didn't, but you just told me." I could've sworn I heard a chuckle.

"That all comes back to me. The last thing I wanna do is lose you, Chad.

I've lost enough people in this life. I'd rather try to keep you around as long as I can."

I was suddenly reminded of the word *loss*. A heavy feeling landed on my chest, but I played along for Grandad's sake.

"So you're not gonna smother me in my sleep for this?" I asked jokingly.

"No promises," he chuckled. "Are you gonna stop hanging around that *sheila?*"

"No promises," I said with a smile.

"The choice is yours, Chad. But like I said, choices have consequences."

We both sat in silence for a few moments before he finally asked the question I was dreading.

"Did you really smoke pot?"

I felt no need to deceive him, but I also didn't need to elaborate.

"Yes."

I half expected a lecture, but what I got instead was totally unexpected. He was nearly beside himself in laughter.

"Okay, I know there's gotta be a story behind this," I said.

Once he finally got a hold of himself, he explained.

"You'd be surprised what a bunch of Aussie kids could get their hands on back in my day," he said with a few more chuckles.

"You smoked pot?"

"Once," he conceded, holding up a finger. "My father about beat the living shit out of me when he found out, and I never did it again. My friends used to tell me 'a little *wacky tobacky* never hurt anyone.' Boy were they wrong."

"What was your dad's name?" I asked. It was a random question, but I was honestly just curious. I could tell that I'd caught Grandad off guard.

"That's some history if there ever was any," he said. "His name was Lee. He and my mother, Ava, were both young when they had me, while still living on the farm in Western Australia."

He had shared his racing story with me before concerning how he'd gotten his start, but he'd left out this tiny detail. I don't know why I was suddenly so curious about it.

"What were they like?"

34

"The complete opposite of how I am with you," he said. "You see how I encourage you to race? That wasn't the case when I was growing up, but then again, motorsport was a *lot* different in those days compared to how it is today."

"How so?"

He uttered one word.

"Guts."

After a moment he added, "Like I said, ancient history. What do you say we put on our tune. We're just about there."

I didn't need a second asking.

"Sure thing, Grandad."

"Roadhouse Blues" by *The Doors* was the song we played on our way to every race. It was our tradition. There may be some history there as well.

As we entered the Dallas/Fort Worth area, the song carried us all the way to the track.

* * *

We arrived at North Texas Karters (or NTK for short) to find a small crowd already there. It was my first time racing there, so I did my best to study up beforehand. That usually meant watching online track footage until I felt like I had the track memorized before I ever set foot there. The half-mile track featured nine turns, including one that—after practicing on it later in the day—I found to be a pain in the ass.

It was a banked left-hand turn that, if you got it wrong, felt like you'd fly off the edge of the world. The rest of the track felt good. After a few laps, I could tell I was getting more and more comfortable with it, but that banked turn was getting the best of me. It always felt like I wasn't getting it right. That and my mind wasn't at one hundred percent after the previous night.

When talking with some of the more experienced drivers about the trouble I was having on track, some of them mentioned that it just takes time and practice before you're able to fully commit to it.

"I thought you were fast?" said one local driver. "You just need to send it."

I didn't take his words very seriously, however. As practice times started coming in, I ended being faster than him on *his* home track.

The day was organized into three separate races. The first two would be heat races, the third was the main race. I could take it slow at first, learn how to drive the track in traffic and then hopefully pick up a few positions as the day carried on. I had no intention of going full wood in the first race and wrecking mine or another driver's stuff. Even if I had wanted to, however, I don't think I could have.

I was off my game by a fair bit. The initial sensation of speed while still feeling the effects of the night before was abnormal. It felt like the world was blurring by while I was also being distracted by what I could only describe as a strange new voice. This voice, however, wasn't friendly. It spoke of a temptation that was convincing me that I needed to hand over control and allow myself to fall under its sway.

The memory of Nora making those two white lines came to the forefront of my mind.

I did my best to ignore it and pressed on. I wasn't as on-point as I normally was on race day.

By the time practice was complete, I was sitting in eleventh out of seventeen karts. Not fantastic and right in the middle of *the kill zone*. It's the place where there's most likely going to be a wreck early on, as you're surrounded by other drivers, and oftentimes you have nowhere to go in the event of a crash up ahead. I'd been caught up in a few big crashes and been fortunate to escape injury each time.

Others hadn't been so lucky.

As we got ready in the hot pits for the start of the first heat race, Grandad came by to check me over. That was his excuse at least. I think he just wanted to be close to the action before the race started.

"Remember what we discussed," he said. "Take it easy at the start and let the race come to you. Study the drivers around you and learn where your marks are on the track."

"Become one with the track, right?"

"That's just nostalgic bullshit to make drivers feel like they've got mystical powers or something." Grandad smiled. "Just go out there and drive your ass off."

He gave me a slap on the helmet, and I took my seat in the kart.

Just as I got settled in, Grandad knelt down beside me.

"Just keep this in mind—to beat Goliath, become David. Be smart, confident and calculated. Plan your moves and commit."

Although I wasn't sure where this sage advice was coming from, I nodded in acknowledgment.

Just then, however, I saw his demeanor completely change.

"What's going on here?"

I turned to see what he was talking about as he gestured towards my right hand, which was gripping the steering wheel.

I noticed that it was shaking uncontrollably.

A pang of fear suddenly gripped me, but I did my best to play it off.

"Just a nervous twitch is all," I replied, grabbing my hand and holding it with my left.

The look on Grandad's face told me he wasn't convinced.

"Are you all right, Chad?"

"What do you mean by that?"

"I mean—" Grandad leaned in close. The look on his face was both serious and accusing. "—I need to know. Are you...under the influence?"

"Influence?" I played dumb. "Of what?"

"Don't make me go there, Chad."

Just then, the sound of engines firing up filled the air.

"Time to roll," I said, closing my visor.

For a brief moment, Grandad just stood there. It wasn't until I gave him the signal that I needed the engine started that he reluctantly fired the kart up.

A moment later, the field and I pulled away onto the track for a few warmup laps. I did my best to set everything else aside in my mind.

Sleep deprived and still feeling the obvious effects of last night's activities, I knew it was going to be the toughest race of my life. On top of all that, the Texas temperature was already starting to heat up, which seemed to compound everything.

I was up for the challenge, though. Even if it was just to prove to Grandad—and maybe to myself—that I was fine.

Each driver took the time to get their tires, brakes and engines warmed up. Nothing fancy. Usually just weaving side to side and dragging the brakes a bit.

Before long, we were formed up side by side several rows back. I was on the inside left of the sixth row.

Even as we were getting ready to race, something felt off in me. I did my best to shake it off. Before long, adrenaline would take over and all would be well.

Game face on.

As we approached the start line, I used my left hand to modulate the brake control on my steering wheel while keeping my right-hand full squeeze on the gas. When the green flag came out to start the race, I dumped the brake and accelerated as the field piled into my least favorite corner.

I was initially caught off guard by the banked turn. I'd gotten so used to going into it at a certain speed that—with this being my first-ever racing lap at this track—I wasn't really sure what to do with myself while still building momentum.

Being on the back bumper of the kart in front of me while having a kart nearly touching my right-side wheels and another directly behind me meant that any mistake I made would be heavy. Despite my uneasiness, I was able to keep things under control.

Still holding the inside, I was able to complete the next left turn while also grabbing a position.

I'll take that and another, please.

We eventually all formed a single file line as we progressed through the course. Thus began the chase.

It usually wasn't wise to go on the attack this early in a race. Getting into a battle early on was a sure-fire way to let the leaders run away and build a gap. But as these were mere heat races and I was starting farther back, I was more obliged to take a risk in order to gain a few positions.

I held my own for the first few laps, getting a feel for both the course and the driver in front of me. I suddenly realized I knew who it was.

The last time we'd raced, Kate had finished just behind Pascal and me in third. She was a fast and experienced driver who'd been karting for a long time. Kate was one of the few drivers we all knew was destined for greater things. Everyone in the paddock knew it was only a matter of time before she moved up to Formula 4.

But right then, however, she was in front of me, and I began to size her up. After a time, I felt like I'd made an appropriate *guesstimation* as to where I could manage a pass for ninth, but I knew it was going to be tricky to get around her. Kate was many things, but a pushover was not among them.

I wasn't letting her get away, but I wasn't exactly on her back bumper anymore either. I quickly glanced over my shoulder to see that there was a pretty sizeable gap behind me, as the driver I'd previously passed was too busy holding up the field trying to prevent anyone else from overtaking him.

Typical.

Even so, losing momentum in karts was a sure-fire way to allow that gap to close back up again. I couldn't afford to make an ill-fated kamikaze move, but I also wasn't content with just sitting back in tenth.

As we completed the final chicane, which led to the long straight where the start/finish line was, I saw that Kate had grabbed too much of the inside curbing on exit and lost a bit of speed as a result. Her kart bounced a bit, and I watched her head and neck bobble as they absorbed the impacts. With her momentum compromised, this was all the incentive I needed.

Getting a clean exit out of the corner she'd just botched, I began to close the gap behind her. As we approached the banked corner, I moved to the left to go for the overtake.

Even if she stayed with me through the corner, I would have the inside

39

line for the next corner, which would allow me to complete the pass.

I fully expected her to back out and not risk a defensive move but Kate was no ordinary driver.

It was a game of chicken in a sense, and if she was willing to play, I was game as well. If she wasn't willing, she'd simply back out, and the position would be mine.

My gut began to get a sinking feeling as we approached the banking at full speed. Everything inside me suddenly screamed to lift off the gas and slot back in behind her, but for some reason I maintained my grip on the throttle.

I began to blink rapidly as my vision momentarily blurred.

Call it nerves, call it anxiety, call it whatever you want, but within the span of what felt like a second, my entire world turned upside down.

As I dived down the left side of Kate while entering the corner, I was carrying too much speed. I felt my kart slowly sliding up the banking of the track towards Kate, who was holding her line alongside me. Any moment now, I knew I'd regain traction and make the pass stick along the inside.

Or so I thought.

I was simply going too fast to be able to give Kate racing room in this corner and as a result, my kart slid up the track and my right-side wheels made contact with the wheels on Kate's left. We both came unglued from the grippy track surface and a second later, I found myself spinning across the nose of her kart.

As we both entered into uncontrollable slides, my kart spun completely around and there was a brief moment when we were both facing each other...just before we both ran out of road as we found the edge of the track.

The sensation of flying off a track backwards was one of the most terrifying feelings I'd ever experienced. What made it worse, however, was seeing Kate's kart begin to spin in the air. As we both came crashing down, I landed hard albeit on all four wheels. The heavy jolt I felt upon landing caused me to see stars but they weren't enough to block out the ability to see what happened in front of me.

The clear visor she wore on her helmet allowed me to see the horror in her eyes.

With her kart spinning in the air, Kate landed upside down as she went head-first into the ground. I watched in horror as her kart rolled several times, throwing her from the kart. Her body landed haphazardly on the ground just as my kart came to a stop.

Rolling out of the seat onto the ground, I looked up and initially began asking myself if what just happened was actually real.

The sky above me was spinning as what seemed like a million different thoughts raced through my mind.

"Chad! Chad!"

I could hear the familiar voice of Grandad approaching, along with several other footsteps of those who were rushing to the scene.

"Kate," I whispered. "Check on Kate."

I wasn't even sure if anyone was with me yet.

Too afraid to know the truth of my present circumstance, I stayed put and didn't move.

Grandad finally showed up.

"Chad! Are you okay?"

I opened the visor of my helmet with my right hand as I also opened my eyes as wide as possible in an effort to stop the spinning.

"I don't know."

"Just stay put, Chad. One of the medics is on the way."

"Grandad... Kate."

I tried to sit up, but he placed his hand on my shoulder to keep me down.

"They're with her now, Chad. It... doesn't look good."

I couldn't see what was happening where Kate was but I could hear enough to put a mental picture together.

"Emergency services are inbound. Get her on the stretcher!"

The sound of a large vehicle pulling up could also be heard, and I assumed it was the trackside ambulance.

Within a few moments, one of the medics ran over to check on me as I slowly began to move my feet and arms again. The spinning had also begun to subside.

The medic did a few checks on me, asking me my name, where I was and if I had any trouble moving. He eventually removed my helmet.

"Does it feel like anything's broken?" the medic asked me.

With the helmet off and fresh air in my lungs, I began to bend my knees as best as someone with an existing spinal injury could. I took a few deep breaths to check if anything hurt. I turned my head from side to side and moved my arms around.

"No, everything feels okay," I said to the medic.

It could've been just adrenaline pumping at the moment, but surprisingly, everything still felt intact.

"How's Kate?" I asked. "Is she okay?"

The medic held my gaze for a moment before he turned to Grandad.

"I need to ask you to sit with him for a few moments while I help out with the other driver," he said in a hurry. "Stay with him and keep an eye on him."

In a flash, the medic raced back over to Kate and joined the crowd of people who had gathered around her.

"Clear the way, please!"

As we watched from a distance, Grandad and I sat in silence for several moments. We exchanged looks, and right away I could tell there was something on his mind.

He knows.

Within minutes, we heard the unmistakable sound of a helicopter approaching. Moments later, it was on the ground as the medical crew began carrying Kate's motionless body via a stretcher.

What have I done?

While all the noise of the helicopter was present, Grandad leaned over towards me.

"Chad, what happened?"

I couldn't answer. Watching Kate being loaded into the back of the helicopter, my mind seemed to be in a few places at once. I felt guilt begin to creep in as my eyes found Kate's parents. Her father held her mother, who was covering her eyes as she wept.

"Chad!" Grandad stood up and stepped directly in front of me. "Look at me."

I turned and met his eyes. "Are you under the influence?" he asked slowly.

Barely able to hold his stare, I knew this was my fault, but I couldn't bring myself to admit it.

You should've never let me get in that kart. You should have grounded me! You should've canceled our trip up here!

I wanted to blame him, but in the end, this was my responsibility. I was the one in the driver's seat.

"Chad! Answer me!"

The propellers of the helicopter began to accelerate as the noise level increased.

"Are you under the influence!?"

I held his stare as I felt a tear water up in my eye.

Grandad must've taken that as an answer because he began to take several steps back. The look on his face was a mix of horror and disgust...but also pain.

As the helicopter took off, I watched as Grandad began to stumble a bit. Reaching his hand up, he clutched his chest as he suddenly fell back and landed on the ground.

"Grandad!"

I quickly stood but without my cane, my steps were clumsy. The world around me was still spinning as well. After just a few steps, I fell forward but crawled the rest of the way to Grandad.

"Are you okay?"

Grandad could only shake his head from side to side.

I could see the pain in his expression. This was more than the pain I'd caused him, however.

Lifting my head, I saw the medics, who were watching the helicopter take off.

"Help!" I shouted.

After shouting a few more times, I finally got their attention. The two of them turned towards me and raced back to Grandad and me.

When I looked back down at Grandad again, his face was unusually pale. "Ch-Chad."

The medics reached us as I managed to get back on my feet and take a few steps away to give medics room.

I watched as Grandad fixed his eyes on me. The look of horror in his eyes made me lose all conscious thought. I could feel this image burning itself into my mind. My stomach tied itself into a knot and I began to feel lightheaded as fear paralyzed my body.

His face strained as he held his gaze at me.

"Not like this," he whispered. "Not like this."

"Go get the other stretcher!"

One of the medics ran over to the ambulance parked nearby and returned moments later.

Together, the two medics carefully lifted Grandad onto the stretcher and moved to either end to pick him up. They stood and began to move to the ambulance.

I didn't have my cane with me, but I followed as best I could. Although I was walking, it instead felt like I was floating.

When they got to the ambulance and loaded Grandad in, I finally caught up.

"I'm coming with you," I said.

"No, sir," one of the medics said. "We're going with sirens on, so family aren't permitted to ride."

They closed the back door as the lights and sirens came on. I watched as they pulled away to exit the track.

I stood there for a moment. Alone.

5

Shadows and Memories

It had been years since I felt like I was truly dead inside. The wretched feeling of being trapped within a cage had been something I thought I'd moved on from. Now, my old demons had returned to torment me again.

This time, however, I was completely alone in my struggle.

I could feel the cage doors closing in around me, seeking to trap me inside just as they once did long ago.

Only now, I offered no resistance. My present circumstance gave me no reason to.

Kate had suffered a severe spinal injury that left her completely paralyzed from the neck down. She would never walk again and her dreams of becoming a professional race car driver were over.

Track officials ruled it as a racing incident. Although it was my fault, they deemed that I'd simply driven into the corner with too much speed.

Truth be told, there was only one person who knew what had actually happened. Unfortunately, his voice could no longer be heard.

Despite the best efforts of the medical team, Grandad died from the heart attack shortly after arriving at the hospital.

Even worse, I didn't make it there fast enough to see him alive one last time.

My mind was mute. I neither thought nor felt anything but complete misery and dread. I was alone.

Completely.

Alone.

My mind couldn't help but wonder what Grandad's last thoughts were as he was in that hospital room surrounded by strangers. Was he at peace? Did he panic?

As I sat at the front row of his funeral at the very grave site we'd both just recently visited, I couldn't take my eyes off his casket.

We were all here in a sense.

I glanced about to see the tombstones of my parents as well as that of Grandma Charlotte. I had only the faintest memories of her.

Now they'd all be lined up, all four of them in a row.

They are only missing one.

As I turned my attention back to Grandad's casket, my mind took flight.

There he was, the man who'd conquered so much in life, who'd been a hero to so many and who was so willing to give as much of himself as needed. Now, he lay motionless inside a wooden box.

Lifeless.

The pastor had said a few kind words. Even so, the words were but a shadow of the man that he was. In the end, I guess that's what we all become. Shadows and memories.

His last words to me surfaced in my mind.

Not like this. Not like this.

Grandad had been an only child. His son and daughter-in-law were both dead and so was he.

I dared a selfish thought.

I was *it*.

The last of his line.

The last of my family.

Well, almost the last of my family.

"Chad!"

Unfortunately for me, there was only one person left. The deep southern accented voice was louder than it needed to be. The way she said my name ignited a silent rage inside of me.

With Grandad passing, this meant that my well-being would be transferred to my next of kin. Being only sixteen, I wasn't legally old enough to look after myself.

"We need to leave. Now. Everyone's gonna be leaving once this little show is done and I don't wanna get stuck in traffic."

She had been the bane of my father's existence, and now Helen would be a thorn in mine. My grandmother on my mom's side, I had nothing but bad memories of her. Controlling, manipulative, demeaning...those were just a few of her finer qualities.

My parents had called her the Texas Chainsaw Massacre due to her innate ability to kill you with her words for an endless amount of time. She would trap you so you couldn't get away and then rain the very words of hell on top of you.

"Chad! Now!"

I turned to look at her, mustering as much hatred in my eyes as I could.

She stood out like a salvaged car in new car lot. While everyone present wore black, me included, her bright yellow, pink and orange flower shirt looked like a potato sack as it wrapped around the various curves and bulges that made up her body. This was complemented by the white pants that stopped just past her knees and her flip-flops, which made the obnoxiously loud *clap-clap* sound against her feet as she walked.

She wanted the attention. She craved it.

As I turned back to look her, all I could think about was violence.

Her big, permed hair shook along with some of her mass as she looked at me and harshly pointed to a spot on the ground in front of her, much like one would do to a dog.

Several people who had come to pay their respects had also turned towards her. In truth, I think that's exactly what she wanted.

I ignored her and turned back around to face Grandad. I had no plans to leave just yet.

I swear I felt the ground shake as she approached.

A stiff grip grabbed hold of my right arm and pulled me close. I could

47

feel her nails digging into my skin.

"Now you listen to me, little boy," she said, her mouth inches from my ear. "I'm not gonna tell you again. Get your scrawny butt out of the chair and get in the car. If you don't, I swear I will leave you here to…"

"Bye."

I wanted to say more, but that was the only word I could get out. Even so, my reply caused her to stop. I didn't make eye contact with her. I just kept my gaze fixed on Grandad. It's what he would've wanted.

The grip on my arm suddenly released, and I felt the deep thud under my feet of Helen walking away. I could hear a few murmurs from the small crowd as she walked by them. Whether she actually left me here or not, I didn't care.

I sighed and looked around again, hoping to see a few familiar faces in attendance. I didn't.

The folks present were mostly his old neighbors, friends from his church and a few local race fans who knew him from TV.

None of the friends I'd come to know as family from my time in Australia were present. Although he'd kept up with them over the years, I doubted they even knew. I was hoping to see Nick and Abby, maybe even Tubbs or Grandad's oldest friend, Greg Foster.

Instead, the crowd of thirty or so people slowly began to diminish as they paid their final respects to the man they called William Watson.

A few people came by and said hello to me. I had no idea who they were.

"If you need anything, just give us a call," said one couple I'd never seen before. They echoed the words nearly everyone who'd come by to talk to me had said. Sometimes, I think people only say things like that to make themselves feel better, to give themselves an out, knowing that they did *something* without ever really doing *anything*. Regardless, I had no intention of contacting any of them.

I felt nothing for them, even as I watched some of them look over the various flower arrangements only to pick one up and take it with them as they left.

As I turned my attention back to Grandad, a few moments had passed before I felt a hand rest on my shoulder. For a moment, I thought it was Helen but quickly dismissed it. The gesture had too much gentleness to it.

"Hi Chad," said a familiar voice.

Even as it carried tones of grief and sadness, I recognized the voice instantly. The monotone voice of my dad's longtime business partner, Pat Henderson, was difficult to mask.

As he stepped into view, I almost didn't recognize him. He was much thinner than I remembered but in a healthy way, and for once, his face wasn't beet red. Despite the situation, he also carried a calmness about him that I found warming.

"I'm very sorry for your loss," he said as he took a seat next to me.

I truly wanted to say thank you and ask him how he'd been or even how the business he and my dad started long ago was doing. I tried but my words were gone. I felt trapped again.

"Your grandad was a great man—one who was loved and respected by many," said Pat.

I turned to look at him, but his eyes were locked on the casket before us. I like to think those closest to Grandad were so used to seeing him full of life and vigor that knowing he was motionless inside of a box was part of the shock.

"You know, I was here with him for your mom's funeral. Both you and your dad were still at the hospital."

Wiping a tear from his eye, Pat continued, "You and your family have certainly been dealt a tough hand, Chad. But one thing I always remember about your dad was his *'never give up'* attitude. Whether it was business, the race at Bathurst or making sure you were taken care of, there are few people I know who are as passionate about life as he was. William was the same way."

He turned towards me.

"I read what happened at the track. Chad, Lord knows I told him to slow down. You knew him better than I did, so you know how much of a force of nature he was. When he made his mind up about something, there was no stopping him. 'I'm just as full of piss and vinegar as I was in my younger days in Straya,' he said to me. We spoke over the phone a few months or so ago to discuss a few things. He went on and on about how much of a joy it was to see you grow into the man you're becoming. More than anything, he loved being at the track with you."

I chuckled at the comment. It was something I could totally hear Grandad say. Deep down, however, the true story remained hidden to all but me.

Pat hesitated before he continued.

"I...I can't get into too much detail but, just know that everything's gonna be all right. Just follow the path, Chad."

Follow the path? What does he mean?

He wiped his eyes once more. Standing, he turned towards me again.

"You've got my number, and you know where to find me. I still do business for business because business is good," he said as he pumped his arm for the latter, reciting the old line I'd heard him say hundreds of times over the years. "Don't hesitate to call or stop by the house if you need anything."

Turning, he walked towards Grandad's casket. I watched as he placed his hand on it, but after a few moments he took a knee and lowered his head. I could see his lips moving, but I wasn't able to hear what he was saying. Not that I needed to know.

Pat's words "follow the path" replayed in my head over and over. I was simply trying to make sense of it amid everything else.

My phone vibrated in my pocket. I pulled it out to see that it was a text from Nora.

[We should talk again.]

There she was. My temptress. My escape.

I probably read it three or four times before I slid the phone back into my pocket. The short but cryptic message was typical of her but even so, I felt an odd sense of comfort and longing from it. That dark voice inside my head told me I needed this and I wouldn't feel better unless I had it.

After some time, the cemetery ground workers came out and began to remove the flowers and the green covers used to cover up the nearby pile of dirt.

I sat still and watched.

As his casket was lowered down into the metal vault, my heart began to race.

I wanted to cry.

I *needed* to.

For some reason, I couldn't. I just sat and watched, like a prisoner watching a piece of his life being torn away from behind caged doors, unable to do anything about it.

Not like this. Not like this.

His words haunted me.

As I watched his casket descend into the vault that would then be lowered into the ground, I swear I could hear screaming. I couldn't tell if it was Grandad or maybe just a chorus of screams from my parents as they looked on from wherever they were.

I wanted to put my hands over my ears. Maybe that would make them stop.

The casket hit the bottom of the vault with a heavy thud, which caused the screaming to cease. The vault cover was then placed on top, sealing Grandad within.

Before long, the vault began to descend into the ground.

As it did, I tried my hardest to recall a memory of Grandad.

Something.

The speech he'd given to Dad's team at the Bathurst 1000, one of the stories he'd shared with me about how he came to the United States, how he taught me how to race a kart with my hand controls when I was younger...

But no matter how hard I tried, his words weren't there. It was like watching your favorite scene from a movie on mute.

The device lowering the vault stopped once it reached the bottom.

One of the workers, a heavyset Hispanic man, turned towards me. He reached down, picked up a handful of dirt and gestured towards the hole in the ground where Grandad would now lie for all eternity.

Using my cane, I slowly stood and approached the hole. I looked down to see the top of the vault and I imagined Grandad kicking and screaming within it.

Not like this! Not like this!

I shook my head, trying to push the thought away.

Reaching down, I grabbed a handful of dirt with my left hand and looked at it.

This was it. The life's work and accomplishments of a great man, snuffed out and buried under shovels of dirt.

As I looked down into the hole, a small part of me wanted to fall in too.

Extending my arm, I slowly released the dirt with my now shaking left hand. The sound of it hitting the top of the metal vault stood out in the otherwise silent graveyard.

Still, there were no tears.

Why? Why can't I have a release from this?

Knowing that there was no comfort to be had and that the cemetery worker would object to me throwing myself into the pit, I turned and walked away.

* * *

Helen had waited for me at the cemetery. I sat in silence as she berated me the whole way back to her house. Several times I'd had the urge to reach over, grab the steering wheel and pull the car into oncoming traffic. Instead, I had gripped my cane in my hands as I imagined beating her to death with it in her sleep. The rage in me began to rise. Pure white hot rage that was so thick I could nearly feel it in the air inside the car.

I had messaged Nora as soon as I got to Helen's house. Having put everything I would need into just one bag, I picked it up and walked out of my room. Heading down the hall, I turned towards the front door, opened it and stepped out into the evening. The peace and tranquility I felt made me feel like I was the only person on planet earth.

Davison's beat up white SUV slowed as it approached. Pulling up beside me, it matched my pace as I continued to walk.

"A little late for an evening stroll, Chad Watson?"

Nora smiled from the driver's seat and my soul leapt with expectation.

"A little young to be driving by yourself, Nora Whitacker?"

"Get in," as she reached over and opened the passenger door from the inside.

Without the vehicle stopping, I climbed aboard.

She leaned over and kissed me as we drove off into the approaching darkness.

6

The Fall

With the window down, the wind blew cross my face and through my hair as I tried to soak in the cool evening. There was a slight chill in the air. The fall season was usually warm this time of year, but the mix of the summer remnants and the approaching winter was perfect.

"I've always thought of you as like a Bruce Wayne or something... minus the billionaire part, obviously," said Nora.

"Why do you say that?"

"Well, both of his parents are dead. You're kind of in the same boat."

My heart sank at the analogy. I did my best to play it off.

"I don't think I'll be swinging from rooftops anytime soon," I replied, holding up my cane for emphasis.

We continued to drive to wherever it was we were going. I wasn't really sure but to honest, I didn't really care at that point. I just wanted to go away. To what end, I wasn't sure.

After several minutes had passed, however, I suddenly recognized the road we were on.

A fear seized me.

"Where are we going?" I asked frantically.

"Back to my brother's trailer. He's gone for a week or so. I think. He doesn't really talk to me anymore."

Looking over at me and noticing my sudden panic, Nora voiced her concern.

"Are you okay? You look like you've just seen a ghost."

I had seen a ghost. Three of them, actually.

Just as the thought entered my mind, the two of us drove past the cemetery where my family was buried. I stared at it in the mirrors, and the pain I'd thought I'd escaped suddenly located me in my moment of peace.

It started in my stomach and worked its way up to my head—a sharp pang of guilt for my irresponsible actions.

"What the hell's wrong with you, Chad?" asked Nora.

I hesitated at first but, given the situation, decided to tell her.

"That cemetery back there, the one we just passed. It's where my family is buried."

Nora was silent. I could tell she wasn't sure how to respond as her lips pursed together.

Continuing to drive, a few minutes passed before she finally spoke up.

"My parents left my brother and me when we were young. Like when I was four or five years old or something. We went through lots of different homes until Davison was old enough to live on his own. I moved in with him soon after."

"Do you remember them? Your parents?"

"No and I don't care to," she replied harshly. "I don't want to talk to them and I don't want to talk to Davison either."

I thought about asking why but decided against it. I'd had enough of family drama for now.

When we finally pulled up to the dilapidated trailer in the woods, Nora brought the vehicle to a stop but didn't immediately get out. Looking over at her, I could tell she was in deep thought.

"Do you ever think, *This is it?*" she asked. "Like, this is all life will ever be? I can't help but think that all I'll ever become is some useless deadbeat somewhere."

I didn't have an answer. My head was in the car but my heart felt like it'd been ripped from my chest and left to rot at my parents' graves.

She suddenly shook her head and seemed to come back to reality.

"Whatever. C'mon, Chad."

Exiting the vehicle, I grabbed my bag from the back seat and followed Nora into the trailer.

As we entered, the foul stench was there to greet me.

What wasn't there, however, was the crowd from the last time I was here for the party.

"Is it just us?" I asked.

"Yep. At least until Davison gets back. Whenever that happens."

"Where'd he go?"

Nora went silent for a moment.

"He—" she hesitated "—owes some money to some people, so he went off to do a job. That's all he would tell me, anyways. Like I said, he doesn't talk to me much anymore."

Okay, I'll bite.

"How come?" I asked.

"He says I'm getting to be too much of a burden. Just before he left, he told me I was the reason he was having to take this *job* or whatever it is he's doing."

"That seems pretty harsh," I replied.

"Yeah, it's a long story, and to be honest, I'd rather forget about it," she replied, walking deeper into the trailer as she did.

I stayed where I was in what I guessed was the living room. I looked around at the stained carpet, the broken windows held together with duct tape, the small light fixture hanging from the ceiling by only two wires (with only one of the three light bulbs still working), and the couch that—without anyone lying on it—looked as if it had been torn up by a sharp knife. There were also small holes in it. Where they came from, I didn't want to guess.

When Nora returned, she carried a small package that I recognized.

The dark voice ignited within me. This is what I needed. A high like I felt last time would take all of this pain and guilt from me.

Instead of cocaine, however, she pulled out a small bag of weed.

"Let's start off with the easy stuff first," she said and smiled as we sat down on the couch together. "It's not like we're in a hurry or anything."

Nora definitely had her reasons, and I certainly had mine. I was tired of running from my past. I wanted to rid myself from it. I wanted to fall, if only to feel something when I hit the ground.

As Nora offered me yet another pathway, I was more than happy to oblige.

* * *

The world spun around me. I felt sick but calm; In the eye of the storm but also above it.

Nora lay next to me. Between the weed and the empty beer cans now scattered around us, my puzzled mind started putting the missing pieces together.

A nearby window with its drapes closed had a small opening, which allowed a sliver of light into the room.

How long have I been out?

Shame landed squarely on my bare chest, but I shook it away.

Glancing at my phone next to me, the time read 5:28 p.m. It was evening...again.

Somehow, a full day had passed since we'd arrived, and I didn't remember any of it.

As I lay there, I began to think of my life.

What in the hell am I doing here?

I felt useless.

Aimless.

I no longer had any direction or goals.

Where I once felt purpose and drive, the only thing that remained was a gaping hole inside me.

My family was gone, all of them buried six feet down. In many ways, I now felt jealous of them. They didn't have to go through any more pain or adversity. The only problem, however, was that I'm now all alone.

Grandad once told me that when Dad was racing at Bathurst, he had a near panic attack while driving. He knew that once the race was done, he—in many ways—would be too.

My mind wandered randomly until it landed on the memory of the first time I stood up from my wheelchair. After nearly a year of feeling like I'd been physically bound to it, I'd stood for the first time since the accident that put me in that chair.

It was like taking my very first steps in life as an infant all over again.

Greg Foster—the famed Australian physiatrist who'd opened his home up to both my dad and me and who'd led my rehabilitation—steadied me from the front as my dad and grandad supported me from behind.

"Every step will seem like a fight, Chad," Greg cautioned me. "But one step leads to another."

I could hear Dad behind me.

"I've got you, Chad. I won't let you go."

I won't let you go.

I physically shook my head to rid the thought from my mind.

Nora stirred next to me as I let go of a breath I didn't know I'd been holding on to.

"What time is it?" she uttered in a groggy voice.

I sighed at the question.

"It's tomorrow."

She sighed heavily as well.

"And yet tomorrow still brings yesterday with it."

Standing, Nora walked with a stagger as she headed down the hall, placing her hand on the wall for balance along the way.

It was more than a hangover. I could tell that she was carrying a weight on her shoulders, but it was hard to say if it was self-imposed or not.

"Where are you going?"

"I think my brother's stash is still in his room," she said from down the hall.

A sudden longing woke up inside of me. A hunger.

I could finally answer the whisper of the dark voice in my mind, a whisper that was beginning to form into a shout.

As I waited for Nora to return, I laid my head back down on the pillow in expectation, and in doing so caused that foul but now familiar scent to arise again as it filled the air and tickled my nose.

I closed my eyes for a moment and tried to imagine a time when everything was right. At least from my perspective...

"You fought like a bloody lion that'd been released from a zoo."

"What can I say? I wanted to win. Instead, I came in second. Again," said my dad.

"Oh harden up, Watson. You finished on the podium at Bathurst. What more could you want?"

Dad turned and looked at me from his hospital bed, having come in just a few days prior due to worsening symptoms. Upon seeing how accelerated his condition was, however, the doctors recommended he stay for the time being.

"Two things," Dad replied, holding up two fingers. "Number one is that I would've loved to have kicked your ass and won the race..."

Derek Renshaw—the fierce rival of my dad's during their Supercars race at Mount Panorama—laughed out loud at the comment.

"Mate, you almost had me. Another few meters and...well. Yeah. Continue, please."

"Two, I'd love to see this guy in a car one day," said Dad as he gestured towards me.

I smiled, feeling like I fit in amongst the two talented drivers who were in the hospital room.

"He's bound to make us both look like amateurs one day," said Renshaw. "Say, if you ever need anyone to give him some driving lessons..."

"Don't even think about it," said Dad. "I can't imagine how the world would react to a second Derek Renshaw on a racetrack."

Both men laughed at the comment.

"Yeah, and knowing me, I'd probably end up hating him too," said Derek. "Plus, I think he'll be in good hands with a bloke like your dad once..."

Derek stopped mid-sentence as an awkward silence filled the room.

Derek cleared his throat.

"Hey, let me get out of your hair, Watson. It was good to see ya, mate."

"Likewise."

I watched as Derek left the room. That ended up being the one and only time he'd ever visited my dad. More than that, however, his conversation had opened my eyes to something.

It was in that moment when I realized my dad was truly going to die.

"Here we go!"

Nora's voice from down the hall pulled me from my stupor.

Moments later, she reemerged in the bedroom carrying a small black backpack with a torn zipper and small holes along the sides. She reached in and pulled out a smaller pouch, which she opened to reveal its contents.

Different from the larger bag she'd pulled out last time, the two small white bags were tied at the top. A small mirror was also in the pouch, along with a razor blade, and Nora wasted no time.

She peered up at me with her seductive eyes.

I felt powerless. Like I'd gone too far down the path to turn back now.

But the more I looked into Nora's eyes, the more enticing it felt. She was leading me, and I was a willing passenger.

Two white lines had been formed on the small glass mirror, neatly aligned by Nora with the help of the razor blade.

She held out a small, rolled-up dollar bill, which I took.

"C'mon," she said. "We'll do it together."

The voice inside of me demanded that I submit. There was no choice in the matter. I longed for the feeling I had when I'd taken my first hit. It was similar to how I felt about racing: no past, no future.

There was only the moment.

More than that, I longed to forget. An image of Kate forced itself towards the front of my mind, followed by the guilt I felt after her accident, and it made me crave this escape even more.

Somehow, I found myself moving closer, as if I really were a prisoner inside my own body. Only now, I didn't know who was in the driver's seat.

Before I could even think about what I was about to do, I found myself side by side with Nora as we each snorted our own white lines.

* * *

No peace.

I was alert but at an alarming degree. After the initial stage of euphoria had passed, Nora and I did several more lines of cocaine well into the evening and into the following morning. I was on edge. I found myself clamping down on my arms with my hands, fingernails digging into my skin. My heart felt like it was about to beat out of my chest, and there was a sudden panic but I had no idea why.

All I know is that I felt like I was in hell.

Screams filled my head. They sounded like my mom and dad. They were screaming my name over and over.

It wouldn't stop.

I covered my ears with my hands, feeling my fingernails digging into my skull. The pain helped.

In a sharp moment the screaming stopped. It was quiet now, and I was alone.

Again.

Sitting up in the bed, I looked for Nora, but she was gone.

With no idea how much time had passed, I stood and reached for my cane. Even as my hand extended towards it, I could see it shaking again.

My hand or the cane? *Both?*

I grabbed it and stood, the first time I'd done so in some time. It took a moment to find my footing and even longer to get partially dressed.

Making my way down the hall, I discovered Nora sitting on the floor of the living room. She was fully dressed with her legs crossed and her phone by her side. I noticed the backpack by her side as well.

There was something about her that was different. This wasn't the same

Nora I knew.

"Are you okay?"

She didn't answer. She just sat there staring off into space, her own infinity that I wasn't able to see or comprehend.

I walked closer but stopped short.

"I'm tired, Chad."

Her words sounded worn and helpless.

"Tired of *this*," she said as she gestured to her surroundings. "The more I think about it, the more I'm convinced that this is all I'll ever be. I want it to be over."

It was a feeling I could relate to.

Over.

To some degree, I'd wanted it to be over ever since my dad died, but something kept me going. Now, that something was gone.

Nora reached into the same worn backpack she previously pulled the cocaine out from. This time, however, she retrieved a handgun.

I wanted to be shocked. Hell, everything inside screamed that I should be shocked, only I wasn't. Not entirely, anyways. Instead, I took a seat on the cut-up sofa next to her.

She turned and looked me in the eyes. Her eyes had a look of sadness and desperation to them.

Longing.

Longing for life to be over? Was I supposed to convince her otherwise?

Her next words shook me to my core.

"I know you, Chad Watson. You're just like me. Abandoned by life and everyone in it."

Her eyes began to water. She looked so alone, even though I was sitting here with her, but there was something else. A resolve seemed to set in. Not suddenly, but more like something she'd been thinking about for some time.

Taking a deep breath, she turned away from me.

"Please, Chad," she said. "Don't try to stop me."

Reaching for her phone, she swiped and opened her camera to record a video. She flipped the camera so she could see herself on the screen. Fixing the backpack on the ground in front of her, she leaned her phone against it so that it was looking up at her.

Pressing Record, she began.

"My name is Nora Whitacker. I'm the daughter of two people I've never met, and I live in this dump trailer with my brother, Davison. I'm a failure."

She wiped her eyes and continued.

"My life is one dead end after another. My brother leaves me for weeks at a time after he tells me how much he hates me and how worthless I am. All I know is that I'm a burden, and I have nothing to offer."

A sudden panic set in within me.

"Nora," I said quietly. I had the sudden urge to close my eyes.

"I hate my parents for bringing me into this life only to leave me behind like I was some damaged product. I hate this piece of shit trailer in the middle of the woods. I hate myself for thinking I could be something in life."

"Don't, Nora."

My words landed on deaf ears as she continued.

"I hate this life. But now, it's over."

I opened my eyes in time to see her place the muzzle of the handgun inside her mouth. It was instinct that immediately led to me closing my eyes again and quickly covering my ears.

The blast was loud. It seemed to hang in time as I sat in internal darkness with my eyes still closed.

I felt a heavy thud of what I could only imagine was her lifeless body hitting the ground.

I dared not open my eyes. Like a frozen corpse I sat there, my heart beating a thousand times a minute on the inside all while wondering how in the hell I'd gotten myself into this.

Even more pressing: *How do I get myself out?*

I'd followed this dark path, and what now lay before me seemed to be the end result.

Death.

All paths seemed to lead there. It was almost as if death followed me everywhere I went. The only thing was that it seemed to touch everyone but me.

This living hell needed to end.

My eyelids slowly opened.

Nora's body was sprawled out in front of me on her back. Blood was sprayed all over the back wall, and the pool coming from the back of her head grew increasingly larger.

Her eyes, once full of beauty and enticement, were half closed—the internal light in them extinguished.

I could feel myself shivering. More than that, however, my eyes were drawn not to the lifeless shell of Nora in front of me, but to the handgun that rested in her dead hands.

It would be so easy. It could all be over.

I found myself looking around at my surroundings when his words came into my mind.

"Not like this. Not like this."

My mind assembled the most twisted thought I'd ever experienced. What was odd, though, was that it made sense.

Not like this.

Slowly, I reached down and pulled the handgun from her dead hands. Upon touching her, a surge of fear and dread crept through my body. I suddenly felt sick inside but pressed through it.

With the handgun freed from her lifeless hands, I slowly rose to my feet and put my plan in motion.

Heading over to the counter, I retrieved the keys to her brother's SUV. With the gun in my hand, I carefully stepped over Nora's body, walked outside into what was now the approaching evening, climbed into the truck and started the engine.

For the first time in my life, I knew exactly where I was going.

* * *

The truck drove like a pile of shit. It plowed in the corners and the brakes squeaked loudly. Even so, it did little to change my mindset. This was, in fact, the first time I'd ever driven a car on the road by myself. Normally, I think I'd be ecstatic about having the freedom of being able to go anywhere I wanted.

In a way, I was doing just that.

It was a relatively short ride. When I pulled up to the entrance, I noticed that the gate that led to Legacy Drive was closed.

Pulling the truck off to the side of the main road, I retrieved my cane and the handgun. I left the keys on the seat and closed the door behind me.

Walking up to the entrance of the cemetery, it took me all of five seconds to figure out I could just crawl under the gate to gain access.

It was evening. The last rays of the sun were just peering through the shifting trees, which swayed in the slight breeze. The temperature was cool as I walked barefoot down the middle of the road on the other side of the gate.

I'd never been here when it was dark. Even so, I knew I could navigate directly to them with my eyes closed.

I turned down the gravel path. It crunched under my feet as I took one slow step after another. Although I could hear my steps, I had the sensation that I was floating above the ground, unable to control where I was going.

I soon found myself standing before the graves of my entire family.

My grandmother Charlotte lay farthest to the left. Beside her, Grandad's freshly laid grave completed the row next to my mother, Lena, and my father, Bill.

I stood between the graves of my mom and dad.

A gust of cool wind sent shivers down my spine, and warm tears formed in my eyes as my lips began to tremble.

The rustling of leaves on the surrounding trees made me close my eyes as I tried to absorb the peace and quiet. That was normally my safe place to go but now, there was only torment.

I imagined the souls of my parents reaching up from their graves and pulling me down. I grasped for words of encouragement from Grandad—

words that had kept me going in the past—but my mind came up empty.

This was it and I knew it. This was the end of the line and the end of the Watson family.

The cane fell from my hands and landed on the ground with a heavy thud. I immediately flinched as I thought back to the sensation of hearing Nora's body hit the ground.

I wanted to shake the feeling away, but I realized that I no longer needed to.

Slowly lifting the handgun, I placed the muzzle against the right side of my head.

I opened my eyes to see the cold stones of my parents' memory before me. They stared back unblinking, seemingly watching what was unfolding before them.

Reading their names over and over, I internally reached for one last possible memory that could pull me away from the edge of this cliff.

No. This was it. My entire life had led to this moment.

I took a deep breath as I stared across the four gravestones. There was no peace. Only fear, guilt, abandonment and shame. My failure was complete and I found no reason to continue on. I'd see them soon. Or maybe I wouldn't. Either way, this would be over.

I trembled. The fear I felt was evidence that I knew how wrong this was. But just like life, there was no turning back.

The only words I had left were as pathetic as my life.

"I'm so sorry."

My final words spoken into the cold dark.

Closing my eyes tightly, my finger pulled the trigger.

Click.

The sound reverberated all around me. It startled me to the point that my entire body flinched.

I had pulled the trigger but the gun didn't fire.

Anger began to rise up inside me.

"No. Don't do this to me."

I quickly repositioned the gun against my temple and, after a deep breath, pulled the trigger again.

Nothing.

My rage took over and I shouted as loud as I could.

"God! Kill me! Let me die!"

I tried a third time.

Click.

The gun still wouldn't fire.

"Dammit!"

I couldn't even kill myself. The shadow of death circled all around me but wouldn't let me fall to its power.

I threw the gun as hard as I could. It smashed against my dad's gravestone, breaking off a small chunk of the stone, and the gun went off. A flock of birds swarmed through the air as the shot echoed through the darkness.

I collapsed face-first onto the ground. A floodgate of tears opened as I began to weep before the graves of my parents.

Dad's words rose up from his grave and seized my mind with their memory.

"Always keep fighting and never quit, even when you fall down and even when the odds are stacked against you. Fight to stand back up because you never know where you'll end up if you keep moving forward. Just know that every time you fall down, I'll be right there with you. I love you, son."

I struck my head repeatedly with my fists as I wept.

"Let me die. Please!"

Watering the graves of my parents with my tears, I had no concept of time. Minutes? Hours? I felt like I was fading. And before long, everything went black.

* * *

The feeling of cold steel awoke me from my tormented slumber. My eyes flickered awake and I found myself face down in the grass in front of my parents' graves but my arms were behind my back, handcuffed.

"Dispatch, suspect is in custody."

I suddenly felt hands grabbing my arms and lifting me up to my feet.

I stumbled, unable to keep my balance.

"Gun," said a voice from behind me. One of the nearly half dozen police officers who were searching the area around the headstones indicated towards the handgun I'd thrown.

"I think that cane is his, too."

Another of the police officers reached down and picked it up. He studied it for a moment before slowly turning towards me. He locked eyes on me before speaking.

"I remember you," he said.

As my eyes adjusted, I fixed my eyes on him. I remembered him as well.

The officer who'd caught me while trying to sneak into Grandad's house at night shook his head at me.

"I told you to get your life back on track. Now look at you."

As before, I had no words. The world still spun around me, but I could see him shaking his head in disappointment.

As he approached, he stopped a few feet from me and put his hands on his hips.

"You're under arrest."

The words landed squarely on my shoulders.

"For what?" I asked.

As he opened the back door to his squad car, I was placed inside by the other two officers, who were holding me up. Once seated, the officer standing at the door looked down at me.

"For the murder of Nora Whitacker."

7

Exodus

I nervously tapped my fingers on the armrest of the chair I found myself sitting in. No matter how hard I tried, I couldn't seem to focus. My mind raced from one memory, one disaster, one heartache to another, only briefly stopping to live in this present circumstance.

She was dead.

He was dead.

Was I dead?

I should be dead. I *needed* to be dead.

Instead, I sat in an uncomfortable chair within an unfamiliar office, unsure of anything. I had a hard time sitting still, and I felt increasingly restless.

Was this even real? Maybe I was dead.

The past few days had been a blur. From being handcuffed and sitting alone in a cell to getting fingerprinted, being put on suicide watch, talking with police officers, counselors, lawyers and now, this person.

The woman seated behind the desk in front of me was typing loudly. The nameplate on her neatly organized desk read *Megan Dulcer, Case Manager*.

My guess is she was in her late thirties. Her shoulder-length auburn hair rested on a navy blue suit jacket, which made her look official. She also wore a small wedding ring on her finger. I glanced over her shoulder and noticed a picture on the wall behind her of what I assumed was her and her husband.

They looked happy together. I don't know why but seeing that picture made me sad.

Would I ever find happiness?

The clock on the wall was ticking loudly. Every second sounded like a damn gunshot to me.

Her body was on the floor in front of me. I heard the gunshot. I watched her die.

When it was my turn to die, I'd somehow failed.

Click...

"All right, Chad," said Megan without making eye contact, her words startling me from my stupor.

The typing suddenly stopped and she looked me in the eyes. The thundering of the clock seemed to amplify and the phones ringing in the background were proving to be maddening.

"What can I do for you?"

What an odd question, I thought.

At first, I didn't know how to respond. She seemed so happy and eager to help but I didn't even know where to begin.

So much has happened.

So much has changed.

I wasn't the person I remembered from my past and I wasn't sure if I could ever get him back.

Now, however, I felt pain for all that had happened—everything that had led me to where I am now. I took it as a sign that I was indeed still alive. But what I craved was something that could only be described as darkness.

I needed a fix. Those white lines Nora drew just before her end beckoned to me. It would fix everything. If I couldn't have that, I no longer wanted to be alive.

I looked down for a moment and noticed my right hand was shaking. I instantly grabbed it with my left and turned my focus back to Megan.

She saw it.

Her concern was expressed on her face.

She wants to help but what can she do?

Despite everything that had happened, I could still feel that there was a small part of me somewhere deep down that longed to be alive. It was barely there—surrounded by death, misery and anger—but there nonetheless. I'd almost snuffed it out of existence.

Maybe I should have.

It was useless, though. No matter where I went or what I did moving forward, I felt like I'd be reminded of my past. I'd be reminded of what I did to Kate and how it led to my betrayal of Grandad. It was like being locked in a perpetual cycle of death.

Everyone around me seems to die.

Everyone but me, that is.

"Chad? You in there?"

"Yeah," I replied, pulling myself from another line of downward thought. "Just thinking."

"About?"

"Your question," I admitted. "I really don't know what you or anyone can do for me."

She turned slightly in her seat to better face me.

"Chad, your situation is rough, but I've seen worse. First off, you've been cleared of all charges after Nora's death was ruled a suicide based on the video found in her phone."

She was crying out for help the entire time. I was just too focused on myself to see it.

"I know it may look grim to you, but you've got to look past the darkness at the light out there."

"What light?"

"Chad, you're a smart kid. I don't have to know you very well to tell you that. No police record, good grades in school, good attendance until recently…"

"What's your point?"

"My point is that you need help, and I'm here to offer that."

I scoffed at the comment. I knew exactly what I needed.

71

I needed all of this to be over.

"Tell me about your parents, Chad."

My head jerked back at the request. It felt like I'd been punched in the gut. My whole world suddenly began to spin even more.

"Wha...my parents?"

Turning towards her computer screen, she replied, "Bill and Lena Watson. Both deceased. Tell me about them."

"So that's it, then. I guess I should just quit because I'll never be good at it, right? I have one thing I enjoy doing. One thing! And now that's not good enough?"

"Is your family good enough?"

"Watch out!"

The last memory I have of them erupted into my mind. It was the final moment before the car crash that took my mom's life. That moment had been permanently etched into the walls of my mind.

It was the last time all three of us were together.

"What do you miss about your parents, Chad?" asked Megan, interrupting my thoughts again.

"Everything."

The word shot out of my mouth before I could even realize I'd said it.

"I..."

There was more to be said. A lot more. The words were certainly there, buried under years of grief and anger. I just needed to dig a bit. I just felt too tired and hopeless to hang on to them any longer.

"I miss my mom. I don't really remember too much about her, but I never got to say goodbye."

I could suddenly feel the psychological shovel in my hands. Instead of digging my grave, however, I was unearthing my past. I'm normally much more reserved than this but I didn't care. Words and memories were suddenly pouring out of me.

"My dad, he was like a damn lion. He never gave up on anything once he set his mind to it."

Another memory surfaced.

I thought of them together. The memory was faint now but I recalled how proud my mom was after my dad's first professional race in Trans Am TA2 at Sebring International Raceway. It didn't end the way he'd planned after his car suffered a mechanical failure, but even so, I remember seeing her embrace him after he'd climbed out of the car back in pit lane. I think it was at that very moment that I thought of my dad as my hero.

"I miss my family. I miss their guidance and…"

There. A spark. A light I felt like I could follow.

"I miss their presence. But they're dead now. And they've been that way for a long time."

"Is that why you were at their gravesites in the middle of the night with a gun and cocaine in your system?"

Even as the words were said, I saw the spark die, and I was reminded again that I needed to, as well.

"You make it sound so poetic. I just wanted to die."

"Why do you want to die, Chad?"

"Simple. Because I don't want to live anymore. Because I have nothing to live for. Because every person I've ever loved or looked up to is dead, and I just don't want to keep going on like this."

"Do you still want to die?"

I sighed.

"I don't know anymore," I lied. "I just want all this to stop."

That much at least was true.

"That will all start with us finding you a place to live with someone who can look after you," replied Megan.

"Don't send me back to my grandmother," I said. "If you do, I'll just leave again."

"So I've heard," she replied. "Unfortunately, there aren't many other options."

I suddenly became aware that I was gripping the armrest very tightly. Lingering memories from my childhood began to surface of how my parents reacted whenever Helen would arrive unannounced at our home. From pretending we weren't home and not answering the door to having to hide as she walked around the house and looked in through the windows, she was a two-legged devil incarnate.

"There has to be another option," I protested. "I may only be sixteen, but I feel like I should have some sort of say in this."

"And where would you go instead?" she asked.

"Anywhere. Put me in a state program. Or in foster care. Or even out of state. I don't give a shit. Just don't send me back to her."

Wherever I go, I won't be there for long anyways.

"What you're talking about is a long and drawn-out legal process, Chad," admitted Megan. "Although yes, you do have a say, a lot of pieces have to fall into place first."

"Such as?"

"Well," she replied. "You would first need to find a suitable living arrangement with someone who can assume legal guardianship. Do you know of anyone who you think would take you in until you finished school?"

I thought about Pat Henderson, my dad's old business partner. His words to me at Grandad's funeral were touching, but that wasn't a good enough reason for me to be unloaded on his doorstep. He'd lived a good life and had taken the responsibility of the business he and my dad had founded in stride after his passing. The last thing I wanted was to be a burden to yet another person.

Greg Foster, a longtime friend of Grandad's, had helped me during my rehabilitation after the accident that had taken my mom's life and resulted in my injury. He had willingly opened his home up to my dad and me, and he was the one who helped me take my first steps out of the wheelchair.

Unfortunately, he was also in Australia. And I was in Texas.

The same was true of Nick Lathan, the man who drove with my dad in the Bathurst 1000. He and his sister, Abby, were so kind. For a time, I thought Abby and my dad had something going. After Bathurst, however, they began to distance themselves from each other. I never really figured out why, but I can only assume it was related to my dad's deteriorating condition.

Even so, I'd spent a lot of time with her while my dad was on the track in Australia. Like my mom, Abby had a way with words. The only difference was that Abby was a bit more blunt. If she felt a certain way about something, she didn't beat around the bush.

My mind suddenly jumped back to the walking tank known simply as Tubbs. He was loud and crude but also the kind of person who would be at your side the moment you needed him. He probably wouldn't be happy about it, but he would be there nonetheless.

He gave the impression that he was an unstoppable conqueror who drank the blood of his enemies and the occasional beer in his free time. Deep down, however, I always knew he was a big softy.

I missed my old friends. When we moved to Australia after my mom died, I'd initially thought it was all my fault. Although I couldn't speak back then, I heard everything. I knew that I was a burden to my dad. I knew the only reason we went there was because of me. Despite this, our time in Australia was something I'll always cherish. Even if it was only for a fleeting moment in time.

Grandad had kept up with them over the years although he mostly talked with Nick. I'd spoken with Abby over the phone on a few occasions but as the years passed, our conversations became fewer until they stopped completely.

How pathetic, I thought. *It's like I'm scrolling through a list of people to see who I can dump this pile of waste on. I wouldn't wish this on anyone.*

I turned my attention back to Megan, who was patiently waiting for a response from me.

"No," I said flatly. "I can't think of anyone."

"That could be a bit of a problem." She sighed. "Unless..."

"Unless what?"

"Well," she said, turning back to her keyboard with a questioning look on her face and beginning to type again. "There are actually residential treatment facilities that are meant for situations like this. They take in troubled youth, help them through school and assist them with getting into a career."

"I'll do it."

"Chad, this is a huge decision that shouldn't be entered into lightly. This will impact the rest of your life. You'd be leaving behind everything and everyone you know and…"

"That's *exactly* what I want."

She sighed.

"It's not that simple, Chad. You're talking about lengthy court proceedings. For the state to remove custody from your grandmother won't be easy."

"I don't care. Just tell me what I need to do."

* * *

I'll never forget the feeling of taxiing to the runway. The brief pause just before takeoff.

My final moments in Texas.

I loved that state. I really did. It would always be my home in many ways. I wasn't leaving *it* behind, but rather all that I had done in it. My grief, my past, my skeletons…my family. I was leaving everything behind in a last ditch effort to make something for myself.

The engines of the plane roared to life and I felt the steady crush of gravity as the plane began to take off. I loved the sensation of speed. As we continued to accelerate, I suddenly felt a rush of emotion land on my shoulders. My parents, my grandad—I found myself mentally saying goodbye to them. As the wheels of the plane lifted off the ground, I was suddenly overwhelmed with emotion as tears filled my eyes.

I was leaving them behind. In many ways, it reminded me of the feeling of taking off another lifetime ago on the trip to Australia with my dad. I felt responsible for that back then.

Now, here I was again. Only this time, I was all alone.

"This isn't the end," he'd said to me back then. *"We'll be back home eventually."*

The plane began to gain altitude, and as it did, I began to feel a sense of release. Years of pent-up anger, sadness, grief and abandonment came flooding to the surface, and I suddenly began to weep. Tears came pouring out, and it was almost as if a weight were being lifted from my shoulders.

Unable to look out the window any longer, I buried my face into my hands and continued to weep.

In several hours, I would be arriving at a new home.

This would either be a new beginning or it would be my end.

II

Part Two

"On a given day, a given circumstance, you think you have a limit ... And so you touch this limit, something happens and you suddenly can go a little bit further. With your mind power, your determination, your instinct, and the experience as well, you can fly very high."

—*Aryton Senna*

8

Process and Procedure

S ecure the vise to the table.
    Slide bolts into t-slot nuts.
    Ensure vise is squared to the table.
Check with indicator.
Tighten down vise.
Recheck with indicator.
Should be squared.
Install 3″ shell mill.
Set tool length offset.
Install material in vise.
Use 3D sensor to set x and y work offset.
Load program.
Raise z work offset up 6″ and dry run the program.
Dry run successful.
Change offset back to zero.
Run program.

Process and procedure gives order to life. There's a correct way to do things and the end result is (hopefully) producing the desired outcome with a finished part. For me, it was running a 3-axis vertical machining center; essentially an automated milling machine.

This was my life now.

And I loved it.

I watched as the machine went to work. The hum of the machine combined with the steady stream of coolant was music to my ears. I watched as the block of steel was slowly but steadily worked away to reveal the part it would ultimately become.

In many ways, I could relate.

Hearing laughter, I turned to see Reggie through a window in his office with someone I didn't recognize. An older gentleman with white hair and a friendly disposition, the two seemed like they knew each other fairly well. Then again, Reggie was as skilled a salesman as he was a machinist. He was responsible for bringing in new clients so he was no doubt buttering this guy up in an effort to close a deal.

My responsibilities were solely the manual sort. Reggie had spent the last several years training me, and he had taught me well. Between creating CAD drawings to running every machine in the shop, I was proud of the skills I'd learned and the work I did. It was something I could pour myself into. Working with my hands was therapeutic. It took my mind off of the present and forced me to focus on process and procedure.

It could be argued that it was because of those processes that I was still alive. My younger self seemed intent on ending things but here I am, still plugging away ever since moving to Wisconsin over four years ago.

Although the program I went through at the Morgan Shipley Center helped me get my life back on track with an intensive therapy program and eventually helped me finish my high school education, it wasn't until I met Reggie that my life seemingly began to take a turn upwards.

Reggie was more than my boss. He was my mentor. And not just in the machine shop but in life as well. In many ways, Reggie was the closest thing I've ever had to a father in my adult life. Reggie was there to shake my hand when I got my high school diploma. The handshake turned into a hug followed by the words I'll never forget.

"I'm proud of you, son."

I don't have daddy issues. Not anymore, at least. But his words gave me a comfort and satisfaction in knowing that I had in fact done something with my life. I had overcome my obstacles, my past and myself.

With Reggie being a black man from Illinois and me being a white boy from Texas, our backgrounds couldn't have been more of a contrast. As he taught me, however, it's not where you come from that matters.

"It's what you do with that experience to benefit the moment. It's about not allowing your past to shackle you down. Be stronger than your past and stronger than those who only want to complain that life isn't fair. Take the cards life's dealt you and play your damned hand. You just may end up taking the house."

As a mentor, Reggie was kind, fair and firm. And he definitely didn't take any shit from anyone, especially me. I may have learned that the hard way on more than a few occasions.

For the better part of two years, I've been under Reggie's wing learning everything I could about the trade and what it meant to make an honest living for myself.

A Chicago-native, Reggie's more or less been involved with machine tools and manufacturing his entire life. He was born into the industry, or so he told me. Because of his background in the manufacturing industry, he in many ways reminded me of my real dad but I tried to not think about that part of my life anymore.

That was the past. And for the first time in years I was happy with where I was at and—more importantly—where I was going. Reggie taught me to keep my eyes forward. He demonstrated that with his own actions in life. Like me, he too had a past he'd rather forget.

He seldom talked about it and I'd never asked him—more so out of respect because he's never asked me too much about my past. And that suited me just fine.

"Watson."

I turned to see Reggie and the older gentleman walking my way. I instantly noticed the other man had an abnormal gait. As I walked towards them both, he stared at my cane.

"I'd like you to meet Mr. Arthur Collins. Arthur, this is my shop apprentice, Chad Watson."

Mr. Collins and I shook hands. A firm handshake, just like Reggie showed me.

"Nice to meet you, Mr. Collins."

"Please," he replied. "Call me Arthur. We'll be friends much longer that way."

He had a friendly smile. The sort that causes his eyes to smile in kind. The southern drawl in his voice seemed to make him feel like a friend right away. There was something else about him that I just couldn't put my finger on.

"Arthur here has just commissioned us to manufacture the parts he and his company will be using to develop a prototype steering wheel."

"A steering wheel?" I asked. "What kind of a steering wheel?"

Arthur smiled as he pointed down towards his feet.

"The kind that allows an old cripple like me to drive safely on the roads," he replied with a chuckle. "Hand controls for gas and brake, mostly. My team's working on a method to ensure it could potentially be installed in just about any modern road car."

He took a few steps forward and looked around the shop as he continued.

"It'll be mostly for people with permanent handicap injuries that prevent them from utilizing the foot controls of a normal car."

"That's certainly interesting," I replied.

It wasn't a lie either.

"I've actually used something similar to what you're talking about several years ago when I used to race go karts."

"Is that so?" asked Arthur.

"I never knew you raced, Watson," Reggie added.

"That was another lifetime ago."

Arthur pointed down at my cane.

"I hope I'm not overstepping my boundaries here but what caused you to acquire that piece of hardware there?"

A mental wall immediately went up within me. I didn't like people probing about my past but as this was relevant to the conversation, I didn't see any harm from hiding it. Plus, Reggie knew most of the details anyway.

"Car accident when I was a kid," I said as vaguely as possible. "Spent the next several years learning how to walk again and I'll probably be spending several more with this thing," I added as I held up my cane.

"Motorcycle accident for me," replied Arthur. "Must be thirty years ago now. More surgeries than I can count, and I still don't have full use of my feet. Figured I'd at least try to make the most of the situation and, well, see if I can help out others who are less fortunate than me."

"We'll let Chad here get back to work," Reggie interjected. "Despite his best efforts, this shop won't run itself just yet."

Taking the cue, I extended my hand to Arthur.

"It was very nice to meet you, sir. I look forward to working with you."

"You as well, son."

I watched as Reggie ushered Arthur off farther into the shop, no doubt giving him the grand tour to assure him that his parts would be manufactured using capable personnel and equipment.

The VMC was still running, as it would be for the next several hours and into tomorrow morning. Gotta love automation. I ran through my end-of-day checklist and began cleaning up around my workspace.

* * *

"What's the ETA on those intake manifolds?"

"Tomorrow morning. They'll be going all night, and I'll be able to monitor the VMC from my laptop once I get home."

Reggie gave a nod as he drove with me in the passenger seat beside him.

"And if there's a hangup sometime in the middle of the night?"

"I've got an alert set to let me know if anything happens and the VMC stops. I'll get a ride back to the shop and take care of whatever it is."

Reggie gave another nod.

"Good job, Watson. I've trained you well."

"Maybe too well," I countered. "This new steering wheel project you brought in isn't like anything we typically do."

"You can handle it," said Reggie as he drove. "If you never step outside the box, you'll never learn anything new. Sure, we can continue making carburetor spacers by the dozens and little nick-nack aftermarket parts for the local shops. But sooner or later we're gonna have to branch out. This seems like it's just the project to get us going in that direction."

I nodded with a full understanding.

"Sounds good to me, sir. I'll make it happen."

"I know you will, Watson."

That pretty much summed up what I loved about working for Reggie. He was a guy who valued business as well as the abilities of his employees. We were a small machine shop punching above our weight, and it felt good to be on the receiving end of challenges like this.

"You seemed pretty smitten with the whole steering wheel idea from Arthur," Reggie added. "How come you never told me you used to race?"

Even though it was Reggie, I still felt an internal barrier go up.

I made an audible sigh that hopefully wasn't too audible.

"It was just a thing I did when I was a kid," I lied. "It really wasn't anything serious, and I guess I didn't think it was ever relevant enough to bring up."

"Must've taken it seriously to have had hand controls designed for you. Don't hear too many people jumping into racing after having to learn how to walk again either. Ever win any races?"

"Just one."

Reggie must've picked up on the fact that I was purposely being short.

"All right, Watson. I'm not trying to probe or nothin'. You know me. Your past is behind you, and it's often better to keep it that way. I was just curious about the racing is all."

I know he didn't mean any harm, and if anything, Reggie was just trying to make conversation. I made an honest effort to at least crack the door open a bit.

"It's a..."

An awkward pause followed.

Shit. I went there.

"It's a what?" asked Reggie.

I took a deep breath and dived in.

"It's a family thing. Or at least it was. My dad and grandad were both pretty involved with racing, so I guess I just wanted to see what I could do too."

Reggie didn't react right away. I knew him well enough to know that he wasn't expecting what I'd just told him.

"This really isn't a sob story or a cry for help, Reggie. I tried my hand at it, and it didn't work out. That's all. I don't have any regrets, and I'm happy with where I am."

Reggie remained quiet.

"What?"

"I didn't say nothin'," countered Reggie.

"No, but you're thinking it. I promise I'm not some basket case wilting in the corner of your shop wishing I was somewhere else as life passes me by."

"I don't doubt your abilities or your heart for a second, Watson," said Reggie. "Like I said, your past is behind you. Probably better to keep it that way. I'm talking to myself too."

"Only crazies do that, Reggie. But I guess it's better than talking to inflatables," I joked.

Reggie didn't miss a beat.

"What you do on your own time is your business, Watson."

"I'm kidding, Reggie."

"I mean, if I pick you up one morning and you've got some blond-haired inflatable you're wanting to put in the back seat with you, then yeah, I'ma start asking some questions."

"Reggie..."

"I may start makin' some damn phone calls too."

"Oh my God."

"Just keep that kinky shit in your apartment with you."

"Wow, Reggie."

Erupting in laughter, Reggie continued to drive his Chevy Suburban towards my place. Luckily, my apartment happened to be on the way to Reggie's house, so it was never an inconvenience. If it was, however, he never mentioned it.

As we got closer, I spoke up.

"Could you drop me off at the corner here?"

Reggie knew exactly where I was going.

"Well it is Tuesday," he replied. "Shit, Watson. You keep eating that stuff, you're gonna blow an O-ring out your ass."

"The flavor is worth the pain," I said.

Pulling up to the corner, Reggie brought the vehicle to a stop, and I climbed out.

"Thanks again, boss. I'll see you in the A.M."

"God help you, Watson. Have a good one."

I closed the door and waved as Reggie drove away.

From here, it was just two stores down to my next destination.

With it being a Tuesday night, I normally grabbed dinner from a small taco shop.

Why tacos? Because it's Tuesday.

I loved this place and I quickly became a regular.

Taco Town was what many consider a mom 'n' pop shop that was owned and operated by an older Chinese man. Yeah, I got a good laugh when I first heard that, but the guy makes the best damned tacos you've ever had.

"Chad Watson!" he said from the kitchen as he noticed me walking in, his broken English accent seeming to add to his charm. "Taco takeout tonight?"

"Hi, Mr. Lee. Yes, the usual please."

"Of course!"

He went to work right away.

Three items.

One beef and cheese burrito, one chicken quesadilla and one hard shell taco along with a side of black beans.

Hey. Variety is the spice of life, or so I've heard.

"Today is a special day, Chad Watson," Mr. Lee said as he prepared my food.

"Special day, huh? Why's that?"

"Today is my daughter's birthday."

"Really? What's your daughter's name?"

"Her name is Grace. Like her grandmother."

"Well happy birthday to Grace," I replied. "Does she live up here with you?

Mr. Lee stopped what he was doing for a moment before continuing.

"No. Grace passed away shortly after birth. I still celebrate."

A five-ton wrecking ball landed square against my gut.

"Lee, I'm sorry. I didn't mean to…"

"*Mister* Lee," he corrected. "You're a good man, Chad Watson. Good young man. Extra taco for you."

"Wha…You don't have to do that."

"No one else cares to ask when I bring up. I won't take *no* for an answer. Kindness for kindness. Good ch'i. Helps make world a better place."

Mr. Lee finished preparing my food and met me by the register at the front counter.

Ringing up my order, he replied with a smile.

"Extra taco on the house. You still pay for others. This isn't a soup kitchen."

I suddenly wished there were more Mr. Lees in the world as I smiled and swiped my debit card.

Throwing the receipt into the bag with my food, Mr. Lee handed it to me and gave a curt bow.

"Good evening, Chad Watson."

Receiving the bag, I turned towards the door.

"Have a good one, Mr. Lee."

I still felt like I'd been hit with a sucker punch as I walked out of the store. A bunch of questions I wanted to ask Mr. Lee suddenly filled my mind, but I decided against it. If anything, I knew all about letting bygones be bygones.

As much as I loved the change of pace that living in Wisconsin brought, one thing I still hadn't gotten used to in the four years I'd been here is the weather. If it wasn't bone chilling cold, it was muggy. If it wasn't either of those, it was probably snowing. Today it was snowing.

As a kid in Texas, I would get excited for snow days. Most Texans weren't used to it and didn't care for it. As a matter of fact, I seem to recall the entire city of Austin pretty much shutting down at one point over a light dusting of snow. But in Wisconsin... the shine wore off pretty quick regarding snow.

I arrived at my apartment, which was on the top level of a three-story complex. Good for the legs, or so I told myself when Reggie and I signed the lease papers. That, and it's a little more difficult for people to take off with your stuff when they know they have to descend two flights of narrow stairs.

I entered, closing the door behind me and taking my shoes off beside the door. Setting the bag of food on the table, I made my way into the bedroom, where I changed out of my work clothes and into something more comfortable.

Workout shorts and old t-shirts are pretty much my go-to.

Grabbing a plate and a fork from the kitchen, I transferred my dinner from the bag. Because why the hell not. From there it was a few steps to the couch, where I plopped down with an audible *sigh*. I reached for the TV remote, cued up the Green Bay Packers game from the previous night and settled in.

This was my life now. Routines, processes and procedures. It wasn't anything glamorous but neither was I.

It was simple.

Clean.

Drama-free.

And after all the hell I've been through, eating tacos alone on a Tuesday night while watching football suited me just fine.

PROCESS AND PROCEDURE

9

Mama

Time passed as it always does. My days continued to offer fresh challenges—the good and the bad kind—but no one ever said life was simple. I did my best not to complain when things got rough, though.

However, I'd be lying if I said I no longer faced issues from my past. Years and long distances can take you only so far. Ghosts have a way of finding you despite how hard you try to ward them off.

There wasn't a day that went by that I didn't think of the accident I had with Kate. The idea that I'd ruined someone's life haunted me. I often wondered what she was doing, how she was going about life, the kinds of struggles she faced…

When memories like these would surface, I would find myself wanting to shut down. I would feel the walls closing in around me, which would cause me to instinctively retreat within my mind. During those times, I often found it difficult to do the most basic of functions.

Despite the life of structure and stability I'd spent years building from the ground up, that dark corner of my life was always there.

It was an ever-present reminder that I was still vulnerable.

In the face of all this, I was grateful to have a support system around me. Reggie kept an open-door policy with me since he knew all about my past in *that* regard.

Sixteen-year-old kids don't just show up to places like the Morgan Shipley Center for getting poor grades. They've got to be pretty bad off, and such was the case with me. It made perfect sense to reveal that part of my past with Reggie, especially since he had agreed to take me under his wing.

From time to time, however, Reggie needed to call in some backup. He would never call it that, but I was no dummy. I knew when I was getting under Reggie's skin. For a man who's never had kids, he sure had a lot of patience, but everyone has their limits. When Reggie and I felt like we were both getting to ours, we'd plan a special trip.

Riding with Reggie was a lot like riding with Grandad. For a guy who was in his mid-thirties, he'd sure been through a lot. He had his storied wisdom that he was always eager to share, but not so much that you got the feeling he was trying to impress you. Reggie simply loved helping people.

Upon arriving at our destination, it was easy to see where he got that from.

"Reggie! Get up here and give your mama a kiss!" We hadn't even exited the vehicle yet, but Reggie's mom was already outside on her front porch greeting us.

We both climbed out, working our way towards her.

"Hey, Mama," said Reggie as the two embraced.

"Good to see you, baby. You been takin' care of yourself?" she asked. Oddly, it sounded more like a demand than a question.

"You know me, Mama. I do what I can."

Unconvinced by the answer, she turned towards me.

"Chad, has he been takin' care of himself?"

I smiled.

"He's doing a lot better job of it than I am, Mama Fuller."

I'd yet to learn her first name. It was always *mama this* and *mama that*, so I just followed suit. Reggie told me it wasn't until he'd graduated from high school that he actually learned his mom's first name. On one occasion after that, he'd referred to her by her first name.

It was the last time he ever did so.

A look of compassion came on her face. I had to admit, there was

93

something very comforting about it.

"Come here, Chad," she said as she worked her way towards me. "You may not be my son but you're still my boy."

We embraced as I kissed her on the cheek.

"You're such a sweet boy," she said as she pinched my cheek.

At once, however, her demeanor changed.

"Now you two go on and get in the house. I've been up too damn long to let the food get cold."

Making our way inside, the inevitable question arose.

"Chad, you met any nice girls up there yet?" she always asked.

"No, ma'am," I replied as I helped set the table. "Not yet, anyways. Reggie keeps me too busy for that."

As soon as the words left my mouth, I realized I'd left the door wide open for Reggie to insert a comment concerning the now-running joke between us about inflatables. He sent a mischievous smile my way and raised his eyebrows so I knew he was thinking it.

As we sat down for dinner, Reggie filled Mama Fuller in on how things were going at the shop. For the better part of the evening, however, it was Mama Fuller who did most of the talking. Both Reggie and I continued to eat as she filled us in on everything from the happenings of her neighborhood to family affairs to eventually landing on telling stories of Reggie from when he was much younger.

These stories didn't last long as Reggie was quick to put the kibosh on them but when they did come out, they were absolute gold.

"Back when this boy was around five," said Mama Fuller, "he really wanted a pet. *Any* pet. He didn't even care. One time I came home to find eggs from the fridge all over the house. They were under chairs, inside shoes, under the couch and even on shelves."

"Mama—"

"Hush! I asked him, 'Reginald, what are you doing with all these eggs?' He said, 'Chickens lay eggs and they turn into little chicks. I thought if I put the eggs out, they'd hatch and I'd have me some chickens.'"

I made a mental note to leave an egg in Reggie's office from time to time.

More than anything, however, Mama Fuller wanted to know how we were doing and how things were going at the shop.

"I'm glad to hear things are going well up there, Reggie. Lord knows you deserve it after everything you went through to keep it."

An awkward silence filled the room. I couldn't tell if Mama Fuller intentionally meant to say that or if she let it slip. The atmosphere had changed.

Luckily, I wasn't the only one to pick up on it.

"Mama, we really shouldn't go there."

"How could we have not told Chad this story?" asked Mama Fuller. "This is where it all began and without that shop, I wouldn't have these two fine young men in here with me now."

"I don't think Chad really cares to know all the details, Mama."

With her eyebrows raised and her chin lowered, Mama Fuller turned to me with a look of disbelief on her face.

"Chad, you strike me as a man who loves details. Am I right?"

"The way I see it, we're all family here. Right, Reggie?" I replied.

Reggie had a blank look on his face as he stared at me while chewing his food.

Mama Fuller brushed her hand in the air towards him.

"Oh never mind him. If you don't know now, I'm sure you'll figure it out eventually. You see, that shop used to belong to Reggie's father, Clarence. He..."

"It was he and his business partner's shop, Mama," Reggie interrupted. The annoyed look on his face was telling as to how he felt.

Mama Fuller shot Reggie a cold look.

"Don't you interrupt me! I'll come over there and slap that look right off your face!"

I sat there, momentarily stunned. I was honest to God scared to move for a brief second.

Now I know where Reggie gets his "take no shit" mentality from.

"Clarence *and his business partner*," Mama Fuller enunciated as she continued, "started that shop a few years after Reggie here was born.

Clarence served in the Army as a mechanic and went to school for manufacturing when he got out. That's where he met Bernard Williamson. Together, they got the idea for their own shop.

"Let's be clear here, though. I had my reservations. I didn't know this man he was partnering with very well, but Clarence…well, he was already having dreams and visions. I didn't fully trust Bernard, but I trusted Clarence. They got rolling and everything was going well for the first few years."

"What changed?" I asked.

Mama Fuller took a deep breath before continuing. Her voice was slightly somber now.

"With every deal they closed and new client they brought in, it gave them more and more reason to *celebrate*. You've been around the block enough to understand what I'm talkin' about, Chad."

"Drinking?" I guessed. I didn't want to venture too far.

"Drinking, partying, lavish business dinners, corporate retreats, you name it. Before long, though, I realized probably a little too late that he and the bottle were more than just friends. He just couldn't stop. Day, night—it didn't matter. He'd try hiding the empty bottles from me but I'd always find 'em. I even went up to the shop one time to try to clean out his liquor stash because I'd had enough. That's when I found out what was going on."

"What you *think* was going on."

"I know what I saw, Reggie!"

"Mama, this is why I didn't wanna talk about this. It's gettin' you all worked up."

"I'm always worked up. You should know that by now," she barked back. "Anyways, I caught that business partner of his, Bernard, bringing him bottles and bottles of alcohol. He was *encouraging* him to drink—pushing him closer to the edge."

Mama Fuller took another deep breath and let it out slowly.

"I tried to warn him. He didn't listen. Said he had everything under control. Then after the first hospital visit, the doctors tried to tell him to stop, but he still wouldn't listen. It wasn't six months later that he…"

Mama Fuller choked up as she covered her nose with her hand.

"Mama…"

Reggie rose from his seat, moved to where Mama Fuller was and sat down next to her.

"…that he died of a heart attack. After that, his business partner just took over. I tried pressing charges, but the lawyers said it would never hold up in court."

Wiping her eyes, she turned and looked at me.

"Let me ask you something, Chad. Is a man any less of a murderer if he puts poison in front of someone and convinces them into thinking it's water? My Clarence was a good man. But when under that kind of influence, even good men can fall. I think you know that all too well, Chad."

The thought of Nora suddenly filled my mind. It was only the briefest of flashbacks, but it shook me. She was the one who led me down the dark path, but I was a willing participant.

Mama Fuller continued.

"Reggie here was still in college over in Virginia at the time all this happened with his daddy. I begged him to stay in school but, well, he's always been wise beyond his years, so he put a plan in motion."

"What kind of a plan?" I asked.

"A foolish and desperate plan," replied Reggie. "I offered to buy the entire business from Bernard. He said *no*. Then I threatened to burn the entire building to ground. I said, 'You can either lose everything or take the money and walk away.' Either way, it wasn't gonna be his shop anymore."

"I take it he bit?"

"Yeah, he bit. Offered me the business for nearly double what it's worth. I tried talking him down, but he wasn't budging. So I did something stupid. Rather than continue to negotiate, I got a business loan. I think I just wanted it to be done with, and I wanted him out of the way."

"Hmm," snorted Mama Fuller. "There's more than one way to get a snake like that out of the way."

"Outside of *going to jail*," Reggie enunciated. "I wasn't about to stoop down to his level. I bought the shop, and it's done."

"Only it wasn't done," replied Mama Fuller.

Reggie sighed, an audible expression of frustration.

"Right before he left, Bernard reached out to all of his clients at the shop, told them all he'd been bought out and if they valued the quality of their products, they should look elsewhere. Probably ninety percent of them left."

"That's right around the time you moved back in with me to save money on rent," said Mama Fuller. "Every day, he'd drive all the way up there, work all day and then hop in the car to drive all the way back here. Even so, the amount of money he owed was just too much. Sooner or later, I thought the bank was gonna take the house from under us."

"I felt like I had to start the business from scratch," said Reggie. "So I did. I gave it a new name, we had a big grand opening party and I started attracting some fresh business. It took several years but eventually and by the grace of God, that loan was paid off."

Looking over at me, Reggie looked stern as he continued.

"Let me tell you something, Chad. When you're desperate and uncertain, it's easy to get worried and feel like the world is crumbling around you. In those moments, you absolutely have to believe that anything is possible. You have to clear your mind, calm your heart and tell yourself that everything's gonna be all right. Sometimes it works, other times it doesn't. Even if it doesn't, that's no excuse to give up. Ever."

"And sweetie," said Mama Fuller. "Don't ever forget that you can always talk to us if you're ever going through anything you feel like you can't handle. Some burdens weren't meant to be carried by one set of shoulders."

I nodded. It was exactly what I'd needed to hear.

It's hard to describe it, but my heart felt better. Relieved. I felt comforted knowing that I once again had a family I could talk to and trust.

I vow not to screw it up like I did with Grandad.

"I've gotta ask—whatever happened to Bernard, the business partner?"

"Dead."

The absoluteness in Mama Fuller's voice seemed to give her a sense of satisfaction.

"Now, before you go off gettin' all sorts of ideas, it unfortunately wasn't me."

"Mama…"

Reggie could only shake his head.

"He got himself killed in some basement after getting into an argument over some damn card game," said Mama Fuller. "Or so I've heard. It's kinda sad when you think about it. After getting all that money from Reggie for the business, he had everything he'd ever need but lost his life while chasing a few dollars."

After a brief moment, Reggie rose from his seat.

"Anyways, that's ancient history. It's gettin' dark, so we best be leavin' soon."

As Reggie started gathering the plates and utensils on the table, Mama Fuller asked, "You boys gonna come down here and see Mama again next weekend?"

I was just about to accept when Reggie held up his hand and spoke up first.

"We'd love to, Mama, but we actually have a commitment."

"We do?" I asked. "On a Saturday?"

"You remember Arthur, right? The man we made that batch of parts for to use on that steering wheel? His team assembled the first prototype, and they're ready to test it out. He invited both of us out to see it firsthand."

"Where are they testing it?" I asked as I handed Reggie my plate.

"Just in the parking lot outside their building. Nothing fancy."

I chuckled at the idea of a parking lot test. "Sounds boring and lacking adventure. Count me in."

Still seated at the table, Mama Fuller spoke up.

"Chad, don't be afraid of the unknown or of stepping out of your comfort zone. I get the feeling that life's gonna take you to a few faraway places. You're a good man and you have a gift. Embrace it, don't fear it. But more importantly, don't squander it."

"She's always right about these things," replied Reggie from the kitchen.

At that, Mama Fuller rose from her seat.

"All right. I know you got that cane in one hand but the good Lord saw fit to give you another hand for cleaning dishes. Go on, now."

10

Ride, Pony, Ride

I 've never been a fan of working on Saturdays. It's not that I haven't done it before, it's that it just feels strange. Regardless, I was waiting outside my apartment at 9 a.m. for Reggie.

"So we're going to a parking lot?"

"Yes," Reggie replied.

"To watch some guy drive a car around with his hands?"

"Yes," he repeated.

"May I ask *why?*"

A deep sigh from Reggie followed. I almost think he was asking himself the same question.

"Because when a client invites you out to see the finished product of something you helped build, it's common courtesy to say *yes*," replied Reggie. "Plus, it builds client relations, and like I said when we first met Arthur, we're trying to branch out."

"I mean I get it. I just don't know what we're supposed to do there."

"Be polite," he said. "Shake hands, act amazed and try not to stand in the food tent the entire time. Plus, I think this may be something you'll appreciate, Mister *I-used-to-race-but-never-bothered-to-tell-anybody.*"

He was still sour about that.

"What would I appreciate about it? Are they gonna have some *dump truck*...excuse me...*stock car* I can stand next to and take a picture with?

I'm always looking for things I can hang on my fridge."

Reggie knew my sarcasm when he heard it. However, he'd long since stopped rising to the bait.

"From what I gathered, they're gonna be testing a car with the modified steering wheel on some course they made in said parking lot. *Traffic cones, speed* and *stop watches* were words Arthur used when I spoke with him about the event."

For some reason, I instantly perked up.

"What do you mean? Like autocross or something?"

"What the hell's autocross?" asked Reggie.

"Basically everything you just described," I replied. "You set a course up with cones and you try to get through it in the shortest amount of time."

Reggie chuckled.

"So...like an obstacle course for cars?"

"That would probably piss off a lot of people but yes, that's pretty much it."

During my karting days, I'd once considered autocross as a means of getting some seat time behind the wheel of a full-sized car. It's relatively inexpensive compared with actually racing wheel to wheel with other cars, and it supposedly teaches you car control. The more I looked into it, however, the more the idea seemed nearly incomprehensible, when you considered that you're literally standing in a parking lot for eight hours with the hope of *maybe* getting six minutes behind the wheel.

I decided to stick with karting.

It wasn't long before we pulled up to our destination on the outskirts of town. It was one of those big fancy buildings with no name on it. The kind you drive past and wonder what the hell goes on inside but turn away and just as quickly forget it was ever there.

We parked close to a small group of about ten or so other cars to make our way towards a red and white tent located nearby. The second I opened the door to exit Reggie's vehicle, I heard it. The unmistakable roar of a V8.

For the briefest of moments, my mind took leave and I was a kid again while sitting in the passenger seat of Grandad's '68 Mustang smiling ear to ear as he floored it. A V8 in full stride is a sound that brings a smile to the face of everyone from little kids to grownups.

I was no exception.

"Well look at you, all smiles now," Reggie noticed. "Should've brought your inflatable friend with you. It'd be good for the two of you to meet some new people."

"All right, all right," I said as I tried to diffuse this conversation from progressing any further. Really, though. I just wanted to listen to that sound all day. The only way I can accurately describe it is like rediscovering a song you haven't heard in ages. All you want to do is put it on repeat and listen to it all day.

As Reggie and I got closer, I got my first glimpse of the car between a small gathering of people as it whizzed by.

At first glance, it appeared to be an older S95 Mustang GT. Probably a '94 by the looks of it.

The closer we got, the more I was able to see it on the course. The worn-out blue paint had seen better days and every time the car hooked a corner, it looked like it wanted to roll over.

Whoever the driver was, they were pushing way too hard in an effort to fight the apparent understeer of…

"Arthur! Good to see you again!"

Reggie's voice pulled me out of my daze as I turned my attention towards the man who'd invited us out here.

"Reggie and Chad! Good to have y'all out!" he replied. What caught me off guard was how he genuinely sounded like he meant it.

"Chad, how you been holding up? Is Reggie here workin' you too hard?"

"You know it, sir," I replied as we shook hands. "Thank you for the invite."

"It was the least I could do after y'all delivered the parts we needed so quickly. I wasn't sure what to expect but as you can see, everything looks to be working as it should."

Arthur indicated towards the blue Mustang that was about to start another run.

I watched as Arthur pulled out his phone and opened a stopwatch app.

As soon as the car took off, he started the timer and closely watched the car as it weaved its way around the cones.

In typical autocross fashion, it was over just as quickly as it began as Arthur stopped his clock.

"Just shy of thirty-two seconds flat. He's getting faster!"

"Who's the wheelman?" I asked.

"Oh, just a local club racer we found on social media. Paid him a few bucks and told him to show up with his gear to drive for a little bit and give us some feedback."

I hesitated before asking my next question.

"Does he...you know..."

"Does he have a paralyzing injury preventing him from operating a normal life?" Arthur finished my question with a smile. "No, I'm afraid not. Folks like us are hard to come by. No, sir, he's a regular old driver who's learning to drive with his hands and not his feet. Pretty impressive, actually."

Reggie just couldn't help himself.

"You should've asked Chad here. I'm sure he would've done it."

"The thought did cross my mind, but I didn't want to assume the man who made the parts for it would also want to drive."

"Oh, I think mister kart racer here would love a chance to show what he's got," Reggie smiled.

Holding up my hands in front of me, I suddenly felt a great fear land on my shoulders. Almost as if every eyeball in the world was looking directly at me.

"I'm fine, really," I lied. "I'm happy enough just to be here."

Reggie didn't give up.

"How about a friendly wager?"

Arthur—seemingly witnessing a side of Reggie he'd never seen before—seemed amused at the display and played along.

"What do ya have in mind?"

Rubbing his chin, Reggie said, "I bet you that Chad could beat your driver's time."

"Reggie," I immediately protested, "I don't even have a driver's license."

"We're in a parking lot, Watson," Reggie chuckled. "What's the worst that could happen?"

Deep down, I think Reggie knew this was going to be a boring day. This was just his way of spicing things up a bit.

"Nothing crazy," Reggie continued. "Loser buys lunch for the other. Oh, and what the hell…if Chad wins, he gets a day off next week."

I wanted to send out a sharp rebuke, something to at least let Reggie know that I didn't enjoy being put on the spot like this. I could feel the walls of my past forming around me again. Walls I hadn't felt in years.

Call it anxiety, call it fear, call it whatever you want. The grip of it all was tightening around my neck.

The screech of tires from the car as it understeered into a corner dragged me out of my stupor.

"What do ya say, Watson?" Reggie added. "You wanna have a run in this thing or what?"

I think he suddenly realized what he'd done. The look on his face said it all.

This is a way out if you want it.

A way out…

A chance to run from my fear.

What I found to be absolutely crazy, however, was that I was somehow drawn to it. Instead of wanting to run from the fear, I wanted to confront it…or maybe run *with* it.

Whatever was happening, my cheeks became flush as I took note of a few others around us turning to see what Reggie, Arthur and I were talking about.

As the car took off to start another run, I was in a position to see it more clearly and instinctively began analyzing the driver's line through the course. Right away, I saw that the driver was getting on the power way too early and causing the car to oversteer through the middle of a corner as the back of the car swung out. Every time it would happen, the driver would have to lift off the gas to get the car back under control before continuing on.

Ending his run, the driver brought the car to a stop and climbed out—leaving the door open as he did. Staring at it for far too long, the open door felt like an invitation. All I knew is that over the last several years, I'd learn to confront my fears. Running from them was what the old Chad would do.

I was done with running.

"Look, Chad," Reggie spoke again, "you don't have to. I just thought…"

"Deal."

My words stopped Reggie in his tracks. A shocked look rose to the surface of his face and dear God how I wish I could've grabbed a picture of it.

Arthur continued to look content as he watched this play out, an intrigued smile creeping onto his face.

"All right, Watson," Reggie finally spoke.

"But I want a few warmup laps," I blurted out.

Reggie turned towards Arthur as if asking for permission.

"Be my guest," replied the older man. "So long as there's rubber on the rims, you can ride it as long as you want."

Without any other words, I turned and walked towards the open door.

It was almost as if my life was moving in slow motion as I made my way towards the Mustang, just as my grandad had at Bathurst all those years ago. I imagined both he and my dad were walking with me.

The rust along the bottom edges of the body was a local characteristic of Michigan, but the faded blue paint looked even more prehistoric up close.

As I climbed into the car, it immediately felt foreign. Having spent the last several years riding in the passenger seat of Reggie's SUV, sitting low to the ground in the driver's seat of a muscle car felt out of place. The car's tan interior had seen better days. Although the front seats had been replaced with aluminum racing seats, the carpet and dashboard remained as a reminder of the car's apparently dismal past.

A noticeable cigarette burn was on the center console and even with both windows open, the smell inside the car was a mixture of what could only be described as *assoline*.

Before I got too comfortable, I looked ahead through the front windshield to see Arthur talking to the driver he'd hired. The younger man looked a bit put out. That is, until Arthur pulled some cash out and handed it to him. All of a sudden, the driver handed Arthur his helmet as the latter turned and walked back towards me.

"You're gonna need this," he said as he handed the helmet to me through the open window. "Make sure it fits you nice and tight. And don't break it... it's a rental."

Slipping the helmet over my head, my memories and raw competitive emotions returned. I felt my adrenaline kicking into high gear for the first time in years and I hadn't even started the car yet. The helmet was a lot nicer than the one I wore while karting.

Just behind him, I saw Reggie with his phone out filming and looking way too cinematic in the process.

A series of taps on the helmet brought me back to Arthur's attention.

"Right here," he said to me as he pointed two fingers on his left hand at his eyes. "Just take it easy at first. If this is indeed the first time you've driven a full-sized car, don't be in a rush to impress anyone and honestly, don't even worry about Reggie's friendly wager. Just have some fun and let me know what you think of the steering wheel."

I nodded as I looked down at the steering wheel, the very wheel I'd built. It looked different out here in the wild but then again, this is where it belonged. This was the first time I'd ever actually used something I'd manufactured. Considering I was about to put my life in its hands, it made me glad I was as thorough as I am.

"Gas is on the right, brake on the left," Arthur continued. "The throttle will automatically disengage when the brake handle is pulled. This is to avoid dragging the brake while gas is being applied."

Reggie was still filming with his phone when he approached to get a close up.

"Smile for the camera, Watson."

Holding out a closed fist towards me, I met Reggie's fist bump and also offered one to Arthur, who chuckled again as he accepted.

Giving a few taps to the hood of the car as he walked away, Arthur shouted out.

"Line 'er up and let 'er rip!"

Turning the ignition, the V8 fired to life as cold chills shot down my spine. I wasn't a kid in a candy shop; I was an adult who stole the whole damn candy truck.

Using the gear selector on the center console, I put the car into *drive* and used the hand controls to slowly accelerate towards the starting line.

Not a bad way to spend a Saturday morning.

11

The Shitbox

Adjusting the helmet, which was entirely too loose, I kept my eyes fixed on the starter. Modern tracks had electronic starters, but what's better than an old man and a stopwatch? I did my best to recall the starting procedures I'd used while karting and relaxed my hands on the wheel as my fingertips rested on the throttle hand control.

"Ready?"

The old man locked eyes with me.

"Set?"

I took a deep breath and exhaled slowly, fully expecting the man to be shouting *Go* on my exhale but he didn't. He let it hang for far too long.

Is this a reality TV show or some....

"Go!"

Caught off guard by my own thoughts, I went full squeeze on the throttle. The tires protested loudly as I succeeded in burning another layer of rubber off them.

At least they're warm now.

The thought barely registered as I accelerated towards the first turn. After all these years, the sudden sense of speed was overwhelming.

The first left turn was taken at a satisfactory speed as I tracked out and looked forward.

Another left...

I pulled the brake handle, which succeeded in locking the front tires. I couldn't have been going faster than thirty miles per hour, but it suddenly felt like I was going over two hundred.

I took the turn way too wide and was suddenly reminded of what it felt like to steer a boat during a trip when I was much younger.

I noticed the right turn far too late as I plowed over the cone to proceed onward. A long sweeping right turn followed, which I negotiated well enough.

Then I came upon the slalom.

Braking again, I used a lot less of the brake handle this time, which felt rewarding as the car actually slowed down.

The only problem was that I had slowed down a tad too late.

It's been a minute, huh, Chad?

I was all over the place as I dived into the slalom. Leveling the first two cones, I got into a rhythm far too late but I did succeed in completing the final two cones.

A hairpin turn was up next but I failed to look far enough ahead to see just how sharp it was and ended up killing a few more cones.

Progressing onward, a high-speed slalom was next, and I was able to see that one well enough. My adrenaline was pumping more than it had in several years and I couldn't wrap my head around getting my entry into the first section correct.

I ended up going in too fast, which caused me to kill even more cones on the second turn of the slalom. I decided to abort the rest.

Another long-sweeping turn, this time to the left was taken successfully but I didn't see the chicane-like corner up ahead just before the finish line. I tried to slow the car down but I once again only managed to lock the wheels up and slid right through it.

Once I crossed the line, I exhaled heavily.

After less than a minute of driving, I found myself breathing heavy and felt my hands gripping the steering wheel so tight one might think my life depended on it.

Bringing the car to a stop, I heard something that lit a fire under my ass so bright I felt like I was seeing red.

Laughter.

Yeah, I get it. I killed a bunch of cones and I was just the snot-nosed shop worker someone thought would be a good idea to stick in the car.

Or maybe everyone knew I would suck at this and just thought it'd be funny to watch.

But I knew who I was and, more importantly, who I wasn't. And I'd be damned if I was gonna be someone's Saturday morning entertainment at my expense.

"All right, Chad," The unmistakable voice of Reggie could be heard approaching. "That was a good show. Let's let the other driver back..."

"What was my time?" I interrupted.

Reggie laughed.

"Numbers don't go that high, Watson. C'mon, let's..."

"What was my time, Reggie?" I demanded.

A sudden pause ensued as we locked eyes, and I suddenly hoped he wasn't planning to beat the shit out of me.

"Shit, I don't know. Hey, Arthur..."

I turned to see the older figure of Arthur heading our way.

"What time did you get *Speedy McChad* here at?"

Arthur raised his eyebrows as he looked down at his timer. It was almost as if those white bushy eyebrows were saying, *Do you really wanna know?*

"The timer says forty-three point four seconds."

"What was the other driver's time?" I asked.

A quick huff of air came from Arthur's nose.

"Thirty-one point eight seconds. You're just a *wee* bit off the pace, it seems."

In an instant, I was somehow able to recall the entire course in my head. I remembered the feeling of getting it wrong, the sensation of the corners I got right.

Why did I get those right? How did the car feel when I did?

A memory of Grandad surfaced. "Remember, Chad, karts are one thing, but if you eventually get into a full-sized car with higher horsepower, just remember

111

these words: slow in, fast out."

"Chad," Reggie's voice brought me back. "I think you've had enough fun for one day. How about we let the driver hop back in?"

"If it's okay with you," I said, trying to be civil after snapping on him earlier, "I'd like to try again. The first one's always a throwaway anyways, right?"

The old saying Reggie used to tell me when I'd first started making parts for him caused him to smile.

Reggie turned to Arthur and gestured towards the car.

"Just don't hurt yourself," was all Arthur said as he turned back.

After seeing Arthur go back towards the people in attendance, Reggie approached and stuck his head through the window. His face was stern, and he once again locked eyes with me.

"Listen to me, Chad. We're not here to play games. They're here testing a product out. Not giving us a free pass to have a joy ride. Be respectful of the situation."

"I will," I replied. "And thank you. I…"

Reggie was pulling his head out of the window and stopped upon hearing my hesitation.

"You what?"

I took a deep breath.

"I know I'm better than what I just did. And maybe I just really want that day off."

That last part caused Reggie to smile as he slapped the roof of the car.

"Get this shitbox on the start line. Make it a good one, Watson."

I nodded and applied enough squeeze to the hand control to get the old pony moving.

I have to admit: Just steering a car again felt weird let alone driving one aggressively. Even so, the feeling began returning to me. It was almost as if a dormant hunger was awakening or maybe it had been there all along and I'd just learned how to ignore it over the years.

Given my present circumstance, there was no ignoring it now.

I brought the car to a stop at the start line.

That same old man with the stopwatch was there waiting for me. This time, he had a smug grin on his face, which caused me to do a double take.

"What in the…"

"Ready?"

Not this time. I turned my attention forward as I quickly replayed my previous run through my mind.

"Set?"

Relax your hands.

Breathe.

Once again, the old man let his previous word hang for way too long, but I waited. This time, I was eager. Hungry, even.

"Go!"

I applied a ginger amount of power to the throttle handle, which didn't cause the tires to burn down.

I accelerated away briskly towards the first section. As before, I took the first left turn well enough but remembered to look ahead towards the braking zone of the next corner.

Squeezing the brakes ever so slightly, I succeeded in slowing the car down enough for me to tip it in to the left and execute the turn successfully.

Breathing: Check

A quick right turn followed but the longer sweeping right allowed me to open the throttle up a bit more confidently.

Then came the slalom. It was one of those things that fall under the *acquired taste* category.

Once again, I failed to get the timing right for the first few cones. I think I murdered a cone or two in the process before I finally got through and towards the next corner.

I'd previously gotten on the power way too early while negotiating the hairpin. I was a bit too conservative second time around. Nevertheless, I came out the other end without murdering any cones.

The next section was the high-speed slalom. The cones were spread farther apart, and I found myself doing a countdown out loud as I approached, wishing I'd taken my music classes in school more seriously, because I had no rhythm.

I barreled into the slalom successfully but couldn't get the timing right. I was looking ahead but still found myself reacting as opposed to planning what my hands were gonna do next.

Slowing down just to make sure I completed the section successfully, I proceeded towards a long sweeping left. I saw the deception in it that time.

The corner tightened up on exit and led to a quick chicane. It had caught me off guard last time resulting in me blowing through the entire section. I lined the car up correctly but I was carrying too much speed and locked the front wheels up. Again.

I nearly killed a cone in the process but managed to keep the car between them instead. Making the final chicane at a slightly lower speed than I'd wanted, I crossed the line feeling a bit happier.

Slowly, I brought the car to a stop. Instead of laughter this time, I was surprised to hear a few rounds of applause coming from the small crowd.

Reggie approached with an impressed look on his face.

"Not too bad, Watson," he admitted. "You've always been a fast learner."

"Time?" I asked. In truth, that was all I cared about.

Reggie shook his head as he turned to Arthur who was just a few steps behind him.

"Nicely done, young man!" he exclaimed. "You managed to shave eight seconds off the clock and got a thirty-five point one. That's pretty damn incredible if you ask me."

"Still not good enough," I said, which I instantly regretted.

Reggie was quick to step in.

"All right, Chad. I think you've had enough fun for one day."

He was right, and I was a man of my word. Reggie had given me one more run and I took it. In all, I was impressed with myself after being out of the saddle for this long.

"Fair is fair."

As I reached for the key to turn the engine off, however, it was Arthur who spoke up.

"Reggie," he looked out of the corner of his eye, "let's let the man go again.

My curiosity is piqued!"

Turning towards me, Reggie was already smiling.

"I don't even think I need to ask if you wanna have another go, Watson."

I flicked my eyebrows and revved the engine slightly causing both Reggie and Arthur to laugh.

"Just take it easy through the slalom," Arthur advised. "You're losing a lot of time by hesitating. If it helps, just enter both slaloms from the same side. Make it predetermined so you can anticipate where you'll be next."

The advice made sense: Remove the guesswork so you can plan the course of action more efficiently.

"Thank you, sir," I replied as Arthur pointed to the start line.

"Give us a good showing, Chad."

I turned to see the hired driver pacing from side to side. Here I was, taking his seat and also wearing his helmet. I guess I'd be pissed too.

As I pulled away and lined up again, the old man with the stopwatch gave me the biggest and cheesiest thumbs-up I've ever seen.

I returned the gesture but wasn't as exuberant about it. Instead, I turned my focus to the task at hand as I mentally prepared for the run.

"Ready?"

For some reason, it really sounded like a question this time.

"Set?"

Damn straight I am.

Another long pause.

"Go!"

I gave the throttle handle a bit more of a squeeze this time. A sharp chirp from the rear tires, and I was off in a much more spirited fashion than previously.

My momentum was carried through the two left corners much better this time as I felt my confidence begin to grow.

The quick but then long sweeping right-handers were taken faster as well. So much so that I could feel the rear of the car getting a bit squirrely.

As I approached the first slalom, time froze for a split second as I recalled my previous runs and what I did wrong.

Pick a side and move.

I moved the car to the right to enter the slalom from that side. Slowing down, I dived it in with a left turn as my hands moved the steering wheel right-left-right-left-right. I exited the slalom with a smile on my face and I imagined all the cones taking a big sigh of relief.

Braking for the hairpin, I did so a bit later than the last time, but used the hand control to modulate the brakes as I slowed the car down. Turning the wheel, I slowly squeezed the throttle with my right hand as I tipped the car in—gradually applying more gas as the car straightened out.

The high-speed slalom was next and as before, I knew I would be entering from the right. Turning in, I used the first cone as a braking zone as I slowed the car down enough to make the remaining turns without so much as killing a single cone. The timing came a bit more naturally. It just kinda clicked.

I sped away towards the final sweeping left followed by the chicane. I monitored my speed a bit more effectively and was able to line up my entrance into the chicane.

It was a feeling of jubilation as I crossed the line to end my run.

Rolling the car forward, I brought it to a stop. As before, I heard cheers but this time, they were more exuberant. Sharp whistles were accompanied by applause.

I looked out the driver's side window to see both Reggie and Arthur approaching.

"Shut the car off, son."

Arthur's word hit me unexpectedly, but I followed orders and turned the car off.

As silence filled the now empty air, I noticed that both Reggie and Arthur were looking at me with a stern look.

"I wanted the car turned off so you could hear me clearly," Arthur added. "The driver I hired—after numerous runs—did this course in thirty-one point eight seconds. You, Chad Watson, somehow managed to finish the course in thirty-one point..."

I waited for an eternity.

"Five."

"A thirty-one point five? I beat the driver you hired?"

"Damn straight you did."

What followed shortly thereafter is a bit of a blur. I recall screaming and getting out of the car. I think I'd planned to dance on the hood, but in all the commotion, I forgot I didn't have my cane with me and nearly fell to the ground. I'm glad Reggie's a good catch.

"Looks like you get that day off too. A bet's a bet."

"Thank you," I managed while still trying to catch my breath. "Both of you, thank you. This was such a fun opportunity."

Arthur suddenly had a perplexed look on his face.

"*Opportunity*. That's a fine choice of word you used. Say, how about you let me buy you that lunch sometime? I've got an idea I've been noodling over for a while now and I think it could present both of us with a few more...*opportunities*."

I shrugged, not really seeing the harm of having lunch with the man.

"Sure. Sounds good to me."

Arthur nodded in acknowledgment.

"What do you say we give that poor driver I hired his helmet back?"

12

Opportunity

"So what exactly are you asking me?"

I paced back and forth in front of my workstation as if the weight of the world were on my shoulders. Reggie—leaning against a nearby machine tool—watched on as someone who had seen this same scene unfold countless times before.

"I just don't know what happens next," I replied.

"How long has it been? A week?" Reggie rolled his eyes slightly. "Chad, you have your talents but patience has never been one of them. Give the man some time."

It had been just that—a week.

A week since that Saturday morning experience, which saw me step into a car and seemingly back into the world of racing. Ever since then, my mind had been going nonstop.

I could still see the look of the hired driver's face when I beat his time.

The sensation of hard braking, clipping apexes, getting back on the power...

All I could think about was being in that car.

Yes, that dilapidated shitbox that had more in common with a dump truck than a road-going motor vehicle, but in that rusty old pony, my senses had reawakened.

I wanted more.

More than anything, however, I wanted to know what the hell was taking Arthur so long to get back to me.

"Maybe I should call him," I asserted. "We did exchange info."

"You could," Reggie retorted. "But then you run the risk of coming across as desperate. For what? I have no idea. I damn sure hope he isn't trying to poach you from this shop, though."

"I don't think so," I stated. "I think it was related to the car thing. Or maybe I just *want* it to be."

Reggie smiled.

"Speedy McChad."

Reggie and I usually would shoot the breeze for a bit on Friday afternoons before we closed things down for the weekend. Our conversations were typically a bit more chill than this, though.

Reggie, being him, made known the fact that he'd posted a video of my first attempt at the autocross course on his social media page in all of its cone-killing glory. He made a point earlier in the day to tell me the video had already gotten over 70,000 views.

A slow round of applause was in order.

Things were a bit more tense, though, at least in my head they were.

"Really though," Reggie brought my thoughts back down to earth, "he may just wanna take you out to lunch and smother you with praise considering how well that steering wheel of his came together with the parts we built."

I let out a loud sigh.

"Yeah, you're probably right. I mean, rightfully so," I boasted.

Reggie rolled his eyes.

"Hey, c'mon. Did you see the low tolerance I got on all of those parts?"

Seemingly having had enough, Reggie pushed off the machine tool he was leaning on and—giving me a heavy slap on my shoulder—walked past me back to his office.

"I've trained you well, my young Padawan."

After a few seconds, he was nearly back in his office when he exclaimed from afar, "But those floors won't sweep themselves!"

I let out a chuckle as I got back to my duties.

Shitbox race cars, dreams, aspirations...they were one thing. But if there was one thing I'd learned over the past four years, it's that the moment that's in front of you is what matters. Focus on the present and let tomorrow worry about itself.

I picked up the nearby broom, put my earbuds in and began to make my rounds, returning to the routine I'd grown accustomed to. There was something therapeutic about it. Maybe it was the safety in knowing that by simply having a routine, I had security. A livelihood. A future.

Or maybe I just liked having structure in my life.

The bright lights of the shop dimmed as I began to turn sections of them off. The shop had been my second home, and as such, I always did my best to take care of it as if it were mine. Routine maintenance on the machines, inventory of equipment and materials, general cleanliness around the work areas...these were just a few of my responsibilities, but I was proud to be a part of the grind of a working machine shop.

A buzz from my pocket ceased my entrance into deeper thought. I pulled my phone out to see a text message.

[Sorry for the late response. Busy week! Wanna meet for lunch tomorrow? You name the place. My treat. —Arthur Collins]

My face lit up as I nearly dropped the push broom. All previous thoughts had suddenly taken flight.

Unsure of what to do next, I did the first thing that came to my mind.

Setting the broom against the wall, I turned towards Reggie's office.

* * *

The door to *Taco Town* squeaked as I stepped in, just as it always did.

"Good afternoon, Chad Watson!"

Mr. Lee was someone who could put a smile on your face at any given moment.

"I don't see you here very often on Saturdays," he added from behind the counter; wiping it down to maintain his store's typical immaculate environment. "You meeting a date here?" he asked.

I smiled.

"Hi, Mr. Lee. No, not a date but I am meeting someone," I confirmed.

With a slight nod, Mr. Lee went back to his duties.

I took a seat in a nearby booth and waited.

Arthur had agreed to meet me at 12:30 p.m. here at *Taco Town*. Although the offer had mentioned that we could meet anywhere for lunch, I tended to stay with the familiar. This was a place I was comfortable in, and I also knew the area. I could only hope that Arthur actually liked Mexican food.

I checked the clock and saw that it was 12:25 p.m. As I was mentally patting myself on the back for being early—just as Reggie had advised—I saw Arthur walk in. His white hair reflected the midday sunlight as he stepped inside. The white button-down shirt and pants he wore initially made me think of Colonel Sanders, but then I thought he looked more like the guy who owned the island in *Jurassic Park*.

I subdued the urge to laugh and stood as he approached.

"Chad! Good to see you again!"

We shook hands.

"Nice to see you too, sir."

"Please," he asserted. "Call me—"

"Arthur," I said, cutting him off. Then I corrected myself. "Sorry, old habits die hard I suppose."

Motioning for me to sit back down, Arthur added, "I must say, of all the places to meet for lunch, I didn't think a place like this would be what you preferred."

I glanced over Arthur's shoulder to see that Mr. Lee had indeed heard that comment.

"What can I say," I admitted. "I'm a simple man. That and this place makes the best damn tacos you'll ever have."

After a bit of small talk, we both made our way up to the counter to order. Arthur looked a bit hesitant for some reason. I got the feeling that this place was a bit below his standards.

"What can I get for you, Chad Watson?"

Mr. Lee waited expectantly as I contemplated my order. I thought about mixing things up and getting something a bit fancier, but hey, why change the habit of a lifetime.

"The usual for me, Mr. Lee. Please and thank you."

Mr. Lee punched a few buttons on the ordering station and just as quickly looked up at Arthur.

"And for you, sir?"

"I'll uh…" Arthur stared blankly up at the menu high on the wall behind Mr. Lee. "I'll have what he's having. Thank you, Lee."

"That's *Mister* Lee," he corrected. "And thank *you*."

After punching a few more buttons, Mr. Lee went to work on our order.

"You come here often, I see," Arthur mumbled to me under his breath.

"Too often," I joked. "I just hope it doesn't start to show." I patted my stomach.

Arthur let out a quick laugh.

"I think it's the other side you should be worried about."

I laughed with him as Mr. Lee turned around and placed our orders on a tray for us. Arthur—being a man of his word—took care of the bill.

As we returned to our seats, I relayed how I first found out about this place through an ad I'd heard on a music streaming service. Mr. Lee had done the voiceover work himself. I saw that it was close by so I stopped in and have been a fan ever since.

Arthur didn't seem too interested in the story.

After a momentary pause, Arthur interlaced his fingers on the table in front of him.

"Chad, I can't get over how impressive you were in that car last weekend," he stated. "When Reggie volunteered you for that, I thought it was gonna be a joke."

"You weren't the only one," I laughed.

"When you finished your first run, I was actually *certain* it was a joke. But you're committed. Even more than that: you're talented. So much so that you put a whoopin' on the driver I'd hired! And he was a fully licensed and experienced race car driver!"

"To be fair," I responded, "I've had experience with hand controls in the past while racing karts. There was a lot of rust to shake off, but I think I found my groove again."

"But last Saturday…that was the first time you'd ever raced an actual car?"

I nodded as a smirk crept onto my face.

Damn right.

"Yes, sir," I actually said.

Arthur leaned back in his seat but held eye contact with me.

"Chad, I'm not a complicated person. Nor am I some elitist who inherited his family's wealth. Not too many years ago, I was working in the IT world as nothing more than a low-level information technology engineer, but I had a love for motorcycles and the open road.

"It was those two passions that led me to be in an accident that involved an eighteen-wheeler."

My eyes opened wide.

"Oh shit."

"I was merging onto the highway," he continued, making the motions with his hands. "The truck driver was merging into the lane I was trying to enter but didn't look. Before I could slow down or move to avoid him, he'd merged into me and sent my motorcycle flying off the road. Long story short, I was beat up pretty bad, nearly lost both of my feet and spent the next several years learning how to walk again."

He gestured towards my cane.

"Considering what you've told me, I think this is something you can relate to."

I nodded, curious as to where he was going with this.

"In the process of rehab, I received a hefty settlement from the trucking company. Now, I could've easily taken all of it and lived out my days in seclusion aboard a fancy yacht somewhere, but I saw my new way of life as an opportunity.

"I wanted to do something that genuinely made a difference for, well, people like you and me. I used my newfound wealth to create tools that would help give people with injuries a sense of normality in life. Some years later, I formed a team that designed and developed the very steering wheel you tested last weekend. If things go as planned, it has the potential to be installed in any car that's used on public roads."

Arthur leaned a bit more towards me as he spoke again.

"This steering wheel has the opportunity to give certain people a new lease on life."

He paused for a moment and looked curiously at me.

"This is all stuff I've told both you and Reggie before, so right about now you're probably wondering where I'm going with this."

I nodded again.

"I'm enjoying the story, but I'm definitely interested to hear more."

He smiled and continued.

"Not only does this steering wheel have a place on public roads, but—as you saw—in other applications too. Outside of destroying our parking lot by hosting nonstop autocross events, I've been looking for a way to put this steering wheel through its paces to show the automotive industry that this thing can hold up to whatever gets thrown at it."

Arthur took a deep breath before he continued.

"Chad, how would like to be on a racing team?"

I swear my heart skipped a beat. Maybe I peed a little bit too.

"A…racing team?" I echoed. "What kind of team are we talking about?"

"This is an idea I've had for several months now, so bear with me on this. I'm looking for young people who are talented but don't necessarily have the means to pursue their passions. I already have a few people lined up, but what I was truly looking for was…well…" He hesitated.

"Someone with a permanent, life-altering injury?" The remark invoked a smile from the older man.

"Couldn't have said it better myself. Chad, those people who were present at the event last Saturday were the ones I needed to convince that this wheel is the real thing. You showed them that. They were impressed, and, to be frank, they wanna see more. What's even better is that you're the perfect candidate for this."

Still curious, I wanted more details.

"So what kind of racing are we talking about?"

"No one's headed to Formula 1 from this, if that's what you're asking. It'd mostly be low-level amateur endurance racing. Probably grassroots racing leagues and maybe some stuff with officiating bodies and what-have-you."

"You said endurance racing. As in multiple drivers sharing one car?"

"Exactly," he stated. "I wanna be able to show how compatible this steering wheel is. I wanna show that typical drivers can still drive the car even when this wheel is attached, but when someone steps in who needs to use the hand controls, they'll be able to drive as well with minimal modification.

"Chad, the whole point of this from a business perspective is product testing and evaluation. But if we're gonna put money into a venture like this, we want people in the car who are capable. Now if this is something you're interested in, you can still work with Reggie and keep your day job, but on race weekends we would take care of you."

Arthur suddenly cleared his throat.

"I should add that my company—Kinetic Systems and Applications— would be footing the bill for everything. We'll get you to the track, take care of accommodation, provide you with the proper safety gear and—fingers crossed—a car that will help you and the other drivers deliver some good results."

"So you'd basically be a...sponsor?"

Arthur smiled with his eyes this time.

"Yes and no. We'll take care of expenses, as in it won't cost you anything, but we wouldn't be paying you to race. The experience you take away from this, however, could potentially lead to other things for a man of your talent."

I should've been elated. I should've been jumping on the table and using my cane as a pogo stick. But for whatever reason, I was cautious.

"I mean this all sounds great, but there's one thing I don't get."

I let my words hang for a moment.

"What's the endgame here? It all sounds fantastic, but are we talking just a few races here and there or something more long term?"

Arthur nodded up and down. I took that as his way of saying it was a good question.

"As far as long-term plans and endgame," replied Arthur, "that's what we at the company are considering a results-based question. It basically means it's really gonna depend on how things go.

"Look, Chad," Arthur continued. "As much as I wanna say this offer is all from the goodness of my heart, I do have to be honest with you. This is a business venture. We're doing something out of the ordinary, and we're definitely going to have a lot of fun, but we should never forget that this is a business first. I'm not just high rolling a bunch of young adults to live out their racing dreams. On top of your driving duties, we'll want feedback and suggestions on the steering wheel as well as support for our company branding as we begin marketing said wheel. But even more than that, I think you know and understand my *why* and the reasoning behind why I started this venture in the first place. I'm here to change people's lives and I think that's a cause someone like you could get behind too."

Grandad had told me once about a time my dad had entered into a business deal for his race at the Bathurst 1000. The sponsor, Higgins Financial, was just entering Australia and had sponsored my dad and Nick Lathan's entry into The Great Race.

It was damned from the beginning, however, as the CEO was as much of a kind soul as I was Abraham Lincoln. He even tried to replace my dad as a driver with his own nephew. Higgins ultimately ended up dropping the team at the first sign of trouble. The ordeal nearly killed the entire Bathurst operation for the team before Grandad and Pat Henderson stepped in.

It was no wonder that Higgins Financial ended up going bankrupt and dissolving a few years later.

But I didn't detect any malice or ill will in Arthur's deal. Granted, this was on a significantly smaller scale than my dad's race but I'd always kept a cautious eye on so-called *opportunities that can appear too good to be true.*

"So whaddya say, Chad?"

Arthur's voice snapped me out of my memory and back into the booth we both sat in at *Taco Town.*

My mind had been fixated on the entire event from last weekend for the past week and now this opportunity was before me.

Call it a sign. Call it the universe responding. Call it the gates of heaven opening. Either way, it was a chance I wasn't willing to pass up on. As Reggie had told me, *Follow your gut.*

I looked Arthur in the eyes

"All right."

A smile slipped onto his face from the corner of his mouth as he extended his fist towards me. I met his fist bump, appreciative of the sanitary gesture as we both turned our attention to our food.

Arthur—grabbing a soft-shell taco—took a bite. A small chuckle soon arose from him.

"Shit, you weren't kidding. That's a damn good taco."

13

Hello There

The plane landed with a gentle thud as it touched down at the Piedmont Triad International Airport in Greensboro, North Carolina. I hadn't flown anywhere since I'd left Texas. I'd barely even left the city. As such, there was a hint of nervousness in my gut as I ventured forward into the unknown.

I nervously tapped my finger on the armrest as I stared out the window, eager to get off the plane and get going.

Months had passed since the meeting with Arthur. During that time, there had been a lot of phone conversations, in-person meetings, photo shoots and even some fitting sessions to get me into a proper racing suit and helmet.

I felt like a damn rock star.

Immediately after accepting Arthur's invitation, I'd let Reggie know. This was the start of a long conversation and one that I'm still not sure we ever finished. Although these races wouldn't affect my work schedule too much, he wanted to take a deeper dive into my reasoning behind joining the team.

He was keen to remind me that I'd previously told him I was through with racing. I also think he was a bit worried about me heading off on my own.

"Look, I know you're young, and this is also a good opportunity to travel on someone else's dime. Just promise me you'll keep a level head, and you'll steer clear of trouble. Never forget who you are and what it took to get you here."

Reggie's words replayed in my head as I took in the green landscape on the other side of the glass—a stark difference to the weather of Wisconsin as the plane turned off from the runway.

As eager as I was to get going, I was nervous. I'd yet to find out what car we'd be driving.

Despite that, I'd been doing my homework on the track. Virginia International Raceway—or simply VIR—was a historic, beautiful and challenging track. All wrapped up in 3.27 miles of elevation changes, tight corners and long straights, it was a track I was a bit nervous to tackle on my first-ever auto race. Track footage, race coverage, on-board camera clips from social media—hell, I went as far as to hand-draw the track outline over and over until I had a muscle memory of every corner on that track.

Arthur took it one step further by having a racing simulator hooked up at his company headquarters. That alone proved to be immensely helpful in not only learning the track but also getting some seat time to refine some lost skills.

I'd nosedived back into the world of racing. I woke up thinking about it, I daydreamed of it at work and I went to bed imagining what it would be like to go racing again. I longed for the competition.

All of a sudden, it seemed like my peaceful life was flipped on its head.

All of the prep work would hopefully pay off when it mattered. However, this first event was by no means a professional race. In fact, it could be considered the furthest thing from.

The ChampCar Endurance Series was a grassroots multiclass racing series that hosted events all over the United States. They ran a smooth operation, but it was an amateur racing series. In fact, the only thing you need to enter a race (outside of having the proper safety gear) is a driver's license.

Our entry into the ChampCar series was fitting though as this was a good place for everyone to meet and see how we work together as a team in a racing environment. But that brought me to my next concern: I still

129

hadn't met the other drivers. Arthur had told me that I wouldn't get to do so until the first event. I never really figured out why he was being so sheepish about it.

The plane finally came to a stop, and everyone stood up at once in an effort to retrieve their bags from the overhead storage and make it off the plane quickly. As I was seated next to the window, I was in no rush.

The same couldn't be said for one particular person a few rows ahead of me.

Standing up from the window seat, the guy—who couldn't have been more than twenty-five years old—essentially climbed over the other two people in his row to get to the aisle. His dark hair—heavily gelled and slicked back—looked like it was permanently molded to his head.

"Excuse me. I have things to do," he said in a slight Indian accent as his dark fuzzy mustache hung just under his nose. Much to the dismay of those around him, he made himself some space by using his body to wedge himself into the aisle.

"What an asshole," I mumbled to myself.

The older lady next to me smiled.

A small argument started after the idiot in question then began to move other people's bags out of the way to retrieve his own but I turned my attention back to my phone.

People being people.

After disembarking, I reached the baggage claim. I hung back at first but as my bag finally slid into view, I walked towards the carousel to retrieve it...until I was barged out of the way.

Nearly falling to the ground, I just managed to find my footing. Rage surged through me as the same guy who'd barged his way off the plane had nearly run me over.

"You walk too slow," he said as he continued towards the baggage claim without stopping. "I have places to be."

It took every bit of discipline I had to not walk up to him and club him with my cane. I shook the thought away, however, as the idea of calling Reggie from jail after beating someone with a steel cane in an airport didn't seem like a fun idea.

As difficult as it was, I brushed it off and headed back towards my bag. I watched as it rolled around again but just as it was about to be within arm's reach, something just ahead of me caught my eye.

Not something. Someone.

Long dark hair.

Tan skin.

Plain white t-shirt.

Faded blue jeans and brown eyes that could kill.

My hand brushed against my bag as it slowly strolled past me while I was in my stupor.

I reached for it but was a bit too slow.

And I may have reached a bit too far.

The fall sideways was slow and awkward. Luckily, the baggage carousel broke my fall as I landed on my ass.

When I looked back at her, we locked eyes for a moment as her eyebrows perked up.

The sight of her seeing me in my present situation hurt more than the act of actually landing on my ass.

I stood back up and watched as my bag made its third lap around the carousel.

When I looked back up towards the mystery girl, however, she was gone.

I looked around but tried not to make it look obvious. I'm not a creep, after all.

Shaking my head clear of the situation, I reminded myself that I was here for a reason and it wasn't for an airport hookup.

My bag finished its three-lap race and crossed the finish line as I retrieved it and extended the handle for ease of wheeling it along.

My phone buzzed in my pocket.

[Van outside of main airport entrance. Leo is the driver who will take you to the hotel and track.]

I made my way towards the exit. I saw that same asshole from the plane just in front of me. Then the girl. She seemed to materialize out of nowhere as she strode onto the sidewalk from my right side.

We were all heading in the same direction.

You've gotta be shitting me.

This was looking like an uncomfortable situation in the making.

"Let's see here," said a large man who exited from the driver's seat of a gray van about a dozen or so feet in front of us.

"Chad Watson?"

"Right here," I replied with a hand raise. I happened to be holding my cane in that hand, which drew quick glances from those around me.

"Ganesh Kirpa?"

The asshole finally had a name.

"Did you honestly feel the need to say my name out loud?" he muttered as he—without waiting for an invitation—climbed onboard the van.

The man shook his head as he read the final name from his phone.

"And…Olivia Calo."

"The one and only."

Her slight accent was hard to place.

"My name's Leo," said the man. "I'll be your driver this weekend. Hop onboard and get comfortable. We've got a bit of a haul in front of us."

Throwing my bag into the back of the van, I realized that I had to say hello to the girl now known to me as Olivia.

As she graced around the corner and threw her bag next to mine, we once again locked eyes. I opened my mouth to speak but nothing came out. A sudden panic fell upon me, and I temporarily froze in place.

Olivia's eyes were wide open in either utter amazement at what was unfolding in front of her, or in dreadful fear knowing that I was someone she'd be spending an unfortunate amount of time with.

Just before she turned around, I was able to gather my senses and say something.

I held my hand up in front of me and said, "Hello there."

I would've been better off shitting a squirrel and holding it up in front of her. I may have gotten a better reaction.

Even so, I could tell she was looking for a way out.

"I'm Chad," I finally uttered.

"So I heard," she replied, slightly annoyed.

What.

A.

Dumbass.

"You're not gonna randomly fall on your ass again, are you?"

The comment seemed to break the ice a bit.

"No promises," I chuckled...or was it a giggle. "Better to be ready just in case, though," I added as I held up my cane.

She didn't seem too amused.

"I'll keep that in mind."

Shit. This is gonna be one long trip.

14

Trepidations

The sheer amount of awkwardness in that van was enough to clog a toilet. It had been a long flight, and I was sure we all were tired, but no one had said a word to each other ever since Leo had closed the van door.

It was strange. I had built up such an expectation about that moment in the weeks leading up to actually being in this van. I'd imagined a cohesive team working together so we could all be fast on the racetrack, helping out where needed, talking things through, working things out... Instead, I was sitting in a van with an asshole who would literally walk over you if you were in his way and a girl who I've already made a fool of myself in front of several times.

It gave me a weird feeling inside. Not worry, but maybe a sense that I'd made a mistake.

This wasn't at all what I'd imagined, and something needed to give.

"So what kind of driving have y'all done?"

I sound squeaky. Why do I sound squeaky? And when was the last time I used "y'all" in a sentence?

"I am a three-time national karting champion."

Ganesh answered before I could even finish my thoughts. The asshole wouldn't even turn around to look at us when he talked.

"I've won races in the rain and in near freezing conditions," Ganesh continued. "I was destined to become a Formula 1 driver but my parents said they could no longer pay for my racing."

I could see his arms flail a bit from the back row of the van.

"I see this opportunity as a chance to show my potential."

"You and me both," replied Olivia.

I still had a hard time placing her accent.

"I also started in karts but went up to Formula Mazda for two years. I eventually got to Formula 4, but my racing dreams went up in the same smoke as my parents' marriage."

Even though she wasn't looking at me, I could hear the despair in her voice. *Perhaps it was something that was fairly recent?* I didn't feel inclined to ask out loud.

"They divorced, and my racing was one of the many casualties."

"Tell me about the karts that you raced," barked Ganesh.

"Nothing crazy," Olivia replied. "LO206 engine on a CRG chassis. A sealed engine made for great racing. It was the perfect office to learn from, if you catch my drift."

"I would do more than catch your drift," Ganesh nearly shouted. "I would pass you and there would be nothing you could do to stop it."

Shots fired.

Olivia seemed to take it in stride, however. She smiled at the comment.

"I guess we'll find out soon enough."

I couldn't help but smile at her reaction. She seemed to have a good head on her shoulders. Any other driver would've gotten into a pissing contest with Ganesh. She was one cool cat.

"What about you?"

I snapped out of it as Olivia turned and looked straight at me. Her beautiful eyes bore straight into mine. I was more than a bit caught off guard.

"Wh-what about me?"

The same beautiful eyes opened wide, and I could see her shaking her head slightly.

"Racing," she said slowly. "What have you driven?"

I'm pretty sure I'd forgotten my own question. She probably could've asked me my name and I'd have forgotten that too.

Well, shit. I am about to disappoint a few people.

"I started in karts too," I said. "Had to get some hand controls built, but I managed to win a race."

It took Ganesh all of one second to catch that one.

"A race?" he sneered. "You've only won one race?"

"Let the man finish, Ganesh," Olivia barked back.

"To be honest, that was about it for me. I raced karts for a few years, but outside of an unsanctioned autocross event in an old beat-up Mustang, that's about it."

"That's it? That is all you have done? This is unacceptable! This…this is shit!" Ganesh finally turned around.

"Well you must've impressed our host enough for you to be here," she added. Turning towards Ganesh, Olivia continued.

"And this is just ChampCar, not Formula 1. Remember that we're just glorified product testers. Not professional race car drivers."

"You may see it that way, but I see this as a gateway," Ganesh countered. "Every race has people who are looking for future drivers. It seems that I will be the one putting on a good show for the team."

Olivia and I shared a smirk, and she cocked an eyebrow as we turned our gaze back to Ganesh.

How Arthur had managed to find this guy was beyond me.

Speaking of which…

"So…" *Could I please just get one sentence in without sounding like a squeaky fifth-grader?* "How did you hear about this opportunity?"

I had to almost give myself a pat on the back when Olivia responded without looking at me as if I were the village idiot.

"Through an online ad. Something about a chance to test racing products in an actual race car."

"Did you know said racing product would be a steering wheel for people like…well…me?"

She smiled, showing her perfect pearly white teeth.

"At first, no. I had to go through several interviews before I got to meet Arthur. He filled me in on what we'd be doing. Seemed like a noble cause, so I said, 'Sign me up.'"

"Where are you from?" I asked, finally sounding normal.

"A small town called Micanopy in Florida. I've pretty much lived there all my life. From what I gather, Arthur had a few ads out at different locations across the country."

Turning and looking back up at Ganesh, Olivia turned back towards me and lowered her voice.

"I'm not sure how *that* character got this gig," she said, gesturing towards the asshole. "Maybe Arthur sees something in him that we don't."

"He seems to have an eye for talent," I said. "I guess we'll find out on race day."

Damn, it felt good to say that.

"Don't take this the wrong way—" she hesitated "—but why are you here?"

"I had a bit of an *in* from the get-go," I replied. "Arthur came to the shop I work at to build the parts for his steering wheel. When he saw my injury, he gave me a chance to drive a car on the autocross course he'd set up. I guess I exceeded his expectations and, well, here I am."

Olivia was shaking her head in what I hoped was astonishment.

"That's incredible. I mean, to just hop in a car and go so well that it impressed Arthur is pretty remarkable. Are you from a racing family or something?"

I immediately tensed up and closed down as a psychological wall formed around me. The feeling was physical as much as it was mental. I know she meant nothing of it and if anything, I should've been excited that this beautiful girl was taking an interest in me.

For one reason or another, I wasn't quite ready to go there just yet. I only managed to get a few broken words out.

"Yeah. My...uh...family...we've...they've done a bit of racing."

Another awkward pause filled the air.

Olivia was slowly nodding her head at me, the way you do when you're expecting more details from someone.

"Okay, so you've got a bit of it in your blood, then," she said.

"You could say that."

With that, Olivia slid some earbuds into her ears. Just before she turned back around and slouched down into the seat, she added, "I guess we'll see how you fare tomorrow."

Yeah, I thought. *I guess we will.*

* * *

Arthur was waiting for us in the hotel lobby and—after some initial greetings—got us signed in and assigned to our rooms.

We each had our own room and my God was I relieved to not have to share a room with Ganesh.

We assembled back in the lobby about an hour later after Arthur invited us all to dinner for what he described as a "special treat."

Boy was he right.

Oak Tree Tavern was just outside of Virginia International Raceway. The bar was affectionately named after the large oak tree that had once stood at Turn 12. Over two hundred years old, the tree eventually kicked the can several years back.

Dinner was mostly spent listening to Arthur describe how excited everyone was to be a part of a project like this. He mentioned something about how they're all counting on us but really, I tried not to listen to stuff like that. At the end of the day, my role was to just drive.

After dinner, Arthur said, "Before we shuttle y'all back to the hotel for the evening, I've got one more special treat in store." He headed for the exit of the restaurant and motioned for us to follow.

We piled back into the van and Leo drove us farther into the track.

All of us stared out the windows in silence.

Coming to a stop moments later, we all climbed out. The sun was just beginning to set over the green hills of the horizon, and seeing the track for the first time with my own eyes, I was awestruck. There was a calming beauty to it.

The distant roar of an engine screaming from somewhere on the track echoed throughout the land as the three of us—Olivia, Ganesh and myself—took in the moment in our own unique way.

Olivia stood motionless, seeming to absorb the scenery into memory. She breathed in deeply as the golden sun danced across her olive skin with gentle winds blowing strands of her dark hair.

Ganesh was like a poodle who'd broken free of his leash. He couldn't stand still if his life depended on it as he did what I can only describe as a chicken dance. Bouncing from one foot to the other, he either had to take a piss really bad or it was the only way he could contain his excitement.

For me, I took this solemn moment to observe and reflect. In a flash, I was mentally back in the garage at Mount Panorama as my dad battled for the win at the Bathurst 1000. Still in a wheelchair at the time, I was sitting on the edge of my seat as I watched the broadcast with the race team. Seeing your dad on TV while also hearing his race car scream by in the background was a sensation I'll never forget.

As a red Ferrari ripped past us from out on track, the noise brought a smile to my face. Hearing a Ferrari in full stride would do that to anyone but this was where I belonged. And I would do anything and everything I could to keep this dream alive.

"Gather around, everyone."

The voice of Arthur just behind me caught my attention.

"I thought it would be appropriate to give you three a bit of a preview of the scenery here before we get things going tomorrow."

"It's beautiful out here," Olivia chimed in.

Arthur smiled in kind.

"It sure is. But I didn't just bring y'all out here for sightseeing. Whaddya say we take a step into our office for the weekend?"

Arthur took off on a brisk walk—possibly unable to contain his own excitement—and headed into one of the nearby garages. After we all stepped inside, he flipped the light switch.

The BMW E36 that sat in the middle of the garage looked to be a 1995 model but I couldn't be sure. It was by no means new. The various dings and scratches along the blue paint gave evidence of being driven many times in anger. The right rear quarter panel was white, as if it'd been recently replaced but not yet painted.

I took in the sight of our race car like a kid on Christmas. As we all walked around it giving the car a nickel inspection, I stuck my head into the driver's window.

The prototype steering wheel we'd be using was already installed. There was what looked like a giant iPad attached on the center console, presumably for race-related information such as lap times and maybe fuel mileage. Outside of that and the various pieces of safety equipment, that was it.

It was rough. But it was ours.

I couldn't help but see it as some sort of battle wagon.

My thoughts were interrupted as the driver door suddenly opened…with my head still in the window.

Ganesh didn't even acknowledge my presence as he used the door to move me aside before climbing into the driver's seat.

Closing it with a heavy slam, he grabbed the steering wheel with both hands and adjusted himself in the seat.

"This is not my ideal seating position," he barked. "My legs are too straight. The seat must be moved forward."

I heard laughter in the background but I couldn't tell where it came from.

"Can you reach the pedals, Ganesh?" asked Arthur.

"I can but that is not good enough. I need…"

"Go ahead and climb out," Arthur interrupted. "Hop on in, Olivia. Let's see how it fits you."

With a demeanor similar to that of an angry child, Ganesh begrudgingly fumbled his way out of the car. Trying to slam the door before Olivia could step in, she took a large step forward and caught the door before it could shut.

She's a badass.

140

I watched Olivia carefully as she adjusted herself in the seat, strapping herself in using the six-point harness. Once the belts clicked into place, she extended her arms and grabbed hold of the steering wheel.

"No complaints from me. If we could leave it as-is, I'll be happy tomorrow."

Arthur smiled and nodded in approval.

"Last but not least, Chad," he said, turning towards me. "Go ahead and step in."

Olivia turned the dial on the harness, which released all of the belts at once. Then she hung her head out the driver's window, grabbed the roll bar above the door and hoisted herself up and out of the car through the window. She swung her legs through the door and walked away with a coy smile on her face.

Even Ganesh had his bushy eyebrows raised.

The car stared back at me as I approached.

How about we just have ourselves a nice and simple introduction. Nothing fancy.

Opening the door, I placed my cane on the ground, grabbed hold of the roll bar Olivia had used to hoist herself out, swung my legs over the NASCAR door bars and used my arms to lower myself into place.

It felt clumsy to me, but I hoped I looked the part.

Resting my butt into the seat, it was snug and surprisingly more comfortable than I recalled my kart seat had been. I followed Olivia's route and buckled myself in and—as I had no need to reach the pedals—grabbed hold of the steering wheel.

The hand controls were much firmer than the ones on the old Mustang I drove back in the parking lot. Everything felt much more polished and refined as if a lot of thought had gone into it.

"How's she feel, Chad?"

"Nice and tight."

"That's what she said," Olivia blurted out.

All of us turned towards her, more than a little surprised.

"What?" she reacted with a shoulder shrug. "I have two older brothers.

Give me a break."

I smiled as I turned my attention back to the car.

Checking the mirrors, I reach out and adjusted the driver's side mirror to my liking.

Other than a few minor things, I felt extremely comfortable.

It took everything inside me to not flip that ignition switch to fire the engine up.

"This weekend's gonna be a test for all of us," Arthur declared. "Sure, we'll be competing against other teams, but we're also testing something that's never been done before. Good results are always a positive but remember to stay focused and give the guys on our crew some good feedback on how things are going. They're here to support you and the car but to also further the development of this steering wheel."

After seeing Ganesh and Olivia gathered around Arthur, I felt compelled to do so as well. I exited the vehicle, mostly glad that the two other drivers had their backs turned to me, as I wasn't nearly as graceful as Olivia.

Picking up my cane, I headed over.

"Just remember: This is a twelve-hour race."

Arthur suddenly turned towards me and met my eyes.

"That's longer than the race your father and grandfather ran in Australia."

The words shook me to my core. I don't know why it surprised me that Arthur had done his homework on me. Considering the resources he was pouring into this foray, I couldn't blame him. Even so, I felt as if I'd been torn open and exposed in front of everyone.

Why did he do that? Why did Arthur call out my family's racing history in front of everyone?

I'd more or less just wanted to blend in during this trip—to take in the sights, to learn and discover, to experience, adapt and overcome. This was all new to me, and I didn't want to draw too much attention to myself.

Both Ganesh and Olivia stared at me while Arthur continued to speak, but that was all out the window now, as my mind seemed to close down.

I could hear words coming out of Arthur's mouth but I was no longer listening. Before long, I noticed everyone heading out of the garage and back towards the van.

I fell into step behind everyone...or so I thought.

"Chad."

I turned to see Arthur off to the side of the garage, motioning me over.

I would tell him off. I would let him know that you don't air someone's past out in front of other people when you're just trying to lie low. You don't...

"Don't be ashamed of your past, Chad," Arthur spoke as I suddenly stopped and met his eyes. He stepped towards me and put his hand on my shoulder. "You've been through a lot, yes. But know that there's nothing to run from over here. The past is there as it always will be. Harness it. Use it. It very well could take you somewhere you never expected."

Before I could respond, Arthur had removed his hand from my shoulder and took off back towards the van.

I stood there for a moment, lost in my thoughts. I was either given wind in my sails or a knife to tear holes in them, I felt. Whatever the direction I took, I just needed silence.

I needed to think.

"C'mon, lonely boy," shouted Ganesh. "I hope you don't lose yourself like this on race day."

As we finally piled back into the van that would take us back to the hotel for the night, my mind was storming with memories and emotions. My dad at Bathurst, his last words to me, Grandad standing against the fence at the local karting track watching me, his insightful racing advice...

Now, I was on the cusp of my first car race. Being the last of my family, I knew I had a legacy to uphold. As I sat there in the back seat of the van and stared blankly out the window, I made a silent promise to myself: I would do everything I could to protect this legacy. Right now, it was all I truly cared about.

15

Slow Motion

Race day.

Those two words jumped into the forefront of my mind as the alarm clock on my phone chimed just before dawn.

My body ached as I peeled myself from the comfort of my hotel room bed; each joint and muscle protesting the process.

The previous day, we had spent hours practicing at the track and it still weighed on me. It was my very first time driving a real race car. It had also been a lot more physically grueling than they make it out to be on TV.

I remembered watching an IndyCar race a few months ago and seeing the winning driver literally jump out of the car and immediately start getting interviewed, all while sporting a smile, speaking clearly and looking like he could run a marathon.

I'd now come to a unique conclusion: That guy must have been an AI-powered cyborg.

After I finished my practice at the track, I was exhausted. I did, of course, try to play it off and not give anyone on the team the impression that I was in such a state. Whether they bought it or not, I have no idea.

At the end of the practice day, Olivia had outpaced us all and was the fastest of the three drivers. Ganesh showed his merit as he was not too far behind. I, on the other hand, was a bit off pace. I wasn't trying to make it a secret that I was still learning so I took things a bit more cautiously.

This wasn't a parking lot surrounded by cones anymore and the other cars around me belonged to other teams. I wasn't about to be "that guy," the guy who plowed into someone else because I was pushing too hard too soon. Despite my pace being a bit behind that of my teammates, I was still plenty fast enough to keep up with some of the other faster drivers who were out there. At least that's what I'm telling myself. And it was a practice for a twelve-hour race so there was plenty of time to get up to speed.

Swinging my legs over the edge of the bed, I followed my typical morning routine and was ready to go shortly thereafter. Grabbing my equipment bag, I noticed that it was unzipped and I immediately knew why. I glanced back at my bed to see my helmet sitting on the edge. I'd somehow fallen asleep with it right next to me.

I used to do that with my dad's helmet the night before his races when I was much younger. I now realized that my helmet was very similar to his: All black, just like his TA2 race car. I told myself I'd add a bit of orange at some point, like the color of the Ford Falcon that Grandad had raced during his Bathurst win.

I picked up the helmet, stuffed it into the bag and double checked to make sure I had everything else.

Before long, I was walking out of the hotel room to meet up with the team and head to the track for my first-ever auto race.

Hell yeah.

* * *

The field roared to life as all sixty-seven cars raced down the front straight of Virginia International Raceway as the green flag waved on a picture perfect day. With Olivia in the car, I watched on from the pit wall as the line of cars seemed to stretch on forever. Arthur had made the call that she would be starting the race. From there, we would simply alternate drivers going from Olivia to Ganesh to me, back to Olivia, rinse and repeat until

145

the checkered flag. No one wanted to be the slowest driver on the team but Ganesh and Olivia had barely said a word to each other since practice yesterday after she'd beaten him. I was beneath their notice for now. I wasn't planning on being the slowest teammate for long but for now, I was more than willing to sit back and let them play their games as I got up to speed.

My heart rushed with awe and eagerness as a smile leapt onto my face. I'd been to lots of races in my life but the sight and feeling of seeing the entire field race by you never got old.

The roar of the engines faded as the field began to navigate the 3.27-mile-long track. I found my way back to my folding chair where the rest of the team took up station. There, we had a TV monitor with a live video feed from the car so it gave us something to look at as time pressed on. The sound of the cars in the background was relaxing to me. It was still early and I nodded off for a bit while sitting there. After some time, however, I woke to see Ganesh staring at me. The asshole was trying to size me up.

Checking the timing and scoring app on my phone, I could see that Olivia had long since moved to the front of the field and was more or less just managing the gap to the car behind. Based on yesterday's lap times, I knew our car had more in it but as this was a twelve-hour race, it didn't benefit us to push things to the max this early on.

What good is setting the fastest lap time if you blow the motor after three hours?

"She's doing exactly what we need her to do."

I looked up to see Arthur talking to another crew member named Craig. I recalled that he worked for Arthur's company.

"You did good by picking her up for this team," said Craig, or at least I think that's what he said based on reading his lips as a pack of cars drove by. He gestured back towards Ganesh and I as he added, "We'll see how these other kids do."

Ganesh immediately perked up as he stood and faced the two men.

"I will be the fastest driver," he said, drawing the attention—and a few laughs—from some of the other nearby teams. "I will also take home the trophy."

This time it was Arthur who laughed.

"I appreciate your enthusiasm, Ganesh, but any and all trophies go back to the shop."

Ganesh wouldn't budge.

"Then I will have my picture taken with it after I win the race."

Arthur slowly approached after seeing that Ganesh was getting a bit too fired up.

"Take it easy, buddy," replied Arthur. "We win as a team and we lose as a team. Now make sure you're all set when Olivia makes her pit stop. You're up next."

Slowly taking his seat, it seemed as if Arthur's previous words had resonated with Ganesh. The asshole reached down, grabbed his helmet and sat it on his lap.

I watched on, more so out of curiosity. I couldn't help but feel like this guy thought he was living a scene from a movie or something.

Does he have a soundtrack playing in his head? Is he...no way. Is he actually moving in slow motion?

Right there before my eyes, my suspicions were confirmed.

Slowly and methodically, Ganesh raised his helmet and slowly...very slowly...lowered it onto his head.

Closing the tinted visor, he sat there in silence...and majesty.

I placed my face into the palms of my hands.

Where did they find this guy?

Before I could contemplate that any further, I heard Arthur speak into the radio via his headset to Olivia as she drove down the front straight.

"Pit next time, Olivia. Great run. Watch your speed coming into the pits."

I couldn't hear Olivia's response, but I imagined it was cool and collected.

Ganesh rose from his throne and took up position along the pit wall.

Before long, Olivia had come to a stop in our pit stall and shut the car off.

Per ChampCar's rules, all pit stops had to be at least five minutes in length. This was to ensure that no one was running around with jugs of fuel and driver changes could be done in an orderly fashion. It basically minimizes the chances of something stupid happening on pit lane. This was amateur grassroots racing, after all.

After about ninety minutes of racing, Olivia stepped out of the car. Ganesh then climbed in and began to buckle himself in. I could only watch the exchange from afar but as Olivia turned to help Ganesh get buckled in, I swore I saw him swat her hand away.

Seeing as she had frozen in place for a moment before stepping over the pit wall, I'm fairly certain she had at least one inkling of violence pass through her mind.

"Great run," I said as she passed by.

Olivia didn't immediately respond.

Unscrewing the lid from a water bottle, she proceeded to pour some of it over her head and then drink the rest.

She then took off on a brisk pace away from the track.

Curious and also wondering if something was wrong, I took off after her.

I looked over my shoulder to see one of the crew members named James standing in front of the car watching the timer on his phone. Ganesh had fired the car up and just as the timer hit the five-minute mark, Ganesh pulled out of the pit stall and proceeded to start his run.

* * *

"Olivia!"

I had to move a bit faster than I normally do but I finally succeeded in catching up to her.

"What is it?" she asked. "What's wrong?"

I was a bit taken back by that as I was about to ask her the same thing.

"Um…well…nothing," I replied like an idiot. "I saw you storm off after

148

you got out of the car and wanted to know if you were okay."

For a moment, she just stared at me with those eyes—probably wondering how I got this far in life without constant adult supervision—before the realization struck her.

"Oh...yeah, I just have to walk things off when I get out," she responded. "A lot of adrenaline is pumping, and I can't just sit down right after a race."

"Fair enough," I admitted. "I also wanted to make sure that...well...I saw Ganesh slap your hand away and..."

"I wouldn't worry too much about Ganesh, Chad," she smiled. "People like him have a habit of taking care of themselves in a not so glamorous way."

Turning, Olivia began to head back towards our pit stall as I followed along next to her.

"Are you nervous?" she asked me as we walked. "I mean, for your first stint after Ganesh finishes up?"

I smiled in her direction, but I don't think she noticed.

"No more than the next person."

I don't know if she bought my response or not. As we continued to walk, I could tell she was gathering her thoughts.

"The traffic out there is pretty crazy, so remember to be patient. It's a long race, so above all, just take care of the car. Always remember that the fastest driver doesn't always win, but the smartest driver usually doesn't lose."

Sage wisdom.

"Thanks for the advice," I replied. "I need all the help I can get."

"No, you don't. You just need to find your confidence. You've got the skillset, Chad. We all see that, even from your practice laps yesterday. For someone who has never turned a lap on a track in a full-sized car, you did great out there. Just feel the car. It'll tell you what it wants. Push when you're able to but lie back when you need to."

Curious, I inquired a bit further.

"Why are you telling me all of this?"

Olivia stopped in her tracks as she turned towards me.

"You know, I could spout the whole 'we're a team' mantra, but deep down, I think I just want you to be faster than Ganesh."

We both smiled as we headed back to our pit area. I noticed that my heart was racing for what I knew were more reasons than one.

* * *

"We've gotta calm this guy down," said Craig. The older man had a weathered look about him as if he'd seen a lot in life. His oil-stained clothes only added to the effect.

As Ganesh drove past us down the front straight to start another lap, he weaved from one side of the track to the other in an attempt to pass a slower car.

I noticed Arthur shaking his head.

"He's fast but there seems to be a price to pay for it," he said to Craig.

This time, I was standing directly behind the both of them so I could hear them both more clearly.

With my fire suit on, I waited with anticipation for Arthur to give the command. Surely Ganesh was running low on fuel and as soon as he pitted, I'd be next to hop in.

As I watched the monitor showing Ganesh's perspective looking out the front of the car, I watched him aggressively pass two slower cars.

I'm no expert but I could tell that he was pushing far too hard and getting little reward for his efforts.

He was creating gaps that didn't exist as he dived into openings to pass slower cars. While doing so, he often caught the slower car by surprise and when the car being passed finally noticed, it would create a bit of a choke point as both drivers tried to assess what the next move should be.

The result was always time lost for both drivers.

When Olivia had pitted, we had a twenty-second lead over the second-placed car: an older Mustang GT. Now, that lead had shrunk down to just

150

five seconds as Ganesh continued to have difficulty maneuvering through traffic.

"I can tell he's got a lot to learn about multi-class endurance racing," said Craig. "You gonna get in there and show 'em how it's done, Chad?"

I was so in the zone getting my mind ready for what was to come that I was caught off guard by the question.

"Y-yuhhh…yeah," I mumbled.

I noticed Craig shake his head slightly as he turned back towards the monitor.

Arthur just smiled.

"I think it's about time, Chad," he said. "Go ahead and get the rest of your gear on. We'll bring Ganesh in soon."

Those words were like life to me as I walked back to my seat to grab my helmet.

I will not move in slow motion.

I will not move in slow motion.

I will not move in slow motion.

As I placed my balaclava over my head and then lowered my HANS and helmet down, I realized too late.

Shit, I'm moving in slow motion now too.

I buckled my helmet's chin strap and placed my cane down across my chair.

It felt weird to be leaving it behind.

Slowly and using various chairs and tool chests to brace myself along the way, I made my way over to the pit wall just as Arthur was making the call to Ganesh.

As Ganesh brought the car to a stop in our pit stall moments later and shut the engine off, I climbed over the pit wall, albeit a bit slower than the guys who had full use of their legs.

By the time I reached the car, Ganesh was already out and waiting for me.

"C'mon, handicapped man," he muttered under his breath as I climbed into the seat. "I'm just glad I got to drive before you crash the car. It was nice while it lasted."

He didn't even help me buckle my seat belts. He just stood there and watched. Luckily, I'd done my homework and had also put the time into practicing driver swaps. That included buckling my own belts by feel alone.

When wearing a helmet, you can't look down to see the belt buckles, so you have to rely on your teammate—or in this case—your own experience to get yourself situated.

Once I'd finished strapping myself in, I gave Ganesh the finger for effect. "Don't forget to close the door for me, asshat."

Before I could fully finish my exquisitely worded line, however, Ganesh had slammed the door shut and walked behind the pit wall.

I checked my mirrors to see the crew still fueling up the car. There wouldn't be any tire changes. I'd have to use the same worn-out rubber that the previous dipshit had nearly torn to shreds. Even so, one of the crew members went around the car and torqued each of the wheels.

Better safe than sorry.

Another of the crew members was working on cleaning the windshield, and I was grateful for that.

"Mic check," I said over the in-car radio.

"Loud and clear," replied Arthur a moment later. "We've got plenty of time."

I took a moment, breathing in deeply and exhaling slowly as I placed my hands on the steering wheel.

I'm not one for prayer, and after all I'd been through, I wasn't even sure if God was real or not. But as I sat there, the words found their way into my mind and I gave voice to them.

"Protection, God."

Before I could get too deep, I heard Arthur on the radio again.

"Thirty seconds. Fire up the engine."

Pulling the clutch lever on the steering wheel, I turned the key as the engine came to life.

At that moment, I missed my family and wished they could be here to see this.

"Ten seconds. Standby."

I put the car into gear as I watched our crew member, James. He stood in front and to the right of the car as he watched the timer on his phone. He held his hand out in front of him but as the timer expired, he gave me the signal.

Giving the car some gas, I accelerated away and brought the car up to the pit lane speed limit. Reaching the exit, I had to verify with ChampCar staff that our five-minute pit stop had indeed fully elapsed but before long, I was released onto the track.

16

Baptized

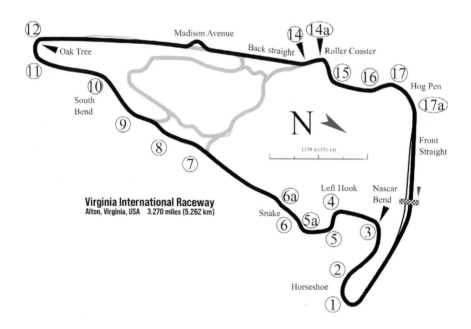

I had often imagined what it would be like leaving the pits in an auto race for the very first time. My mind conjured up visions of getting up to speed, feeling my way around the track, getting comfortable and then chasing down the leaders en route to a glorious victory.

The reality of it, however, was very different.

Immediately upon exiting the pits, I was swarmed by a pack of cars from all different classes. Some of the cars were in the slowest class but as they were in front of me, I couldn't just drive through them.

Others were from classes that were still slower but had cars that were very capable in the corners. As such, they were trying to get around me as I was just trying to get up to speed.

My mind was racing, my breaths were short, and I could already feel my heart beating rapidly. As I maneuvered through *NASCAR Bend*, I must've had six cars swarming me from all sides. I was just trying to make sure I could see my brake markers while also not smacking into another car.

I was in a near state of panic as I made *Left Hook* and headed towards Turn 5. By that point, all of the cars in the pack had passed me.

All of them.

I took a long slow breath in an effort to calm myself. It was then that I noticed that my hands had a death-grip on the steering wheel. All of that and I hadn't even made it through half a lap yet.

I relaxed my hands as the road opened up a bit. With me now at the tail-end of things, the pack I was in all headed into the climbing slopes of *Snake*. I went full squeeze on the gas and the car showed its worth.

The slower traffic was no match for the top speed of this car. Even so, there were inter-class battles going on in front of me and some of the drivers were heading towards *South Bend* side by side.

I waited, heeding Olivia's earlier advice on patience.

Eventually, the traffic went single file and I went hard on the gas. As we headed into the *Oak Tree* hairpin, I could've sent it into the pack in front of me with the hope of passing them with a dive into the corner but that would have been foolish. After completing the turn, I knew a long straight awaited me and I'd be able to pass them cleanly.

I opened up the throttle and passed the remaining cars in the pack as I exited the hairpin. I was still freaking out and constantly checking my mirrors. I also had the sudden realization that I was going really fast and remembered there was a hard braking zone approaching.

I started to question just how hard Ganesh had pushed these tires.

It was a moot point, however. Braking just a bit earlier than I had during practice the day before, I made the corner and felt like there was plenty more time to chip off in the coming laps.

The rolling hills sloped up and down as I navigated through *Roller Coaster*, and my stomach shrank a little bit as I plunged down through *Hog Pen*. As I crossed the line to start my first flying lap, the track before me was clear.

I'd passed my trial. I didn't crash on the out-lap like I feared I would. I'd found my confidence. Now it was time to settle in.

Deep down, I knew that I didn't need to panic. I'd already been through my own hell in life and came out stronger.

I knew I was going to be okay.

Now I just needed to stay focused and tune everything else out.

As my dad's former team principal once said to him over the radio, "Head down, eyes forward."

* * *

Arthur nodded his head up and down as Chad raced by, completing another lap as he did.

"He's getting the hang of it and staying out of trouble," Arthur said. "He's turning out to be more than I could've hoped for."

"He's not too far off the other two, as well," said Craig. "Last lap was only a half second off Olivia's fastest lap, and he's only a tenth off Ganesh. I had my doubts at first, but I'd say he's gonna fit in nicely."

Just behind the two men, Ganesh sat with his back to them. Despite the cars that had been driving by, he was able to hear every word being said.

Maybe the cripple isn't as slow as I originally thought.

It didn't matter. Sooner or later, he knew that Chad would show his inexperience….and incompetence. He just had to wait patiently although he knew that was something he wasn't good at.

He thought about waking Olivia, who was taking a quick rest back in the team's trailer, maybe disrupt her sleep so she wouldn't be as sharp for her next stint, but that would be frowned upon. That and he had the sneaking suspicion that Olivia and Chad were teaming up against him.

He could see the way the cripple looked at her.

Ganesh, however, had no interest in pursuing relationships. To him, there was racing, and that was it. Everything else was a distraction.

As Chad clocked another lap, he heard cheers from the two men behind him.

"This kid's fast! He just beat Ganesh's time!"

Arthur turned around to speak directly to the driver.

"Don't worry, Ganesh. I know you've got more in the tank."

Inside, however, Ganesh sank away a little bit.

He would have his victory. Even if it meant beating Chad at his own game, Ganesh would be victorious.

* * *

I should've been tired. The longest I'd ever been in a race car up to this point was the thirty-minute practice session I had done the day before.

Passing the one-hour mark, however, I was still going strong. Better still, I was laying down consistent lap times as the digital screen inside the car displayed each time around.

On top of that, I was doing my best to take care of the tires.

This wasn't sprint racing so we all had to play the long game. And seeing as I'd be handing the car off to Olivia in a short while, it wouldn't be very beneficial to set blistering lap times only to melt the damn tires off in the process.

The radio had been quiet for the majority of my stint. I didn't receive any special instructions or feedback outside of the occasional message from Arthur that we were still in the lead and I took that as a good sign. The gap to the car behind us remained steady at around fifteen seconds, which—after about five hours of racing thus far—was impressive.

Over the course of my stint, I could feel myself getting more and more comfortable behind the wheel. The hand controls on the steering wheel began to feel second nature, and the thought of passing slower cars wasn't nearly as horrifying. I found myself focusing on the next corner, which helped me to stay sharp throughout my stint.

In all honesty, I don't think I'd ever been that focused in my entire life. That in itself was calming.

My confidence began to grow as well.

As I pushed the car just a bit harder, I was beginning to find the limits of the tires. In a way, it was like a conversation between me and the car. I was asking her what she needed to operate at peak efficiency, and she was telling me through the behavior of the car. It was all surprisingly natural to me.

As I took a deep breath after completing the final corner, Arthur finally chimed in.

"Excellent run, Chad. Pit next time by."

"Copy," I replied.

Speeding towards *Horseshoe*, I suddenly realized just how tired I truly was. Knowing that one single lap was all that separated me from a break made me feel anxious. I'd tried to conserve my energy but as the sun continued to rise and the temperatures began to climb inside the car, the heat alone was enough to drain you and there was no escape from that.

The fancy teams had equipment inside their cars to keep the drivers cool during these long races.

We weren't one of those teams.

The final lap on my first stint was uneventful although I managed to pass nearly a half dozen slower cars while going down the long *backstraight*. I kept a calm state of mind as I traversed *Roller Coaster*, not trying to do anything fancy or unpredictable.

Just be consistent.

Coming out of *Hog Pen*, I reduced my speed and ducked to the right side of the track to enter pit lane.

It was a strange feeling to be going slow all of a sudden. I almost felt like I was doing something wrong. There was the ever-present desire to give it a bit more gas but exceeding the pit lane speed limit was a good way to flush your race down the shitter.

I spotted one of our crew, James, waving me down as I approached our pit stall.

Don't miss the pit box, Chad.

Don't miss the pit box.

Don't miss the...oh, shit!

I drove it in a bit too deep. Slamming on the brakes, I went full NASCAR and slid the car into the pit box. As far as I could tell, however, the car had come to a stop within the boundaries.

I played it cool, brushing it off to make it look intentional. I noticed that Olivia was already over the wall as I shut the car off.

Swinging the door open, I unbuckled my belts and grabbed the door frame roll bar to pull myself out.

Right away, Olivia climbed in.

Bracing myself against the car for balance, I gave my legs a few shakes to get the feel back in them as I leaned in and helped Olivia get buckled in.

"How are the tires?" she inquired.

"I did my best to take care of them," I replied. "Same with the brakes."

"If the way you slid the car in just now is how you take care of things, remind me to never let you borrow anything."

With her helmet on, I couldn't tell if she was smiling or not.

"Temps looked good and the car wasn't sliding around...on track, at least. You should be good to go."

With her strapped in, I grabbed the door to close it when...

"Hey."

I stopped and ducked my head back inside the car to see what Olivia needed.

Our eyes met.

"Good laps out there," she said, her eyes beaming as she spoke. "You're only a tenth off my fastest lap, and you've got Ganesh in a panic. All that in your first-ever car race. Consider me impressed, Chad Watson."

For a moment, I froze. *Should I say something? Should I...*

"Now close the damn door and get out of here."

"Yes, ma'am."

I think I may have performed a slight bow as I removed my head from the car and closed the door.

Hobbling back over the pit wall, I began to remove my helmet when Arthur came over.

"Helluva run, Chad. *Helluva* run! Are you sure this is the first time you've done this?"

Damn. I knew I had done a good job, but am I that good?

"The first of many more to come," I said.

Arthur patted me on the shoulder. "We've got a long way to go, but you maintained the lead and brought the car back in one piece. How did the steering wheel hold up for you?"

"It was great," I admitted. "After a while, I grew accustomed to it and forgot it was there. It just became a part of the process."

Nodding in approval, Arthur headed back to the folding desk he and Craig were running the show from. Sliding his headphones back over his head, he added, "Go get yourself some rest and something to eat. You'll have at least one more stint before the end."

"Copy that."

I had to admit...it felt good.

Not just running a good first stint in what was my first-ever foray into auto racing but also receiving a bit of praise from my teammates, it was a breath of fresh air. It also gave me the continued confidence that I was indeed where I belonged.

Hobbling my way back to my folding chair, I heard Olivia exit the pit stall to begin her second stint, and I immediately noticed that something was missing.

My cane.

Placing my helmet and gloves onto my chair, I began to frantically look around to see if maybe it'd fallen off and someone had propped it up somewhere. I peeked around the nearest tool chest when…

"You ran good."

I turned to see Ganesh spinning my cane in his hands.

"I thought for sure you'd be dead weight, but it looks like you're not as worthless as we all originally thought."

I tried to contain myself, but I couldn't. With the adrenaline of racing still pumping through my veins, I decided that I'd had it with this guy's shit.

Grinning, I leaned up against the tool chests.

"You talk…a lot," I said. Turning towards the racetrack, I pointed in its general direction before facing Ganesh again.

"I can't wait to hear what you have to say after I finish destroying your lap times out there."

I let the words linger in the air for a moment. I could see Ganesh's eyes wandering a bit, more than likely trying to formulate a response he knew he didn't have.

"You should get used to being the slowest driver on the team, Ganesh," I added. "I'm only gonna get faster. I just can't imagine what it must feel like to have your ass handed to you by…what did you call me again? 'Handicapped man'?"

The look on his face—as well as the lack of a snappy comeback—made me feel like I'd taken the wind out of his sails.

I could've pressed further, but there was no need. Not right then, at least. I'd let those words simmer with him for a bit.

We held each other's gaze for a moment longer before I sat down…in his chair. I leaned my head back and closed my eyes.

"Go ahead and set my cane down for me, please and thank you."

I didn't even bother to see where he would set it down. He knew I'd defeated him. What's more was that we both knew that Arthur was watching the entire exchange.

After a few moments, I opened my eyes to see my cane right back where I'd originally placed it on my chair. I also saw Ganesh, fully suited up with his helmet on while pacing back and forth in the area behind our pit stall.

He had his visor cracked open about an inch to hide his eyes.

He was drawing a lot of stares and even a few laughs as he walked with slow but methodical steps, like one would do just before entering a fight. I just shook my head while secretly wondering if he'd stayed up all night doing this same thing in his hotel room.

Does he realize this is just ChampCar? No one's winning a world championship from this.

Either way, I was fine with letting him sweat a bit before his next stint. He was inside his own head. My best guess was the only problem he truly had was the inability to get out of his own way.

I slowly stood up and grabbed my cane as I headed back to the team trailer to get a bit of proper rest before my next stint...not even bothering to make eye contact with Ganesh as he mumbled incoherent words to himself as I passed.

I must say, it felt good.

I'd bested Ganesh.

I'd bested the entire field.

I'd exceeded my expectations...

...and I was just getting started.

17

Ground Control

The door to the trailer swung open, which caused me to promptly awaken and sit up straight. My heart raced for a moment as Olivia walked in and headed for the fridge, grabbing a cold water.

Oh shit! Did I sleep too long?

"Everything all right?" I sounded groggy.

"Yeah, all good," she replied calmly, taking a nearby seat. "Just finished my stint, and our boy Ganesh is back in the car."

I sighed, probably a little too loudly, but Olivia didn't seem to care. Unscrewing the lid, she took a sip of water as she looked about the trailer.

Although it was just a rental trailer for the weekend courtesy of Arthur, it was a good respite from the noise and craziness that was unfolding just outside the door.

And it was nice to just sit there with Olivia one on one.

"You said your family's done some racing, yeah?"

Her sudden question caught me off guard, but I guess I was just tired enough to not get too caught up in it.

"Yeah, you could say that."

"You've obviously got a talent for it, too," she added. She was tapping her index finger against the bottle and her eyes looked far away as if she was deep in thought. There was a long pause. Her thoughts finally materialized, and I couldn't help but think this was something that had been on her mind for a while.

"If things continue and, I don't know, you had a chance to do something with racing, where would you want to go?"

I furrowed my brow slightly as I slid to the edge of the bed.

"That's a pretty loaded question."

"Not really," she responded. "I'm just curious is all."

"I don't know. Wherever it takes me, I suppose," I guessed. "There are a few places around the world I'd like to have a chance to race at if I was ever given the opportunity, but that all seems pretty far off. What about you, Miss 'fastest driver on the team'? You planning to drive race cars for the rest of your life?"

Olivia's eyebrows raised at the question.

"Me? Hell no. I only got into this to prove I could do it."

"Prove to whom?" I asked.

"Maybe to my parents when I was younger, but for now, mostly myself. I'm from a small town, Chad. Girls there graduate from high school, get married and make babies. I wanted more, so I took it. And it damn sure wasn't given to me either. I earned my way to where I am. But that doesn't mean I wanna stay here forever."

"Well, where do you wanna go?"

Her eyes spaced out again as she took in the question for a moment.

"Back home. I wanna tell those little girls that there's a big wide world out there outside the borders of their hometown. We live in a world where you can make something of yourself despite where you come from but you've gotta be willing to beat the pavement sometimes. I wanna show them how. I wanna help them make something for themselves."

Her words made me think about Austin. I'd spent a big chunk of my life there and, despite the heartache I still felt because of it, that place would always hold a special spot in my heart. Did I want to go back? Hell no. Too many ghosts lingered back there and I'd dedicated my life to moving forward.

Still, Olivia's words made me think of other potential kids who may be going through far worse than I ever did.

Can I help them? Inspire them? Is that even something I'm supposed to do?

I thought about Kate, the girl whose life I'd seemingly destroyed in the karting accident all those years ago. I wondered how she was doing, and right away, a sharp edge of guilt seemed to cut into my heart. Even after all these years, I still thought about her on a regular basis.

"Hey. You in there?"

Olivia smiled at me as I returned from my past.

"Yeah, I'm here."

A pause followed. And I assumed Olivia was thinking I was going to expand on what I was thinking about. She shook her head slightly.

"Anything you need to talk about?"

I slowly stood up, grabbing my cane and doing a quick stretch as I did. Walking past her, I put my hand on her shoulder as I headed for the door.

"Maybe one day. But not today."

* * *

Ganesh put the power down while coming out of Oak Tree. The rear of the car—fighting for grip on the hot track surface—swerved a bit as Ganesh applied a bit of countersteer to keep it pointed straight.

The protesting tires ultimately fell into line as Ganesh raced down the long backstraight.

About halfway through his second stint, he couldn't help but feel that the car was behaving worse this time around. Everything felt used up.

His top speed was down, his cornering speed was reduced, the grip was severely limited...

As a result, his lap times were a far cry from what they'd been earlier in the day. Every time he crossed the line to complete another lap, he glanced down at the data screen in the car to see his time and immediately saw how far he was off from Chad's time.

"Too slow. Too slow!"

He could picture it now; Chad sitting in *his* chair that he moved next to Arthur as they watched the lap times. They would be shaking their heads at Ganesh after every lap and Chad would be laughing.

"Car behind is now seven seconds back," Arthur's voice chimed over the radio. "We're falling off the pace a bit but you're doing a good job, Ganesh. Keep it on the pavement and bring 'er back in one piece."

Arthur was lying to him.

He knew it.

He knew that Chad was probably telling him to say that.

Make him feel better about how slow he is.

What Arthur probably wanted to say was, "Ground Control to Ganesh: Pick up the pace! You're too damn slow!"

Diving into *Horseshoe*, Ganesh suddenly felt the pressure from what the team was *surely* saying about him and took the corner a bit deeper in an effort to make up some time...and nearly drove the car off the track.

The left-front tire came within two inches of the edge of the grass as Ganesh had to go hard on the brakes to get the car back under control. A large puff of white smoke filled the cabin as the tires squealed in protest.

Ganesh's eyes bounced from the road in front of him to his mirrors multiple times per second.

All of his experience in karts had gotten him here but as he was finding out, the same tricks he'd used in a kart were not working in a full-sized car.

Out of nowhere, a pack of cars had run him down as one succeeded in passing him on the left side through *NASCAR Bend*.

As he tried to maintain his momentum through the corner, he nearly drove the car off the right side of the track going into *Left Hook*. As a result, another car overtook him.

Driving his way through the next few corners, the winding road of *Snake* was ahead of him.

"Car behind is for position."

Arthur's voice again. Letting him know that's he'd somehow managed to lose seven seconds within a handful of corners.

The black Mustang GT behind him looked to have seen better days. With a patchwork of stickers and what looked to be a very homemade livery of a faded white stripe down the middle of the car, the driver behind the wheel was applying a good amount of pressure to Ganesh.

Ganesh's eyes were fixated on the mirrors as he navigated *South Bend*.

Racing down a brief hill, the braking zone for *Oak Tree* was up hill, which invited drivers to try their skill at braking just a bit deeper.

Ganesh obliged.

Once again, however, the tires protested, which forced Ganesh wide.

The driver in the Mustang—now seeing a wide-open door on the inside of the corner to make the pass—moved into position for the overtake.

But Ganesh wasn't about to lose the lead.

Moving down to close the door at the last second, Ganesh was rewarded with a loud *clunk* as the right-side door of the car met the front left corner of the Mustang.

Immediately, Ganesh felt he needed to let the team know.

"I'm hit!!" he shouted into the radio.

The Mustang driver, not willing to give up, pressed on and completed the pass, coming out of *Oak Tree.*

Now in a panic after causing contact with another car, Ganesh came out of *Oak Tree* with the aim of quickly catching the Mustang.

Smashing the gas down, the engine revved high but the surrounding scenery didn't move any faster. Instead it moved laterally as the back of the car swung out to the left.

Applying a fair amount of countersteer, Ganesh kept his foot in it with the hope of catching the slide. The tires, however, chose not to participate in Ganesh's efforts.

The car proceeded to loop as it rolled backwards off the track. Ganesh soon found himself in a cloud of brown as dirt and grass filled the cabin.

Pushing his feet onto the brake and clutch pedals, the car eventually came to a stop. Ganesh was soon met with the sight of a train of cars passing by him on the track.

Eager to make up the lost ground, Ganesh put the car back to first gear and hit the gas. The engine, however, was silent.

Noticing that somewhere along the line he'd stalled the car out, Ganesh quickly put his foot back on the clutch and tried to fire the car up.

He caught a glimpse of the local yellow flag waving from a flag stand.

Looking down, he also noticed that his hands were shaking.

"Ganesh? Are you okay?"

The entire incident had occurred in slow motion to him but in reality, it was covered by the span of a few seconds.

Arthur's voice over the radio sounded concerned.

Still trying to fire the car up, Ganesh responded.

"I...I spun out of the corner. The...tree. Big tree. Of Oak."

The humiliation he felt had manifested itself through his voice.

After several tries, Ganesh finally got the engine fired up again.

Slowing accelerating out of the dirt and grass, Ganesh rejoined the track just behind a large pack of cars.

So much time had been lost.

"I'm back. On track. I'm driving. Racing."

Ganesh was embarrassed by the sound of his own voice.

He knew Chad and Olivia would be in the pit stall, probably sitting with their feet up. They would be laughing at him.

Laughing together.

In his mind, Ganesh was certain that all of the photographers at the track would've traveled to the wreckage site, taken thousands of pictures and already posted them online. Video of his spin would be going viral by now. The fans would all be pointing at him, taking selfies from the stands with his car while it was parked in the dirt.

Ganesh shook his head and widened his eyes in an attempt to bring his focus back.

"So long as you're okay and the car's still driving, feel free to keep going," said Arthur over the radio.

The backstraight seemed to last forever as the sound of small rocks along with clumps of dirt flying off the car slowly decreased. The cloud of brown dirt trailing behind him diminished as well just as another pack of cars passed him.

Eventually, Ganesh worked his way around to the line to complete the lap. Doing so had updated live timing and scoring.

"We're down to eighth but we're still going. Keep your chin up and finish up your stint."

Ganesh didn't respond. He had no words.

The next several laps were done at a greatly reduced speed as Ganesh tried to find the appropriate balance of the car while also handling his own fears and shortcomings.

As the thought of crossing the line to win the race slowly vanished from his mind, so too did the prospect of standing on the podium and claiming his hard-fought trophy.

Although there was still plenty of time left on the clock, Ganesh knew that for all intents and purposes, this race was over.

18

The Road Thereafter

The coolant sprayed in a steady and controlled burst. I watched on, mesmerized by the methodical process of the VMC as it slowly worked the block of aluminum down to what would eventually be one of several intake manifolds for one of our customers.

As I watched, my mind constantly bounced back and forth just as it had done for the past several weeks.

On one hand, I was mentally checking to make sure my duties back in Reggie's shop were being fulfilled. Although much had happened in the previous weeks, my commitment to my job and to Reggie still took precedence. The high standard Reggie had set for each and every part that his shop manufactured needed to be maintained.

On the other hand, my mind was still in the race car.

Although our first race in Virginia had been cut a bit short and we didn't finish where we wanted thanks to that idiot Ganesh, it was an experience worth celebrating.

At least for me it was.

Since that first race, we'd gone on to race at Hallett Motor Racing Circuit in Oklahoma. We managed to finish the race just off the podium in fourth. Once again, Olivia was the fastest, but I was only off her quickest lap by three hundredths of a second. Ganesh had been about a half-second back, but I didn't really care.

Our most recent race, however, marked the first time we all stood on the podium. Just on the other side of Lake Michigan from where I lived, Gingerman Raceway saw us racing in two events: an eight-hour race on Saturday (where we finished fifth) and a seven-hour race on Sunday (where we crossed the line to finish third).

Although it was great to get a trophy and stand on the podium, there was something else I was particularly proud of. After the dust had settled, a look at the lap times had shown that I had set the fastest lap. And not even by a small margin.

I had bested Olivia by nearly a second.

And Ganesh? I mean who the hell cared? The guy was dead weight to the team, and I let him know it every chance I got. The guy just didn't seem to have the goods when it came to racing a car. For me, I felt like I'd made the transition naturally.

It felt like the more I was in the car, the faster and more comfortable I was getting. I felt at one with the car. It sounds cliché, but it's true. It was that unique feeling of almost sharing a consciousness with the car as you and this chunk of metal form one physical creation made for speed and conquest.

Now if I could just get these other two drivers on the team to catch up, we'd be unstoppable.

After our race at Gingerman, we all reconvened for dinner before catching our respective flights home.

"It takes a village—even at the grassroots level—to get onto the podium," Arthur proclaimed as he stood from his seat at the head of the table. "Today, you all did fine work and earned us our first trophy. Well done to all!"

Everyone clapped.

Everyone, that is, except Ganesh.

Once the applause had stopped, I just had to bite.

"What's your problem?" I asked him. Everyone turned towards the both of us.

Ganesh, however, kept his head lowered and his eyes downcast.

"I wouldn't take being the slowest driver on the team too personally,

Ganesh."

Arthur held out his hands in front of him towards me.

"Okay, Chad," he said in an effort to diffuse the situation.

"Yeah, it takes a village," I continued, "but every village needs an idiot."

"Chad!"

Arthur's outburst caught me—and probably the rest of the team—by surprise.

Ganesh, on the other hand, didn't even flinch.

I felt like I might have pushed it too far, but even so, I couldn't—and still can't—escape the feeling of being the fastest driver on our team. Doubly so after everything Ganesh had said before we'd even turned a lap as a team.

After the dinner, Arthur pulled me aside. I braced for a scolding, knowing that insulting a fellow team member in front of everyone was frowned upon, and yeah, Arthur gave me a bit of an ear spanking. He did, however, have another point to make.

"Listen to me, Chad. You have the ability to tune things out and focus," said Arthur. "But that seems to be the issue that Ganesh is struggling with the most. So, to help you two *bury the hatchet,* so to speak, I want you to work with him."

Shocked, I immediately protested.

"You want me to work with Ganesh? Arthur, the guy's an asshole. He thinks he knows everything, and he wouldn't even be receptive to anything I have to say."

"I think you'll be surprised," he replied. "I've spoken to Ganesh in private, and he's wanting some help. He *wants* to improve, Chad. Now the way I see it, you have the tools that he wants to learn. He needs help translating his experience from racing karts to cars, and he needs help staying focused. You have experience in both of these matters. Teach him. By doing so, I think you two can finally move past the rough start you both had."

I contemplated the situation.

"Arthur, I'm more interested in improving myself. As far as Ganesh goes, I don't like the guy, I don't wanna work with the guy and I'm content with him staying out of my way."

For a moment, Arthur just looked at me. He held my gaze as he sighed and then slowly nodded.

"Well that's disappointing, Chad. A village can't function if everyone goes rogue and doesn't serve the bigger picture."

I knew that Arthur was making a good point so I decided to play a card. After a moment of perceived contemplation, I nodded as if I took his words to heart, exhaled slightly for effect and spoke up.

"Let me at least think about it," I offered, knowing full well that my mind was indeed already made up but it was what Arthur wanted to hear.

Arthur took the bait.

"That's the least I can ask for."

He patted me on the shoulder and returned to the table.

"Watson."

The sudden voice caused me to find myself back in the shop.

"You keep daydreaming with your mouth open like that, you're gonna make a mess on my machines," Reggie joked.

"Sorry," I replied. "Just lost in my thoughts is all."

"You seem to be lost a lot more than usual," he added. "But then again, you're mister racer now so I can understand."

"That's *mister* with a capital *M*, please and thank you."

Reggie only shook his head. I found that he had been doing that a lot more regularly as of late.

"If that head of yours gets any bigger, I'm gonna have to widen the damn door just to get you inside."

Reggie—turning and looking around the area—pointed towards the floor.

"Let's get the place cleaned up a bit so we can get out of here. Preferably on time tonight.

As he turned to walk away, a thought hit me and I decided to give voice to it.

"You know, if my head *does* get any bigger, that would mean this racing stuff is taking off. If that were to happen, I really wouldn't *need* to come in here at all."

The words caused Reggie to stop dead in his tracks. He slowly turned back towards me.

When our eyes met, there was a moment I thought he was going to charge towards me and kick my ass. He just looked at me, holding my gaze as he seemingly contemplated his words.

After several seconds, however, he spoke almost somberly.

"Just remember who signs your damn paychecks, Watson."

Turning back towards his office, he continued although his walk was noticeably slower.

I felt bad. This newfound confidence I had as well as the attitude I needed on the track was one thing, but I couldn't let it jeopardize my relationship with Reggie. Not after all he's done for me.

"Reggie," I said with a raised voice so he could hear me over the hum of the machine tools running in the background.

Once again, Reggie stopped but this time, he didn't turn around.

"I'm sorry."

He remained still, probably processing the line of thought that got us to this awkward moment.

After a few seconds, I could see Reggie's head nodding slowly as he continued on towards his office.

* * *

It was a quiet ride with Reggie as he dropped me off that evening. We'd shared a few words when we first hit the road but deep down, I think I'd managed to hurt him, which certainly had not been my intention.

Reggie had been my number one supporter those past several years, and we'd learned to talk through nearly every situation. But I'd made it seem like I was ready to cast him and his efforts aside in my quest for glory.

I wanted to explain myself, but I thought it best to just let silence take the lead. Sometimes it's best if we just move on.

174

I made the climb up to the third floor and walked into my apartment, threw my things down, devoured my dinner as if I hadn't eaten in days and then freshened up a bit.

With a few minutes to spare, I had my laptop set up for the video chat—even going so far as to check to make sure the lighting was optimal.

Maybe I was excited to see Olivia again.

Maybe I wanted to look the most professional in front of Arthur.

Or maybe I'm just a stickler for details.

Either way, I got connected to the video chat to find both Ganesh and Arthur already there.

I seemed to have interrupted a conversation they were having.

"...but I certainly do appreciate you bringing this up to me," Arthur said to Ganesh just as I connected.

Noticing that I was now in the video chat, I could see both of them change demeanor a bit.

"We'll...chat about this again later, Ganesh," Arthur added.

This was one of those weird moments where I felt like I was interrupting something important. Rather than just maintain silence until the meeting had officially started, however, I felt compelled to chime in.

"What'd I miss?" I blurted out, a bit more obnoxiously than intended, which created another odd moment.

Just then, Olivia's face appeared.

"Let's keep it on topic tonight, Chad."

Olivia looked surprised.

"Um...hi everyone," she said.

"Welcome, Olivia," Arthur continued. "That's everyone, so let's go ahead and get started. This shouldn't take too long.

"As the three of you know, this entire racing venture all started from the idea of testing out the prototype steering wheel for use in road cars. This has been a resounding success as we've not only shown the wheel's durability through several racing environments without a single failure, but it's also been adapted to fit into several different cars along the way. You could say that our primary goal has been accomplished as the wheel is now ready for market but considering the level of talent I have before me so to speak, I don't think we should just abandon ship just yet."

I found myself sitting on the edge of my seat for some reason.

When Arthur began, I thought it was a precursor to him closing the team down. But now I was eager to hear where he was going with this.

"Before I get too deep, I wanted to get a read on where y'all are at with racing. Do you want to continue? Is the schedule getting a bit too crazy?"

"I'm golden, Arthur," I immediately blurted out. "So long as there's a seat to fill, count me in."

Arthur's eyes went a bit wide, but then he gave a nod, which seemed to say *I expected as much*. Olivia's brow had furrowed a bit as she let a moment pass before speaking up.

"I like the idea of being a part of something that genuinely makes a difference," she stated. "Yeah, we're racing and we're all having fun but at the same time, we're talking big picture stuff here. We're testing something that has the ability to allow people with devastating injuries to have a sense of normality by driving again. I'm honored to have a continued role in this."

Arthur was smiling from ear to ear at her words. He was a believer in what he was doing and it looked as if Olivia was as well.

Her words, however, made me feel like a chump for my lack of sensitivity to the situation. I was indeed proud to be a part of this team and the efforts they were making to help people. Had I never stumbled onto this opportunity, I would've been someone who'd eventually be benefiting from a steering wheel like this. For the first time, I'd be able to drive on public roads.

You'd think I'd be a bit more invested in the actual project rather than just having my butt in the seat of a race car.

"I know I ruffled some feathers when I first joined the team and for that, I'm truly sorry."

Ganesh's words caught me by surprise although I did my best not to show it.

"Where I grew up racing, this kind of attitude was needed to attract attention," he continued. "It was almost frowned upon if you didn't do...oh what do you call it...peacocking? Now, however, I see this sort of behavior can be toxic and detrimental to a team. I know that I also have a lot to learn but in all, I'm humbled and honored to not only have been selected for this team but to also participate in something that will change people's lives. If you'll have me, I'd like to stay with you all."

I nearly had to pick my chin up from the table after hearing those words. Part of me wanted to feel like a pompous asshole for how I've been treating him these past few races. The other part of me, however, knew that I'd essentially beaten him into submission.

And honestly, why would I stop now?

"Good to hear, everyone. I'm glad to hear we're all still onboard and—more or less—have a noble cause we're pursuing with this."

Pausing for a moment, Arthur cleared his throat.

"Now, with all of that being said, how would you all like to participate in a race that's on what one could describe as a slightly bigger stage?"

The three of us drivers all paused for a moment, seemingly wanting to ask the same question.

"Don't leave us hanging like that, Arthur," Olivia joked. "What kind of a race are we talking about?"

A smile slipped onto Arthur's face.

"I'm talking about the longest auto race you can run on a racetrack in North America. I'm talking about the 25 Hours of Thunderhill."

My heart nearly burst from my chest and fell on the floor at hearing those words.

The 25 Hours of Thunderhill was more than just a race on *a slightly bigger stage*. It was an event that drivers from all over the world traveled to. It was considered by many to be America's toughest endurance race. Although it was run by the National Auto Sport Association, *"The 25"*—as it's come to be called—consists of everything from Mazda Miatas all the way up to prototypes that cost as much as a house. Traffic management was always an issue but that's what made multi-class racing so unique.

It was a far cry from the races we did in ChampCar, and it was a significant step up.

"I think I'm gonna puke."

Olivia played it up a bit as the rest of us laughed.

"So a big race like this begs the question," I interjected. "What will we be driving?"

Arthur tilted his head back and smiled, which, from my experience, meant he'd been waiting for someone to ask that question.

"We'll be renting a car from an established team that has some seats they need to fill. Just like with the previous races where we rented, this team will provide the support for the car and for us. We're essentially their customers.

"The car, however, is a good one. A bit of a step up as well. You all ready?"

Ganesh had literally started to beat the table his webcam was on. Looking like he was suddenly in an earthquake as his camera shook, he shouted, "C'mon, Arthur!"

The older southern man smiled with his eyes as he chuckled, presumably finding a bit of joy in holding this info for as long as possible.

Finally, he relented.

"You'll all be driving a McLaren 570S GT4."

"Holy shit!" Olivia yelled. "A McLaren? A GT4?"

"Oh hell yeah!" I barked.

"Arthur, how in the hell did you pull this off?" Ganesh asked, his mouth still hanging open.

"Our results speak for themselves and the mission we're on with the company is picking up a bit of a fan club out there. We're still having to pay, mind you, but as with before, the company will be covering your entry. Y'all just be sure to do your homework and do what you do best."

I was ecstatic, elated, damn near moved to tears and also anxious as all hell. My wildest dreams were seemingly at my doorstep.

I'll be driving a purpose-built GT race car in one of the most legendary and grueling races on earth.

I paused for a moment as I let my thoughts sink in.

As Ganesh and Olivia soaked up the situation, Arthur looked like a dad watching his kids open presents on Christmas.

"All right, Arthur," I said, which caused everyone to stop. "When do we start?"

19

Thunder

The air was cold and hard as it bit down on my exposed skin. Despite being in Northern California, it was early December and the cold was enough to slowly wear you down if you weren't careful.

I had reached a point beyond exhaustion. I was tired, sure. But as the 25 Hours of Thunderhill raged on, so too did my desire and passion for speed and victory.

A large pack of cars raced by where I was seated in our pit stall, the sound of the engines now vastly different from our time racing in ChampCar. My eyes followed a white and blue Audi as it screamed by. Even after all these hours, the sound of it was still music to my ears.

Despite the signs that I was paying attention, however, my mind was doing anything but. I sat by myself, alone with my thoughts and memories from the start of the race.

Although Arthur had decided that Olivia would start the race, I demanded that *I* be the one who starts. This was promptly shut down, so I had to think outside the box and do some lobbying.

Olivia and I had gotten to know each other fairly well and I told her just how important it would be for me to start the race.

I didn't exactly have to twist her arm. She was always the more practical one and given the fact that I had been the fastest in the practice events leading up to the start of the race, having me start was an obvious choice.

Olivia approached Arthur who later conceded and allowed me to start.

After qualifying in fifth position in our class of twelve cars the day before the start of the race, I'd put us in a good position to fight. That and a bit of drama hit two of the GT3 teams in our class during qualifying as the rain started to fall. One of the BMWs went into Turn 10 too fast and couldn't get it slowed up enough. This resulted in it sliding into the back of a Porsche the driver had been following around the track.

The result was an early trip home for both teams and a whole lot of money lost.

That night, I was more than a bit restless given the weight of what I was going to attempt the next day but as it turns out, so were Olivia and Ganesh. Since we were all sleeping in an RV together, it was a good moment for us to chat a bit.

Minus Ganesh, of course. He dealt with his inability to sleep by stepping out of the RV and into the cold night to "walking amongst the race cars."

I had grown close to Olivia over the past several months. There was a deeper connection now. So much so that I found myself opening up to her about my past a bit, albeit in private. In truth, I deeply cared about her. That and maybe I was feeling a bit more open than usual.

"It's ancient history," I said. Having told Olivia a few of the details about my previous life, her eyes were locked on me.

"You're honestly the last person I would expect to hear about drugs from," she commented, an astonished expression on her face as she did. "You just don't seem like the kind of guy who would do something like that."

"We all have our secrets. I can trust you, right?"

Her smile back to me lit up my world.

"Of course you can trust me, Chad."

I felt safe around her. She was a light to me and my vulnerabilities seemed to fall by the wayside when she was around. I think that's why I decided to open up to her about my darkest secret.

"The drugs weren't the worst of it," I admitted. "Remember when I told you I'd raced karts? I never actually told you why I stopped."

Olivia's eyes were glued to mine as she waited in expectation.

"At my last karting event, I was racing the morning after a night of... partying."

"Were drugs being used at this *party?*" she asked.

I nodded.

"That...was the first time I'd ever used cocaine."

A long pause followed.

"Shit, Chad. And you raced the next day?"

I nodded again. Suddenly, however, I wasn't so sure this was a good idea, but I kept going.

"Look, I don't wanna get into the weeds here, but something bad happened."

"Something bad?" she echoed with a laugh. "Like what? You crashed your kart after driving while high on drugs?"

"Actually, yes," I admitted. "But I wish that was the end of it."

Olivia's laughter suddenly stopped.

"I hit someone while diving into a corner too fast. Sent both of us flying off the track. The other driver, she..."

I hesitated, feeling the old pain resurface once again.

My eyes must have revealed the pain I was hiding inside, as Olivia put a comforting hand on my leg.

"It's okay, Chad."

I huffed through my nose.

"That's the problem. It's not."

Olivia furrowed her brow as I continued.

"The wreck was bad and she—Kate Roberts—ended up being paralyzed from the neck down."

I watched as Olivia's hand slowly withdrew. The look of horror on her face caused me to turn away.

"You must think I'm a monster but know this: There isn't a day that goes by that I don't think about her. I regret every single decision that led to me doing drugs for the first time. I was young, stupid and impressionable. I hope that, one day, I can muster up the courage to apologize to her in person, but until then, I'm forced to carry the weight of this everywhere I go."

Olivia and I both sat in silence for several moments, presumably lost in the memory I'd just shared. She was probably wondering what this Kate girl was doing right about now. I, on the other hand, was wondering what that sound was on the other side of the door to the RV.

"You're the only person alive who knows about this, Olivia," I whispered.

The door suddenly swung open as Ganesh stepped inside.

"Cold night," he said as he walked past us on the couch. He headed straight to his bed.

I turned to look at Olivia, who gave a gesture with her head towards Ganesh and then shook it. I, too, felt that he hadn't actually heard anything.

She then leaned in close to my ear and whispered, "I won't tell a soul."

I patted her leg as I mouthed, *Thank you.*

We both ended up hanging out together until about 2 a.m., before we finally signed off to get some sleep.

* * *

The day of the race came like a thief. Before I knew it, I was in the car and lined up on the grid. My mind was so focused that I could hardly remember getting to that point.

Watching the green flag drop to start the race from behind the wheel of a McLaren GT4 was an experience I hoped I'd never forget.

The rush of speed while that close to other cars from various classes, the fear of smashing up a car that costs over $150,000, the thrill of making passes while also being passed by the faster prototype classes... They practically had to pry me out of the car after my first stint.

Racing in the GT class, we were accompanied by other types of cars, including other GT4s from various manufacturers, such as Porsche, Audi, BMW and more. Additionally, we were also classed with various GT3 cars, which had more horsepower, less weight and more aero but also cost significantly more.

To top it all off, there were even a few stock cars out there that were classed with us, such as the three TA2 cars similar to the ones my dad used to race.

And that was just our class.

The fastest class—the EP class—consisted of various makes and models of prototypes and sports racers. These were usually center-seated monocoque-designed cars, but as always, there were variations in that.

The four classes below ours were E0 through E3.

With each class having a fair amount of cars, it goes without saying that it was a busy field, and no two laps were the same.

On top of that, by having six classes out there at once, it meant there were essentially six races happening at the same time, with each class having a winner at the end.

There was also the unpredictable weather, including high winds, occasional showers and fog, and that was on top of it being just plain cold.

Right now, Olivia was in as I watched the McLaren race by, counting the time before the second placed car passed the line.

Ten seconds.

It sounds like a lot, but in the grand scheme of things, it wasn't much at all.

The blue Audi R8 LMS GT4 was playing catchup after an earlier incident in which it went off track in the slick conditions of the night. We'd played our cards right, and while Ganesh was in the car, we passed them for the lead in our class while they were in the pits.

For the next several hours, we'd just maintained, focusing on hitting our marks and not getting caught up in other people's mistakes. It all sounds a lot easier than it actually was. During the night hours, visibility was difficult. Doubly so when the rain began to fall.

Much to my surprise, Ganesh had begun to show his worth. Where he was once an unpredictable mess, he now seemed controlled. I don't know where he'd discovered his newfound speed but he had it nonetheless.

For the first time since our inaugural race in Virginia, I felt like I needed to perform against him. Ganesh's fastest laps were now just 0.2 second off mine, which made Olivia officially the slowest driver on the team.

I took that with a grain of salt, however, as she was less than a tenth of a second off Ganesh. We had all indeed upped our game and the results were showing it.

Ganesh was back in the trailer, getting ready for what would be the final stint of the race. I was technically *done* as I'd finished my final stint just before Olivia had jumped in but if I was being perfectly honest, I didn't like the sound of that.

As such, I sat with my racing suit, gloves and shoes on and a jacket over the top of me. My helmet lay in a chair next to me.

I pictured Ganesh in the trailer getting ready. He would be doing his slow-motion shit again—more than likely pretending he was a Formula 1 ninja warrior preparing for Armageddon.

Only this time, he wouldn't be participating.

A sinister smile crept onto my face.

The trailer Arthur had rented for us during the race week was nice. It was spacious, warm, had multiple beds for us drivers, room to have team meetings, a place to relax with a nice couch…yeah. The works.

There was only one problem with it.

As the temperature outside would fluctuate, the door to get into said trailer would stick every once in a while.

At first, it was just a matter of applying a fair amount of force but as the race progressed, I needed something to occupy my mind during the time that I wasn't resting up. I had found creative ways to get the door to stick even more. It was amusing to watch Olivia or Ganesh trying to open it with increasing frustration. At one point, Ganesh had to ask a few other people to help him open it.

With Olivia currently in the car and a plan for her to pit soon with a little over an hour left, that meant that Ganesh would be getting in the car next and he would be the one to finish the race. That just wasn't something I could let happen.

While Ganesh was taking a bit of a rest before the next driver change, I popped my head in to see how he was doing. I said my *hellos* and *how ya doings* and *best of lucks.* On my way out, however, I powered off and hid his phone. I also lined the bottom of the door with a mixture of super glue and baking soda, which creates a faster setting and curing time.

Sometimes those things just get stuck at the worst possible times.

"Chad, have you seen Ganesh?" Arthur's face was filled with concern.

"I haven't," I lied. "He could be back at the trailer. How much time before Olivia pits?"

"No more than five minutes," Arthur replied. "We need him here now in case we need to pit sooner. We'll be coming up on a pack of slower cars soon so I'm thinking we'll bring her in a lap early."

I looked concerned. Or at least I tried to.

"I can head back and check on him if you'd like." I held up my cane for effect. "No guarantees I'll make it there and back in time, though."

Arthur contemplated for a moment.

Time to play the final card...

"Have you tried calling him?" I asked.

"I have. Several times. He must've turned his phone off or his battery is dead because it's going straight to voicemail."

...and go in for the kill.

"I mean I hate to say *you snooze, you lose* but I'm here and I'm ready to go."

I had to keep myself from jumping up and giving away the fact that this may or may not have been my doing all along.

Stay calm. Be intentional but act helpful.

"I'd be happy to hop in and get us to the finish."

Arthur continued his contemplative look. It only took a moment, however, for him to come around.

"All right, Chad. You're up. Get your helmet on and get ready to jump in. You're gonna take us home."

Damn straight I am.

"Yes, sir," I replied with a slippery grin.

After Arthur turned to head back to the pit stall, I jumped up faster than

I can ever remember doing and threw my jacket aside.

Within a moment, my balaclava, helmet and HANS were on and I'd grabbed my specially made steering wheel as I took my position by the pit wall.

I looked back just in time to see Arthur making the call to Olivia.

"Pit this time. Pit this time."

A moment later, I saw Olivia bringing that sexy McLaren into pit lane.

It was a borderline crawling speed on pit lane.

Twenty-five mph.

After racing a GT4 for a stint, slowing down that much felt like a sin.

As Olivia puttered down pit lane, I noticed the Audi that was in second place choosing to stay out and pass us, taking the lead of the race.

This was expected, however, as they would still need to pit soon too.

Bringing the car to a stop squarely in our stall, the crew went to work refueling the car. Olivia was already unbuckled and nearly out of the car by the time I'd reached her. She was a bit shocked to see me but she knew what needed to be done. Reaching back in and quickly disconnecting the steering wheel, Olivia ran over and placed it on the pit wall before turning and heading back to help me get buckled in.

As I jumped into the car, connected my hand-control steering wheel and started getting strapped in, I had a smile on my face.

She picked up on the proverbial stink in the air right away.

"What the hell did you do to Ganesh?" she asked as she tightened the crotch strap on the harness a little too tight.

"Wish me good luck," was all I said…with a smile of course.

One of the crew pulled a windshield tear-off away giving me a clear field of view in front of me.

Not wanting to jeopardize the race, Olivia made sure I was properly strapped in, closed the door to the car and jumped over the wall.

I did my slew of processes: connecting my helmet to the radio, pressing the left button on the steering wheel and performing a radio check, making sure the driving mode of the car was still in *track* mode…

There would be no tire change as Olivia had taken on fresh tires just before her previous stint. With the temperature still pretty cold, the time it would take to warm up fresh tires on track would be costly as opposed to simply managing one-stint old tires.

"Standby."

Arthur's voice caused me to put my game face on.

I took a deep breath, exhaling all of my worries and breathing in the sights, sounds and feelings the car was giving me. The steering wheel vibrated through my hands as I held on to it, my fingers resting on the handle control for the gas.

I felt the car shake slightly as the fuel connection separated.

"Go, go, go!"

Before Arthur could finish, I was on my way.

As I reached the end of pit lane, I disengaged the pit lane speed limiter. Going full squeeze on the gas, the 3.8-liter twin turbo V8 roared to life.

20

Dances with Race Cars

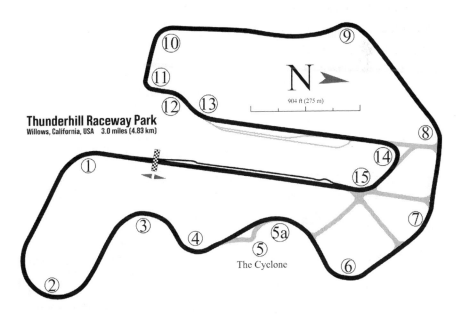

You would've expected the GT3 cars that had started the race to have been fighting for the win in our class. A person of reasonable and sound mind would think that would be the logical explanation.

But most people of reasonable and sound mind don't look at the 25

Hours of Thunderhill and think, *Hmm, that sounds like fun. What could go wrong?*

As multiple teams up and down pit lane had found out during an eventful night of racing in slippery conditions, anything can happen. Of the five GT3s that had shown up to race, two had been wrecked out in qualifying, and the other three were victims of attrition. Between getting caught up in slower traffic or getting dive-bombed into a corner by a faster prototype, the nearest GT3 to us was over seven laps back and were not a factor. Our only opposition for the win in the GT class was the blue Audi GT4, and it had yet to pit for its final stop of the race.

I accelerated out of the blind corner of Turn 3, which snaked its way through a left turn before another blind rising-then-falling Turn 5. That entire turn complex was tough to get right as the race wore on. After a while, the corners would all start to bleed together, and it was easy to forget where you were as fatigue set in.

Now, however, I felt a buzz in the air as I charged the McLaren around Turn 8—using all of the runoff on exit as I continued on. The lap had been clean so far, but looking up the road, I saw a pack of slower cars ahead.

I would need to get around them as fast as possible.

Corners 10 and 11 were the slowest on the track, but once I unwound the wheel, the track opened up to a nice backstraight, which led you under the bridge. A final hairpin to the right and you found yourself crossing the line again.

I went through the gears as I brought the car up to speed down the front straight. Passing two slower classed cars in the process, I'd come up onto the pack and tried to make a late dive down the inside of a third car while heading into Turn 1.

The car was too far ahead and I wasn't about to throw away just over twenty-four hours of racing in one corner. I bided my time and completed the pass before getting to the sweeping left of Turn 2. Although I'd completed the pass, I'd lost a bit of time in the process.

Judging by the small pack of cars in front of me, I was looking to lose a bit more.

The time of cordial passing was over, however. We were fighting for the win and I wasn't about to give it up just to be friendly to a few Miata drivers.

Navigating Turns 3, 4 and 5, I glanced at the mirrors to see the overall leader coming up on me as I completed the dog-legged Turn 7.

The leader was being pursued closely. Both cars looked to be LMP3 prototypes.

Racing onward towards the fast Turn 8, the leader dived in just before I was going to turn in, which forced me to brake unexpectedly.

"Damn dentists."

If you know, you know.

Keeping the McLaren on the track, I'd lost even more time as both LMP3 drivers were already a ways down the road.

"The leader's pitting now, Chad."

Arthur's voice sounded both excited and stressed.

I did my best to remain calm. Breathing deeply, I focused intently on the next several corners up the road.

"They're putting their pro driver in."

Well shit.

"They'll be exiting the pits about—"

I waited for Arthur to look up the data.

"—four seconds behind you."

Shitty McShitballs.

I'd managed to lose heaps of time fighting with traffic and I was now about to get into a dogfight with a pro driver.

Rounding the final hairpin, I raced down the front straight and navigated Turn 1. Before long, I noticed the headlights of the Audi behind me.

"Fight's on," I said.

To be honest, I'd never been in an all-out battle on the track before. And especially not for a win.

The next several laps allowed me to maintain the gap to the Audi, which surprised me. However, once the Audi had completed about three laps, it was like the driver had pressed the Turbo Boost button from *Knight Rider*.

My gut told me they had taken tires during their pit stop, and they were now up to temperature.

"Three seconds to the car behind," Arthur chimed in.

Although the clock was winding down towards the end of the race, I was still losing time, which was unacceptable.

I doubled down and did my best to capitalize on the potential the car had for every corner. In truth, I was pushing as hard as I could.

When I crossed the line, the lap time lit up as a 1:55.8.

That, of course, wouldn't matter at all if I got passed with twenty minutes left in the race.

"He's right on you!"

Arthur's voice interrupted my concentration while heading into Turn 1.

"I know! I know!" I shouted. "Leave me alone!"

Between Turns 1 and 2, the car reached about 115 mph before easing onto the brake and transitioning back to the gas to fire into the blind corner of Turn 3.

The driver behind was getting a bit bolder.

Just before going into the braking zone, the Audi swerved to the right to fake a dive and get me to look in the mirrors with the hope of me missing my braking point.

Cheeky, but I would've done the same thing.

Things were getting close, and with each passing moment it felt like the Audi was inching its way up to my back bumper.

Finishing the lap, we managed to come up on more slow traffic. I was planning to just make the pass as normal, but the slower driver did the stupidest thing imaginable. Heading into Turn 1, the slower driver moved off the preferred driving line in an effort to give us racing room.

Racing 101 teaches you that it's the overtaking car's responsibility to complete the pass. You don't move out of the way for faster traffic.

As I attempted to pass the slower driver around the outside of Turn 1, the driver effectively blocked me by going offline and moving directly in front of me. This opened the door for the Audi, which easily made the pass on the inside.

Giving the slower driver the finger as I went by, I now found myself in second place with a fresh dose of fury running through my veins. I stayed on his tail through the short shoot to the sweeping left of Turn 2. Everything inside me told me—screamed at me—to be aggressive and force a pass. If I could get a nose in, the position would be mine.

A small voice inside me, however, told me to be patient.

Wait for the opportunity and then strike.

Against my better judgment, I decided to play the long game, but I sure as hell wasn't going to give up any ground in the process.

I was practically glued to the back bumper of the Audi—its high-pitched V10 engine screaming as it accelerated out of the corners with me in hot pursuit. When we crossed the line again, Arthur notified me that there were only fifteen minutes left.

Pushing the rising panic aside, I stayed patient and waited. I felt like a damn lion waiting to pounce. As soon as that door opened...

More prototypes were coming up on us. Not the leaders, mind you, but still a faster class. As we braked for Turns 10 and 11, the two prototypes passed both of us down the left side.

The door was open.

Before we'd completed the corner, I slotted in behind the second prototype and followed them through the inside line. By the time we'd exited the corner, the Audi and I were racing side by side down the backstraight, but I was now on the wrong side of the track.

With the next turn being the final right-hand hairpin, I was offline and didn't have the grip to maintain my spot alongside him. I was forced to back off. This wasn't over...but it soon would be as I was running out of time.

Two more laps ticked by and nothing had changed. I was able to catch the Audi but not get enough of a nose in to make any sort of move stick.

I breathed deeply and relaxed my hands as best I could.

Whoever this driver was, they were good. They were able to anticipate all of my moves and didn't seem bothered at all by my presence.

"Five minutes left," Arthur spoke over the radio the next time around.

"About three laps."

The Audi had since managed to pull a bit of a gap on me. It seemed like it was on rails as it navigated the track with pinpoint precision. I was pushing as hard as I could just to keep up, but it just wasn't enough. Slowly, I was beginning to realize that I wouldn't be able to catch up.

We caught up to slower traffic while heading through Turns 7 and 8 but were able to negotiate our way through it without incident. Heading into the braking zone of Turn 10, however, I noticed something.

I'd stuck my nose out just the slightest amount, and in doing so the Audi driver had moved to cover even though there wasn't a chance I'd be able to make the pass. I took that as a sign that the driver may not be driving in cruise control after all. Maybe I was indeed putting the pressure on.

As we crossed the line, two laps were all that remained for me to try my hand.

I had to be careful. Play my hand too soon and I could very well end up losing the spot again. Play it too late and I risked not having enough time to make anything happen.

I took a deep breath, calmed my nerves and focused on what I needed to do.

On the penultimate lap, I watched and observed. I feinted slightly heading into some of the corners and the driver covered down...every time.

When we crossed the line to start the final lap, my stomach was in my throat and my heart was pushing its way up next.

"This is it, Chad!" Arthur practically shouted over the radio. "Last lap to make it happen!"

He very well could've said we were under an alien invasion and I wouldn't have known as I was laser focused on my newfound plan.

I stayed on the back bumper of the Audi through the rising and falling turns. Going into the light braking zone of Turn 6, I even managed to give the driver a slight tap in the rear to rattle his cage a bit.

Then, the opportunity opened like a beacon in the night.

Heading towards Turn 10, I moved the car over to the left side to feint an overtake and the Audi promptly covered.

That's when I slid back over to the right and went side by side with him. His entrance into the corner was compromised as was his exit.

My entrance could've be taken a bit faster but I managed to squeeze as far down as I could onto the Audi. We may have traded paint but I wasn't sure. Regardless, I hit the gas coming out of Turn 11, and we were side by side.

This time, however, I was on the right side of the road and ideally placed to take the apex of the final corner.

Braking, the Audi tried an ill-fated pass around the outside as we both turned in but momentum was on my side.

I squeezed down on the gas and, for a moment, the world stood still.

The checkered flag waved in the air as I raced towards it. My eyes began to water up a bit as I saw everyone from the team already cheering with their hands in the air.

Then, I crossed the line...and won the 25 Hours of Thunderhill.

"YES!! We did it!"

My shouts on the radio were nothing compared to the chorus of screams that came back.

"We won, Chad! We won!!"

Arthur's voice was nearly gone as the cheers and commotion in the background drowned him out.

I screamed inside my helmet as loud as I could. No one would hear me. I'd beaten all the odds, mastered all that was thrown at me, overcome the might of a professional driver and come out on top. The tears were already flowing from my eyes as I coasted the car around the track.

My mind couldn't fully grasp the enormity of what I'd accomplished until I brought the car around to a stop in the pits. I stayed in the car for a moment, hoping this wouldn't be the last time I drove a GT car.

The door swung open and the team swarmed me. They nearly pulled me out of the car as we all shared a giant hug amidst our cheers. When I didn't notice Ganesh, I knew I'd have to deal with that at some point.

Olivia embraced me for the first time ever. It only lasted for a few seconds but to me, it might as well have lasted for hours.

"What a master stroke move you pulled on that guy!" Olivia shouted. "Where in the hell did you learn that?"

My mind went back to the time Grandad told me about *selling a dummy*. Basically making someone buy into a move that was never going to happen and then they feel like a dummy when they realize they'd been played.

"Oh, just watching too much racing on TV," I said instead. "You know how it is."

I wanted to say something else but instead, Olivia and I locked eyes for a moment. She just smiled at me.

"C'mon, hero," she said. "Let's go collect our hardware."

21

As Fate Would Have It

After taking the win at Thunderhill in December, I crossed into the new year with my head held high. If there was such a thing as a breakout year, it's safe to say that was mine.

Notching my first win at Thunderhill had earned us some time in the spotlight, and I was keen to make the most of it. We had done a number of interviews, and even though it was mostly smaller publications and podcasts, it still made me think that I'd arrived. Whenever Olivia and Ganesh were involved, I did my best to take the lead during those interviews, feeling as if I'd earned the spot as the team's lead driver. I even did a few solo interviews as several motorsport publications wanted to talk to the "handicapped driver," as some called me, who had beaten a professional racer.

At first, interviews were rough for me, so I had to do a bit a fake confidence, doubly so when Olivia and Ganesh were around. By nature, interviews are all about asking questions. The only problem with that was, by nature, I was a private person. I didn't like people meddling in my personal affairs. As such, a part of me was a bit hesitant to open up, but after a high-profile win like that, people started connecting the dots.

When word got out that I was the son of Bill Watson and the grandson of William Watson, I thought I would retreat but this time, it was different. I was being celebrated for it and for good reason. I felt as if I'd embraced the legacy of my family and I'd earned my spot among them.

Olivia had known, but like with everyone else, I hadn't divulged any of the details.

People thought they knew the story of my family, but from what I was gathering, it was all just surface-level information. Nobody really knew too much about the struggle my dad went through, and few people alive knew about how Grandad got his start in racing back in Australia. The way I saw it, those were *my* stories to share with the people I believed had earned the right to hear them, and only when the time was appropriate.

The next several months saw the team trying a few different things, which included sprint racing. These were much shorter races and didn't involve driver changes. Once the green flag waved, you just go until the end. We continued to rent our cars for these events, but more importantly, I continued to win.

Spec Miata, Spec Racer Ford, ST2 and even a wild race in a 1968 Mustang Trans Am with Corinthian Vintage Auto Racing (CVAR) at Eagles Canyon Raceway back in Texas. Whatever I could get my butt into, I was in. It was also great for Arthur and his company, as they continued developing iterations of steering wheels that had been very successful.

Although years had passed, it felt weird being back in Texas—doubly so in a Mustang that was the same year as Grandad's. If I said the ground felt shaky under my feet while I was there, most people wouldn't understand, but I wasn't comfortable in Texas. Not yet anyways.

Too many ghosts and too many skeletons in the closet.

Regardless, I won two of the four sprint races I'd entered—the Spec Miata and ST2 races—and finished on the podium for the other two.

Olivia and Ganesh both did some sprint racing as well but the best they could manage were mostly top ten finishes. I think Ganesh somehow got a top five in a Spec Miata race, but whatever.

Speaking of Ganesh, the incident involving a certain door on an RV at Thunderhill never came up. How I managed to slip through on that one was beyond me, but I was perfectly fine with it.

People also started to recognize me. I signed my first autograph at one of our SCCA race weekends, and plenty of people were even asking if I could sign their cars.

To top it all off, my twenty-first birthday was coming up soon.

By the time early June had rolled around, we had one of our normal video team meetings when Arthur mentioned he a special announcement to make. It was so special, in fact, that he'd decided to fly everyone into town for it so we could all be together. Right away, my mind began to wonder about the various possibilities of what it could be.

The morning of the meetup, I was late getting downstairs to catch a ride with Reggie. I was so excited at what the possibilities could be that I'd hardly slept.

Going pro? Racing in Europe? Offering us paid positions as drivers?

"I've told you this before, Watson," he barked at me after climbing into his SUV about fifteen minutes late. "I'm the one signing your damn paychecks. You've had your head so far up in the clouds lately that you're losing track of where your feet are."

As much as I wanted to believe he was right, I honestly felt that I was a part of something bigger now.

Maybe, just maybe, I didn't need Reggie anymore.

"Look, I said I was sorry," I retorted. "You know I've got a lot on my mind, and this is important to me."

Reggie took a long slow breath.

"You've got a lot on your mind? Chad, Mama's in the hospital after taking a fall. While you've been off dreaming about race cars, I've been doing my own race back and forth to her house and the hospital. I've got a lot on my mind too, but do you see me complaining or running late?"

He paused and looked over at me as we were at a stoplight for a moment.

"It's about responsibility, respecting the situation and the people who are involved in it. I've got a shop to run. This is my *business*, Watson. My life! But more than that, I've got people in my life who depend on me to do what's right. Not just Mama but you too. I take that seriously because even though you're some renown race car driver now, you've still got bills to pay. Last time I checked, our man Arthur hasn't paid you a dime."

"All right, Reggie," I surrendered, holding my hands up in defeat. "I'm sorry for slacking off. Really."

"Are you just telling me you're sorry or do you genuinely mean it?"

I huffed through my nose as I smiled.

"A little bit of both, I think."

Reggie shook his head but chuckled soon after.

"Shit. Now there's the Chad I know."

After a brief pause, I asked, "How is she?"

Reggie sighed.

"Good but not great. She was asking about you. When I told her you were off driving race cars now, it made her smile. She said, 'I always knew that boy was made for greater things.'"

I smiled to myself.

At least one person saw it.

* * *

I climbed out of the rideshare vehicle and gave my legs a quick shake more so out of habit. The back seat was a bit cramped during the ride from my apartment to Arthur's company but in truth, my mind was elsewhere pretty much the entire ride over.

Was this the ride to a destination that would change the course of my life?

I couldn't help but see *destiny* written all over the wall.

It was almost as if every event I'd faced in life—good or bad—had led me to this very moment.

I walked towards the main entrance of the nondescript building and couldn't help but admire my reflection in the glass doors as I approached. I'm not one for dressing up, but this event seemed to call for a nice collared shirt, some black slacks and a matching sport coat.

A line from one of my favorite movies echoed through my mind. *"I look good. I mean really good."*

As the automatic doors slid open, my heart skipped a beat—and maybe my feet did too—when I noticed Olivia standing in the foyer. I'd never seen her in anything other than either a fire suit or a t-shirt and jeans, but the blue form-fitting dress she wore now had my eyes buzzing in their sockets.

"Well look at you, Chad Watson," she replied as she turned towards me.

I did a little flourishing spin as I approached her, and I was just happy to not fall flat on my ass in the process.

"Not too bad for a Friday night around these parts," I admitted. "You look amazing."

"Thanks," she replied, not seeming to think too much about it. "I'm just glad this old thing still fits me after all these years."

I leaned in a bit closer and lowered my voice.

"So have you heard anything? About tonight's announcement?"

Olivia slowly shook her head and lowered her voice as well.

"I haven't heard much, but whatever it is, a friend I have inside the company say it's *big.*"

I huffed through my nose.

"What kind of *friend?*"

She chuckled but didn't respond.

I wasn't too sure what to make of that, but I faked a smile nonetheless.

"You think we'll be going pro or something?" I asked.

Olivia only smiled and raised her eyebrows.

"I don't know. I was just thinking it'd be a bump to our current nonexistent salary, or something along those line. I wasn't even thinking about the racing stuff."

"That's all I wanna do," I replied. "It's all I've been thinking about."

"Why does that not surprise me?" Olivia smiled.

I turned and held a cheesy attempt at a superhero pose.

"What can I say? This racing stuff is in my blood."

At that, Olivia rolled her eyes.

"You're starting to remind me of what Ganesh used to be like when we all first met up. And vice versa. Did you two swap personalities when I wasn't looking?"

Her comment made my head spin.

"If you see a lot of me in him," I expressed, "then maybe that's why I hate him so much."

Olivia didn't immediately react.

I pointed my cane towards a set of doors.

"Have you been farther inside yet?" I asked, wanting to change the subject. "I know we're a bit early."

"No, not yet," she answered. "I didn't wanna look like a lost dummy wandering around by myself."

Having been to the building several times in the past, I was more than eager to volunteer my services.

"C'mon, I'll take you in and give you the grand tour."

We were about to head farther into the building with my heart leaping for joy as we did when I heard the main entrance doors slide open...and my stomach sank.

"Hey! I'm glad I found you both!"

The voice of Ganesh echoed through the entryway.

Shit.

"Ganesh!"

Olivia's voice rang with joy and for some reason, I could feel myself getting angry.

By the looks of things, he'd somehow mustered the common sense to dress up as well. Taking things a bit further than I did, he had a tie on and his suit jacket and slacks looked neatly pressed.

The asshole looked good; I'll give him that.

"Go figure," I said. "The slowest guy gets here last."

He didn't take the bait.

I may have caught a side-eye glare from Olivia as well.

"Hey, I'm still early," Ganesh said with a smile, seemingly paying no mind to my comment. "I'm just glad I was able to find this place. There's no sign out front or anything."

"Well, we're glad you made it," Olivia said as she cast me a glance. "It's so weird that we're all together but not racing. We get to just be *us* for a change."

"Hopefully there's more racing to be had, though," I added.

"Even if there isn't," Ganesh replied, "just how many people do you know who get to have opportunities like the ones we've experienced?"

Gesturing towards the trophy case that was prominently displayed in the center of the foyer, Ganesh continued.

"Look at all this," he said as the three of us took a few steps closer to it.

The glass cabinet had lights affixed above each trophy and the wooden frame around the trophy case gave it an elegant but classy look.

"We did this."

Having been here a few times since our trophies were added, it didn't take me by surprise but this was the first time both Olivia and Ganesh had seen it in person.

"It's beautiful," replied Olivia.

"And there's room for more," I added.

"Either way," Ganesh retorted, "I'm just happy to be here."

I couldn't help but laugh.

"You *should* be happy, considering how you nearly wrecked all of our chances early on in this endeavor."

"Chad, seriously," Olivia exclaimed. "Give it a rest."

"I'm hit!" I laughed as I mimicked Ganesh's radio comment from Virginia. I may or may not have turned that into a viral video.

"Look I've had my rough patches," said Ganesh. "I like to think I've pushed through them. If that wasn't the case, I don't think Arthur would've flown me out here to be with you all."

"Oh..." I sighed. "Lucky us."

I think Olivia was about to fire back at me when the doors on the other side of the foyer opened and Arthur stepped through. He was dressed formally, which made me realize I should've put a damn tie on.

"There's my race team!"

We all greeted him with hugs and handshakes.

Looking all of us over, he commented, "Y'all look great!"

He turned towards me and gestured the length of me.

"Going a bit business casual are we, Chad?"

Both Olivia and Ganesh laughed.

"What, this old thing?" I tried to play it off.

Arthur got a laugh out of it, and then he looked like he was ready to get down to business.

"I hope y'all haven't eaten yet. I've got dinner being catered. I've also made this an all-staff event, so everyone should be here tonight. I know the folks who work from the offices here are really looking forward to meeting y'all."

Olivia began to bounce up and down.

"This is so exciting!"

"Before we all head inside for the big announcement," Arthur said as he turned towards me, "can I speak with you alone for a moment?"

The time has come.

I guess I didn't think it would happen this soon.

"Of course!" I said, eager to get the news out. "Lead the way, sir!"

Arthur forced a smile as he turned back towards Olivia and Ganesh.

"Y'all can go ahead on in and make yourselves at home." He turned and gestured toward the direction from which he'd come. "Just through those doors and to the right. You can't miss it."

As the two of them headed off, I added, "Better if Olivia leads the way. Ganesh isn't used to being up front."

The two only shook their heads as they passed through the double doors.

"All right, Mr. Watson," said Arthur. "Right this way."

I fell into step behind Arthur as he led me through the maze of halls. Having visited several times, I recognized some of the rooms we passed, but before long, I was somewhere completely unfamiliar to me.

Arthur was unusually silent as I followed.

"You're not gonna take me out back and shoot me, are you?"

I laughed at my own comment.

Arthur did not.

"Should I?"

I was suddenly on edge as we turned a corner and then made a right into a large office.

Arthur flipped the light on, and I noticed it was his office. Or at least one of them

I'd been in his main office before, but as he liked to work with various departments of his company, he'd long since set up additional offices throughout the building. He liked to stay close to the action and be a part of the team whenever possible.

"Take a seat," he said as he gestured towards a nice leather chair as he sat down behind his desk.

For a moment, we simply stared.

It was making me uncomfortable.

"I've been a racing fan for as long as I can remember," Arthur disclosed, gazing at some of the racing-inspired artwork on the walls around his desk. "When I was younger, it was all NASCAR, but as I got older, I got an interest in road racing and haven't looked back. Hell, that's part of the reason I got a motorcycle. You could argue that I'd watched too many Isle of Man events and decided to give it a go, but I was also into sportscar racing as well."

Arthur paused for a moment as he fixed his eyes back to mine.

"You've come a long way, son," he said. "A helluva long way from when you turned your first laps in the parking lot right outside here."

"Experience is the best teacher," I blurted out. "Thanks to you, I've been able to refine my driving into what it is today."

"That's great," he added. "But what about you as a person? Do you think you've changed?"

I shrugged my shoulders.

"I like to think I'm the still the same ol' me that I was when we first met back at Reggie's shop."

Arthur didn't respond right away. After a few breaths, he finally spoke up.

"Chad, we have a word for people with your level of talent: prodigy."

I gleamed at his words as I sat up a bit taller in my seat.

"But...we've got another word for people with your *attitude...*"

Arthur paused as he locked his eyes on mine and uttered one word.

"Asshole."

I felt a kick to my stomach.

What the hell! After everything I've given to this team?

I held my tongue, eager to hear where he was going with this.

"You're here tonight to hear the big announcement, and here it is."

Arthur placed his hands on the desk and leaned forward.

"We're going to be racing in one of the biggest endurance races in the world: The 24 Hours of Daytona."

My eyes shot wide open.

One of the pinnacle races in all of motorsport, racing in the 24 Hours of Daytona was a dream not just for American drivers, but international racing stars from all over the world and from several racing disciplines.

For those who've achieved victory at the Daytona 24, they were more than just race winners: they became legends.

Ken Miles, Dan Gurney, A.J. Foyt, Al Unser, Mario Andretti...

To even have a chance to be among the greatest drivers of my time— much less racing against them—was more than I could've ever dreamed for.

"We'll be running in the GTD class in a GT3 car. It's a big step up from the GT4 we ran at Thunderhill."

I was nearly shaking in my seat with excitement.

"What...uh...car...manufacturer?"

My words were nearly gone.

Arthur, for one reason or another, wasn't amused.

"We're looking at a few options, but that's not why I called you in here."

Wait, there's more?

I sat waiting with expectation.

"Early next year, the team will indeed be racing at Daytona."

Arthur took a deep breath before continuing.

"You, on the other hand, will not be joining us."

My heart stopped for a brief moment.

"Wha...why? Is it because of this?" I asked as I held up my cane.

"No, no, no, it's not because of that," Arthur replied. "Chad, your attitude has taken a downward spiral ever since you started picking up speed. It's almost like the faster you got, the more you began to look down on those around you. You've become a detriment to the team. Between your constant flow of negative comments, that stunt you pulled on Ganesh at Thunderhill..."

Shit, he does know about it.

"...and your continued unwillingness to be a team player, I have no choice but to cut you from the team. I don't want you representing my company on an international stage like the 24 Hours of Daytona."

I sat motionless, feeling as if my soul had left my body and all that remained was an empty husk.

"You've got skill, sure, but you weigh Olivia and Ganesh down—particularly Ganesh," Arthur continued. "These are your teammates, but you've somehow made them your enemies, especially Ganesh, who's tried repeatedly to make amends with you. I've given you multiple chances to improve, but you seem determined to make people not like you.

"You've been a great asset to the team, but I'm sorry, Chad. You've run your last race with us."

I could have dropped dead right then and there and been perfectly content with it.

Once again, my words were gone but this time for very different reasons.

"Whether you decide to stick around this evening and say goodbye or slip quietly out the back door, it's up to you. But before you go off and paint a target on me, I want you to know that I'm proud of what you've accomplished for this team and that it brings me no joy to do this. You're an incredibly talented driver, but you've lost your way, son.

"I'm sorry."

22

Old Shadows

He'd used me, and I knew it.

He knew a handicapped driver like me would draw attention to his company.

He knew we'd inevitably win races and his damn steering wheel would take off. He'd be rolling in money. Then he'd cast me out and I'd be rolling in the dirt.

This was his fault, and I'd find some way to make him pay for it.

As I stepped out into the evening air, the rain had just started to fall. That unique aroma from when the first drops of rain hit the ground was rich in the air.

I didn't make any attempt to shield myself from the rain as it progressed from small drops to a consistent shower. I remained still, letting the sound of the rain drown out the music that was now coming from inside the building that was just behind me.

I'd gone from a semi-skilled shop laborer to a race-winning driver in the span of a few months. Now, I was seemingly right back to where I'd started, without a damn thing to show for it.

The question that lingered in my mind wasn't anything like "What should I do next?" or "Where do I go from here?" Instead, it was something far deeper.

Whom do I have to blame for this? Have I truly become a pompous asshole whom people loathe to be around?

Am I that one guy that everyone just tolerates, but deep down they can't wait for me to go away?

Just as my thoughts were beginning to storm inside me, I heard the sound of the sliding door behind me open as someone ran out into the rain.

"Chad!"

* * *

Although the evening had yet to officially kick off, people had begun to filter into the large conference room that was being used for the celebration. Many of the people who were present also worked in this building and, as such, weren't immediately familiar with the two strangers standing off in the corner.

"They're talking about us," Ganesh whispered.

"That's because they're probably wondering who we are," Olivia responded.

"You're wrong. Surely they've heard of our endeavors. We're the reason they're here tonight!"

Ganesh spoke just a little too loud, which succeeded in attracting a small group of people.

"Excuse me," said an older woman. "Do you know where we can find Chad Watson? Is he going to be here tonight?"

Ganesh took a slight step back as Olivia chuckled to herself.

"He should be around here somewhere," she kindly responded. "I'm Olivia Calo, and this is Ganesh Kirpa. We're…"

"These are the drivers who've carried us to victory!"

The voice of Arthur as he entered the room drew a few rounds of applause as a few others cheered.

"Yes, but we've heard so much about Chad," the woman said. "Is he here tonight?"

"Well—" Arthur seemed to be choosing his words carefully "—he unfortunately won't be joining us this evening."

A shocked look appeared on Olivia's face. Ganesh, on the other hand, seemed to have immediately put two and two together as a twisted smile lined his lips.

"What are you talking about?" Olivia inquired. "We just…"

Before she could fully respond, however, Arthur held out his hands before him.

Turning to the small group that was beginning to form around them, Arthur addressed them.

"Would you all excuse us for just a few moments? I need to have a quick powwow with the team here."

Before everyone was fully out of earshot, however, Ganesh's apparent excitement couldn't be contained any longer.

"He's gone, isn't he? You finally sacked him!"

"Keep your damn voice down, Ganesh!"

"Arthur!" Olivia shot back, albeit a bit quieter than Ganesh's previous comment. "Please tell me this isn't true! Tell me you didn't fire Chad!"

Taking a deep breath, Arthur spoke up.

"It's true. I don't like it any more than you do, Olivia. But Chad is no longer a part of this team."

"Yes! Goodbye to him!" Ganesh announced as he began jumping up and down. "And good riddance!"

"That's enough, Ganesh," Arthur rebuked. "That's the very attitude that got him off this team."

"Of all the nights, Arthur," Olivia responded. "He had such high hopes for whatever it is you'll be announcing, and you just threw it back in his face!"

"I don't like it either, Olivia, but considering what I'll be announcing tonight, it was *go* or *no-go* for him, and I went with the latter. I don't want his negative attitude on this team."

Olivia wanted to take things further but bit her tongue. Suddenly aware that this meeting couldn't have taken place more than a few minutes ago,

Olivia took off towards the main entrance as fast as her heels could carry her.

"Olivia!" Arthur yelled but in a subdued manner. Before long, however, she had marched out of the conference room leaving Ganesh and Arthur alone for a moment.

"You did the right thing, Arthur. I'm glad to see him go."

Like an unfamiliar aroma, the comment seemed to hang in the air on its own.

Arthur simply stared off into space for a moment as several lines of thought seemed to pass through his mind. After a long sigh, Arthur turned towards Ganesh.

"C'mon," he responded, his expression sour and disconcerting. "The party's started."

* * *

"Chad! Wait up!"

I turned to see Olivia running out into the rain after me, her beautiful blue dress immediately getting drenched.

I should've been happy or even relieved to see her.

Instead, I felt anger.

"Did you come out here to send me off too!?" I shouted.

Olivia suddenly stopped in her tracks as a look of disbelief filled her eyes.

"Is that what you really believe? Do you really think I came out here just to mock you? Chad, what's happened to you?"

A rumble of thunder erupted in the skies above.

"Since you're out here, you know damn well what happened to me."

Now completely soaked, Olivia held her hand out towards me.

"It's not too late, Chad. Come back inside with me. We can talk to Arthur. We'll do it together."

The thought of taking Olivia's hand lit a candle in my now dark world.

The thought of speaking with Arthur, however, seemed to snuff the small light out of existence.

"You're going to Daytona, Olivia. The 24 Hour. That's the big announcement."

Olivia didn't immediately respond, so I continued.

"I got the team here! Where we are now, all the success we've had…"

I began pacing back in forth in front of Olivia. Pointing my cane towards the building behind her, I shouted.

"That sonofabitch used me!"

"Do you even hear yourself?" Olivia countered, her wet dark hair now matted to the sides of her face. "No one's using you, Chad! You've pushed, shoved and bullied your way through every race weekend we've been to. Your attitude, the way you demean other people…You've managed to push aside and belittle everyone around you. Even those who…care for you."

We stared at each other as the words I was ready to send her way were suddenly lost within me. I cared deeply for Olivia. That much was true. Right then, however, I felt like I'd been betrayed by the very thing she was representing.

I couldn't take it any longer.

Turning, I headed off deeper into the night.

"Chad, stop!" Olivia shouted. "Come back in and talk to Arthur! Ask for forgiveness! Tell him you'll change!"

As I marched off into the darkness before me, I forced myself to ignore Olivia. Even so, I couldn't help but wonder if there was any truth to her words. *Maybe she's right. Maybe I can go back in, ask Arthur for forgiveness and promise to be different.*

No. Arthur was no dummy, and he'd already given me too many chances as it was.

Feeling as if my heart were being ripped out of my chest, each step I took away from the building seemed like a small struggle; my cane offering stability but also indicating the support that right now, I felt I truly lacked in life.

I have Reggie, Olivia…I *had* Arthur. I knew this support existed but right now, it didn't feel like it was enough.

By the time I'd stepped off the concrete walkway and into the parking lot, I'd made up my mind that I would be walking home tonight.

Reminded of the night when I'd barged out of Nora's shithole trailer and had walked several miles by myself, the feeling of failure returned to me.

This time, however, I didn't have anyone waiting for me when I got home. No parents ready to scold me for screwing up. No grandad ready to check out the latest contraption I'd developed to aid in my escape.

Nothing.

No one.

I'd give anything just to have someone to scold me.

Instead, I was walking home in the rain on the night before my twenty-first birthday.

Dark thoughts entered my mind. Thoughts that reminded me of the past trauma I'd experienced followed by the pain I still feel from it. In that moment, I thought of Kate. She knew what it was like to have her dreams ripped away...because of me.

I shook the thought away, purposefully trying to bury it somewhere deep. My heart began to ache as I felt new scars forming within me. My old life had shown me how to deal with this.

Ways to ease the pain.

Ways to numb and deafen the sting of defeat.

A dark voice I'd not heard speak with such clarity in many years entered my ear.

I knew what it wanted: my absolute surrender.

The heavy thunder from above rolled again, which aided me in escaping from this line of thought.

Look at you. You failed at one thing, and now you're ready to forsake everything!

I shook my head as water dripped from my hair and face. My clothes were soaked through and my shoes were now filled with water.

As I continued to walk and got farther and farther away from the building, the only sound that was heard came from the steady fall of the rain around me. I suddenly stopped in my tracks and simply breathed.

"What do I do now?" I asked. "What do I do now..."

23

Somber Celebration

The glass slid across the bar and stopped right in front of me.

It looked like something straight out of an old western film.

The bartender nodded back at me but I couldn't tell if it was because he'd seen hundreds of people in this very seat with sadness on their face like I had or if he was simply admiring his handiwork.

Either way, I nodded back.

The small hole-in-the-wall bar was mostly empty, which was surprising given that it was an early Saturday evening. I was sure the crowds would work their way in here as the night progressed, but for now I was content with the relative quiet.

I'd been eyeballing this place ever since I'd moved up here. The thought of coming in here after a long day and having a drink seemed appealing. Now my reasons were very different.

Grabbing the glass in front of me, I held it up and gazed at the golden liquid inside.

Happy Birthday, Chad Watson.

My phone had buzzed a few times today. Several times from Reggie and even more times from Olivia. The former probably calling to say *happy birthday.* The latter probably calling to talk about how I'd been dropped from the team.

Either way, I didn't answer. I really didn't want to deal with people. Or maybe I just didn't want people trying to deal with me.

I lowered the glass and brought it close to my lips.

"Here's to the next twenty-one years," I said to myself. "May they be better than the first."

I was about to take a sip when…

"No one should drink alone."

The familiar voice caused me to stop and turn.

Reggie walked up and took a seat next to me at the bar.

"I'll have whatever he's drinking," he said to the bartender.

If I looked stunned to see him seemingly materialize out of thin air, my face must've shown it.

"Don't let your mouth hang open like that in public, Watson," he said. "It's anti-social."

"How?"

"I mean would you want to be chatting with someone who had their mouth hanging open like some damn bird waiting for food to fall in or…"

"No," I stopped him, suppressing a laugh in the process. "I mean how did you find me? How'd you know I'd be in here?"

The bartender slid a glass towards Reggie, and it stopped directly in front of him.

Even Reggie looked impressed before he turned back towards me.

"This was the place you said you wanted to have your first drink when you turned twenty-one."

Lifting his glass, Reggie waited for me to follow suit.

I really wasn't in the mood but I obliged. He'd come out here looking for me, which is more than anyone else on this earth had done.

"You want me to sing 'Happy Birthday' or will a dance on the bar be enough?"

We both laughed as we clinked out glasses together.

"Cheers to you and happy twenty-first birthday, Chad," he said. "Here's to many, many more."

At that, we took a drink…and I about spat that shit right back out.

"Good God…this is awful!"

Reggie about fired a nose full of beer out as he tried to contain his laughter.

"If this is what I think it is, you picked a drink with a ten percent alcohol content," Reggie laughed as he took another drink from his glass. "The hell you think was gonna happen?"

I placed my glass down on the bar.

"I guess I thought I could power through it." I considered the meaning behind my words. "I guess that's how I ended up here to begin with."

Reggie paused for a moment.

"I heard what happened," he replied. "With Arthur and the team."

I shook my head.

"Let me guess: Did he call you up to tell you we wouldn't be doing business anymore?"

"No," Reggie flatly replied. "One of our clients from the shop who's been following your progress sent me an article about it. Apparently it made some headlines in the racing world. Arthur and his team are going to the big time and the driver who got 'em there got kicked to the curb."

Reggie took another drink.

"In a nutshell," he added.

"That about sums it up," I said, pushing the beer glass in front of me around with my fingers. "Reggie...I don't...I."

I still had trouble finding my words.

"Get the shit out of your mouth, Watson."

"How did I get here!?"

The words came out louder than I'd expected.

Reggie simply held my gaze for a moment. He slowly placed his glass down on the bar and turned towards me. When I looked over at him, I could tell that he was lost in a thought and a memory.

"Pride," he said, his intense eyes locked onto mine as he spoke from his heart. "Pride takes all of us at some point in our lives and if we listen to its words, it can destroy us without so much as lifting a finger.

"In many ways," he continued, "it's like a drug. We get addicted to it and crave it. We begin to need it in our lives. All the while, we fail to see that it's been destroying us from the inside all along."

I nodded, agreeing with his words.

"You know, it's kinda funny," he added. "I've always thought it was unique that your birthday is on July eighth."

"Why's that?" I asked.

"July: Seventh month of the year, eighth day. Seven, eight. When I was younger, Mama used to read this scripture to me from the Bible. The book of Micah, chapter *seven*, verse *eight*: 'Do not gloat over me, my enemies. For though I fall, I will rise again. Though I sit in darkness, the Lord will be my light.' When I think of that verse now, it makes me think of you. I think about how you had to learn to walk again after your accident, how you picked yourself up from drug use and pulled yourself back from the brink of suicide. You fell and you rose again. Now, here you are once more. You may have fallen, but how you pick yourself up from here is completely up to you."

Reggie's words resonated within me as he leaned in close.

"Let me give you some advice, Chad," he continued. "A wise person once said that when you hear people say *bad* things about you, don't listen to them because you just might start to believe it. And when you hear people say *good* things about you, don't listen to them either because you just might start to believe it. You catch my drift?"

I nodded. "I let it go to my head, didn't I?"

"You did. I've seen it before. Pride comes before the fall, Chad. And when you fall, those you lorded over always get the last laugh. I saw it in my own dad, and now I see it in you."

I lowered my head as his words seemed to pierce my heart.

"Stay humble, Chad. In victory and defeat, *always* stay humble. We are the learners, never the masters. Let other people call us that if they want, but like I said, don't listen to them. Stay grounded on who you are as a person and always seek to lift up those around you. *That* is the mark of a true leader."

It was exactly what I'd needed to hear but also a lesson I feared I'd learned too late.

"Thanks, Reggie. For everything."

"You don't need to thank me, Watson. You're a good kid...*ahem*...man, excuse me. You've got a good head on your shoulders. You just need to figure out what you wanna do next and how you wanna move on."

"Is there a moving on from this?" I asked. "It's safe to say that the greatest opportunity I've ever had has just sailed past me."

"C'mon," Reggie asserted. "You're a Watson. I know you haven't dived too far into your family history with me but if what you've told me about your lineage is true, you're not one to give up. It's not in your blood. You've gotta pick yourself back up and press on, son."

"But how? Where do I go from here?"

Reggie took another sip before setting his glass down.

"You're old enough to make that decision on your own, Chad. But from my experience, sometimes you don't know where to go until you remember where you've come from."

His words struck me for a moment.

I don't know how, but a sudden sensation of comfort that I hadn't felt since my early childhood suddenly overtook me. It was almost as if I'd been transported back through the pages of time in an instant.

At the same time, there was a haunted feeling close by as several old ghosts seemed to be waiting just below the surface.

Regardless, it was a part of my past and therefore, a part of me.

A word I'd said countless times in my life suddenly had a different meaning to me.

As I sat in that bar with the man who was now the closest thing to a dad I'll ever have, I instantly knew where I needed to go and what I needed to do next.

It was time. Time to confront my past; time to confront my old demons. More importantly, it was time to confront myself.

It was time to go *home*.

24

Released

So much time had passed, so many things had changed. Where I was right now, however, everything remained the same.

The overnight flight was uneventful as was the ride over to the cemetery. The rideshare driver—who stopped along the side of the road just outside the gates—waited patiently for me. Unlike the last time I was there, I had plans to actually leave afterwards.

Reggie's words were still ringing in my head.

Sometimes you don't know where to go until you remember where you've come from.

The Texas summer heat had scorched some of the grass, despite the groundskeeper's best efforts. I had only just set off from the car and I was already starting to sweat. I walked slowly—the gravel always giving me trouble when I walked on it even with my cane.

My heartbeat began to rise the closer I got to them. Already I could feel a well of emotion building up inside of me, something I felt like I'd secretly been holding on to ever since leaving Texas years ago.

As I walked down the rows, I counted subconsciously even though I still knew exactly where to find them. The four long-stemmed roses I held in my left hand as I walked released a fragrance in the air.

I'd been here so many times in the past, but now I was here on my own.

And as I stopped in front of their graves, all of the Watsons were together again for the first time in several years.

I breathed deeply, taking in the silent ambiance of the surrounding area. It was always so quiet here yet so full of memory and emotion. Even so, the stillness brought a sense of comfort to me as I gathered my thoughts.

Birds chirping from a row of nearby crepe myrtles as a slight breeze swept through were the only sounds to be heard out here.

There they all were. My mom and dad, side by side. Next to them were Grandad and Grandma Charlotte. I stood before all of them as their headstones seemed to watch me, unblinking, in eternal silence.

"Hey…everyone," I said as I gazed upon the graves of my parents and grandparents. "I really don't know what I'm supposed to say. I thought I'd have something ready by the time I got here but…here I am."

I lowered my head, staring down at my feet as I ran my shoes through the grass.

I turned my attention towards the headstone of the man who'd watched after me for many years after my dad died.

"Grandad, I want you to know that I miss you. I regret all the times I mistreated you and thought of you as…well…just an old guy. Thinking back, you were one of the youngest people at heart that I've ever met. You would always remind me of the words that mom and dad used to say to me when I was younger—words I've long since forgotten. I despised you for it because I just wanted to forget, but now I wish you were here to share their words with me again."

A silent thought gave way to my spoken words.

"What I would give to remember once again."

I took a few steps over towards my parents.

"Hey, Mom…and Dad."

I could begin to feel it rising up within me. Not anger this time. No. This time it was something different.

"I just…I wish I could hear you. I wish I could talk to you both. Just one more time."

Tears welled up in my eyes, tears that came from someplace I didn't fully understand.

"Mom, I admit that I don't remember much about you. It's been so long. I've forgotten the sound of your voice, and all I have left are distant memories. Even so, there's a feeling in my heart when I think about you, and it's joy. Even though you'd probably tell me I'm starting to act like Grandma Helen, I know you'd be able to pull me back down to earth."

I smiled at a memory. "From what Grandad told me, I know you had to do it with Dad more than a few times."

I wiped my eyes with the back of my hand as I looked at the wording on my dad's tombstone. I noticed the small chunk of stone that was missing from where I threw the handgun at it after failing to take my own life.

In many ways, the cracked headstone reminded me of him.

Scarred but solid.

"I...I miss our long talks, Dad. From the time I learned to speak again to our last conversation, I learned so much and just enjoyed the time we got to share together. Now, I feel lost. I followed a path, a path that both you and Grandad followed but I've managed to squander it. Now I...I don't know what to do."

Wiping my eyes again, I shook my head slightly to clear my thoughts as I took a step towards my grandparents' headstones.

"Above all, I just want you all to know that I'll be okay," I said as I placed a rose on Grandma Charlotte's tombstone.

"Reggie has been keeping an eye on me and I think you all would really like him."

The rose I placed on Grandad's tombstone blew in the wind slightly.

"Mom, I didn't go crazy on my twenty-first birthday." I cleared my throat. "You're welcome," I said, placing a flower on her tombstone.

As I came to stop in front of my dad, I froze in place—suddenly overtaken with emotion.

I stared at the words on his tombstone once again.

BILL WATSON
Loving Husband, Father and Friend
First American to Podium at the Bathurst 1000

The old me used to look at those few words and think how minuscule they were. *How can one's entire life be summed up into that?*

Now, however, I read them and thought of the enormity behind each and every one of them. In the end, we wouldn't be remembered for the deeds of life as much as for the person we were. My dad never won a race in his entire life, yet he managed to change the lives of so many people in the process. His "never quit" attitude, his positive outlook, his ability to make friends with anyone...that was how he would be remembered.

As I thought of how I've recently been treating people, I felt ashamed. I'd let pride overpower who I'd become as a person, and as a result, I'd managed to push away nearly everyone around me.

Letting my cane fall to the ground, I soon followed suit as I dropped to my hands and knees in front of my father's headstone.

I didn't cry at my father's funeral, and I never knew why. Now, however, I felt that every tear that had been locked up inside of me was being released.

They fell from my eyes and landed on the grass, perhaps making their way down several feet to the wooden coffin that contained my dad.

My fists clenched large chunks of the grass but not in anger. It was more of a longing, a desperation to see him and hear his voice just one more time. It felt as if my soul were weeping, but in doing so, I felt a great sadness melting away from me.

"I'm so sorry, Dad," I cried. "I'm sorry for who I've become. You, Mom and even Grandad raised me better than that."

Wiping my eyes after a moment, I sat down on the grass in front of their tombstones.

"From now on, I'm going to make you proud. No more of this pointless pride and arrogance. That's not who I am. Even if it means I never race again—which is pretty much a reality—I'm gonna change *me.*"

I pondered a thought.

"Because what's the point of being proud of something you did when everyone around you despises you in the process?"

I somehow felt a strange sense of peace, the likes of which I don't recall ever feeling before. I came here with the purpose of coming to grips with my past, with the hope of gaining a sense of where I needed to go next.

Instead, I felt as if I'd received something far better and perhaps the very thing I needed the most.

My eyes, body and soul had wept. I finally felt as if I'd mourned the loss of my family.

In doing so, I felt that I'd been truly released.

As I slowly stood—grabbing my cane and using it help me up—I rose with a renewed sense of purpose.

Not with a mindset of chasing dreams or driving fast cars, mind you, but of simply being a better person.

Stepping forward once more towards my dad's headstone, I placed the final rose on top as I rested my hand on the stone. It had been over ten years since he'd passed away, but the lessons he taught me in life were still rooted deeply. I just needed to remember.

"Thank you, Dad. For what you did at Bathurst all those years ago, for what you did for me in life and for who you still are to me. Whatever happens from this point forward, I won't disappoint you."

Stepping back, I gazed at their four graves and made a vow to them...

...and to myself.

"I promise."

As I turned to take my leave, I headed back towards the driver who was still waiting for me outside the gates of the cemetery. I was ready to head to the airport and make the long flight back up to Wisconsin, but before doing so, there was one person I wanted to visit.

I owed him that much.

25

Follow the Path

T he old car on the driveway didn't match the house it was parked in front of. I faintly recalled some of the stories about it from my dad but even so, it was the first time I'd seen it in many long years. The house was beautiful. Tan stone filled the gaps between the darker wood trim around the two-story house. The side-load garage that wrapped around the opposite end looked to have three bays, and by my untrained estimation, the house was probably close to 4,500 square feet.

I walked up to the front door; the motion-activated doorbell illuminating before I could press it. When I did, I heard its chime ring. It was a few seconds later that a familiar voice spoke up.

"Can I help you?"

The voice on the intercom was louder than I'd expected, which caught me off guard. Even so, it was difficult to mask the empathy and kindness of the man I'd known for many years as Mr. Pat Henderson.

"Hi, Mr. Henderson. It's me, Chad Watson."

A few seconds passed before a response came.

"Chad?" Pat's voice sounded astonished. "Is that really you?"

I held up my steel cane to the camera.

"The one and only."

A few moments later, the front door opened to reveal my dad's old business partner. The last time I saw him was at Grandad's funeral, and truth be told, I still couldn't believe how much weight he'd lost.

"Chad! What a surprise!"

"Hey, Mr. Henderson. I was in the neighborhood and thought I'd stop by to say hello. I hope I'm not intruding."

"No, no, no, no. Please come on in!"

I'd been to Pat's house before, and to be honest, the interior wasn't much to talk about. As a person, Pat was all business inside and out, and that also carried over into his choice of home decor…or lack thereof. After all these years, he was still living the simple bachelor's life.

The last time I was there, however, was for the reception he'd hosted after my dad's funeral.

"You remember the old place, I hope," he said as he led me in. "Not much changes over here."

Walking into his kitchen, Pat retrieved a bottle of sparkling water and offered it to me. He motioned towards his family room, and we both took seats on his very comfortable sofas.

"So how's Wisconsin life treating you?" he asked. "I imagine coming back to this Texas heat is a bit of a shock!"

How does he even know that I'd left in the first place?

"It's going well," I answered, sharing the details with him about my work as a machine tool operator and shop assistant.

"That's where your dad and I got started all those years ago. Good to see you're learning a skill. That's something he—your dad—really wanted."

There was an awkward pause as Pat started messing with the label on his glass bottle.

"You, uh, drive any fast cars lately?"

I leaned my head back in suspicion.

"You already know, don't you? About the situation with the race team."

Pat nodded.

"I do. I promised your father I'd keep an eye on you. Nothing creepy, I promise. It was just to make sure you're doing okay. So yeah, I've heard about your racing and your…let's call it an *unscheduled departure* from the team you were on."

226

I sighed.

"That's why I'm back in Texas," I admitted. "Call it soul searching, call it whatever, I needed to settle a few things with my past. Things that were affecting me in various ways."

"Yeah?" Pat seemed intrigued. "And how did that end up going?"

I took a breath before continuing.

"If I'm being honest, I haven't been myself lately. I haven't been the person that my mom and dad or even grandad wanted me to be. I guess I needed to be reminded of not just who I was but where I came from. So, *how did it end up going?*" I said, echoing his question. "Coming back home reminded me of the great people who raised me, the kind of person my dad was, but more importantly, the kind of person he wasn't. I mean—" I hesitated "—I feel like I've been turning into my grandmother Helen."

Pat's eyes perked up at the mention of her name.

Curious, I asked, "How is she, by the way? I mean, if you know."

He held my gaze for a moment before his eyes dropped towards the bottle in his hands, his index finger slowly tapping the glass.

His blunt response shocked me.

"It wasn't six months after you left Texas that she passed away."

"What?"

A sudden kick to my stomach brought with it a harsh realization.

Helen was dead.

Now I really am the last of my entire family.

All of the pain and suffering she caused when I was younger, all of the horrendous things she'd said about my dad and the constant harassment of my mom for marrying him in the first place; my memories of it all were vague but even so, I should've been glad she was gone. I should've been happy that she wouldn't be able to inflict her venomous words upon anyone else.

I should've. But I wasn't.

Pat seemed to have been wondering what was going through my mind.

"How does it feel for you to hear that?"

I pondered his question for a moment, unsure of how to respond.

"This may sound strange given all that she did to my parents...and I honestly don't even know how I can feel this way...but I feel pity for her."

For one reason or another, Pat didn't look surprised.

"Why's that?"

I didn't even have to think about the answer.

"She'd pushed everyone away with how she treated people. She carried resentment in her heart towards my dad and when my mom died, Grandad said she'd hung that over his head every chance she could. In the end, though, she had no one."

A thought surfaced within my mind.

"After the way I've been treating people lately, I guess I see things from a different perspective now."

My mind raced back to the fateful meeting with Arthur. His words still echoing in my head and heart.

You've become a detriment to the team. Between your constant flow of negative comments..."

I had indeed become the very thing I'd despised. I'd succeeded in pushing away nearly everyone who'd cared about me.

In truth, however, this was the sharp wakeup call I needed—even if it was a bit too late.

Pat nodded slightly.

"You couldn't be more correct about her. She died broke and, from what I gather, had no will to her name. Because of that, the state seized all of her property. She died alone and penniless."

A part of me wanted to have what I morbidly construed as the last laugh but instead, I felt another kick to my stomach.

"When I found out," Pat continued, "I took care of her funeral costs. The funeral home held a wake for her but no one showed up."

I sat there with my mouth gaping open, once again unsure of how I was supposed to feel.

"I made sure she was buried next to her husband. She was no friend to me either, Chad, but it was the very least I could do."

We both sat there, seemingly lost in our thoughts. I couldn't shake the

228

feeling that I was really it; the last of all there was in my family.

Perhaps Pat was thinking along the same lines when he posed a question to me.

"What do you want, Chad? Out of life, I mean."

I shrugged my shoulders at first, ready to give some half-ass answer. Instead, though, I took a peek inwards. Considering where I'd come from just before stopping by to see Pat, the answer was there waiting for me.

"At first, I think I just wanted to follow in my dad and grandad's footsteps. I wanted to race cars and be a part of our family's legacy. Now, though, I can see that our legacy isn't just racing. It's about who we are as people and the impact we have on others along the way."

I paused, recounting what few actual memories remained of my dad during my childhood.

"I wanna honor them. I mean, they sacrificed everything for me. The least I could do is live a life they'd be proud to see."

After a moment, I looked over at Pat. He seemed to be in deep contemplation, as if he were deciding something. Then he suddenly stood. Pausing for a brief moment, Pat held up his index finger before heading off towards another room.

"Hang here for a second, Chad. There's something I think you should have."

I watched as Pat headed off into what appeared to be an office. From the silence of the house, I heard yet another door open followed by some inaudible mumbling. A fair amount of shuffling around could be heard as if Pat was moving things around.

"What in the world is he doing?" I whispered to myself.

Moments later, I heard what sounded like something heavy was sliding... followed by a crashing sound.

"Oh no."

Pat's monotone voice—although diffused by the various walls between us—sounded disappointed.

"Pat? You need some help in there?"

"No, no. I'll be fine. Just give me a...found 'em!"

229

A few moments later, Pat emerged from the office, and I noticed that his hair was more than slightly disheveled. What's more was that he carried two items in his hands.

The first item I immediately recognized.

As Pat stopped in front of me, he held out both items and handed them to me.

"These are for you."

In what was a flashback to my days in Australia, I reached forward and grabbed the small die-cast toy race car that was given to me long ago by Greg Foster—the man who'd been instrumental in my physical therapy to literally get me back on my feet.

Taking it in my hands, I looked at the slightly worn-out paint, which featured the number "28" circled in black with *Holden Dealer Team* written along its side. Once described by my dad as a "small piece of history," I recalled this car belonging to a legendary Australian racing driver named Peter Brock.

The second item, however, was one I didn't recognize. The brown leather cover of the book was soft to the touch. On the bottom right corner of the front cover, the name of my mother, Lena Watson, was embroidered in gold print. As I picked it up, I could tell it had been well used. The red ribbon sticking out of the bottom of the pages grabbed my eyes as I placed the small car down on my lap. Opening the book using the ribbon to see a hand-written entry, my eyes opened wide.

"My parents' journal. Pat, where did you get this?"

"Your dad gave both of these items to your grandad, who later entrusted them to me for safekeeping. Words and memories fade with time. It's inevitable. In saying that, I feel like they should be returned into the hands of someone who would both appreciate and cherish them."

As I began to flip through the pages, it felt as if both of my parents were suddenly sitting next to me. Their presence was soothing as I held their thoughts and memories in my hands.

Before I could get too far into it, however, Pat spoke up again.

"I think you deserve to have some time with them," he said, nodding.

Heading back towards his office, he added, "I'll be cleaning up the mess I just made in there if you need me. Take your time. No rush."

I nodded as my attention returned to the once familiar handwriting of my parents. I flipped back through the dozens of pages and saw even more handwritten entries, a few more from my dad but mostly from my mom.

This was originally her journal.

As I flipped back to the page where the ribbon was, I turned another page forward but saw there was nothing else. The words written by my dad were the last entry. I took a deep breath and exhaled slowly as I read:

To my son, Chad.

Well here goes nothing. I'm not the writer in the family (your mom was much better at it than I am) but given my present circumstance, I want the words that are still on my mind to come out before they're lost forever.

I don't know how much time I have left as even now, my memory is starting to get a bit fuzzy on things. Just in case things take a turn for the worse, I want you to know just how proud I am of you, Chad. In such a short amount of time, you've overcome so much. From taking your first steps since the accident, to gaining your speech back, to looking after your old man, you've come such a long way but deep down, I know this is only the beginning of what will more than likely be a long and oftentimes rough road. I can't tell you that the future will be full of promises and rainbows. That's not how the world works. One day, you'll wake up to realize that both your mom and dad are gone.

There will inevitably be dark days ahead of you where you both weep for and curse your past...and maybe even your own life. I have no doubt there will even be days where you'll be angry at me and I understand that. But like I said before—that time I finished second in the Bathurst 1000 (which still feels pretty cool to even write)—I told you that every time you fall down, I'll be right there with you. You'll always be my son and I'll always be your dad. Nothing will ever change that. Just know that whatever happens—whether it be tomorrow or twenty years from now—it's never too late to start again. One day you may find yourself in a situation you don't think you can get yourself out of but trust me, you can. You've always been resourceful. Sometimes a little too resourceful (like that time you rented your old comic books to your friends and classmates to make money). You're a part of a family that's deeply rooted in strength and determination. We're pretty fast on the race track too, but I want you to know that our family's legacy doesn't define you. You can pursue whatever passions you have in life but whatever you decide to chase after, do it relentlessly. This is who we are, Chad.

As you go thought life, always remember to: 1) Be kind to others because you never know what they may be battling beneath the surface. 2) Right your wrongs. To the best of your ability, don't give anyone the chance to use your past deeds against you. Own up to your mistakes, forgive others and move on. And finally, 3) step up to the plate. Take those big chances, Chad. As cliché as it sounds, you miss every shot that you never take. Dream big but don't stop there. Pursue these dreams relentlessly because if there's one thing I've learned in my later years, you never know how much life you have left to live.

I love you, son.

P.S. There's plenty of room left in this journal. Feel free to add to it.

I closed the book, wiping a stray tear from my eye after doing so.

These were the first words I've read from my dad in many long years and I didn't want them to end. This time, however, they didn't have to. Although I had trouble remembering the sound of his voice, I still felt like we had reconnected despite him not being with me anymore. I was reminded of who he was and therefore, I knew who I needed to be.

"You were a man of integrity," I said quietly to myself. "If there were ever any footsteps I'd want to follow, they'd be yours."

Placing the die-cast car into my pocket and holding on to the book, I pushed off with my cane and stood.

In doing so, the words *right your wrongs* suddenly pushed forward into my mind and I immediately thought of one particular moment; a moment that's been haunting me ever since.

The crash, the aftermath, the guilt from long ago that I still carried with me.

A guilt I don't think I could ever escape from...

The feeling of dread immediately filled my heart but even more powerful than that was the call I now felt in my soul. I knew what I needed to do.

It was time to face this ghost head on.

26

Purpose

Pat's car had a *vintage* feel to it, as he described it. He loved it but it was in fact an old shitbox. As I rode along in the passenger seat, I *absolutely* wasn't paying attention to its worn-out suspension as I felt every bump in the road or the fact that he was pulling the wheel slightly to the right due to a bad alignment.

Instead, my head was still trying to make sense of what I was about to do.

The sun was hanging low in the sky as we pulled up to a house I hadn't seen in many years. Even so, I'd been over here only a handful of times—mostly after karting races to celebrate her various wins.

"I have no idea how long this will take," I cautioned as Pat pulled into the driveway and put his car into park.

"I also don't know if they'll just shoot me on sight."

Pat smiled, seemingly unaware that I was actually serious.

"I've got a few phone calls for work I need to make so you go right on ahead and take as much time as you need."

I wanted to tell him to run if he heard me scream but decided against it. Slowly, I stepped out of the old car and—giving my legs a quick shake—made my way to the front door by following a short path made of stone.

As I walked, I recalled the accident in detail as well as the fallout. I even recalled one of her friends at school calling me a murderer just before Grandad's funeral.

My steps felt heavy. I wasn't exactly sure what I was gonna say but I kept going and before I knew it, I was knocking on the front door.

My heart was racing and I felt my hand nervously tapping against my cane as I heard the door unlock. A middle-aged woman with blond hair appeared.

I recognized her instantly.

Kate's mom. She immediately recognized me as well. How could you forget the face of the boy who'd wrecked your daughter's life? Kate had been of the most prominent up-and-coming drivers on the grid at the time, and the accident I caused had left her paralyzed from the neck down.

"How dare you show your face around here!" she raged, years of unspoken anger seemingly rising to the surface. "Haven't you done enough? After all these years, you never so much as apologized for what you did! Not a single *I'm sorry*, not a visit to see how she was doing, nothing!"

I wanted to speak up but decided against it.

"You ruined her life, Chad! She never did anything to you! She had worked so hard to get to where she was! She had a future ahead of her, chasing her dreams, and you stole that from her! Now you think you can suddenly show up and..."

She stopped venting as she took notice of the tears that were forming in my eyes.

As I lowered my head and wiped my tears away, there was a brief pause. Lifting my eyes, we both held each other's gaze for a moment, and I could see the anger and resentment in her eyes. Even so, I knew this was as good a time as any to let my heart speak.

"Mrs. Roberts, there isn't a day that goes by that I don't feel the guilt and absolute misery for what I did. Not a single day passes where I don't think of Kate and the life she's now forced to live because of me. It sometimes feel like there's a shadow following me; like a damn ghost reminding me of the terrible thing I'm responsible for and rightfully so. I deserve to bear this weight for the rest of my life."

Mrs. Roberts was beginning to cry as well as she placed her hand over her mouth.

"As much as I wish I could, there's nothing I can do that will change the past. I offer a thousand apologies to you, to Kate and to your family, but it won't change the fact that I made a mistake."

Holding up my cane, I continued.

"I know what it's like to lose the ability to walk. I know all about the physical therapy, the pure hell you have to go through just to be able to put one foot in front of the other, catching the stares of people everywhere you go and not being able to live a normal life like everyone else. I wouldn't wish this upon anyone! Not my worst enemy and *certainly* not Kate."

I paused for a moment as I thought about everything that happened after the crash. Images of Grandad's funeral flashed before my eyes. Memories of my suicide attempt caused me to shake my head to clear my thoughts.

"I lost everything after that crash…everything except for the memory of the fact that I'm the one responsible for it. I'll never escape that. The only thing I can do is ask for your forgiveness."

I stood there fully expecting her to slam the door in my face. She could've lashed out at me, told me to rot in hell or leveled me with a stiff right hook to my face and I wouldn't have been surprised. Nor would I have blamed her.

The sound of a voice coming from within the house caught me off-guard. "Chad?"

Peering my head around the entryway, I saw Kate for the first time in years.

She approached the door in her motorized wheelchair and as our eyes locked, the tears in my eyes began to fall once more.

"Kate…"

She smiled at me; that same smile I'd seen on the grid during our time racing against one another.

"Hello, Chad. It's been a long time."

"Yeah," I said as I wiped the tears from my eyes. Her long blond hair was tied back into a ponytail and the *He-Man* shirt she wore had *I Have the Power!* written across the front. It made me laugh. "It sure has."

"Well," she said as she looked up at her mom, "don't just stand there.

Come inside."

Reluctantly, Kate's mom stepped aside and motioned for me to enter. Before entering, however, I spoke up.

"Kate, I'm so sorry. I..."

"I heard everything you said, Chad," she interrupted. "I've shed my tears. Believe me. I don't like it, but this is my life now. I had to learn to deal with it or give up."

She wheeled herself closer to me.

"You should remember from our days of racing that I don't give up."

Taking a step closer to her, I used my cane for balance and support as I slowly knelt down in front of her and placed my hand on top of hers.

"This is hard for me to ask and probably even harder for you to answer, but...can you ever forgive me?"

Kate looked at me as she nodded.

"That was a long time ago, Chad," she said. "I forgive you..."

Slowly wheeling backwards and turning to head farther into the house, she added, "But I'll forgive you even more if you come inside and talk with me."

As Kate headed in, I exchanged a look with her mom, who nodded for me to enter.

"The doctors say I'll never walk again, but I'm not giving up, Chad," Kate declared as I followed her into the living room. "The moment you give up, everything they tell you becomes true."

"Ain't that the damn truth," I said, sitting down beside her.

We spent the next few moments sharing our stories with each other and the various things we'd been up to over the past several years.

I was surprised to learn that Kate hadn't actually given up on a career in motorsports.

"I never made it pro, but I still have experience," she conversed. "Once you realize that racing is less a sport and more of an industry, it can feel like you're in shark-infested waters. I enjoy being able to help some of the younger kids get started on the right foot."

I remained silent. It took Kate all of two seconds to catch on.

THOUGH I FALL

"I heard about your departure from the team," she added.

I nodded.

Kate seemed to catch on.

"We don't need to go into the dirty details, but I am curious. What exactly are your plans now?"

"Plans?" I asked.

"Yeah, plans. Are your sponsors gonna help get you into a car with another team?"

"Sponsors?" I shrugged, frowning at the same time.

At that, Kate's face dropped.

"You...don't have any sponsors?"

I shook my head. "Not a one."

Kate's head fell back as she laughed.

"Chad, how in the hell have you won all those races and not picked up a single sponsor along the way?"

Holding my hands out, I admitted, "I had someone cash-rolling the entire thing. I didn't have to worry about it. Until now, I guess."

Kate appeared to be in deep thought as she looked elsewhere for a moment.

"All right," she said. "We've got some work to do, then."

Shaking my head, I asked, "What are you talking about?"

She turned back towards me.

"Racing is a business, Chad. Not a charity. This may come as a surprise, but very few people in the industry actually care about your abilities as a driver. What they *do* care about is your story. Your story is what makes people money and if you can get people and businesses to see the opportunity in partnering with you, you'll start finding some open doors. You, fortunately, have both skill *and* a story. It's time for you to market that."

I instinctively shook my head.

"Kate, I got lucky. The team I was on, the racing, the opportunities I had...it was one of those *once in a lifetime* deals that I had going."

"Yeah, well, you blew it and now you're here," she fired back. "If you're content with being kicked off your old team and never driving again, then by all means, go enjoy your life. But I've raced against you, Chad. You're a driver and a damn good one at that. If you wanna have a prayer of getting back to where you were, you're gonna need funding. If you want that, you've gotta learn to beat the streets, knock on the right doors, talk to the right people and work the boardrooms like a pro. The question is: *how bad do you want it?*"

The thought alone made my head spin. I had no experience in seeking out sponsorship and didn't even know where to start. I suddenly became aware of just how good I had it on Arthur's team.

"Do you still wanna race, Chad?" asked Kate.

My response was immediate.

"Yes."

Kate nodded.

"It's not too late. I've been there, in the boardrooms with CEOs. I had sponsorship lined up from multiple companies. If I can do it, someone with your talent and credentials can do it too. I won't do the work for you but I can at least get you pointed in the right direction."

As I contemplated the strange order of events that had led to us meeting up after all these years, I asked, "Why do this, Kate? Why help me?"

The question didn't seem to catch her off guard. I noticed, however, that her eyes suddenly locked with mine.

"I'll answer your question if you answer mine," she responded. "During our last race, just before our accident, why did you go for that pass?"

My heart sank as a sudden uneasiness filled me.

"My dad filmed all of my races and I've watched the footage from the accident countless times now. There wasn't any way you were going to make that pass stick at the speed you were coming in. Why did you go for it? And so early in the race too? It seems so unlike you..."

I realized that I'd left out the fact that I was under the influence while I was racing. That would've opened an entirely new can of worms. For one reason or another, I couldn't bring myself to confess this detail.

"That was a...a long time ago and I..." I stuttered. "I guess I didn't like that

I'd started…so far back in the field. Maybe I saw some daylight and…you know…I…decided to go for it?"

Kate held my eyes for a moment.

"It was a kamikaze move, Chad; one that was destined for failure."

There was a large part of me that wanted to tell her the truth but for some reason, I couldn't bring myself to do it. As she continued to look into my eyes, I felt as if she relented.

"But," she finally replied. "back to your question. Why would I help you, you asked?"

I suddenly had a hard time formulating my words. I nodded in response.

"It sounds to me like you're looking for a renewed purpose," she stated. "If I'm being perfectly honest, helping *you* can potentially help *me* get to pro-level drivers who need help on the business side of things. Let's see if we can help each other out."

III

Part Three

"You only get over your fears if you attack them head on."

—Mika Häkkinen

27

Connections

"No."

The word was simple yet absolute, leaving me struggling to formulate a response in my mind.

I'd just spent the better part of thirty minutes spilling my guts and explaining my proposal to the group of four people in a small, muggy boardroom. Together, they represented an international manufacturing machine tool supplier who had sponsored drivers in the past.

I'd come prepared as well. Using the advice given to me by Kate, I'd arrived early wearing a suit and tie and had a full presentation I'd rehearsed a few dozen times in my apartment.

"Chad, we really do appreciate you coming down here but we just can't help you. The amount of money you're looking for is well beyond what we're able to do."

I was ready to respond.

"Let's negotiate, then. What would be a fair investment from your perspective based on what I can offer and what you've offered to other drivers in the past?"

The team of four individuals exchanged a few looks before the CEO—an older man with a patch of white chest hair sticking out of his open-collared company polo shirt—responded.

"To be honest, the other drivers we've worked with were mostly kids whose parents worked with us. There have even been a few employees of ours who drive as well. There really wasn't an exchange of funds. They just wanted a big name to put on the side of their car. We certainly don't mind the free advertisement, but what you're looking for is at a level we're just not prepared to enter. I'm sorry, Chad."

Having dealt with that type of rejection multiple times already, I knew there was no point in pressing the matter. Companies can't make money appear out of thin air, so if it wasn't something they could do, that was simply the end of the meeting.

"I understand," I replied. "Thank you for your time. It was a pleasure meeting you all."

I shook hands with them. As the four men stood from their chairs and exited the room, I began to gather the presentation materials I'd used, and I also took a brief moment to collect my thoughts.

This was the eighth meeting of this kind that I'd had in the past month. Eight times I'd made it past the gatekeeper of these companies—which is usually the person at the front desk—set up phone calls, made face-to-face appointments with local companies and video calls with others, researched the individuals I'd be meeting with and showed up to make my pitch.

Every single one of them had ended in failure.

I was getting desperate and truth be told, it was starting to get to me. So much so, that even my old demons were beginning to speak to me once more.

I could feel the world shrinking and the walls slowly closing in around me. The fear of abandonment began to grip my throat as my voice longed to diminish under the shadows that still seemed to surround me.

I took a deep breath in and exhaled slowly. I suddenly became aware of the cold sweat dripping down my back and beading up on my forehead, so I tried to distract myself. Pulling my phone out, I sent Reggie a quick text.

[Rejected again.]

He'd been the one who I'd initially practiced my pitches with. Reggie was great at playing the role and asking the hard questions I would expect to receive in a boardroom. He was a business owner, after all, as well as one helluva salesman, so I was grateful for his support.

I even made a pitch that was directed at him and his company. He got a good laugh out of it and even admitted that I made a good case. The funds, however, just weren't there. He had a small advertising budget that he'd used on social media and even hired a local film crew to produce promotional video content.

The amount of money I was asking for was simply out of the question.

A minute later, my phone began to vibrate.

"Hey, Reggie," I answered. My voice was surprisingly shaky.

"You doing okay, Watson? I know all these rejections must be getting to you."

Sometimes I think Reggie knew me better than I knew myself.

"I'm...struggling," I admitted.

"Stay where you're at, then. I'll come get you, and we'll go get some lunch. We could both use a break."

Just as I was about to respond, one of the gentlemen who'd been in the boardroom earlier stepped back in.

"Sounds good, Reggie. I've gotta go, but I'll see you in a few."

As we ended our call, the man approached.

"Chad, I've gotta say you made a good presentation."

I felt bad that I had no idea what the man's name was. We shook hands at the start of the meeting but it was all I could do to simply remember my own name at times.

"Thank you," I replied. "And I totally understand the company's position on this. It is indeed a lot of money."

The man nodded.

"You mentioned this would be on a global stage too?"

"Yes, sir. The series I'm aiming for races here in North America, but many of the drivers actually come from all over the world, so it's also broadcast as such."

I could've started off small. I could've asked for a much smaller amount of money and raced in a lower series. I could've spent years working my way up, and maybe one day I'd have the chance to make the step into the big leagues. But I was on a mission. I had a target in mind, and I was either going to hit that target or go down trying.

I was going to race in the 24 Hours of Daytona. I was going to meet Arthur's team on the field of battle.

That was the plan, anyway. As Kate had so eloquently put it, however: "You need money to race, you big dummy!"

"Your experience does speak for itself. Winning so many races in such a short amount of time is impressive."

"Thank you, sir. Racing is in my blood, and I plan to pursue this with everything I have."

The older man laughed but not in a condescending manner.

"With someone of your talent, I believe it."

Pulling out a small sheet of paper, the man began to write on it.

"I've got an old friend who works in broadcast. Animation, to be specific. I can't make any promises, but we spoke on the phone not too long ago, and I know they're working on a new animated series."

"As in...a cartoon?"

This elicited another laugh from the gentleman.

"That's not incorrect, but I'll let him decide that."

Handing me the slip of paper, I studied it for a moment.

"Here's his name and phone number. Like I said, no promises but I know they're looking for new ways to promote this new show. He may be able to help you out, and since they're backed by a major network...well, I don't wanna get your hopes up, but I thought this would help you out."

I smiled, but deep down I could already hear Reggie laughing at the prospect of me getting sponsored by a company that makes cartoons.

* * *

Just as I predicted, Reggie was about beside himself with laughter when I told him about the prospect.

After making a stop at Taco Town, we both headed back to the shop, where I put in my hours with the altered work schedule Reggie agreed upon. I would come into work after lunch on some days and work into the evening. If that wasn't possible due to meetings, I would be there on the weekends getting things caught up. The last thing I wanted to do was get Reggie behind.

As Reggie headed out around 5 p.m., I was still there setting up an automation sequence when my phone rang. I looked to see that it was Olivia. We'd spoken on a handful of occasions after my departure from the team. I was just glad to have not burned that bridge during my moment of rage.

"Hey, you," I answered.

"What are you up to?"

"Working. Setting some programming up so the machine tool runs itself."

"Sounds fancy," she admitted.

It was and I'm glad she saw it. I played it off, though.

"I for one welcome our AI overlords."

She got a chuckle out of that. The sound of her laughter brought a smile to my heart.

"Any luck with the sponsor hunt?" she asked.

"Nothing so far, but I've got a promising lead. I reached out to the guy, but I'll probably follow up tomorrow."

As we continued to talk, joy entered my heart whenever she spoke.

After I finished relaying all of my recent rejections, for one reason or another I felt emboldened.

"Can I tell you something without you getting mad at me?" I asked.

"Depends on what it is. If you tell me that—being the prankster you are—you dunked my toothbrush in the toilet, then yeah, I'll probably get a little mad."

"I mean your breath hasn't changed at all so..."

"Chad!" she laughed. "Well, don't keep me waiting. What did you want to tell me?"

I could tell she was smiling. I took a silent breath as well as a chance.

"I miss you."

The pause that followed was longer than I would've liked.

"I miss you too."

Her response made the sun rise for me. If ever my heart could smile, it was doing so right then.

"But…I do have to tell you that there's someone else vying for my attention now."

Just as fast, I felt a sharp pain in my heart as I tried to play it off.

"What, did you get a cat or something?"

"No," she responded calmly. "His name is Anton."

A silent rage began to rise up within me. *Who the hell is Anton? Is he the driver replacing me? Some German model-turned-racer? Now he wants to steal Olivia from me?*

"He's strong, handsome and has a smoking voice," she continued.

"What in the actual hell," I huffed.

"There's just one problem."

Yeah, me.

"What's that?" I said instead.

After a moment, Olivia made an audible and slightly exaggerated sigh.

"Anton also just happens to be a Porsche 911 GT3 R."

I emptied my lungs as my rage subsided.

She got me.

"Okay, your toothbrush is going straight into the toilet."

At that, Olivia laughed out loud.

"Really, though, Chad. You should see this thing. It's blue and—" she paused "—and I just remembered you won't be racing with us. I'm so sorry, Chad."

"Way to rub it in," I said, hamming it up a bit.

"Really, Chad. I didn't mean to."

I could hear the excitement in her voice, and honestly, she had every reason to be.

"You know," I mused, "you could always just leave Arthur's team and come race with me."

She laughed a little too loud at that one.

"That is a tempting proposition, Mr. Watson. Would I be the one pushing the wheelbarrow, or would I get to ride in it?"

Now it was me who was laughing.

"Our metaphorical wheelbarrow has a flat tire, so I don't think we'd get too far in it."

Laughing at the comments, she added, "Maybe one day, Chad. For now, I think you and I would agree that I need to make the most of this opportunity."

I was just about to respond when my phone began to buzz.

It was the call I'd been waiting for.

"Olivia! Can I call you back?"

"Chad!" she responded. "Yes, you can!"

"Talk to you soon!"

Hanging up, I switched over to the incoming call and took a deep breath. *Business face on.*

"This is Chad."

"Hi, Chad. This is Dennis Yates, CEO of InfiniteMotion. You left a cryptic message earlier in the day about race cars and sponsorship?"

Was it cryptic? I honestly don't even remember what I'd said.

"Y...yes, sir. I did. I was hoping to talk with you about the potential of a partnership between InfiniteMotion and myself on the global stage of motorsports."

Dennis listened carefully over the next thirty minutes, only stopping to ask a question or two here and there. The time seemed to pass quickly as I made my presentation, outlining my experience and explaining how I could be a benefit to the company as a race car driver.

"Would you be interested in discussing this partnership in more detail?"

My closing arguments probably needed some work, but in truth, I'd only made it here once before. Most companies shot me down long before I got this far in my presentation.

"Actually, I would."

"Wha...you..."

Stop talking, Chad!

I honestly about shit a golden brick. I was so flabbergasted that someone was actually interested that I didn't even know what to do next. Luckily, Dennis carried the conversation forward.

"Let's talk again sometime next week. I'll have some other members of the team on the phone and they can ask a few more pointed questions. If things progress from there, I'd love to bring you up here to New York and show you the studio, have you meet the team and also show you some of the content we've been working on for the upcoming show."

I was now pacing up and down the row of machine tools at Reggie's shop, ready to burst with excitement. Before we ended the call, though, there was one more thing I wanted to know.

"Can you tell me about the show? What's it called?"

There was an awkward pause, and I swear I heard Dennis laugh in the background.

Then he laid it on me.

"The show is called *Bubble, Bubble, Fish, Fish*. There's an exclamation point at the end of it too, for emphasis. It's…about a shy fish who lives in a bubble."

In my head, I could already hear Reggie pissing his pants in laughter.

As Dennis explained the details of the cartoon about a fish, a lone thought circled through my mind.

What in God's name have I done?

28

Moving Forward, Looking Back

After weeks of discussion, traveling to New York to meet the team and even watching the first few episodes of the show, an agreement was reached and I was now officially sponsored by *Bubble, Bubble, Fish, Fish!*, the upcoming animated series that would be plastered all over everything I did for the foreseeable future.

With the help and advice from both Kate and Reggie, I'd worked my absolute ass off, stepped out of my comfort zone, fought through rejection and failure, and acquired a major sponsor that not only agreed to a sizable deal, but was also genuinely passionate about what it was I was trying to accomplish.

For the first time in my life, I was a sponsored race car driver.

I should've been elated. I should've been over the moon. Hell, I should've been doing the happy dance on top of my kitchen table for the next several days and been posting about it all over social media.

Every time I thought about it, however, it came into my mind:

I was sponsored by a cartoon called *Bubble, Bubble, Fish, Fish!*

As predicted, Reggie physically fell out of his chair with laughter when I told him about the deal. He was excited that I'd secured funding to chase my dreams, but it seemed like every five minutes he would sneak up behind me and start singing the catchy little jingle that went along with the title of the show.

One of the many perks about acquiring a major sponsor, however, was that it seemed to open the door to other smaller deals. As the weeks ticked by, I'd managed to pick up smaller sponsorship packages with a sunglasses company, a major motor oil brand, a popular energy drink, a watch company and an obscure coffee company based in Mississippi, just to name a few.

I'd even secured a partnership with a nonprofit group that supported athletes with disabilities. There was no money involved, but it was a means of public support and a good cause I could stand behind.

Things were picking up steam fairly quickly.

With funding secured, finding a ride now became my primary focus. Much to my surprise, however, it was proving to be a difficult task as well.

With my primary target being entry into the upcoming 24 Hours of Daytona, many of the teams I spoke with already had their driver lineup filled in. On most occasions, racing teams were more than eager to take the money of an overly enthusiastic driver, but if there wasn't a seat available, the only thing I could do was move on to the next team.

Day after day, I was turned down by nearly every team. One team, which fielded a pair of Lamborghini Huracán GT3s, actually gave me the time of day. They had an open seat after one of their international drivers fell through, and I actually started to get a bit optimistic about my chances.

That is, until I told them about my primary sponsor. I'll never forget the laughter on the other end of the phone.

Another team I'd chatted with, after asking me to repeat my name a few times, soon let me know: "Scuttlebutt says you're the guy who got kicked off his team for being an asshole."

Doubt began to set in as I started having a serious concern about finding a seat. I was running out of options, and I needed to inform Dennis of my progress. I soon circled back around to a team that I'd originally skipped over.

They fielded a single McLaren 720S GT3. This wasn't ideal. Teams with multiple cars had a better chance for success, as they could test on multiple platforms once practice sessions began. The team also only ran major events. It looked like they lacked the funding to race a full season.

Owned by a former pro racer and his wife—Ron and Shayla Jolis—they were both kind and very welcoming. They were the kind of people who genuinely had a heart and passion for racing. Together with their crew, they were a small operation with a true underdog vibe that I was attracted to.

They were a mom 'n' pop setup, being a hodgepodge team consisting of a skeleton crew and a shoestring budget. Unfortunately, they appeared to be on their way out.

Getting involved with a team that was *possibly* in the process of closing its doors was risky. You could end up dumping a load of cash into something, only for the team to close up shop, causing you to lose every nickel you'd put into it. As Kate told me recently during one of our business calls, "There are no refunds in racing."

In short, it wasn't an ideal situation.

But I was nearly out of options.

I began to put a game plan together before reaching out to the owner of the team. Over the course of several days, we spoke in great detail regarding the state of the team, which was far worse off than I'd originally thought. They were in fact just weeks away from selling off parts of the team due to the loss of a major financier. This financier, as it turns out, was the last thing standing between them and a liquidation sale.

But we agreed to a deal.

I had done it. I'd successfully punched my entry ticket.

I would be racing in the 24 Hours of Daytona.

Well, that was the plan at least. There was still a lot of work to do with the car and the team as a whole. The sponsorship money I brought to the table breathed new life into the team. Yes, they got a good laugh about having to slap an animated fish onto the side of their McLaren. Even with funding in place, however, one of the major hurdles ahead was the other drivers on the team.

In short, there weren't any.

To race in the Daytona 24, each team needed a minimum of three drivers.

With the many teams in IMSA already having had the pick of the litter from the pool of available drivers, what was left were mostly underfunded and inexperienced drivers. I hadn't just put of ton of someone else's money into a team only to have an inexperienced driver bin the car in the first practice session. I also wasn't looking for someone who just wanted a ride. I was in it to win it, not scratch off a bucket-list item for someone.

We were only months away from the start of the race in January. If we were going to make this a reality, we would need qualified drivers and fast.

I was at home after work one evening, just enjoying the silence in my apartment while reading my parents' old journal. I'd come to find it comforting to read their words, especially when I considered what I was up against.

I stumbled upon a particular entry written by my dad just after the Bathurst 1000. He was highlighting the various people in his life who'd encouraged him along the way, going so far as to name a few when—like a lightning bolt from the sky—it hit me. It was almost as if he were reaching out to me from beyond the veil and giving the answers I was seeking.

With a renewed sense of clarity, I now knew exactly who I could reach out to.

I could only hope they would be interested.

* * *

The phone rang loudly, which caused him to wake with a start. Gazing at the nearby clock, he had to wait for his eyes to adjust before he saw that it was just after 3 a.m.

"Who in the bloody hell!"

Caller ID showed it was a US number. Even during normal hours, it would be unusual for him to receive a call from the States. Everything inside of him told him to hit the ignore button and go back to sleep. But for whatever reason, he decided to answer.

"Yeah?"

"Nick?" said the voice on the other end. "Nick Lathan?"

Curious, Nick asked, "Who in the hell is this, and why are you calling me at three in the bloody morning?"

After a brief pause, the strange voice spoke again.

"It's me, Chad."

Confused and getting irritated, Nick gestured with his hands as if the person on the other end could see.

"Chad who?" he demanded.

"Um…Watson. I'm…Bill Watson's son."

Nick's stomach tied itself into a knot. It had been many years since he'd heard that name.

"Chad?"

Nick shook his head, unsure how he should respond as the weariness of sleep still held onto him.

"Are you drunk or something?"

The laughter Nick heard indicated this was a distinct possibility, but the response that came back changed his mind.

"No, I'm not drunk."

"What…I mean, why are you…how are you doing?"

The voice on the other end spoke.

"It's been a long time, Nick. I just…"

"You could say that," Nick fired back, surprising himself at just how aggressive it sounded outside of his mind.

"I know it's been a bit," said Chad. "And I apologize for calling you so early."

Taking a deep breath, Nick rubbed his hand through his dark hair as he sat up in his bed. Slowly waking up, he knew he wouldn't be falling back asleep anytime soon.

Reluctantly, he responded, "No worries, mate. To what do I owe the pleasure?"

The awkward pause that followed gave Nick the impression that the younger man on the other end of the phone was trying to figure out how

255

to start the conversation.

"Well," the voice began, "are you still doing any racing?"

Nick furrowed his brow at the question.

"Racing? I mean, yeah, from time to time. Why?"

"I was wondering if you'd be interested in doing a race with me. Here in America, that is."

"A race? In America?" asked Nick. "What are you on about?"

"I'm talking about the Daytona 24."

Nearly dropping the phone, Nick got to his feet. He began pacing around the dimly lit bedroom.

"Chad, what? You're…racing now? At Daytona?"

"Yeah, but it's not NASCAR or anything. These cars turn left and right and…"

"I know what the bloody 24 Hours of Daytona is, Chad. What the hell does this have to do with me?"

Another pause followed before Chad continued.

"I've secured a seat on a team racing a McLaren GT3. We need some more drivers and—" Chad hesitated "—I was wondering if you'd be interested in racing with me."

Letting the phone drop to his side for a moment, Nick let his head fall back as he sighed. After a moment, he raised his phone back up and continued.

"You mean to tell me that you're calling me for the first time in years because you need me to be a seat-filler on a damn race team?"

"I know it's a bit out of the blue, but—"

"It *is* out of the blue," interrupted Nick. "I'm happy to hear you're following in the footsteps of your old man but isn't this race just a few months away? Who's funding this? And what kind of sponsors do you have for this?"

There was an unusually long pause in the conversation before Chad finally responded.

"I've…secured funding from a major television studio. They're releasing a show soon, and I've partnered with them to promote it."

"Yeah?" asked Nick. "What show it that?"

"The show is called—"

Another long pause.

What is this kid's problem?

"—*Bubble, Bubble, Fish, Fish.*"

Nick froze in place for a moment, in disbelief.

Bubble...Fish... Nick mouthed the words, thinking they'd start to make sense.

"There's an exclamation point at the end," added Chad, embarrassed. "For emphasis."

At that, Nick felt compelled to simply hang up the phone.

"Chad, is this a joke? I mean points for creativity, but have you actually fallen on your head recently or something?"

"I'm serious, Nick. The team I'm on, they're really good people, and we've got major sponsorship."

"From a fish..."

"Yeah, from a fish."

At that, Nick let out a heavy sigh.

"If this were as amazing an opportunity as you're making this out to be, every driver from Toowoomba to Tucson would be beating your door down. Since you're reaching out to me this close to the start of the race, it's got to mean that you're pretty desperate."

The other end of the phone was silent. Taking a seat back on his bed, Nick rubbed his weary eyes.

"Chad, it's good to hear from you after so many long years. I can't say I appreciate the three a.m. wakeup call, but in all honestly, this isn't something I'm interested in. I'm sorry, mate."

Chad remained silent, and Nick could feel that he'd possibly deflated the kid's hopes.

"I get it," Chad commented after a moment. "And I totally understand. Just let me know if you change your mind, all right?"

Exchanging goodbyes, Nick was grateful that Chad didn't put up a fight, as they hung up the phone.

He was now alone with his thoughts.

Alone with himself.

Nick lay back down on his empty bed and recalled the vivid memories of all he'd sacrificed for racing. Memories began to flood his mind of his long-ago race at Bathurst with Bill. Chad was just a small child at the time, unable to speak and also in a wheelchair.

Now this same kid was calling him up trying to talk *him* into doing a race.

My, how the tables have turned.

It had been Nick, along with a few others, who had to persuade Bill to race at Bathurst. He'd been reluctant based on his lack of experience but also because of his dark secret, the cancer that gripped his mind and numbered his days.

A few years ago, Nick would've leapt out of bed and been on the next flight if given the opportunity to race at Daytona. It was one of the biggest races in the world. Taking a win in the 24 would possibly trump the victory he'd achieved in the Bathurst 1000 a few years after Bill had passed away.

Now, however, he lay in quiet discontent, his mind racing back and forth to determine if he had indeed acted rashly or not.

A loosely put-together team scrambling for drivers this late in the game? And sponsored by a damn fish?

It screamed field-filler, and that was something he couldn't accept.

No, he had made the right choice.

Even as he told himself this over and over as he tried to go back to sleep, the feeling in his heart offered him no rest.

29

The Friend and his Enemy

I t would be a drastic understatement if I said that Nick's rejection had been unexpected. I fully believed that he would jump at the opportunity to race at Daytona. But on reflection, I couldn't help but feel that it wasn't executed very well on my part. The middle of the night wasn't the best time to receive a blast from the past.

As the days passed, there was bit of good news on the driver front. After getting turned down by Nick, I reached out to another international driver who was more than eager to come to the United States and race with our team. We were still working out all of the finer details for his contract, and the stress of trying to make all of this happen on top of still looking for our final driver was something that constantly kept me up at night.

We were close now, less than a month away.

"Maybe we should let in a younger funded driver," said the team owner, Ron Jolis. "It would be a good opportunity for them. We could also use the additional funds."

Racing isn't cheap. Doubly so when talking about a twenty-four-hour endurance race. Each team will spend upwards of $75,000 on tires alone, so any additional injection of cash you could get would oftentimes go a long way.

Ron and Shayla didn't have to listen to me, but I was grateful for the fact that they did. The idea of some trust fund kid stepping into the driver's seat without ever having to earn or fight their way in just rubbed me the wrong way. Even so, the owners began lining up a few "potentials" as they called them, as we gave ourselves a deadline to find someone more experienced.

The more I sifted through the profiles and credentials of some of these young kids who—because of their wealthy parents—would have life handed to them on a silver platter, the more I found myself ruing the fact that I'd screwed up. I was previously on a team where monetary means had no part on who had a seat at the table.

Even though I was extremely proud of the fact that I'd since secured my own sponsorship and gotten a seat on a team because of it, I don't think I would ever be able to truly escape the fact that I'd royally screwed up what was an opportunity of a lifetime.

This combined with everything else that was going on with the team and with me personally caused me to often find myself lying awake in bed until the early morning hours. Being alone with my thoughts was often one of the worst places to be, especially during difficult times. Even though I felt I'd mostly made peace with my past, there were still dark parts of my old life that often came out during these alone times. These thoughts and many more were making their nightly rounds through my mind when one early morning just before 3 a.m., my phone suddenly rang.

Gazing at the caller ID, I could hardly believe my eyes as I quickly answered the phone.

"All right, Watson," said Nick. "I'll do it."

I pulled the covers back and shot out of bed. Momentarily forgetting my cane, I came close to performing a full faceplant onto the floor of my apartment, but a nearby bookshelf broke my fall.

"Let's get one thing straight, though," added Nick. "I'm not doing this for nostalgic reasons."

"Of course," I replied, finally letting go of the bookshelf I'd suddenly found myself clinging to for balance.

"I did my homework on both you and the team and yeah, this does indeed look like a good opportunity," Nick commented. "When do I need to be there?"

"Yesterday."

"Fair enough. I've also got a bit of something I'm working on for the team but I won't divulge too much until I have things a bit more carved in stone."

Now he's being mysterious.

"Can you at least give me a clue?"

Nick laughed as he replied, "It involves an old British bastard and one of his longtime friends who works in the motorsport industry. That's all I can say."

It was vague, but I was just happy to be securing the final seat on our team.

"Can I ask you something?"

"Shoot," replied Nick.

"What changed your mind?"

"That was one hundred percent Abby. You remember her, right?"

A flood of emotions filled my heart at the mention of Abby. It had been many long years since I'd seen her. We'd spoken on a few occasions after Grandad and I moved back to Texas. A long time had passed since our last call but even so, she would always hold a special place in my heart.

"Who could forget?" I responded.

"Yeah, well, she berated me for hours after I told her I'd turned you down. I mean, it was borderline harassment, mate."

I laughed at the comment.

"That sounds like the Abby I remember." Taking a seat and actually feeling like I could actually be getting some rest tonight, I breathed a sigh of relief.

"Nick, I'm grateful for the opportunity to race with you. We'll definitely be doing some catchup once you get over here but for now, it's a bit early here so..."

"Oh," replied Nick. "I'm sorry, did I call you at...well, it must be close to three a.m. over there."

Well played.

"I think we're gonna get along just fine."

* * *

I waited patiently, just as I'd been doing for the past hour. Okay, *patiently* may be a bit of a stretch but I was there nonetheless.

Checking my phone again, I took note of the fact that the flight I'd been waiting for was now over forty-five minutes late.

Orlando International Airport was busy, which I assumed was typical for this time of day. The crowds of people rushing to their destinations made it difficult for me to relax considering what was about to happen.

My finger began to impulsively tap against my phone as I waited. I was eager and excited, but also nervous and anxious. I checked the clock on my phone again and when I glanced back up, I saw the face of someone I hadn't seen in many long years.

He looked like a hitman on a mission as he strolled into view. Nick's black form-fitting t-shirt and jeans showed that he was still taking good care of himself. The aviator sunglasses he wore inside made him look like a badass. He looked every inch the race car driver who'd raced with my dad in the Bathurst 1000.

Rising to my feet, I walked forward to greet him.

"Hey, Nick."

"As I live and breathe," Nick said, coming to a stop in front of me. Lifting his glasses and placing them on top of his head, Nick smiled. "Chad 'son of Bill' Watson. Look at you, mate! You're all grown up!"

I could tell the excitement in his voice was genuine. I had nothing but good memories of Nick from my time in Australia with Dad. He was instrumental in getting my dad back into racing and also into the race at Bathurst.

Nick extended his hand in greeting. Meeting his handshake, I replied, "Welcome to America! You look...almost exactly the same as the last time I saw you."

"And still handsome as ever, I hope. Still hard to believe, this is. I never thought I'd be coming to the States and racing at Daytona!"

I looked around.

"No Abby?" I asked.

Nick's face puckered, the glimmer in his eyes fading just a bit.

"She, uh, decided against it. Don't take it personal, mate. I just don't think she's ready to open up those old wounds if you know what I mean."

Nick's sister Abby and my dad had a special bond, but it never materialized into any sort of relationship. Although I had my theories, it was the one thing Dad never truly explained to me.

"I understand," I responded, a little disappointed to not be able to see the woman who was essentially a *mom* to me when I was in Australia. "So how's everyone else doing? Tubbs…Greg…"

"Oh, Tubbs is Tubbs," Nick sighed. "He's still a walking tank that everyone's more or less scared shitless of. He'll still bearhug you to death if you're not careful, it just takes him a bit longer to get to you. Age is a cruel mistress."

I smiled at the memories of the massive veteran-turned-bar-owner. He was the kind of guy you wanted by your side if you found yourself in a dark alley but from what Grandad said of him, he was a softy at heart.

"And Greg?"

"Greg Foster? Retired now, last time I checked. I haven't spoken to him much in the past several years, but last I heard, he'd sold the house and moved out to Tazzy, but I couldn't tell you if that's true or not. Speaking of which, I'm…sorry to hear about your grandad."

I nodded. "Thank you. I know you two kept up for a time after we came back home."

"We did. That man was a bloody legend, Chad. He'll always hold a special place in my heart."

After a moment, Nick looked around and smiled.

"Right, then. Shall we get going?"

I hesitated. What was about to happen next would either end poorly or be a complete disaster.

"Actually, no," I said. "There's someone else on the same flight as you that I'm waiting for."

Immediately, Nick got suspicious.

"Someone on the...What are you on about, Chad?" he replied, turning around to also take a look at who I was expecting.

"Well, after you initially turned me down, I reached out to another driver from... let's call it the same era as when you and my dad raced and..."

Nick's brow suddenly furrowed, his eyes telling me that he was mentally narrowing down the possibilities of who I could be speaking of.

The realization seemed to smack him in the forehead as his eyes widened. "No..."

"I needed two drivers, Nick. I needed someone else with experience. He fits the bill."

"No, just...are you shitting me, Watson? Is this one of those pranks your family's known for?"

A smile crept onto my face as I caught a glimpse of who I'd been speaking of. I indicated with my head for Nick to turn around.

"No, Watson! Hell no! Absolutely not!"

He'd let himself go a bit. He was heavier than I remembered, and the dark, full beard protruding from his jaw made him hardly recognizable. Even so, there was no hiding the shit-eating grin from the unmistakable Derek Renshaw.

He was the arch nemesis of my dad during his race at Bathurst. I even recall a story of the first time the two had met; Derek reaching into his own pants and rubbing his balls before extending that same hand to greet my dad.

Now, an older Derek Renshaw was coming to a stop in front of both Nick and me.

"It's like looking at a bloody ghost," said Derek towards me, setting his bag down on top of Nick's feet. Extending his hand towards me, Derek added, "You look just like your old man. How are ya, little mate?"

"You didn't just rub your balls, did you?"

I thought Nick would get chuckle from that but he didn't respond.

"No, mate. I washed my hands...mostly."

"Okay," Nick exclaimed. "Are you shitting me, Watson? You flew me all the way out here to surprise me with the fact that I'll be racing in the 24 Hours of Daytona with you and this colossal pile of shit?"

"Nick Lathan," Derek uttered slowly as he turned to face his fellow countryman. "I saw you on the plane, you know. Walked right past you in your fancy first-class seat. How was the legroom up there?"

Nick's face began to turn red as he turned back towards me.

"Watson, did you do your homework before you decided this was a good idea? This plus-sized man wrecked my chances of winning a Supercars championship! After that, the entire country hated him so much that he got sacked from his team and he hasn't ran a Supercars race ever since."

Derek simply shrugged.

Turning back towards him, Nick asked. "What are ya up to nowadays, Derek? Selling used cars in a three-piece suit?"

"Oh eat shit and let the past go, will ya?" barked Derek. "That was years ago and you've done well for yourself since then. Remember, we're both Bathurst winners!"

"You won the 1000 by a whisker against Chad's old man after you nearly wiped out the entire field and then biffed and barged your way past him!"

"Are you still whinging about that? A win is a win, Lathan!"

"A win is even more special when you team doesn't have to rebuild the entire car because you smashed half the field up to get there."

"It's called getting your elbows out! Something you never quite figured out how to do! Maybe I should show…"

"Enough!"

My intervention was louder than it needed to be, but it got both of their attention…as well as a few passersby.

I took a deep breath, extending my hands in front of the two of them after the gap between them was beginning to close.

"I'm not asking for you guys to become best friends. I'm not even asking for you guys to like each other. All I'm asking is that you bring your A-game to one of the biggest races in the world. You two raced in some of the most challenging cars to drive in all of motorsport and were among the best at it. You each have unique traits that make for valuable assets to this team.

Please, for the love of God, just tolerate each other until the race is over. That's all I'm asking."

The two seemed to cool down a bit after that. They locked eyes, Derek giving his signature smile, which didn't look quite as refined as it used to be.

"We're gonna be racing against some of the best GT drivers in the world. Trust me when I say that we're all gonna end up needing each other's help if we're gonna make this work. Can you two do this for me? Because I sure as hell can't do it without you."

There was a brief pause as the two seemed to analyze everything I was saying. Or at least Nick was as I purposely didn't tell him about Derek until now.

"You play a dangerous game, Chad," Nick replied. "This is a race I've wanted to do for a very long time so I'll play along for now if he's willing to do the same."

Derek's smile turned into an overly dramatic look of surprise.

"I knew you'd come around," he said, patting Nick softly on the shoulder. "It'll be just like our old Formula Ford days."

Nick patted Derek's stomach.

"Hard to think about those days, mate. You've had a few too many burgers and fries to fit into one of those. Hopefully you can fit into the same seat as us for the race. Have you thought about pitching a sponsorship deal to McDonald's?"

Derek raised his eyebrows in surprise.

"Jokes, huh? Fair game then. While we're here in the States, you should send a sponsorship proposal over to Kleenex considering the amount of whinging you still do."

"Guys..."

My protest caused Derek to hold his hands out in front of him in a form of surrender.

"All right, all right. I'm sorry."

At that, Derek picked up his bag from the ground.

"Let's get rolling, yeah? Off we go to see some 'Murica! Beers, babes and bald eagles await!"

Derek strolled ahead of Nick and me towards the baggage claim. Nick turned and looked me in the eye.

"Let's get something straight, Watson," he said. "Your old man and grandad were legends. They earned their place and hold a special spot in my life. You've got a lot to live up to, but between you and me, this stunt you just pulled with Renshaw doesn't put you off to the best start. Just remember that respect goes both ways. More importantly, it's earned, not given."

That was fair. I knew it was a bit of a cheeky move, but truth be told, I was simply out of options.

"I understand."

Gesturing towards Derek, Nick added, "Keep that man on a short leash. He'll either be one of the fastest drivers in the field or he'll get us all kicked off the grid."

Repositioning his bag over his shoulder, Nick turned to follow Derek as he muttered under his breath, "I can't believe I'm racing in the same car as Derek Renshaw. Derek bloody Renshaw."

I stayed for a moment as I watched the two men walk away. As bad as I'd thought this was going to go, it could've gone a lot worse.

Granted, I still had to get them to their hotel and I may have failed to mention that they'd have rooms right next to each other for the next week.

Nick's words echoed in my mind. I knew I had a powerful driver lineup. If all the pieces fell into place, we'd have a good shot...

...if I could keep those two from killing each other.

30

We Shall Meet Again

Ganesh stood stoically, lording over the white porcelain. In one hand, he held his phone as he leisurely scrolled through his social media feed—mostly to see what his old friends and family who had previously not taken him seriously were up to.

It was always so typical.

Baby pictures of their latest crotch monsters, last night's dinner, selfies with people he neither knew nor cared about and one random douchebag who stood with the collar of his pink polo shirt popped, sunglasses down on the bridge of his nose as to peer over the top of them and his tongue partially sticking out while posing with someone else's Porsche 911 GT3 in the parking lot of a gym.

Pathetic.

They'd doubted him in the past. Family…friends…they'd all cast him and his dreams for greatness aside as they pursued their cookie cutter lives of fake-bake tans, clothes that made them look just like every other idiot they saw on their phones, the latest trends so they could feel like they actually belonged to something and babies. Lots. Of. Babies.

It was all such a ridiculous act…and Ganesh wanted nothing to do with them.

As he continued to hover over the white porcelain bowl while releasing the contents of his bladder—splashing about here and there—the mindless scrolling continued. It was always more of the same.

Every once in a while, his scrolling would reveal a story regarding another GTD class team he'd be racing against.

Although they—himself, Olivia and the newest member of the team, Daniel Stephens—were one of the newest teams to hit the grid, Ganesh knew they'd be able to punch above their weight, even amongst the more experienced GTD Pro drivers.

His confidence was strong. Ganesh had been taking driving lessons from some of the best coaches in the business who'd all reassured him that he had the tools to be a force to be reckoned with.

As he finished relieving himself, he then came across an article that made his entire body jerk.

'The Watson Legacy Continues'

Underneath the headline, the face of Chad Watson looked back at him. There he was—the face of the cripple he'd worked so hard to manipulate into getting sacked from the team—staring back up at him.

So the rumors were true.

The cripple was back.

Somehow, he'd found a way to get into the Daytona 24. He'd probably lied, cheated and stolen his way there. The little shit had humiliated him in the past.

Ganesh would never forgive him for Thunderhill.

The more he stared into the face of Watson, however, the more his curiosity was piqued. It finally overtook him and he decided to read a bit more. He tapped the screen with his finger, but with a bit too much enthusiasm. The phone slipped from his hand and for a brief moment, life seemed to move in slow motion.

His phone tumbled into what would surely be its watery, urine-infested grave.

Not quick enough to catch it, the phone plunged into the toilet bowl causing the yellow water to splash across the floor and onto his bare feet.

Once the ripples in the water ceased, Chad was still there—looking up at him once again.

Taunting. Menacing, even.

Ganesh's face got hot.

He would meet his foe on the track at Daytona, this he knew for sure. The little boy he'd plowed over in the airport in Virginia would be no match for him, not this time.

As Chad Watson's smirking face smiled up at him, he swore he saw the image wink at him just before the screen on his phone went black.

31

Off to the Races

With the Daytona 24 now fast approaching, there was a running checklist of things to do.

Nick and Derek's trip from Australia had gone as planned, with the two only having one scrap that nearly resulted in a fistfight. They did, however, manage to get their individual seat inserts made, get sized for their new fire suits and also began the media exposure with various interviews from sporting outlets so that was a plus.

As news of my newfound team began to make headlines, stories about my past started to crop up. I did my best to answer the questions directed towards me about my family. It's wasn't every day you had a third-generation racer on the grid at Daytona so I did my best to honor that. But I knew they were just hunting for headlines. As far as I knew, no one knew too much about my *actual* past…and that suited me just fine.

Many of the interviews I did were via phone or video chats, and Reggie was more than accommodating given the fact that I was bringing a bit of publicity to his shop. He was not only able to bring in more business but also hire some experienced machine tool operators to fill the new demands.

Reggie wasn't one to normally give much slack to anyone, me specifically. When I heard, however, that he was under strict orders from Mama Fuller to give me as much leeway as I needed, the only thing Reggie continued to harass me about from that point on was that stupid little jingle.

Bubble, Bubble, Fish, Fish!

At home and zipping up the last of my suitcases, I picked it up and placed it with the others by the door of my apartment. I lived a spartan lifestyle and didn't have much in the way of material possessions. I'd always been a jeans and t-shirt kinda guy who didn't like to have too much excess. Packing for what would be an extended stay in Florida was easy.

I did one last check to ensure I'd grabbed everything I would need. I didn't need to say any goodbyes or rub any door panels for good old sentiment. I'd be coming back here after the race was over.

I stopped in the hallway between my bedroom and the kitchen.

The thought of the race being *over* caused a foreign feeling to enter my mind. Once I left this apartment, the next time I would walk through this door would be after the race was complete.

How would I fare? Will I walk in with a massive trophy and a new Rolex watch that's only given to the winning drivers? Or would I come back here defeated with my tail between my legs?

Another thought soon followed.

What will happen when it's all over? What would be next?

My phone vibrated, ceasing that train of thought.

"Didn't think I'd be hearing from you until we were both in Florida."

The sound of Olivia laughing on the other end of the phone made my heart leap with joy.

"So it's true, then. You're really racing in the 24."

"Guilty as charged," I replied. "Don't act like you won't be happy to see me on track."

"I welcome any and all competition. Just know that this time, you'll have a giant target on your back."

My brow furrowed at her comment.

"Geez, I would at least hope for a clean race from you."

"It's not me you need to worry about," Olivia replied. "Ever since the news broke that you'd be racing with a pair of old guys from Australia, Ganesh hasn't stopped talking about you. He says he's been training his entire life for this moment."

My eyes rolled as I sighed.

"Dear Lord, that guy. Well, I'm looking forward to the chase, then."

A slight pause followed.

"He's wanting more than that. It almost seems personal. He said he's out for blood, which has Arthur—and me—a bit worried."

We chatted for a bit longer, catching me up on how everyone was doing. In truth, I just liked hearing the sound of her voice.

"I just saw the pictures of our team's Porsche with the livery on it; and Chad, it looks sexy."

A chill shot up my spine. I may have noticed some goosebumps on my arms as well.

"Yeah," I managed to get out, "but does it have a giant fish on the side of it?"

Olivia burst out laughing.

"I still can't believe it. Chad Watson; the winner of the 25 Hours of Thunderhill...sponsored by a fish."

"Hey, you don't see what the car looks like when you're driving it."

"Yeah, but I will," Olivia smiled. "And it'll give me a good laugh every time I pass you."

"Such confidence!" I exclaimed.

Right then and there was the first time I'd ever heard Olivia giggle. An awkward pause followed as I smiled. I think she caught herself in the act, as she immediately took a serious turn.

"This is more just curiosity, Chad, but *why* are you racing? Are you trying to prove to Arthur that you're capable of beating us? Is this about some twisted plot for revenge?"

I thought for a moment, letting the question hang in the air.

I'd never really thought about it. It was more of a gut feeling. Something that hadn't truly manifested into words, but I guessed it was about time that it did.

"It's about redemption," I began. "It's about looking myself in the mirror, knowing how much I've screwed up, but then being able to tell myself that I still came back, showed up and gave it my all. It's about believing I can make my own destiny, not content with simply accepting what life hands me. Sometimes we need to make calculated risks but when push comes to shove, you've gotta be willing to roll the dice and take your chance when the time comes."

A thought came to mind—an image of the person who personified why I believe the way I do.

"It's what my dad would've done." I added. "I think he would've liked you."

I heard Olivia laugh a bit on the other end. "If he was half as tenacious as you are, I'm sure we would've gotten along just fine."

The image of Olivia meeting Dad for the first time created itself in my mind. For some reason, I felt like it gave me a sense of boldness.

"I still miss you, you know."

The words seem to kill the energy in our conversation. That certainly wasn't my intention and part of me immediately regretted saying it. What came next, though, was completely unexpected.

"Look here, Watson. I'm not gonna go easy on you out there. We may be friends but don't expect that to save you when we're racing on track."

"Just friends?" I joked.

Call it a sixth sense but I swear she was smiling on the other end of that phone.

"Watch yourself, Watson. Once that helmet goes on, you're just another car out there to me."

"I'd be disappointed with anything less," I smirked. "Hopefully after all this is over, that helmet will come off and I can buy you a drink. You're twenty-one, right?"

This time, I heard it. The laughter under her breath was like a beacon I wanted to run to. It was short-lived , however, as Olivia soon put her game face back on just before she hung up the phone.

"Chad, I'll see you in Daytona."

32

The Locked Door

My hand twitched nervously as I sat towards the center of the long table. The black tablecloth I rested my forearms on concealed the cheap folding table that shook ever so slightly with each minuscule movement of mine.

Dozens of reporters and journalists sat in chairs in front of me. Some of them I recognized as personalities embedded in the world of motorsport media. Many others were strangers to me. They would soon be asking a lot of questions.

Nick and Derek were flanking me on my left and right.

The months leading up to where we presently found ourselves had raced by in what felt like a single lap of Daytona. When we weren't doing physical training to ensure we were in top shape, we were training with the crew so we could nail down our pit stops to a science. If there was one way to throw away a perfectly good race, it was from a botched pit stop. When we weren't focusing on the real car, we were on the simulator we had installed in the shop. The sim featured a motion chassis that moved as the real car would. This was extra handy for the high on-track banking at Daytona, and having a simulator allowed us to start working on our racing line and braking points. Any sort of extra practice you can get is never a bad thing.

When everyone on the crew wasn't training, we were prepping the car, ordering spare parts, analyzing data, working on marketing and branding, fulfilling sponsorship and media commitments, crunching numbers, spying on the other teams...it was enough to make your head spin. With all the pressure, I wasn't getting more than a few hours of sleep every night.

I shook my head to wake myself up. There comes a point where even chugging copious amounts of coffee does nothing.

Nick's face was set like stone. He looked like he could murder someone, and the only thing he'd be worried about would be getting a stain on his fire suit.

The Nick I faintly remembered back in Australia, the guy who loved to joke around and play video games in his spare time, seemed to have been replaced with someone whom I often wondered might be a cyborg of sorts. He was focused, disciplined and took his racing very seriously.

Derek, on the other hand, looked like a kid standing at the entrance to a candy shop with a pocket full of quarters. It had been a hot minute since he'd received any sort of media attention. It had probably been an even longer minute since that attention had been *positive*.

On the other side of Nick were three empty seats. The media—the slippery bastards—thought it'd be cute to put me in a press conference with not only my current team but my old team as well.

As if on cue, Olivia stepped in from one of the side doors.

She looked good.

It had been several months since I'd seen her in person, and if anything, she was more beautiful now than before.

"She's cute, mate," Derek whispered in my ear as she walked in. "You hit that?"

I turned sharply towards him as I jabbed him in the ribs with my elbow.

Olivia was followed in by their new driver, Daniel Stephens. He was slightly taller than me. His messy light-brown hair looked like he'd just rolled out of bed and his fire suit looked as if it were meant for someone about twenty pounds heavier. He looked like he'd be knocked down by a stiff breeze. But his record stood up.

A two-time SCCA National Champion in Spec Miata and the winner of multiple XGT races in the Trans Am Series, Stephens was someone who

276

tended to do most of his talking out on track, which is something I could respect. It seemed fitting that Arthur selected him as my replacement.

Then *it* entered.

Just behind Stephens, Ganesh strolled in. The shit-eating grin on his face ignited a fire in my gut. He immediately locked eyes with me as he headed up towards the small platform we had all taken our places on.

As they went to take their seats, Ganesh leaned over towards me and, in a stage whisper, said: "Good to see you again, Nora...I mean, Chad."

My heart jumped as if I'd received an electrical shock. A one-ton wrecking ball landed squarely on my gut. My world began to spin as a dizzying feeling entered my head.

What in the hell just happened?

Nora?

There was only one explanation for this.

He knows.

The bastard had dug up my past and used it to fire a shot across my bow.

What else does he know?

I suddenly saw Nora's dead body on the floor in front of me. The blood from the gunshot wound was still pooling up around her. My eyes closed instinctively, and I felt my hands reaching up to cover my ears as her final words surfaced in my mind. I couldn't take my eyes off her, even as I knew Ganesh was laughing at the other end of the table.

"Chad, you okay?"

Derek wasn't the sharpest tool in the shed, but even he could see that something was off.

I muscled my way back to the present as Nick leaned over and whispered.

"Game face on, gents."

A short, chubby, middle-aged fellow approached a small podium towards the right side of the room.

"Thank you all for joining us here today. Up here with us we have two of our newest teams to enter the GTD class for this year's Rolex 24 Hours of Daytona."

My mind was back in the trailer with Nora. I shook my head again in an attempt to free myself, knowing that many eyes would now be focusing on my every move.

She's gone, Chad.

You're here.

Focus.

"Going from left to right we have Derek Renshaw, Chad Watson, and to his left we have Nick Lathan. Next, we have Olivia Calo, Daniel Stephens and Ganesh Kirpa."

Doing everything I could, I somehow was able to return myself to the present. Ganesh had unsettled me, pulling a string from my past to get me off balance in front of everyone.

And it worked.

Right then, I wanted nothing more than to shrink down into nothingness.

"Before we open the floor up to questions," the speaker continued, "Chad Watson, I'd like to start with you. Tell us about what got you interested in racing in the 24 and how you ended up partnered with both Lathan and Renshaw."

I leaned into the microphone that was on a small stand on the table in front of me. My eyes suddenly didn't know where to focus, and my hand was shaking on my lap.

Just before I started to speak, I felt a slight kick from Derek, which seemed to pull my head up from the dirt.

"My heart has always been guided by the footsteps of my family," I began. "Even though I took a few *detours* along the way…"

A few murmurs of laughter helped to calm me down a bit.

"…I met some great people who helped me get to where I am now. I couldn't be more thrilled to be racing with two Bathurst 1000 champions in Derek Renshaw and Nick Lathan. I can speak for the three of us when I say we're all eager to get out there and get amongst it."

It was a generic response, but I tried to play the game and give some short headliner material.

Move on to the next person.

My internal pleas went unnoticed.

"You've had an interesting foray into racing," the man continued, as I could feel myself continuing to tense up. "In fact, you were, at one point, on the team that's on the other side of the table. How does it make you feel to know you'll now be out there racing against them?"

"It was never about racing against them or anyone," I quickly fired off my rehearsed response. "It has been and will continue to be about winning races. That's what we're here to do. Nothing else."

I took note of Nick approvingly nodding his head after my statement.

I also heard a snickering laugh coming from the other team.

"We miss you over here, Chad," Ganesh blurted out. "We've sure got some stories to tell."

Several people in the room started laughing.

In that moment, dread filled my heart as the world seemed to darken around me. It was as if I were standing before a doorway—one that I'd tried to keep locked, fortified and hidden away for several years. But I could see the locks, bolts and chains falling off the door as it slowly creaked open. I stood at the brink, staring into the shadows of my old life.

My fists lay on my lap, balled up so tightly the bones in my hands popped. I needed to respond, but I suddenly couldn't find my words.

Thankfully, my team was there to save me.

"From what I've heard," Derek uttered, "you really *do* miss him. Especially considering your team hasn't come within a mile of a podium ever since he left."

I deep chorus of *ohhhh* sounded through the crowd of journalists seated before us, several of them plucking away on their laptops.

"We've only done three races since then, and they were all at a much more advanced level than we've previously ran," said Olivia. "Chad's undoubtedly a talented driver, but even he would've struggled against the competition we've faced."

"Much like he will here."

The voice of Daniel Stephens was finally heard. His voice caused him to sound much older than he was. His words were so confident and absolute that I even started to believe them.

"You kiddos talk...a lot," Nick spoke up, still maintaining an ice-cold look about him as he stared straight ahead. "If I were you, I'd save all these emotions for when it actually counts... on race day."

"Nick here's being generous," Derek replied, causing Nick to roll his eyes. "I say we get it all out in the open. Chad, let's start with you."

I knew exactly what he was doing. Derek was effectively hijacking the press conference and was about to set me up for an easy, softball question.

Something that would hopefully get my head back in the game.

Although my head was still spinning, I smiled at the prospect.

Or at least I *was* smiling...

"Yes, Chad. Let's get it *all* out into the open." Ganesh stole any hope of rescue. The shadow of dread suddenly felt as if it were gripping my throat. "Why don't you tell everyone about your days in karting? You know, like when you showed up to a race with cocaine in your system."

At that, a few people in the room began *booing* Ganesh.

With all my heart, I wished he would've taken the hint and stopped, but this was Ganesh after all. I had a distinct feeling that he'd been preparing for this moment for some time.

I felt helpless as I was forced to sit there and listen.

"Didn't this lead to an accident where you crashed into someone so badly that it caused them to be paralyzed from the neck down?"

The *booing* stopped as every eye in the room suddenly turned towards me. The weight upon my heart was astronomical, but it was nothing compared with the guilt I now felt once again.

"What's her name, Chad?" asked Ganesh, a sinister tone to his voice. "Do you even remember? How does it feel knowing that you destroyed someone's life because of your negligence?"

"Let's keep things under control, shall we?" the man at the podium finally asserted. "This isn't a criminal trial. Let's keep questions and comments related to the event, please."

"I don't see how this *doesn't* concern everyone out on track with this guy," Ganesh continued. "Would you want someone on track with you who nearly killed someone because he was under the influence of cocaine while racing? To top it all off, the guy tried to kill himself shortly after! Is that the kind of irresponsible person this series wants? There are literally millions of dollars' worth of race cars out there, not to mention the lives and well-being of the other teams, drivers and fans. Can anyone assure them and their families that they'll be safe with someone like Chad Watson on the grid?"

"Those are some strong words, mate," announced Derek. "What proof do you have that you'd like to share?"

"The only proof anyone needs is the look on his face," hissed Ganesh as he pointed directly at me.

At that, both of the teams began shouting at each other as Nick and Derek stood. A few members of the press who were present even went so far as to physically stand between the two teams as the heated exchange seemed to intensify.

Despite the chaos that was unfolding all around me, my eyes locked on one person.

An anger fueled by betrayal suddenly ignited a fire within me.

There was only one other person alive who knew the full story; just one person I'd ever shared the truth with.

As my mind drifted back to when I'd shared my past with her in the trailer at Thunderhill, I held my gaze at Olivia.

* * *

Back in our team's trailer, which served as our official meeting space—away from the prying eyes and ears of other teams and wandering fans—Nick, Derek, Ron and Shayla sat in silence with me.

The sun was setting, and cascading slivers of golden light slipped through the openings in the curtains, allowing our otherwise dark room to have a small bit of light.

I felt numb. My deepest, darkest secrets had been thrown out for all to see. As much as I'd tried to course-correct my life along the way, I now felt like a horrible stain on my family's name.

There would be no coming back from this.

"Is it true, Watson?" asked Nick as he finally lifted his head after holding it in his hands.

Everyone turned in unison towards me, undoubtedly waiting for me to say it was all made up. From there, we could get a plan together and move on.

I realized right then and there that I could easily lie to get myself out of this situation. There would be no proof, as no drug tests were ever done after my crash with Kate. It was Ganesh's word against mine, and the people who write about these things would more than likely dismiss it as hearsay.

It would be easy, but after all I'd done, I just couldn't bring myself to do it.

"It's true," I said, the defeat in my voice apparent. "All of it."

A heavy sigh came from Ron as he turned to look at his wife.

"I was sixteen," I added as I rubbed the sides of my head, trying to fight off the onset of a migraine I felt forming. "My life was a mess back then, and I was in with the wrong crowd."

"Chad, we're on your side, but you've got to understand that this doesn't look good," replied Ron. "IMSA will more than likely start an investigation and also order a drug test from you. On top of everything from the press conference today, there are more rumors going around too. Drugs, running away, some dead girl named Nora, the suicide attempt..."

"My God," Nick whispered under his breath, undoubtedly wondering what he'd gotten himself into.

"Is there anything else you can tell us?" asked Ron.

"Yeah," I replied. "I could say I'm a different person now. I could say I've made mistakes, got caught up with the wrong crowd, done some horrible things to others and myself, but would it matter? Ganesh doesn't have a case against me. He's just trying to destroy my character. I just need you all to know I've turned my life around."

"Look, we all have a past, Chad," said Shayla "We've all made mistakes, but the crash, the one involving the girl who's now paralyzed. Is this true? You were using cocaine when this happened?"

With downcast eyes, I nodded my head in acknowledgment.

There was an awkward moment of silence before I heard Ron speak up again.

"We're on your side, Chad. But it looks like we've got some decisions to make," said Ron as both he and Shayla stood. "Nick? Derek? Could you follow us, please?"

As the four of them exited the trailer, I was left alone in my thoughts and misery. The sound of the trailer door closing reminded me of Kate's body impacting the ground head-first as I shook with fear. I fell out of my chair to the ground as I felt the world around me fall to pieces.

I'd worked so hard and come so far.

In the end, however, I feared it would mean absolutely nothing.

33

Her Voice

Olivia marched along the rows of trailers belonging to the various teams up and down pit lane. Casting a long shadow as she walked in the evening sunlight, the casual smiles and waves she made masked her true purpose as she continued her trek forward.

He was so predictable. All that bullshit about his convictions, passions and purpose in life. It was laughable.

A quiet rage pumped through her blood. As every step brought her closer to her destination, a calm sense of purpose gave her the clarity she knew she would need.

There would be no more playing games. Now, the only thing left to do was take action.

She arrived a few moments later.

With a heavy hand, Olivia applied three sharp knocks on the door to the trailer.

"Who is it?" shouted the voice within.

He didn't take visitors very often, so she needed to be convincing.

"It's Olivia. Open up, dammit."

Seconds later, the door swung open, and the figure of Ganesh came into view.

"What do you want?"

"I have something for you," she said. "Something that'll be the last nail in

Watson's coffin."

A smirk slipped onto Ganesh's face as he stepped aside, an open invitation for Olivia to come inside.

Before stepping in, Olivia cast a few glances around and saw that she was clear of onlookers. Stepping inside, she waited.

"All right," said Ganesh, just as the door of the trailer clicked closed. "What have you got?"

Olivia smiled.

"I've got your ass."

At that, Olivia turned, leaned her body to the side and thrust her leg straight out into Ganesh's stomach.

Toppling over to the ground, Olivia pounced again. Moving to the ground and placing his head close to her stomach, Olivia slid her arm underneath Ganesh's armpit and across his neck while clasping that hand in the crook of her other elbow. Clamping down, Ganesh immediately began gasping for air.

"What in…the hell is…this?"

"It's called having two older brothers who study Brazilian Jiu Jitsu. My turn, dipshit. Where'd you get the dirt on Chad?"

Upon asking the question, Olivia squeezed her arms even tighter. Ganesh continued to squirm under her control and even let out of short squeak.

"Answer me!" she demanded.

"I won't…tell you…anyth—OOOWWWW!"

Planting her knee sharply into Ganesh's side, he howled in pain as Olivia advanced the move forward.

Rolling Ganesh onto his back, Olivia slid farther down while maintaining the chokehold, further compressing his neck in the process.

"Back at Thunderhill. When Chad shared that story with me that you just spewed out to the world. Did you spy on us?" challenged Olivia. "Is that where you heard the story from?"

After a moment, Ganesh managed to get a single word out amongst the various groaning babble and wheezing sounds.

"Y-yesss."

285

Finally relenting, Olivia rolled away and quickly sprang up to her feet.

"You're an eavesdropping little shit! You would ruin his life just to satisfy some pointless feud you two have? Just wait until Arthur finds out!"

As Ganesh slowly began to catch his breath, however, the sound of laughter soon came from his voice.

"Arthur?" he echoed, laughing again while still on his back. "You stupid girl. Arthur was the one who gave me permission to break the story."

In the span of a moment, Olivia felt her world turn upside down. Arthur—the man who'd been like a father to her—wouldn't stoop down so far.

He couldn't.

"You're lying."

"No. You just can't see past your own emotions. He's tired of this *Watson* story. We're all tired of it. Do you know how close Arthur came to shutting the entire program down because of Chad? He *was* and still *is* an embarrassment. Now that same embarrassment is gonna be out there competing against us? After all he's done?"

Suddenly it all clicked for Olivia.

How bad would it look if the guy who got kicked from the team joined an underfunded team and then beat us at our own game?

She knew Arthur was all business, but she was also convinced that there was a solid, beating heart underneath.

"It's about time his story faded away, Olivia," Ganesh continued. "You just need to ask yourself which side of history you want to be on."

Her mind told her it should've taken her more than the briefest of moments to decide. By the time her mind had finished speaking, however, her heart had already made up its mind.

Stepping towards Ganesh, Olivia smiled internally as she watched him squirm out of her way. Marching past him, she climbed down the short stairwell towards the door to the trailer.

"You still support him, don't you?" asked Ganesh. "You still stand by the side of that crackhead who nearly killed someone and then tried to kill himself?"

Opening the door, Olivia let her smile show as she uttered a single word before slamming the door to the trailer behind her.

"Yes."

* * *

If only the world would rip open and swallow me up. After the psychological beating I'd just endured, that was beginning to feel like the only way out.

The press conference had gone viral.

After it had aired, there had initially been a public outcry that Ganesh had gone too far and that he should be removed from the upcoming race. He was, after all, a rookie in the series who hadn't yet earned his place. The criticism was short-lived, however, as a police record of my arrest after Nora's death as well as lab results from the drug test that followed conveniently surfaced.

People could live with the drug use. That was a long time ago, and as Shayla put it, we've all made mistakes.

What people were having a difficult time looking past was how it all culminated in the accident that left someone permanently scarred for life.

To top it all off, old footage of the accident involving Kate also began making the rounds.

It was all out there now. The sins of my past had been exposed for all to see. It was soul-crushing to see my life being shattered before my eyes and all of the tiny fragments being inspected by strangers who didn't know me or even care about the kind of person I was now. To them, I was nothing more than the failed end of a third generation racing family.

I had the distinct feeling that Ron and Shayla were pulling my seat out from under me. They had been on the phones immediately, trying to limit fallout. A few of the smaller sponsors I'd picked up in the previous months had expressed their displeasure with the situation. One of them— an organic bubble gum company called Big Green Chew—pulled their support outright. The folks at *Bubble, Bubble, Fish, Fish!* had yet to respond to me or to any members of the press. It felt like they were undoubtedly formulating a plan to withdraw their support.

Nick and Derek were getting hounded in every interview they gave. No one wanted to know how they were preparing for the race, they all just wanted to know how they felt about the claims against me. As more and more allegations and rumors began to spread, I could sense both Nick and Derek slowly distancing themselves from me—not wanting to tarnish their reputations.

Rumors had spread online about my supposed involvement in Nora's suicide as well as the attempt on my own life. Despite a lack of evidence and being cleared of all charges, people were formulating a story with the narrative that I somehow encouraged Nora to push herself over the edge.

I tried to put on a brave face to let everyone know how much I'd overcome and that I was no longer the person they were hearing so much about. The entire situation made me feel like I was some sort of damaged good. Like I somehow wasn't even qualified to be here.

As much as I was willing to bear the burden for the sins of my past, the people around me weren't able to escape being tied into this mess as well.

The worst part about the entire situation was the undue heartache it had brought upon Kate. Local news stations had parked themselves outside of her house and had been knocking on the door. No one had answered, though, and any phone calls had been met with silence.

I had sent Kate a message, but she never responded.

It was almost as if the floor was falling from beneath me. I was running out of ground to stand on and I felt like I was nearly down to my last straw.

Sitting alone in the trailer, it was as if I were alone with a madman. My thoughts were as dark as the room I was sitting in.

I needed an escape.

My body was shaking, and even though I was just sitting down, the sweat was beading up on my face. The thoughts of racing and of honoring my family's legacy were gone.

I thought of people I could call. Maybe Reggie would pick up?

A soft knock on the door startled me.

"Go away!"

The last thing I needed was company.

My response was more aggressive than I'd intended, but I got the point across.

Another knock on the door. This time louder and more intense.

I shot up from the chair and grabbed my cane, ready to let the person on the other side of that door have it for disturbing me. Marching down the short staircase, I swung upon the door and...

"Chad? Are...you okay?"

The concerning eyes and voice of Olivia seemed to put a dagger through the heart of my dark thoughts.

Instead of the joy I normally felt when seeing her, however, anger rose up in its stead.

"You betrayed me," I whispered. "I trusted you."

I stared into her eyes, the sweat still beading up on my face. My eyes began to water as I took a small step back inside.

Olivia was smart enough and took the hint.

Looking from left to right, she saw that the area around us was clear of bystanders.

"Get back inside," she whispered. "Quick before someone sees you like this."

I turned and headed back as Olivia followed. Closing the door behind her, she climbed the stairs to find the dark room I'd been sitting in. Before turning on a few lights, she closed the blinds so no one could see inside.

"Do you really think I would do rat you out like that, Chad?" asked Olivia. "And to Ganesh, at that?"

Taking a seat on the couch across from me, she continued.

"I just paid him a little visit, and he admitted to eavesdropping on us at Thunderhill when we were in the trailer and you were sharing the whole story with me."

Shaking my head, I admitted, "I'm surprised he confessed."

"Yeah, well, I can be pretty convincing when I want to be."

For the next few moments, we simply sat along together in silence. This was the first time we'd been together since I was kicked off the team several months ago. I should've been over the moon to have this time with her and deep down, a part of me now was. The other side of me, however, knew that my life was in turmoil and I didn't like anyone seeing me like this.

"I wanted to stop by and check on you," she admitted. "I know you've been through the ringer lately and I wanted you to know that I'm really sorry you're going through this. Ganesh is a piece of shit for doing this to you."

Leaning back into my seat, I let out a deep sigh.

"There's nothing to be sorry about," I confessed. "Like I told you before, everything is true. The accident, the drug use and yeah, even trying to kill myself…I spent years of my life trying to let go of my past and start again only to have it resurface and used as a weapon against me."

I leaned forward in the chair, resting my elbows on my knees and holding my hands together.

"But now…it's like torture. To be constantly reminded of who you were and what you did, I just don't know how to get out of this one."

I took a deep breath and leaned back as I exhaled.

"Tell me what happened, Chad—and I want the whole truth."

"I was just sixteen at the time. I got mixed up with Nora—the mystery girl everyone keeps talking about. After the accident with Kate, it all ended with me running away after my grandad's funeral and finding myself a willing participant in Nora's life. She offered me a way to forget the pain I felt."

As the words left my mouth, I felt a bit of relief. Olivia listened intently as I continued with the story, explaining my fall into cocaine use and how Nora ultimately ended her life in front of me.

"I guess I didn't realize just how far gone she already was but also how willing I was too. I wanted to follow suit, but I guess you could say I still valued myself to some extent. I didn't want my life to end in some disgusting trailer in the woods."

"And that's why the police found you at your parents' graves," Olivia connected the dots, obviously having read the police report that had surfaced. "You went there to end your own life."

I nodded as my eyes remained downcast.

"My father once told me that every time I fell down, he'd be right there with me. When I went to pull that trigger, I had every intention of doing just that; falling down before them and being with them again. Only the gun didn't fire."

I exhaled again, lifting my eyes to meet Olivia's.

"That's everything," I admitted. "That's who I was but I'm ashamed to admit that a piece of that person still exists within me today. I own up to my past and take responsibility for it. I just don't know what to do. Ever since Ganesh opened his mouth, everyone thinks I'm a rotten little shit who's getting what he deserves."

"Everyone doesn't think that, Chad," Olivia countered. "There are a lot of good people out there pulling for you. Other teams, drivers, people in the media...Don't let Ganesh fool you into thinking that the world shares his similar viewpoint."

Her words brought me a much needed sense of peace. Even just her mere presence was soothing to me.

"I know you, Chad. You're a sweet and caring person. I wouldn't be in here alone with you if I thought you were even close to how you just described yourself. Yeah, you're a racing driver so yeah, you're just a bit egotistical. But I'll let that one slide."

I laughed as she smiled at me.

Olivia's expression suddenly faded as her face turned serious.

"Years ago when my parents divorced, I can remember how hard they fought not for me or my brothers, but for money. They each hired lawyers but the heated arguments over our family's wealth erupted at every meeting. In the end, I felt like I was just part of the sideshow waiting to see who I was gonna get pawned off with."

Her eyes stared past mine as if looking at a distant memory.

"I told you my original racing endeavors ended with their divorce but more than that, I'd thought about running away too. I wanted my own

291

escape, Chad. I made plans and decided to put them into action. On the night I was planning to pack up and hit the road to God knows where, I remember sitting there and suddenly realizing that it wasn't them I'd be giving up on. It was me."

Olivia shook her head free of the memory as her eyes locked with mine.

"Chad, every race we've ever been in is a battle. Whether we're fighting for the win or some mid-pack position, the battles taking place out there always find us whether we're ready for them or not. I've learned that life is the same way. The only difference is that with life, it's a race we all have to run whether we want to or not. Instead of flat tires or engine failures, we have various obstacles and setbacks. But just like in a car, how we negotiate those setbacks defines how our race will go. Once I gained the mindset that life is nothing more than a race, I stopped thinking about how I could escape my problems and started finding ways to beat them—just like we do out on track."

Her words seemed to speak directly to my soul.

Life as a race.

This was indeed my race and just like any long endurance race, things happen along the way. In this race, however, I was the driver but that didn't mean I was alone in this fight.

I sighed again, but I was beginning to think clearly and logically once more.

"How do I beat this, Olivia?" I asked. "How do I turn this debacle around?"

The question caused her to lean forward towards me.

"This isn't something you can just beat. You have to step in front of it and take control. Ganesh has it, but you can take that back from him. You just have to decide how."

I huffed out of my nose, and Olivia seemed to take the cue.

"Hey, no one said it would be easy. If there's one thing you can beat, though, it's Ganesh. Beat him out there on the track. He won't give you an inch… but you're Chad Watson, so I know you'll take it from him anyways."

I smiled even as Olivia held her gaze.

"Just don't stoop down to his level, Chad. Not again."

Meeting her stare, I slowly nodded my head as my past actions and words towards Ganesh surfaced in my mind. I suddenly knew exactly what I needed to do.

It was as if a great weight had been lifted off my shoulders once again. Although I wasn't out of the woods yet, I'd at least found a path, which is more than I had just a few minutes ago. .

I sat up a bit taller in my seat as I felt my shoulders relax a bit.

"Thank you, Olivia."

She smiled back, her beautiful eyes seeming to siphon every ounce of fear, worry and dread away from me.

"Don't thank me yet," she stated. "There's still a long race ahead of us, and we just so happen to not be on the same team anymore. Although a part of me wishes that wasn't the case."

"I mean, we can technically have four drivers on a team," I teased.

Olivia smiled back but shook her head.

"I may not like it anymore, Chad, but I need to finish what I started with the people I started with. After Daytona... well, let's just take it one day at a time. There's a lot of racing to come between now and then."

"Well I'll be sure to give you a friendly wave every time I pass you."

Olivia gave me a coy smile.

"You can do more than that. How about once all of this is done, you buy me that drink you'd mentioned."

I cracked a smile as my heart lit up in her presence. Extending my hand towards her, she met my shake as I agreed to her terms.

"Deal."

34

Rise Again

The following morning, I was up early making phone calls with the media and the officials at IMSA. I had a lot of work to do and a short window of opportunity to do it.

A few hours later, I found myself heading towards that same small conference room where the entire ordeal had initially began. Several members of the media were already standing outside the door when I arrived but naturally, so was someone else.

"Ah, the cripple is here."

Outstretching his arms to convey surprise, Ganesh's shit-eating grin was ever present and still so punchable, but I resisted.

"I heard you were making a big announcement. Are you finally realizing there's no place for you here? Maybe dead mommy and daddy left you a bit of money and you can buy yourself a plane ticket home. Either way, I felt like I should be here for you. You know, to see you off once again. I have to admit, it's been fun watching you limp away again after failing."

Just then, I noticed Olivia talking with Arthur off to the side. Whatever she was talking with him about, she was laying it into him.

With my own concerns to worry about, I ignored them for now as I took a small step closer to Ganesh. With my cane gripped tightly to suppress my aggression, I spoke softly to him.

"Before all of this is over, I just want you to know something…"

"What's that, crackhead?" he whispered.

I took a subtle deep breath.

"I want you to know that I'm sorry, Ganesh. For everything."

Momentarily stunned, Ganesh's expression did exactly what I thought it would. His surprise lasted all of two seconds before he turned right back to his old ways. He smiled back at me and uttered two words.

"I'm not."

The venom in his voice was obvious.

I held his gaze for a moment, knowing full well that this was no longer the battle I needed to fight. I turned and headed inside but was stopped along the way.

"Chad."

I turned back to see a noticeably upset Arthur heading my way. His eyes were bloodshot and the usual pep in his walk was replaced by weary steps, a testament to the weight he appeared to carry on his shoulders.

Slowly, he reached out and put a hand on my shoulder. Looking me in the eyes, he uttered two words.

"I'm sorry."

Olivia had relayed to me that Arthur had a hand in the story Ganesh had broken. Judging by the look on the face of Arthur, however, something told me he'd gotten a bit more than he'd bargained for.

Nodding, I didn't respond as I turned back towards the conference room.

The room buzzed with the hum of journalists who were eager to hear what they hoped would be newsworthy detail.

There was a single seat at the center of the same long table I'd previously sat at towards the front of the room. In the audience—aside from members of the media—I noticed Nick and Derek as well as Ron and Shayla as they each gave me a thumbs up. Nodding back to them, I turned to see Olivia and Arthur taking their seats. As I saw Ganesh take a seat, I shot him a wink.

I took a deep breath, gathering my thoughts and doing my best to slow my heart rate. The eyes of everyone in the room were on me but this time, I was prepared.

Leaning forward towards the tabletop microphone, I began:

"Good morning, everyone. There have been a lot of stories going around about me. I come before you all to confess that before the untimely death of my grandad, William Watson, and for a time afterwards, I had indeed fallen into a very dark place. I was lost and in need of guidance."

Audio equipment was pushed towards me as I continued, recording my every word.

"As my life began what can only be described as a downward spiral, it ultimately led to me being involved in a serious karting accident with Kate Roberts."

I paused; my heart needing to find the words as I felt a rush of emotions wash over me.

"There isn't a day that goes by in my life that I don't feel the guilt and regret for what I did on that day. Kate was a fantastic racer who—despite her current condition—is still involved in the industry today. As a matter of fact, I wouldn't be here today if it wasn't for her. She was the one who pushed me to face my shortcomings head on and to step out of my comfort zone. She guided me in my quest for sponsorship, which ultimately allowed me to..."

I stopped dead in my tracks as something caught my eye. Coming through the doorway at the rear of the conference room was Kate. She smiled. It was the same smile I'd known during my years of racing karts. And as her motorized wheelchair came to a stop behind the back row of media personnel, I noticed the *Bubble, Bubble, Fish, Fish!* t-shirt she wore.

Keeping my eyes on her, I continued.

"I know how difficult life can be when you have to navigate it from a disadvantaged position—all while hoping, praying and working to get even the most basic mobility back. Someone like Kate gives me courage. When I see her tackling life's hardships and helping people achieve their dreams with a smile on her face, I know that anything is possible if we have the right attitude."

As if on cue, everyone in attendance noticed that I was looking at someone as I was speaking. Turning, they saw Kate for the first time.

What happened next caught me completely off guard and nearly caused me to break down in tears. Standing to their feet, nearly every person in the room began to cheer for her.

Right there in that moment—as the crowds shared their praise for someone who had overcome so much in life—I learned a valuable lesson.

It was never supposed to be about what *I* can do for *me*. That selfish attitude and outlook I'd once had on life had nearly destroyed me. Instead, I learned that life was about who we can help along the way and who we can take with us.

When you surround yourself with people like that, the fires and storms of life suddenly don't seem as fearful as they once did.

"Hey, Kate," I smiled.

"Hi, Chad!" she replied.

"For any young drivers who may be watching or listening," I remarked, "be sure to reach out to Kate if you're wanting to get serious about motorsports."

The sounds of fingers plucking away at keyboards filled the air as I gathered my thoughts to continue.

"My old life is not something I'm proud of, and more than that, it's a part of my life I've worked very hard to move on from. For me, *moving on* was enrolling in a school called the Morgan Shipley Center, which is designed for children like I was at the time—kids who've had traumatic experiences. Once there, I received the help I needed and ultimately found my mentor, Reggie Fuller, who is now more of a father to me than anything. Although I'm ashamed of some aspects of my past, I'm also grateful for the many people in my life who've helped me to move on and realize my true potential."

I breathed, allowing the room to also take a breath and process the information I'd just shared.

"I'm by no means perfect, nor will I ever claim to be," I continued. "But I am clean, sober and of a sound mind. I haven't touched drugs since I was sixteen, and I'm eternally grateful for all of the second chances I've received."

My voice caught for a moment as my eyes met Olivia's, silently conveying the depth of my gratitude towards her. My next words were said to all but directed towards one.

"Thank you."

Her smile back gave peace to my rapidly beating heart.

The silence that followed was deafening. You could probably hear a mouse fart in that room but after a long moment, the voice of the organizer drew everyone's attention.

"Thank you, Chad. I'll now open the floor to questions."

I braced myself for what I felt was surely to be the equivalent of a shark attack. My blood was in the water for all to see. My hands trembled slightly—betraying my vulnerability—but I felt a glimmer of relief in my eyes.

A few hands were raised as one person received a microphone to speak.

"Chad," the journalist announced, "I think it's safe to say that you're an inspiration to everyone here. Am I right?"

The comment was met by a resounding applause from those in the room, which nearly brought a tear to my eye.

"I think it's time we all moved on from this. My question to you is in regard to preparation. With this being your professional racing debut, how are you and your team handling the stress of being a late entry to the 24?"

Though I fall, I rise again.

The words of scripture that Reggie had shared with me surfaced in my mind.

My face lit up with an ear-to-ear smile as I leaned towards the microphone once again.

"I think the best way to answer that would be to have my fellow cohorts join me up front. Nick? Derek? Can you guys bring your chairs up?"

Seconds later, the two were working their way through the crowd while holding their chairs over their heads. Getting to the front, they took seats alongside me as I felt a sudden wave of confidence and pride in my team.

"We won't hide the fact that we're a bit late to the party," Derek began. "I can say with confidence, however, that we've made leaps and bounds in the development of the car."

As both he and Nick gave in-depth answers regarding the state of the team's preparation for the upcoming race, I caught Olivia's eyes in the crowd once more.

For a moment, it was as if we were the only two people in room as we held each other's gaze. I could feel my face beaming as she smiled back at me.

That all changed when I suddenly turned my attention over towards Ganesh. The grin that typically adorned his face was gone now. Taking its place was an emptiness in his expression that made it seem as if the wind had been taken from his sails. I held his stare for a moment longer, even as a subtle grin formed on my face.

In that moment, I was more eager than ever to get into a race car.

35

Perfect Makes Practice

F*ire.*
That's the only word I could use to describe the relentless beast that had awoken inside of me.

While most fires rage uncontrollably and consume everything around them in a wild onslaught of flame and ruin, the fire within me was mine to control—contained within the confines of my body but exploding into existence externally through my actions and purpose. It was almost as if I'd been given a brand-new lease on life. My confidence, eagerness and willingness to join this team in battle had been renewed.

Even better was how it showed in the team. I was proud of the fact that they'd stuck with me during my trial by fire. As such, I felt that we were united in our efforts to take the fight to the larger teams. When combined with the news that Nick shared with us shortly thereafter, our chances became that much better.

The secret project he'd once mentioned involving, "an old British bastard and one of his longtime friends," had finally been revealed.

Reaching out to his longtime racing mentor, Nick was able to get in contact with the one and only Richard Mayfield. The team principal during my dad's race at Bathurst with Nick, Richard was a brute of a man who had long since retired from racing.

I didn't remember much about him other than the fact that he towered over most people and that he had big, yellow teeth.

Even so, Nick was able to somehow convince Richard that helping us would be advantageous. Helping us, it turns out, was having Richard connect us with one of his old British friends who just so happened to work at McLaren Automotive in the UK. One connection led to another and before long, the word came through.

Nick had been able to work out a deal to get us official manufacturer support from McLaren.

It was a game changer.

Additional funding, track support, engineering, expert data analysis...the support we were now receiving would give us an incredible edge over the competition. To see our once small team getting this type of support brought joy to my heart, especially seeing how the team owners Ron and Shayla were at one point just weeks away from closing their doors.

The days leading up to the first practice sessions before qualifying—commonly referred to as the ROAR Before the 24—had been a blur. I was there when the big rig carrying our team's race car and equipment pulled into Daytona International Speedway and parked.

It may seem insignificant to most but to us as a team, seeing the rig pull up was the culmination of all our efforts. Despite the bad press and various dramas that threatened to undo us, we'd arrived as a complete team and with a car that was ready to roll off the truck.

To me, showing up was half the battle.

Once the car had arrived and we were set up, work was underway to prepare for the first of five practice sessions.

The night before the first practice, the drivers met with our team's head engineer, Jason van der Berg. Part of McLaren's factory program, Jason could best be described in Derek's own words as a "hot tits engineer" who knew his shit.

However, despite his extensive experience, Jason had never been part of a team that ran the 24. None of us drivers had either. So we definitely had our work cut out for us.

"One thing to keep in mind is that we're not alone out there."

Seated in the garage on a cool evening, we reviewed some of the data and preliminary setup information. I was laser-focused, despite the hustle around the paddock as the various teams prepared for the first practice set to take place tomorrow morning.

"Of the three McLaren teams in the paddock, we're the only one with direct factory support," continued Jason. "The other two are private teams running their own programs but we've got an entire operation behind us back in Woking. The factory sent us a good baseline setup to start with. Once we get the car on track, we'll start making the appropriate adjustments to get things dialed in."

Nick, Derek and I nodded, eager to finish up as the evening hours began to weigh on us.

"We've got the hand control steering wheel set up, so tomorrow will be the time to get you all up to speed. It's a ninety-minute session, so we'll try and capitalize on as much of it as possible."

The briefing dragged on as Jason took us through the details of the baseline setup on the car and the things to watch out for. Despite all of this, we were all keenly aware of the one varying factor that could throw everything for a loop once the on-track sessions began: the infamous Florida weather. At one moment, it would be a cool breezy day. An hour later, it would be pouring rain.

Throughout our entire brief, I could hear Derek's finger rapidly tapping against his chair as he looked on. I looked over at him to see a blank look on his face.

"Hey," I asserted. "You all right in there?"

We could tell Derek was a bit caught off guard.

"I'm all right, mate," he confessed. "Just getting the jitters is all."

"It'll all come back to you once you put your lid on and climb in," commented Nick.

When Jason spoke again, he seemed a bit nervous.

"I don't wanna talk to you guys like you're amateurs, so forgive me if it comes across that way, but keep in mind that we're all first-timers here. You all have also never raced in an event where you're the slowest class on the grid. Believe me when I tell you that the first time one of those GTP cars rips past you, you're gonna feel like you're standing still."

I think all three of us took a deep breath at the same time.

"That's all I've got for you guys tonight," Jason concluded. "Get some rest and I'll see you boys bright and early tomorrow morning."

* * *

I woke up more tired than when I'd lain down.

I'd barely slept a wink. I was hours away from hopping into a race car that costs more than some people's homes and driving it on a track I'd never so much as turned a lap on with roughly sixty other cars.

It was gearing up to be a day to remember. Hopefully for all the right reasons.

The sun was bright but the air was cool and the clear blue sky above offered us a perfect day to be at a race track.

In the team garage, the crew had the car pulled out onto our pit stall. The orange McLaren glistened in the sun as I approached, with Nick and Derek in tow. It made my heart pump faster just by looking at it. It was the kind of car that looked like it was going 200 mph while it was sitting still.

It's blacked out hood and side markings gave it a formidable appearance but this was all overshadowed, however, by the giant fish on the side of the car.

As I approached, its beady little eyes smiled at me from inside the protection of its bubble. As my eyes followed the leading lines of the car, they led me to the inevitable words of *Bubble, Bubble, Fish, Fish!* on the rear quarter of the car.

I recalled first acquiring the sponsorship and how I felt afterwards. Happy, yet embarrassed. If I thought long enough, I could still hear Reggie's laughter in my head.

After Ganesh's failed character assassination attempt on me, however, something very strange happened.

What had once started off as a source for a seemingly endless stream of jokes and internet memes had somehow transformed into a cultural phenomenon. The images of Kate wearing her *Bubble, Bubble, Fish, Fish!* t-shirt began appearing in various motorsport articles, which sparked a surge in popularity. There was an endearing level of enthusiasm that stemmed from this stupid little fish that I was starting to relate to.

At least, that was the story I was telling myself. It didn't make walking up to a McLaren GT3 race car and seeing a fish on the side of it any less awkward.

Despite all of this, I approached the car and felt a beam of pride within me. Cartoon characters aside, this was the vehicle I'd be riding into battle. As I ran my fingers along the various curves of the car, I pictured my mom, dad and grandad here with me. In my mind, no words were said. They just watched as joy and pride filled their eyes.

As much I carried a part of my family with me, there was another part on the car that was equally as important.

Seeing as I was officially the first driver to be signed to the team for this event, Ron and Shayla were kind enough to ask for my input on many factors. One of which was the car number.

Inspired by Reggie, the car was numbered 78. Yeah, it's my birthday, but more than that, I used it as a testament to Reggie, who'd relayed the story from the Bible to inspire me to press on after I'd been kicked off Arthur's team.

Micah 7:8 would always hold a special spot in my heart now.

Though I fall, I rise again.

Thanks to Reggie, it would now hold a spot on this team.

"She looks ready."

I turned to see Derek standing behind me. He took a few steps and stood by my side as we both gazed upon the machine we'd essentially be riding into war.

"Ever thought you'd be here, Watson?"

"Yeah," I confessed. "Just not with you."

The remark elicited a laugh from Derek as he slapped me on the shoulder.

"You're all right by me, Watson. Now let's see how you fare on track. You ready for this?"

I shrugged my shoulders.

"I'm looking forward to getting up to speed," I replied, the butterflies doing their work in my stomach. "Lots of time to get things set for qualifying at the end of the week. Practice makes perfect, as they say."

"No."

The sharp reply from Derek caught me off guard.

"Practice *doesn't* make perfect," Derek expressed. "Because if what you're practicing is flawed, all you're doing is reinforcing bad habits and you'll never achieve perfection. Instead, be perfect at what you're practicing. *Perfect* makes *practice*. My old man told that to me when I was younger. Never forget that, Chad."

It was sound advice, but in truth, it made me scratch my head a bit. I think Derek took notice.

"Don't worry, mate," he added. "You'll figure it out."

As the sounds of engines firing up filled the air around us, smiles formed on both of our faces.

Turning towards me, Derek leaned in and gestured towards the track just beyond.

"Shall we?"

36

Objects in Mirror

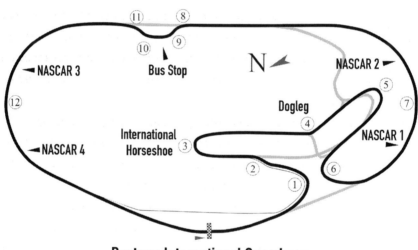

Daytona International Speedway
Daytona Beach, Florida, USA   3.560 miles (5.729 km)

The thunder of the field roared to life and I gripped the steering wheel of the McLaren from the driver's seat. As the first practice session was about to get under way, all of the team's work and preparation had led us to this moment.

"Radio check."

"Check," I replied back to Jason.

"All right, follow the field out and take your time getting up to speed. No need to set the world on fire in the first few laps. It's a ninety-minute practice session so settle in. I'll make the call for you to pit and then Nick will hop in."

"Copy."

I kept my responses short. My mind was focused on the task at hand but if I'm being honest, I was more nervous than I thought I'd be.

I closed my eyes for a brief moment and took a long, slow breath. Even though this was just a practice session, there was an enormous amount of pressure on my shoulders. You didn't need to be in an actual race to completely wad up your car. Crashes could happen anywhere and at any time.

I looked up the field that lined pit lane. At the very front, the cars that made up the fastest class—the Grand Touring Prototypes (or GTP)—were poised to break track records. In this class, the best and most talented drivers in the world would be fighting to take the overall victory in the 24 Hours of Daytona.

Behind them were the Le Mans Prototype 2 (or LMP2) class. Despite the lack of a hybrid powertrain system, the LMP2 cars were incredibly fast and agile. The class attracted professional racing teams from numerous countries as well as drivers from various motorsport categories.

Next were the Le Mans Prototype 3 (or LMP3) class. Although I hesitate to call these cars entry-level, that's essentially how they were marketed. As such, many of the drivers who lacked the professional experience but possessed the funding to buy their way into a prototype class found their way into LMP3. It was rumored that the only people who could afford to fund their way into this class were dentists and lawyers, thus earning the nickname "the root canal wagon," but you didn't hear that from me.

Behind them, the various manufacturers made up the largest and most diverse classes of the field. Split into two GT3 sportscar classes, the GT Daytona (or GTD) and GTD Pro classes consist of FIA GT3 race cars that more align with their road-going counterparts. Although the cars used in both classes were identical, the difference could be found in those behind the wheel.

GTD Pro teams consisted of drivers referred to as works drivers, basically a fancy word for professional or factory-backed. These drivers typically had years of experience under their belts and were usually partnered with a specific manufacturer. The GTD class—the class I was in—was either a mix of works drivers and amateurs or just exclusively amateurs.

Nick classified as the professional driver on the team while myself and Derek—due to his prolonged absence from professional racing—were both considered amateur drivers.

Despite the fact that GTD and GTD Pro were technically two different classes, the field was not split and cars in these two classes competed for spots on the qualifying grid. During the race, however, they were scored separately.

Each of the individual classes were only racing against the cars in their respective class. In a nutshell there were basically five different races happening at the same time on the same track over a period of twenty-four hours.

Before any actual racing began, this week would feature five practice sessions followed by qualifying on Sunday. Once qualifying was complete, another round of practice sessions would begin the following week, which gave teams a chance to test their cars out in race trim before the official start of the 24 Hours of Daytona.

I glanced up pit lane to see the GTP cars starting to file out onto the track. I waited for what felt like an eternity as the entire flock of over sixty cars across the various classes began to pull away before I did something I'd been waiting to do for months.

Using the custom hand controls, I put the car into gear, applied a bit of gas and slowly let the clutch go as the McLaren 720S GT3 Evo rolled away with the field.

Thank God I didn't stall it.

My heart was already beating through my chest. I followed the field out and made the initial left turn out of pit lane while following the blue and white Porsche in front of me. This was followed by another left turn, which was much sharper than I anticipated—nearly scraping the wall on the right side in the process.

I checked my grip on the steering wheel and forced myself to relax my hands a bit as I took a quick but sharp breath.

Straightening the wheel out, I followed the line of cars out until we eventually hit the track and opened the gap up a bit.

Once the field had hit the open track, no one was in a rush to just smash the gas down. So much work had gone into just getting here for many of the teams, and no one wanted to be the laughingstock of the paddock who crashed on the out-lap with cold tires.

I let the car in front of me open the gap up a bit as we filed in and out of *International Horseshoe*. The car behind me—a red Ferrari—did the same as I picked the pace up a bit in an effort to warm the tires. Right away, I could tell how responsive this car was compared with the McLaren GT4 I'd raced at Thunderhill. Even on cold tires it seemed much more nimble.

Heading through the dogleg, I was still only about half throttle as to not close the gap to the car in front of me. I continued to wind my way through the long right-hander of Turn 5 as I opened up the throttle a bit heading towards the hard braking zone of Turn 6.

As the field filed onto the high banks of Daytona for the first time, the 31-degree banking made me feel like a bug clinging to a wall. As I squeezed the throttle on my hand controls, however, the twin-turbo V8 engine in the McLaren came alive as I began working my way through the gears and gaining speed.

The sound of the McLaren at full stride was music to my ears.

I may have giggled a bit at the sound.

Approaching the infamous bus stop, I got off the gas early and braked a long way from what I felt was normal. I knew from my experience in the GT4 that the tires and brakes weren't up to temperature yet so I took it easy.

Powering out of the bus stop, the field had successfully spread itself apart so it was time to start logging some laps. I still needed to take it easy for the next lap or so but I didn't need to baby this thing so much.

Going full wood through NASCAR 3 & 4, I approached the start/finish line to begin my first flying lap at Daytona.

Braking hard for Turn 1, I took it wide and trail-braked my way through. Once slowed, I turned in towards the painted white line on the inside of the track as I got back on the power. The grip wasn't fully there yet so the car understeered a bit and ran wide. I didn't fight it, though. I knew she was still warming things up and the track was also still getting rubbered in.

Over the next several laps, I began to find my groove as the engine, tires and track got to ideal operating temperatures. It had been months since I'd been in a race car and even so, nothing I had ever driven compared to the speed of a GT3. Although we were considered the slowest class in the field when compared with the various prototypes out here, a GT3 is still an incredibly fast vehicle.

As fast as I was going, however, nothing in this life or the next could've prepared me for the first time the field of GTP cars fell upon me. I had only completed a handful of laps by the time the GTP cars had succeeded in catching up to the back of the GTD field.

The best way I can describe it is to picture yourself swimming as hard and as fast as you possibly can. You then turn around to see a pack of angry whales plowing head-on towards you. By the time you turn back around so you can make a life-or-death decision, one of the giant whales has already engulfed you. In this case, however, it then fires you out of its ass and carries on about its business. That's how fast those cars seemed. They're here and then they're not.

I carried on with getting a feel for this car. Even though I was going faster than I ever had in my entire life, I knew there was plenty I was leaving on the table. This was evident as the red Ferrari who'd exited pit lane behind me as well as an Aston Martin and Porsche had since overtaken me.

I didn't fight it, though. If anything, I let them go so I could then use them as a benchmark on how to get around the track. This was a huge help, as by simply following them I learned where I was braking a bit too early and where I was losing speed.

"Pitting in two laps."

The voice of Jason from pit lane came over the radio as I raced towards the start/finish line to start another lap. The practice session had been a success for me so far. First off, I hadn't shit my pants, which—believe it or not—was a legitimate fear of mine. Second, I'd been able to keep pace with the field towards the latter part of my practice stint while still feeling like I wasn't going at one hundred percent. Truth be told, I'd be willing to bet that every other car up the field wasn't going one hundred percent just yet either.

I finished up my next lap as Jason's voice sounded over the radio. "Pit next time around."

Knowing from previous discussions that this pit stop would be a full-speed driver change to practice what it would be like in racing conditions, I began to run through the mental checklist of things I'd need to do while navigating the course.

Loosen the belts.

Unplug the radio and drink straw from helmet.

Reset the brake bias.

Disengage the steering wheel hand controls.

By the time I got to the pit lane entrance, it felt like I'd taken the lap on autopilot as I eventually pulled the car into our respective pit stall. Nick was there waiting alongside the crew, who stood behind the pit wall as I brought the car to a stop. They sprang to life and began running through a full pit stop, with fuel and tire changes all around.

Opening the driver's door, Nick waited as I climbed out—using his shoulder for balance just as we'd practiced. It only took a moment for me to find my footing, which Nick used to place his seat insert into the driver's seat. Once secured, he proceeded to climb in and get buckled up. Another team member assisted Nick with his belts as I made my way over the pit wall and grabbed my cane.

As the crew finished up and Nick pulled away, I heard the team give a mild celebration as to what must've been a smooth first pit stop.

The feeling I had was similar to how I felt when I climbed out of the car after my first-ever laps at Virginia International Raceway. Even as I hobbled my way into our team's tent, which was set up on the other side of the pit wall, I had a smile on my face as I set my gear down.

"Good run, Watson."

Derek sat in front of a timing and scoring screen as he waited for his turn to hop into the car after Nick. Sipping on what I hoped was water, he sported one of our team's hats as the upper torso of his fire suit was wrapped around his waist.

"You brought the car back in one piece. Hey, that's more than your father did when he was practicing at Bathurst."

Chuckling at his own comment, Derek turned his gaze back towards the monitor as I approached—giving him a quick jab on the shoulder for his remark.

"Your lap times put us in eighteenth overall in the GTD classes with a 1:49.236," Derek remarked as I took note of my fastest lap compared with that of the other teams. "We're a bit off pace, but it's early days and I know we've all got a bit of rust to shake off. How'd the car feel?"

I thought for a moment, recalling the memories and notes I'd mentally gathered while driving.

"I wasn't exactly pushing, but it felt like we're a bit off balance with the aero," I noted. "I was catching the field in the corners, but they were pulling away from me on the straights."

"Pass that along to Jason," said Derek. "He and the crew will—"

"Already on it!"

From the back, Jason had overheard my comment. "The data coming in confirms what you've said, Chad. We're working on a solution as we speak."

Putting his head back into his work, Jason resumed his train of thought as both Derek and I caught each other's wide-eyed gaze.

Leaning in close, Derek whispered, "I used to pick on nerds like that when I was younger. Now I thank God they're on my team."

Patting Derek on the back, I grabbed a water bottle as I cast another quick glance at the timing monitor and noticed a familiar name in eighth and a full two seconds faster than me.

Ganesh Kirpa, 1:47.389
"Shit."

37

Final Warning

The wreck had occurred at the bus stop just moments after I'd stepped out of the car and handed the driving duties over to Nick. As a GTD Pro driver was heading full bore into the tricky *bus stop* section on the backstraight, he was a bit ambitious and went in too deep under brakes. Unable to slow the car down in time, the driver ran his Mercedes AMG GT3 into the back of the Porsche 911 GT3 R in front of him, which caused them both to slide off the track and into the nearby tire barrier.

The incident triggered a red flag as all of the cars from the various classes returned to the pits.

Over the radio, Nick was none too pleased with the incident, as it would greatly reduce the amount of time the team had to develop the setup and for the drivers to get up to speed. He had only managed to complete one flying lap before the incident had occurred.

Electing to stay in the car during the red flag, Nick worked to maintain the same focus he had when he'd first stepped in. As such, he kept the visor on his helmet cracked open slightly, which I always took as a universal sign of "leave me alone."

It took the safety crew roughly ten minutes to get both wrecked vehicles off the track and to make sure the area was clear of debris.

Once cleaned up, the cars were once again released from pit lane and the practice session resumed.

Due to the amount of time lost, Nick ran for only about fifteen minutes before pitting and performing a driver swap with Derek.

I stood by, watching the swap from the other side of the pit wall as it happened. There they were—two drivers that in many ways hated each other and who'd also played such key roles in the life of my dad. Nick Lathan—the man who drove *with* my dad at Bathurst—hopping out of a GT3 car at Daytona while Derek Renshaw—the man who drove *against* my dad at Bathurst—was hopping in.

I snapped a picture on my phone for safekeeping.

As Derek accelerated away, I suddenly felt the need to say a short prayer. *God help them all.*

Derek Renshaw—the terror from down under—had just been unleashed in America.

As Nick entered the tent and grabbed some water, he immediately shared his thoughts and feedback with Jason on how the car was handling while it was still fresh on his mind.

"There's a bit too much understeer for my liking and I'm willing to bet Derek out there will say the same thing," Nick commented. "It just doesn't have the initial turn-in I'm looking for."

We compared thoughts as I mentioned my feedback, which he agreed with. As Nick glanced over at the timing and scoring, he noticed that his fastest lap was a 1:48.923, roughly three tenths of a second faster than me.

"Glad to see we're both in the same ballpark," Nick said. "I've gotta say, I'm genuinely curious to see how our boy Derek fares out there. It's been a number of years since he's been behind the wheel."

Within a few minutes, the lap times started coming in.

1:55.124

1:52.549

1:50.735

1:49.981

"He's certainly not wasting any time getting up to speed, that's for sure."

As the time continued to pass, we waited for Derek's next lap to post, but it didn't happen. Nick raised his eyebrows as he glanced over at me.

"He should've crossed the line by now."

After several additional seconds had passed, Derek finally crossed the line as the live timing screen updated.

1:59.258

Nick and I both exchanged perplexed looks.

"What the hell happened there?"

In unison, we both turned towards Jason, who appeared to be analyzing data. As if he had somehow detected that he was being watched, Jason turned towards us.

"Derek got into a little scuffle out there heading into Turn six," Jason stated. "He dived for a pass and the other driver squeezed him a bit. They both ended up spinning but no contact. He has carried on."

Jason promptly turned his attention back to his array of monitors.

Nick, however, turned towards me and leaned in.

"I'm starting to think that Jason is a cyborg of some sort. Like some artificial intelligence that eats batteries when no one's looking."

We both shared a laugh as we waited for Derek's next lap to post.

"He'll be thoroughly pissed now," said Nick. "It's not wise to get on Renshaw's bad side. Most drivers become unpredictable when they're angry. Derek just gets incredibly fast."

As Derek crossed the line, the timing screen updated once again.

1:48.231—a full seven tenths of a second quicker than Nick's previous best lap.

Nick couldn't help but laugh.

"He's gonna make us look like amateurs," joked Nick.

By the end of the session, Derek had improved his time even further, with a 1.47.891. I was officially the slowest driver on the team. I was okay with that.

For now, at least.

As the crew went to work on getting the car prepared for the final session of the day, Jason debriefed us. We all agreed on the changes needed and the crew locked into step to make it all happen.

By the end of the second practice session, all of our times had improved and we were getting more comfortable in the car. The warmer weather gave us some additional data to consider, and we also were pushing things a bit harder. I found myself driving closer to the other GTD cars to better utilize the draft down the long straights and even managed to perform a few overtakes.

At a track like Daytona, the draft was crucial. When you're chasing a car down a long straight, the car in front of you is basically punching a hole in the air and while doing so, creates an area of low pressure behind it. This low pressure works like a vacuum of sorts, pulling the trailing car forward while also reducing the leading car's drag. What this basically means is that when two cars work in tandem together, these two cars are faster than one driving by itself.

When the session had concluded, I had somehow gotten my time right in between those of Nick and Derek. It was satisfying to see that we were all so close to each other on times. I fought back my ego, which wanted to fill my head with self-proclaimed praise. However, the ego wasn't difficult to fight off considering that—despite our improved lap times—we were still only thirteenth fastest in the combined GTD classes, with still a fair bit of pace to find.

Even so, the first day of practice concluded on a positive note. We'd all gotten a good amount of time on track, the car was still in one piece and the team had made the appropriate changes to the car based on our feedback, which caused it to move in the correct direction.

The excitement of being back in a race car and doing so with my friends and teammates was what I needed in life. I felt connected, and more importantly, I felt like I was a part of something.

That night, I slept better than I had in a long time.

* * *

The next day was more of the same. We worked the track, improving our lap times and we finished the session with the tenth fastest time in the two GTD classes. Much to my surprise, I'd succeeded in setting the fastest lap between the three of us.

We were closing in on what we wanted the car to do for us. With each session, the car was getting more and more to our liking and with us finishing the next session out in 8th, it was safe to say that things were looking up.

As we entered the final practice session of the day, the sun was beginning to set, which caused the track to cool off a bit. Driving at night wasn't new to me after my experience in the pitch black of Thunderhill, but for Nick and especially Derek, it was taking some getting used to.

Having to use the headlights of the car while also having faster traffic coming up behind you under low light conditions was tricky. Even more so when you factor in the closing speeds of the GTP and various LMP cars.

"We're just inside the top ten, and we're inching our way upwards," said Derek, sitting behind the pit wall. I stood just behind him with my driving gear on and ready to go. Nick would be finishing his practice stint soon and I'd be hopping in.

Just then, I noticed a gray and blue Porsche 911 GT3 R drive past our pit stall. It was Arthur's team. I noticed Olivia's custom red and white helmet with the letters of her initials OC painted on the side. She would be laser focused on the pit stop she was about to perform and wouldn't have had time for a casual wave, as much as I wanted her to.

Looking farther up the pit lane, I saw something I really didn't want to see.

Ganesh.

Wearing his ass-ugly blue-and-green helmet, he was waiting to hop in once Olivia jumped out.

A sudden fire began to rage through my veins. Turning back towards my pit stall, which was currently unoccupied, I closed my eyes briefly and— doing my best to think of something else—ran through the motions in my head of what I needed to do in the coming driver change. The last thing I needed was to get distracted by a petty rivalry. Yes, this was only practice but as Derek so wisely stated, perfect makes practice.

Several minutes later, the pit crew were in position on the wall as I waited just behind them. One of our tire changers, Ryan Hess, didn't mind me using his shoulder for balance as we all waited since I was without my cane.

Nick brought the McLaren to a stop squarely in the pit stall as I stepped over and opened the driver's door for him. As he climbed out and removed his seat insert, I stepped in and made ready.

"Track's cool and fast," said Nick as he helped me get strapped in. "Have some fun."

I remained silent, performing the acts I'd mentally rehearsed just moments ago.

Nick closed the door as I performed a radio check.

"Loud and clear," replied Jason.

Roughly twenty-five seconds after the car had come to a stop, I was rolling down pit lane towards the track entrance.

More confident in the car after all the seat time from today, I still needed to take it easy on the cold tires but I did so as if it were a race. I pushed the tires hard enough to warm them up but not so hard as to defy the laws of physics.

Working through the track, I saw a few sets of headlights coming up behind me. Holding my line, I was still in the infield section during my out lap when a few LMP2 cars drove past me on the inside of Turn 5; taking the apex from me in the process.

Offline and on cold tires, the McLaren fought for grip but I managed to catch her and keep her on course. It was my out lap after all, so I wasn't concerned with the loss of time. I was still going, which was all that mattered.

Another set of headlights was also behind me, and I could tell by their shape that they belonged to a Porsche.

Still getting up to speed, I turned onto NASCAR 1 & 2 and went full squeeze on the hand throttle.

The headlights of the car behind were inching closer as it was well within the draft. As we both headed towards the bus stop, the Porsche suddenly dived down the inside for what I considered to be an aggressive dive bomb of a pass, doubly so considering this was only practice.

Then I saw which car it was.

Ganesh.

I gathered my machine back up and chased after him, fully aware that I was still warming things up. He had the advantage of tires that were already a few laps old and more than likely up to ideal temps.

Going in NASCAR 3 & 4, we both raced towards the front stretch as I worked the draft and closed in on the back bumper of Ganesh.

Tempted, I backed out of an attempted dive into Turn 1; content with simply showing him my headlights in his mirror in an attempt to distract him.

Staying on his back bumper through Turns 1 and 2, we both braked for *International Horseshoe,* which I did with a bit too much gusto. Sliding the tires just a bit as I turned the car in, I could tell that things hadn't yet reached the right temps. The evening was cool, and as such, the warming of the tires was taking a bit longer than normal.

I continued to stay locked in just behind Ganesh, more so to study him but also keenly aware that the car wasn't ready to go on the assault.

The voice of Jason came over the radio.

"Take it easy, Chad. Control the temps."

Following Ganesh onto the oval section of the track, our speeds climbed as I used the draft to close the slight gap that I'd allowed to open.

Momentum was on my side and I had the room to make a pass if I dived the McLaren into the bus stop where Ganesh had previously passed me.

I hesitated, deciding to back out and wait another lap instead of risking the move.

Ganesh, however, braked earlier than I'd anticipated. Moving to his left to avoid him, I suddenly found myself side by side with the Porsche as we both entered the bus stop.

He should've backed out but he didn't. Instead, I was nearly shoved into the grass on the left side as Ganesh didn't give me the room I needed. When we got to the center of the bus stop, we banged doors together. The impact wasn't anything crazy, but it was just enough to cause my tires to come unglued from the road.

Squealing in protest, I was suddenly a passenger as the McLaren slid off the track...and planted itself into the tire barrier.

The feeling of suddenly becoming stationary on a hot track was both dizzying and humiliating.

"That sonofabitch just shoved me off the track!"

I was nearly shouting over the radio as I found the reverse gear. Easing onto the gas, I heard the engine rise in pitch but the car remained stationary.

Trying a few more times, along with rotating the wheel while applying the throttle, the car didn't budge.

Jason's voice came over the radio next.

"Shut the car down, Chad. Red flag is out."

* * *

"I don't give a shit what's going on between you two! The next time I see you two idiots coming together, swapping paint or even *looking* at each other in a way I don't like, you're both out of this race!"

The race director's eyes bore into those of Ganesh and me as we found ourselves standing before him after the incident.

Although it was deemed a racing incident with neither myself nor Ganesh labeled at-fault, our past was enough to invoke the wrath of several racing officials. They had little in the way of sympathy for rookie drivers coming into their series and running amok.

Promptly summoned to race control—a place, one would argue, that you only saw the inside of when you screwed up—Ganesh and I both glared at each other before we entered but hadn't said so much as a word since.

"I won't let the integrity and reputation of this race and series be ruined by two entitled rookies. Consider this your final warning. Do I make myself clear?"

"Crystal clear, sir," I replied.

"Yes."

Ganesh's short reply caused the race director to shake his head at both of us.

"God help you if I catch either of you causing trouble on my track again. Now get the hell out."

I performed an about-face without falling on my ass and headed for the door. While I was walking, I overheard the race director mumble under his breath.

"Damn rookies."

Making our way outside so our respective team members could shuttle us back to our pit stalls in golf carts, Ganesh just couldn't help but say something.

"I can't wait until race day, Watson," he said as he climbed onto his team's golf cart. "Considering your pace so far, I don't imagine I'll be seeing too much of you."

I just smiled and waved. I wasn't about to play his games again. I'd worked too hard and truth be told, I had other things on my mind.

As we were both driven off, the crew member who was driving me in the golf cart took us past Arthur's pit stall en route to ours.

Olivia waved as we drove by.

Giving her a casual wave, I turned my attention forward, wondering how our car was and how this incident might jeopardize our chances in the qualifying session tomorrow.

I just hoped my little *incident* hadn't ruined our chances.

38

Ghost in the Machine

The constant tapping of my hand against the armrest of my chair drew Derek's stare.

"Sorry."

Derek held my gaze for just long enough for it to be awkward before he returned his eyes forward.

Derek was still stewing at the fact that I'd been the one to wreck the car during the previous practice. Although the team was able to get the car repaired in time for the qualifying session, the advances we'd made to the car had seemingly been lost in the process. There just wasn't enough time to get it dialed back in like we'd had it.

He gazed up towards the screen. There we were…mired back in eighteenth position in the combined GTD/GTD Pro field after qualifying. *The kill zone.*

When you're in the kill zone at the start of a race, you effectively have nowhere to go should a major incident occur. If you were in the front of the field, you had the open track to avoid said incident. In the very back of the field, you typically had time to avoid it. In the middle there was no such luck.

"You got caught up in drama we don't need to be involved in," Derek said. "You went into a practice session and thought it was a race. What the bloody hell were you thinking?"

"It was an accident, Derek," I'd fired back. "No one was at fault."

Derek could only shake his head at me.

"Just because the suits up in their high tower say no one was at fault doesn't make it true, Watson. It takes two to tango, but it helps if you both know how to dance."

Turning to walk away, Derek took only a few steps before he stopped short and turned to face me once again.

"You're a fast driver, Watson. Just like your dad was. But sometimes, you just don't get it. You don't get it because you've forgotten the glory. You've forgotten the pain and hell your father went through to stand on that podium at Bathurst."

His words stung, but they also rang true in my heart.

"Remember what it is that you represent out there. Remember the shoulders you're standing on that got you here. Pride, ego, selfish ambition...look where these things got me! Don't go down the same path and expect a different outcome. You're smart enough to know that you need to let go of these petty squabbles. Or at least I thought you were."

Turning to walk away, I realized Derek's words hit me hard. It was a swipe, yes, and one that I deserved after chasing Ganesh the way I did in a practice session and effectively ruining our qualifying chances.

But his comments also made me second-guess myself.

Am I in over my head? Did I get to where I am too quickly? Have I truly earned my spot on this grid?

"Look, mate," replied Nick after Derek's exit. "Don't let him get to you. You got swept up in a moment, and we've all been guilty of that. Just remember that we're all in this together. Everything you do out there on track affects both Derek and me. I understand you're young and you're full of piss and vinegar. But just be mindful of the fact that there are other drivers on this team too. What affects one of us affects all of us."

"I'm sorry, Nick," I responded. "I should've just backed off and let him go. Like Derek said, it was just a practice session."

"You're all right, mate," said Nick. "I just hope it didn't kill our chances. The car was doing wonders up until that point. The crew got everything put back together, but we all know it's not the same anymore."

The crew had indeed performed an incredible feat in getting the car back into operating order and looking the part. During qualifying, however, Nick had commented over the radio that the car felt *off*. It just didn't drive the way it had in previous sessions. By the end of qualifying, we'd only managed to get our once top-ten capable car into eighteenth in the combined GTD/GTD Pro field. The only consolation was that within the GTD class we were racing in, we were actually in eleventh.

I couldn't help but smirk as I noticed that Arthur's team was inside the top-ten in the combined GTD field with an eighth place starting position, fifth in class. Even better, it was in fact Olivia who had piloted their Porsche to said position.

Although I was proud of her, I wanted nothing more than to beat her.

I'm nothing if not competitive.

As we rolled into the race week, with it came a fresh dose of practice sessions before the race kicked off on Saturday afternoon and went twenty-four hours nonstop until Sunday afternoon.

Even as we began the first of the race week sessions, the car continued to feel a bit off and we found ourselves chasing mechanical gremlins because of it. We later found out that the wheel bearings on the left side had been loose due to the impact from the crash. The crew were able to get things repaired and we lined up for the second practice thinking we had things under control.

We were wrong.

During the second practice session, we experienced a serious issue that caused the car to grind to a halt on track. It's never good to see your car on the back of the tow truck twice before the race had even started.

After getting the car back to the garage, Jason and the crew did a deep dive and found another lingering issue. Due to the nature of my previous impact, the rear axle was pushed into the ring and pinion inside the gearbox, and the crew discovered that the ring gear had been fractured. We'd been driving around with it until those fractures finally turned into broken bits.

The crew worked diligently. Within forty minutes, they had a new gearbox installed, and we all prayed it would be the end of our mechanical woes.

By the end of the day on Thursday, we'd had managed to get the car back underneath us and stuck it in eleventh by the end of the third practice session. Friday saw us further refining the car, testing out full fuel loads during our practice runs, conducting numerous pit stops and driver changes and still more track time. Although it was only a one-hour session, the boys worked their asses off and it was starting to show.

As I crossed the line to finish up the final practice session before the start of the race, we'd managed to get our McLaren in seventh on the leaderboard, ahead of Arthur's team, which finished in ninth.

When we got the car back to our garage, it felt as if we'd won a race of sorts. The celebrations that began were well deserved. Although drivers are often the ones who get the praise from the fans and media, it was truly these guys and gals on the crew—the ones behind the curtain making sure all of the bits and pieces work and are put together correctly—who make it all possible.

Stepping forward, Ron addressed the team.

"I just want to say how proud I am of all of you," he announced. "You're all the embodiment of relentlessness and your work ethic is a testament to this. Tomorrow, we'll be going into battle against some of the best drivers and teams on earth and I couldn't be more honored to have you all by my side. I know it's been a bumpy ride at times but if we continue to fight, to stand up every time we're knocked down and bring the *'never quit'* mentality, I believe we've got a good chance to let the world know that we're not here to just fill out the field. Because of you all, we're contenders. We've got a good shot at a strong result."

A few cheers erupted all around us.

"We'll stay focused," continued Ron. "We'll pick our battles and we'll run our race,"

"And maybe even grab ourselves some new Rolex watches if we're lucky," Derek chimed in.

The crew cheered in response to the idea of receiving the coveted watches given only to the winners of the twenty-four-hour race.

Gesturing towards the car, Ron continued.

"Let's get this thing ready for war. Time to bring the fire, everyone. Tomorrow, we fight."

39

Green Flag

No more practice sessions.

No more development briefings, no more talk of qualifying and past blunders.

That was all behind us now. In front of us, a mammoth task and a grand battle lay just over the horizon.

It was race day.

I woke at dawn feeling refreshed. Much to my surprise, I'd managed a decent night's sleep.

As I rubbed my eyes and swung my legs over the side of my bed, I rested my elbows on my knees and took a moment to reflect on the road that led me here.

In that moment, I thought of my family as I recalled a few words from my parents' journal.

"Set your personal feelings aside," my mom wrote. *"Focus on the big picture."*

"If you can beat the track and the expectations you put on yourself," Dad had written, *"no one will ever be able to truly defeat you."*

Grandad, on the other hand, would be reminding me to relax my hands when I drive.

"You can't be smooth and precise if you're tense and holding the wheel with a death grip. Relax your hands and don't forget to breathe. Your body will handle the rest."

A memory surfaced: Grandad teaching me to drive a kart after I'd first received the hand-controlled steering wheel. Truth be told, I'd been really bad at it. My mind couldn't grasp steering the kart and using the hand controls to accelerate and brake.

Having just spun the kart after braking too hard while entering a corner, the back end had looped around, and I'd found myself facing the wrong way on the track. Although we'd been out there by ourselves, I recall feeling like there was a great weight on my shoulders and several eyes watching me.

"I suck at it, Grandad!" I'd said in frustration. *"I can't do it!"*

Approaching, Grandad had laughed as he put his hand on top of my helmet and knelt beside me.

"Believe it or not, there was a time when all the greats were just starting out. Did you know that Aryton Senna didn't start karting until he was thirteen years old? Later that same year, he was out there beating other drivers who were both older and more experienced than him. He stuck with it, Chad. He learned his craft and honed his ability."

"But what if I just don't get it? What if I don't ever get as good as you and dad were?"

"It's not about being as good as anyone. It's about finding out who you are and what you're made of. You'll never find that if you're constantly comparing yourself to other people. Remember, when you slip that helmet on, close out the world around you. When you close that visor, it's just you in there. The only thoughts and emotions you carry are the ones you take with you."

I'd sighed deeply, conceding to the fact that I may have gone into this thinking too highly of myself.

"I guess it's just harder than the video games."

Grandad had laughed at the comment.

"We don't have to do this, you know," he'd reminded me. *"If racing isn't something you wanna do, we can stop at any time."*

The feeling of not racing was about as foreign to me as not breathing. My desire to be a part of it came naturally, even if the skillset didn't.

At the same time, I had other reasons for wanting to be on track.

I could feel my eyes watering as I longed to hear his words again; words that in time, were starting to fade from my mind.

"I miss him, Grandad," I'd admitted. *"But I feel like he's out here with me. When I'm on track, I feel closer to him."*

Grandad had held my gaze for a brief moment before he lowered his sunglasses from the top of his head to cover his eyes as he stood to his feet.

"C'mon," he'd replied. *"Let's get you facing the right direction so you can give it another go. Never give up, Chad. Never, ever quit."*

Shaking my head, I reached over to the nightstand to grab my phone and noticed I had a text waiting for me.

[Go out there and do your thing, Chad. Mama and I are cheering for you.]

The smile that filled my face was the evidence of the pure happiness I felt in that moment. Knowing I had my friends and family back home cheering for me gave me a sense of pride as well as a boost in confidence. Reggie and Mama Fuller were about the closest thing I had to family. Given all that I was about to attempt today, I needed all the help I could get.

[Glad to have you both in my corner.]

Sending the message, I was suddenly reminded of someone else. Scrolling through my messages, I found Olivia's name and sent a brief message.

[Good luck today.]

She was probably still sleeping. I knew I would be if I could.

Seconds later, my phone buzzed as a response from Olivia came back.

[You too.]

My heart leaped at those two little words and the smiley face response. Grabbing my cane, I stood and stepped into the day and all that it would hold for me.

* * *

At the Bathurst 1000, my dad had taken me on nearly every pre-race media commitment with him before he actually climbed into the car. I vaguely recalled how tired he was before the race had even started.

Since then, not much had changed in the world of racing. As the mass of crowds flowed up and down pit lane to see the cars lined up, the camera crews, motorsport personalities and journalists were making their rounds as well. I honestly wished I could've simply kept out of sight but I know the team and our sponsors had expectations I needed to fulfill.

The atmosphere on the grid was energetic to say the least. With only a few clouds dotting the sky, the air was cool as the sea of people flooding the pit lane were enough to cover the entire surface. Between the celebrity interviews, the voices over the loudspeakers and the music playing in the background, the energy circulating up and down the grid was contagious.

For many families, coming to the 24 Hours of Daytona was a time-honored tradition that was shared across multiple generations. For others such as myself, it would be the first time.

I never enjoyed large crowds, much less being one of the centers of attention. Despite this, I had to admit that I was getting a kick out of the overly enthusiastic *Bubble, Bubble Fish, Fish!* crowd. Scores of people had their fish t-shirts, and many seemed to be carrying a clear balloon with that stupid fish inside of it. It must've been the hot item to have because they were everywhere.

I found myself simply standing by the car as people stopped by to have their picture taken.

Nick and Derek, however, took a different approach.

During one particular interview where a reporter was attempting to talk with both of them together, Nick and Derek legitimately hijacked the camera crew. Watching from a distance, I couldn't help but think this was planned as Derek seemingly produced a small jar of Vegemite out of nowhere. The duo then led the camera crew up and down pit lane as they conducted their own interviews with various teams to see if anyone wanted to try what they described as an Australian delicacy.

They had a few takers. Needless to say it made for some entertaining content.

Despite all of the fun we were all having, my mind was already locked and loaded with the info Jason had briefed us all on beforehand.

Because of his extensive racing experience, Nick would be starting the race with the hope of getting us through the opening stages unscathed. We had our work cut out for us but everyone up and down the grid knew that qualifying for a twenty-four-hour race was more of a formality. It was all about running your own race and staying out of trouble. If you could succeed in keeping the car out of pit lane as much as possible, you had a good chance of a strong finish.

The hours passed, and before long, Nick and Derek had released their captive camera crew, having emptied the entire bottle of Vegemite in the course of their adventures.

"That should digest nicely throughout the race," Derek laughed as we all met in front of the car.

Slowly, the crowds of families, fans and reporters walking up and down pit lane began to diminish as the butterflies began doing their work in my stomach.

As Nick climbed into the car to prepare for the start, I was envious, but in my heart I knew he was the right person for the job. Standing by the car with him, the magnitude suddenly hit me as I felt a heavy hand across my shoulder.

"This is it, mate," said Derek. Nick stared up at me from the driver's seat.

"Whatever happens from this point forward, I'm proud to be a part of this team. I never thought in a million years I'd be racing with Nick Lathan and Bill Watson's son but here we are…and I'm grateful. Thanks for bringing us here."

I fought off a tear as—above everything that was happening—I wished my dad were here to see this moment. I could only hope he was looking down and proud of me. Shaking the feeling aside, I elbowed Derek in his ribs for good measure.

As I turned to see his response, my eyes suddenly became fixed on someone who'd met my stare across pit lane.

Arthur.

He was staring at us while we shared the moment together. I couldn't help but wonder what was passing through his mind.

Despite all that had happened regarding his alleged involvement with Ganesh and his smear campaign against me, there would always be a part of me that would be grateful for Arthur.

He was the one who'd given me another shot at something I'd completely given up on. Even though I'd screwed it up, he'd given me a chance that ultimately led to where I was. Now, however, we were on opposite sides of the fence, and I would show him no act of friendship on the track.

The grid was nearly clear as Jason made sure Nick was set up. Giving the car a few pats on the hood, Jason closed the door for Nick. I gave him a thumbs-up, and Nick returned the gesture as the team and I headed back to our pit stall.

Moments later, the roar of engines filled the air as the cars rolled out.

Derek and I sat near the wall, watching the entire field go around the track once again. After the various prototype classes passed the start line, we finally saw our McLaren in the mid-pack.

Tuning into the broadcast, we got to see a brief glimpse of Nick in the car as he swerved side to side, accelerating and braking in an effort to warm the tires.

As the pace car lights turned off, the entire field formed up double-file. The race was about to get underway.

Coming out of NASCAR 4, the pace car turned down onto the pit lane. The green flag waved and at once, the roar of the GTP field filled the air as everyone in attendance stood to their feet. Watching those rocket ships fly by stirred my envy once more, and I began to hope that maybe one day...

After the GTP field had shuffled into Turn 1 without incident, the LMP2 field followed shortly thereafter as well as the LMP3 field. The latter, however, had a brief mix-up as two cars made contact entering the first corner. The car on the outside of the corner was shoved wide, losing several positions in the process.

Just behind them, the entire GTD field raced past the start line and into the first corner to start the race. Everyone on our team applauded not just the effort it took us to get here but also the fact that Nick was already on the move.

The 24 Hours of Daytona had begun.

40

A Hill Worth Dying On

Nick waited patiently as the field worked its way towards the start line. From the outside of the ninth row, he received word that the lights on the pace car had turned off and promptly straightened the McLaren out to line up directly behind the car in front of him.

For Nick, the green Lamborghini Huracán GT3 EVO2 just off the nose of the McLaren might as well have had a target painted on its back. He avoided fixing his eyes upon it, however. Any mistake made by the car in front while he was fixated upon it could cause Nick to replicate or even follow it farther into the mistake. Despite the fact they were only racing other cars in the GTD field, Nick saw them *all* as opposition.

His breaths shortened. His mind was ready and his right foot wanted nothing more than to feel the vibrations of the McLaren going full stride.

"Standby."

Hearing Jason's voice, Nick did his best to focus on what was before him. Forcing himself to relax his hands on the wheel, Nick splayed his fingers for a second before grasping the wheel once more. Thinking back in time to when the great William Watson once advised him to "Close your mind and open your eyes," just before the start of the Bathurst 1000 he'd raced with Bill, Nick meditated on the words for a brief moment.

"Pace car's entering the pits. Standby..."

Taking a deep breath, Nick exhaled slowly.

"Standby....Green Flag! Go, go, go!"

Punching the accelerator, the McLaren came to life as the entire GTD field raced towards the start line.

Approaching the treacherous first corner, the entire pack braked and Nick saw an opening down the center between two cars in front of him. Modulating his braking pressure, he slipped through the middle of the two cars and the green Lamborghini on his outside suddenly became aware of Nick's presence.

Losing grip on the outside of the track, the Lamborghini was forced to concede track position to Nick and the driver fell back and slotted in behind the McLaren.

Now on the right side of the track, Nick was ideally placed to have the inside for the *International Horseshoe*. Going into the corner side by side with a BMW M4 GT3 on his left, Nick once again had track position and the ideal racing line as he powered out of the corner clear of the BMW. The short shoot towards the dogleg found him on the back bumper of a Ferrari as he began making decisions on when his next move should happen. He could've tried a daring pass by braking later while entering Turn 5 but decided against it; not wanting to risk a heavy braking maneuver this early in the race and while still on tires that were still warming up.

Staying just behind the Ferrari, Nick accelerated cleanly out of Turn 5 and into the braking zone of Turn 6. He let the McLaren drift wide while tracking out onto the high banking of NASCAR 1 for the first time.

The McLaren's V8 screamed as Nick powered his way through the gears and around the high banking before the track leveled out on the backstraight. Now in the draft of the Ferrari, Nick got a good run and decided to go for the overtake while heading into the *Le Mans chicane*. Twitching the wheel to the left and braking heavily, Nick succeeded in slowing the car down while also maneuvering to the left side of the Ferrari. Tipping the McLaren in towards the left corner, the Ferrari yielded as Nick slowed the car down further to make the sudden right corner to exit the bus stop.

It was a clean getaway. Although the pass was successful, it had cost him some time and a slight gap had opened up towards the next group of cars in front of him. Racing out of NASCAR 3 & 4, Nick crossed the line to finish the first lap of the 24 Hours of Daytona.

Immediately, he was on the attack again as the pack in front of him cautiously braked for Turn 1 at the start of the second lap.

Only about 700 more to go…

* * *

Nick was on fire out there and making up solid ground after qualifying saw them starting farther back than they'd liked. He was pushing when the opportunity presented itself and laying back when the doors closed. The decisions he was making were smart, calculated, and effective. These moves were a testament to Nick's prowess behind the wheel and it truly showed his experience on the motorsport battlefield. Just fifteen minutes into the race and we were already up to twelfth overall in the combined GTD field and eighth in class. As I searched the timing and scoring screen a bit further, I noticed that Arthur's team was still fifth in class with Olivia behind the wheel.

Even though they hadn't moved up the field like we had, I knew the most talented and experienced drivers were up front. The fact that Olivia was maintaining position with them said wonders about her skill level.

Still, these were early days and although we were off to a solid start, there was a long way to go.

As Nick's stint wore on, Jason and the team were hard at work running fuel numbers and preparing for the first pit stop.

As they worked, I watched the broadcast monitor, which was focused on the GTP leaders who had already spread out quite a bit. With no battles going on up front, the broadcast shifted suddenly to Nick. He was in full defense mode as a silver Aston Martin Vantage GT3 was quickly gaining on him.

Upon crossing the start/finish line, Nick elected to not fight too aggressively. As the Aston Martin pulled up along Nick's left side, he gave up the position and slotted in behind the overtaking car.

"That's all right," Jason uttered, although I wasn't sure if he was speaking to Nick or just talking out loud to himself.

Turning around to face me, Jason continued. "That wasn't a hill we needed to die on. Had he fought too hard, we would've lost touch with the pack in front."

Initially stunned to see Jason turn around so suddenly to face me, I could only manage to say, "He's...uh...yeah, he's good."

Jason—possibly detecting that I did in fact have nothing useful to say— turned back towards the plethora of data he was monitoring.

Regardless of my thoughts on the race engineer's remarks—an engineer I was more and more beginning to think was indeed a cyborg in disguise— he was right. It's one thing to go on the attack in a race, but what I was beginning to discover was the difference between the *good* and truly *great* drivers.

Wisdom.

The great drivers knew when to fight and when to lay back; when to yield and when to defend. Time would tell where both Derek and I would fit into this.

Almost as if on cue, Derek appeared from around the corner, and I couldn't help but laugh out loud.

With an energy drink in one hand and a basket of food in the other, the Aussie smiled back as he held up his goods.

"Sausage, anyone?"

* * *

I slid the helmet down over my head and connected the two straps that held it in place. Pulling my racing gloves over my hands, I took a moment to make sure they were pushed down as far as they could go.

After one last adjustment to my helmet, I set my cane aside and cautiously made my way to our pit wall.

The crew were readying their equipment, test firing their air guns for the tire changes and getting into position for our first pit stop of the race. So far, the race had gone on without incident, outside of a few local yellows. As such, the pit stop would be done under green flag conditions.

Nick was still sitting in thirteenth position in the overall GTD field, as he'd elected to lay back and save fuel by drafting off the pack of cars in front of him. We were confident that other cars were doing the same as they played the long game. Even saving just a bit of fuel during each stint could pay dividends down the road.

The overall leaders in the GTP field ripped past the start/finish line as several of the leading GTD and GTD Pro drivers soon dived down pit lane. In the McLaren, Nick along with a large pack of GTD cars stayed out; having saved enough fuel to go one more lap around.

Moments later, the McLaren came into view as it exited the driving line and made the slight left turn down pit lane. Engaging the pit lane speed limiter, Nick cruised the short distance from the pit entrance to our stall before turning in and coming to a stop squarely in the box.

Right away, the crew hopped the wall and went to work servicing the car. I reached the driver's side door just as Nick was exiting. The actual climb inside the car was always a bit of a challenge for me but the sheer amount of time we'd spent practicing driver changes had caused us to move with a well-orchestrated efficiency.

I connected my radio, cool suit and drink straw as Nick helped me to get buckled in. Connecting my shoulder and waist buckles to the six-point harness, Nick then gave me a slap on the chest.

"Good luck, mate!"

The crew was still fueling and getting the tires changed as I made ready to accelerate away once the car dropped from the air jacks.

Seconds later, four new tires connected with the ground. Easing onto the power with the hand controls, I accelerated away down the long pit lane. As I was leaving the pit stall, the cars that Nick had pitted with were also leaving their stalls. I wasn't sure if I'd gained or lost any positions during the stop. All I knew was that I wasn't giving an inch during the exit.

While exiting, a few cars from the LMP2 and LMP3 classes ran us down. Wanting to get by us slower GTDs as quickly as possible, the prototypes dived down the inside of *International Horseshoe*, but they caught up too quickly to a Lamborghini that was still on cold tires. Not anticipating the slower speeds enough, an LMP3 driver collided with the Lamborghini, which knocked it sideways, collecting an LMP2 car as well as two GTD cars in the process.

For a brief moment, the track in front of me was completely jammed. Cars and various components that had come detached from said cars littered the apex of the corner. There was nowhere to go. My heart sank into my stomach.

At the last moment, one of the LMP2 cars that had been collected in the incident rolled off into the grass, which created the opening I needed. Going for the gap, I managed to clear the incident and proceed on just as the double yellow flags began to wave.

The full course caution brought the entire field to a crawl, which—after a few deep breaths—allowed me to fish my heart from my stomach. It was moments like this, I knew, that brown underwear were invented for.

Putting the car into a higher gear to save fuel, I cruised around until I caught up with the field.

"Good heads-up reaction, Chad."

I nodded, more so because I didn't have words. I was just happy to have not wadded up the car two corners into my first stint.

In all of the excitement, however, I'd somehow managed to slip past a few cars—one of which was the blue Porsche that belonged to Arthur's team. They must've gotten mixed up in the earlier incident as well. Glancing in my rearview mirror, I now had the view I'd been wanting to see for some time.

That blue Porsche was now behind me.

Knowing that Olivia had started the race, I half expected to see her still in the driver's seat. But it wasn't Olivia's helmet that I saw, nor was it Ganesh's ugly green helmet.

That meant only one thing: I was about to go toe to toe with the driver who'd replaced me on Arthur's team.

It was true that Daniel Stephens was an experienced driver...

...and I was keen to see how I fared against him.

41

Golden Reflections

I leaned my head back against the headrest; the constant roaring of the numerous cars circling the track that surrounded me was only slightly deadened by the walls of my trailer.

Having just finished a double stint, I felt that a rest was definitely in order. I recalled what it was like when I drove at the 25 Hours of Thunderhill. The race was longer than Daytona, but it was also far less stressful. Thunderhill was definitely a great event, but you didn't have to worry about television crews, millions of fans watching around the world and multimillion-dollar race cars zipping by you.

The battle with Stephens had been intense. He had gone on the attack right away in an attempt to get by me, but it was unsuccessful. He followed that up with some kamikaze dive into the *International Horseshoe* and nearly wiped out me and another car in the process, but he'd failed to complete the pass.

One thing he probably didn't count on was my uncanny ability to make whatever it was I was driving seem like it was the width of a bus. As much as I loved the feeling of hunting down the car I was in pursuit of, I was also a defender.

Every gap he went for, I would promptly close the door. When he would show his nose down the inside, I was able to judge when it was a feint and when it was going to be an actual dive for a pass.

It wasn't blocking as that's illegal. You're allowed one move to defend in response to a possible pass. When it came to defending against some of the more experienced drivers at a track like Daytona, it was often a fool's errand. You were only delaying the inevitable and losing heaps of time in the process. Sometimes, it's just better to let them go and use their draft to help you catch up to the next pack.

For someone like Stephens, however, this wasn't the case.

He telegraphed his moves far too early. It was almost as if he was expecting me to see him coming and jump out of the way out of fear of contact. The only thing it actually succeeded in was building up his own frustration.

After about five laps of this, he'd finally decided to strap on a pair as he tried to muscle his way past me at the Western Horseshoe. He threw his car down the inside and I *did* actually move out of his way this time when I saw the move coming.

He had to have known he wasn't going to make the corner. Either that or he'd gotten so tired of my shit, he'd just had enough and decided to ram me or something. Whatever his reasons, or possibly the lack thereof, he'd fired his team's Porsche down the inside with so much speed that he wasn't able to slow the car down in time.

Stephens found himself in the grass on the outside of the corner and a bulk of the field had passed him before he eventually re-entered the track. It was like seeing a monkey swing through the branches but ultimately smacking itself directly into a tree.

Yeah, okay. I may have gotten a bit of satisfaction out of that. Maybe too much. My head must've still been back in that corner when I entered the bus stop as I nearly missed my braking point. In doing so, I went into the first left corner way too hot and locked the inside tires up. Trying to still make the switch back to the right corner, which takes you out of the bus stop and back onto the oval proper, I had to over-slow the car in order to make the corner.

The move cost me a position as an Acura NSX GT3 managed to overtake me around the outside. The driver had been waiting patiently just behind

Stephens and me, probably waiting for one or both of us to take each other out. It was a GTD Pro car, so it technically didn't count for position, but I think I was just telling myself that as an excuse.

"Be good to the tires, please," came the immediate response from Jason over the radio.

I knew from experience, however, that it was his way of saying, *Open your damn eyes!*

The remainder of my stint was spent just managing traffic, staying out of trouble and saving fuel where I could. Getting passed after my little *episode* actually worked to our advantage. Having a car in front of me afforded me the opportunity to stay in the draft and save loads of fuel.

At one point in the stint, however, the Acura I'd been following actually pulled off to the side while we were entering NASCAR 3 and let me by. He promptly slid in behind me in what I could only guess was the driver's way of saying, *You've saved enough fuel; now it's my turn.*

With Derek in the car now for what would undoubtedly be a double stint for him, I was beginning to wonder if he would be as friendly as I was out there. Derek was fast but he was also unpredictable. We never really knew what kind of Derek we were going to get on any given day.

In practice sessions, they would turn into full intensity race sessions to Derek. Although I'd done a bit of homework as to why Derek was no longer racing in Australia, it was tough to get him to open up about it. Because of this, it was almost as if he were racing against a damn ghost every time he got in the car.

* * *

The feeling of having his hands on the steering wheel of a race car in a major motorsport event took him back to his days as the star driver in the Supercars series. He recalled the success he'd had; being a two-time Supercars series champion, winning the Bathurst 1000...

At the time, businesses flocked to Derek with the hope of gaining his support via sponsorship. There was plenty of money flowing around as well as national fame and notoriety even. Sure, he had a reputation as a bit of a bad boy in the series but everyone needs their gimmick if they're going to stand out in the crowd.

Peacocking is what he'd heard it called from a performance coach he'd hired. At first, it was all just an act. He'd talk louder than the other drivers, act more flamboyantly but he also backed it up with his actions on the track. He'd certainly received his fair share of penalties over the years, but it seemed that before long, the crowds loved him for it.

The more he went against the grain, the more support he'd receive. What was crazy is that it eventually paid off. Before long, he'd secured a seat in the best car on the Supercars grid and with the most well-funded team.

There was a time, he recalled, when he seemed untouchable. He'd start from pole in nearly every race and was able to convert the vast majority of those starting positions to race wins. He'd even heard one broadcaster call him the *golden boy* of Supercars.

Then came Bill Watson.

An American, the son of a legend, a man whose confidence was at times strong enough to face a charging bull but at other times, weak enough to be knocked down by a stiff breeze.

In truth, Derek had nothing to fear from Bill but for reasons unknown, people wouldn't stop talking about him. For months it was *Watson this* or *Watson that*.

"How do you think he'd fare in a proper Supercars race?" one reporter had asked Derek.

It was lunacy. An American coming to Australia and racing in the Supercars series? And challenging him, the defending series champion, at that?

The thought alone was pure madness. What Derek hadn't counted on, however, was just how skilled Watson truly was. More than just his skill as a wheelman and his decision-making process while under pressure, however, he had heart.

Indeed, Derek had never faced an adversary who'd pursued him with such fire and conviction. Although Derek had come out on top of the exchange at the Bathurst 1000—even if only by a whisker—the act had allowed him to gain a level of respect for the American.

He'd be lying if he said the event hadn't changed him. Because of Bill Watson, he'd been able to look inside of himself and in doing so, soon found a desire to get his personal life back in order.

In the months that followed his victory at Bathurst, Derek reconnected with his childhood girlfriend, Lola, and the two eventually moved in together. His victory in the Great Race had also earned him much in the way of fame and additional support for his team.

He had found a peace he'd never experienced before. Derek had even gone so far as to say that Bill Watson—his once fierce competitor and bitter rival—was now one of the few people in life he could refer to as a friend.

Then, that friend passed away.

For Derek, it was difficult to comprehend. How could such a person, a human being that genuinely deserved the title of *"good man,"* die so young and leave behind so much? How could one of the few people Derek had ever regarded as a friend be gone?

In truth, Bill's death shook Derek to his core. He bottled up these emotions, however, but they couldn't stay hidden for long.

It began as outbursts towards his partner. Although they were engaged to be married at the time, it was eventually called off due to Derek's constant berating.

He hid his mounting grief behind a veil of anger and resentment. He was no longer able to maintain his focus on track. When things began to look bad, Derek turned to aggression. The penalties soon began to stack up as Derek's reputation as a hard but fair racer was soon replaced with that of being a hazard to himself and to other drivers on the track.

He still remembers when Nick Latham—the man who was now his co-driver in the 24 Hours of Daytona—had passed him for the lead on the last lap during a race at The Bend Motorsport Park in South Australia. The win would've secured Nick's first Supercars championship.

The two had grown up racing together. From karting to Formula Ford, Nick had always shown speed and Derek knew that his fellow countryman had big aspirations in motorsport.

Instead of helping him, however, Derek fed him a bumper at Turn 14. The ensuing crash wasn't just the end of Nick's race, but of his championship hopes as well.

Nick—the man who'd gone from a driver who was seemingly out to pasture to a championship contender—had the backing of the Australian racing community behind him. He was a bona fide underdog with a Cinderella story as he faced off against the giant.

This time, however, it was giant who'd come out on top. Able to press on after the incident with Nick and cruise to a victory, the crowd soon turned against Derek. Throwing bottles at him, spitting on him, threatening him…it was almost as if the world had aligned itself against him. Although the series had penalized Derek and the win was eventually stripped from him, that was of little consolation to the one who'd paid the biggest price. For Nick, winning that race was a chance to secure a lifelong dream of being a Supercars champion.

Now that dream was gone.

It was a crushing way to end his season and truth be told, Nick was a changed man afterwards. The entire ordeal had hardened him on the inside. His typical youthful and oftentimes playful attitude was replaced with that of coldness and a stone-faced disposition.

He spoke less and turned up the aggression on track. Not in an out-of-control sort of way but more so in a manner akin to a man with a single but calculated purpose to his life now. He saw meagerness as a weakness and he told himself that he would never again give an inch on the track.

For Derek, however, he experienced a different kind of loss. Being the unapologetic person he was didn't help his cause as Derek attempted to carry on in the only way he knew how. Following the incident, Derek's team began to separate themselves from him. Sponsors began to pull their support and by the end of the season, Derek's team had decided they'd had enough.

Terminating his contract with immediate effect, Derek Renshaw—once the golden boy of the Supercars series—was now without a ride.

Despite his talent and his impressive resume as a driver, no other teams showed interest in him as the series headed into a new season.

He still remembered the feeling of watching the next season begin without him. No one seemed to care. Instead, they almost seemed relieved.

Having no sponsors, no ride and no prospects, a feeling of brokenness entered Derek's heart. For the first time in his professional racing career, Derek felt what could only be described as vulnerability.

He'd given his entire life to getting to the top level of Australian motorsport only to be cast aside so quickly. He knew he only had himself to blame, however. As Derek looked for other options, he began coaching aspiring drivers who hoped to siphon his skill and energy, but not so much his attitude.

As the years passed, however, his clientele dwindled as he faded into obscurity. Now, most of his students were far older than him as they attempted to get a few thrills in their big-dollar sportscars.

Cars—Derek knew—that now had more in common with caged lions than the fire-breathing dragons they were designed to be.

Perhaps it was fate, then, when Derek's phone rang early one evening and the sound of a young man was on the other end.

Chad Watson—the son of his friend Bill—was offering him a much-needed lifeline to race in one of the most iconic events in the world.

Although the opportunity had indeed revealed to Derek just how much time had passed since his glory days, he was confident he'd be able to reignite the fire that once burned within him. It was an open door he truly could not afford to pass by. He needed this race—for himself and for his future.

Even if this race was to be his swan song in motorsport, Derek knew that racing with the son of his friend and also with his former Supercars rival at Daytona in a GT3 car was better than being cast aside and forgotten. This was his redemption drive, even if it was only he who knew how much he needed it.

If there was one thing he'd learned during his time away from racing, it was that you sometimes never knew when you'll step out of a race car for the last time.

* * *

Derek accelerated onto NASCAR 1 & 2 with a pack of GTD cars just off the nose of the McLaren. Having been catching this pack rather quickly over the course of the past two laps, Derek was already formulating a way to get past them.

Things had been progressing well for the team so far. After witnessing Chad narrowly avoid an accident, the young driver managed to pick up a few spots and then maintain his position for the remainder of his stint.

The boy is good, Derek thought. *Just like his old man.*

Derek was continuing to pursue the pack of GTD cars that were getting closer with each corner.

His efforts to brake a bit later and also harder were paying off and Derek closed the gap on the group. Roughly five cars—a mix of GTD and GTD Pro cars—were now close enough to mount an offensive.

Going on the attack, Derek positioned the McLaren on the back bumper of the Mercedes, which was at the rear of the pack. Entering the dog leg, Derek fired his car down the inside of Turn 5 and held the racing line— forcing the Mercedes driver to take a wider line and ultimately yield to the Australian.

Turning his attention to the next car in line—an Audi R8 LMS GT3—the V10 engine of the Audi screamed as Derek pressed on towards its back bumper.

Entering NASCAR 1 & 2, Derek hoped the slipstream would allow him to get a run on the Audi, but as all of the cars in the pack were lined up, they all seemed to benefit from this advantage.

The cars at the front of the pack dived for position as Derek looked for an opening. All he saw were cars going not two, but three wide into the bus stop.

"You stupid shits."

Derek mumbled under his breath as the entire pack had to drastically slow down while the three cars sorted themselves out in front of him.

Because of this, he was under attack from the very Mercedes he'd passed back at the Western Horseshoe.

Now in the slipstream, the Mercedes driver used the long road and high banking of NASCAR 3 & 4 to complete the pass on Derek before braking for Turn 1.

Getting frustrated, Derek stayed on the tail of the Mercedes as the driver held the inside line going into International Horseshoe.

"What in the hell are you doing!?"

Why the driver was defending this early in the race when a position wasn't even at stake was beyond Derek's understanding; although he did have a few theories, which were of the unkind nature.

Flashing his headlights at the driver, Derek's frustration grew as he noticed a pair of headlights growing brighter in his rearview mirror.

They belonged to a Porsche.

Continuing to be held up by the pack of cars, Derek followed closely as they entered NASCAR 1 & 2 again. Still unable to get a run on the pack, he checked his mirrors to see the Porsche driver who was wearing a blue and green helmet. He was taken off guard as the Porsche—which had gained enough ground behind him—cut to the left before the *Le Mans chicane* and went full send down the inside.

It was a borderline kamikaze move but much to Derek's surprise, it paid off. After building up enough momentum in the draft, the blue Porsche then succeeded in passing an incredible two cars as the entire pack clumsily slowed for the bus stop.

Derek witnessed the driver hang back on exit, only to gain another advantage that allowed him to out-brake the next car in the pack while heading into Turn 1.

"Shit balls," replied Derek, who was still at the back of the pack.

Whoever was in that car was making some serious moves.

A pack of three GTP cars—the overall leaders of the race—ripped past Derek as he braked for Turn 1 as well. Dicing through the pack in front of Derek, the GTP cars created an opening heading into *International Horseshoe,* which Derek was able to capitalize on.

Following the faster cars through the slow corner, Derek completed the overtake on the Mercedes once again.

Looking up the road, however, he witnessed the blue Porsche pass the final car in the pack and get clear of the traffic. The GTP leaders soon caught the Porsche as it entered NASCAR 1 & 2, giving it a good draft down the backstraight until they pulled away.

As Derek watched in awe at how the Porsche managed to clear the entire field of slower GTD cars, he continued to struggle with them. While the setting sun was beginning to cast hues of gold across the surface of the track, Derek could only watch as the blue Porsche was soon nothing more than a set of taillights driving off into the coming darkness.

42

Driven by Reasons

"We need you to back it off, please. We're above our target fuel numbers."

Nerds.

Pimple-faced pencil-pushers telling him how to run his race. Had he not just made up more ground and gained another position?

After the inadequate driving by their newest teammate, which saw him get passed by that idiot Chad Watson, Daniel Stephens then proceeded to allow Watson to slip away unopposed.

What an embarrassment, thought Ganesh. *Maybe I should lock him in a trailer.*

After Stephens's stints were complete, however, it was up to Ganesh to take back the ground they'd lost.

Or at least that was the way *he* saw it.

"Ganesh, did you copy? We need you to back off."

And then there were *those* guys.

They were always telling him to do this, don't do that, back off, drive like this, not like that, speed up, slow down…

At some point, Ganesh knew, they were just going to have to trust him. Was it not merit that had earned him the seat he was currently occupying? Had he not succeeded in becoming the fastest driver on the team?

It was just like back home. Everyone from family to friends always felt like they needed to tell Ganesh what to do next and how to do it. More than that, they seemed to be more inclined to tell him what *not* to do.

He still remembered winning his first national karting championship here in the U.S. Having paid the extra money to travel back home to India with his championship trophy, he was eager to show his friends and family the rewards of his success.

The responses were not what he expected.

"Driving cars in circles is for the rich and the stupid," his father told him in front of all his family and friends. "Get an education and a career. In the end, you'll get more satisfaction out of life than you will from that large piece of golden plastic."

Feeling as if his greatest accomplishment in life was suddenly worthless, Ganesh could feel himself sinking back while those around him laughed as he stood with his championship trophy.

He hadn't returned home since.

Even after winning two more national karting championships, Ganesh hadn't bothered to even bring it up to his family.

When he would have the occasional conversation with his family over the phone or through video chat, they would often ask what he was up to. Ganesh, of course, would bring up his racing accomplishments and endeavors.

Like clockwork, however, an awkward silence would always follow. If the conversation was through video chat, Ganesh would witness this silence firsthand as all the heads of those in the chat would drop at once.

They didn't say it, not out loud anyways, but he heard their message loud and clear. Over time, he stopped bringing racing up, as he knew they had no interest in it. What followed this, however, was a different kind of silence.

The phone calls with his family became fewer and further between until one day he realized they'd stopped completely.

Instead of feeling despair, however, this drama with his family seemed to fuel Ganesh.

He would show them.

More importantly, he would show himself.

As he pressed forward with his dreams of becoming a professional race car driver, there would be no relenting.

He knew his purpose, his reason for being.

Although he'd had a rocky start during his initial foray into cars, he soon found the right coaches, who told him what he'd needed to hear.

As one of his previous driving coaches once told him, "You win races by driving faster than the other driver. It's that simple."

Just like racing, Ganesh saw life as a sprint race. This attitude suited him.

Considering how easily he'd just passed one of the old men Watson had recruited for his team, Ganesh was reassured that this was the way to get what he wanted.

A win.

Not just a class win against the amateurs in GTD, mind you.

No, Ganesh wanted the grand prize. He wanted to best the entire GTD field. The GTD and GTD Pro classes were separated by skill, not by technology. A Porsche driven by a GTD Pro team was essentially identical to that of one driven by a GTD team. Although winning in the amateur class would be great, besting all of the GTD Pro teams to win overall in the sportscar class was the goal.

After all, what good is a win if identical cars finish in front of you? Is that really a victory?

However, this was all just a distraction as there was still plenty of racing left to do. Of the two other drivers on his team, he trusted Olivia the most. Despite the fact that she had nearly choked the life out of him, he had grown to respect her skill behind the wheel. Although he hated the idea of having to give up the car to another driver, Ganesh knew she would be fine and more or less keep his car out of trouble.

As he pressed on and started another lap, Ganesh took note of traffic coming up behind him.

The LMP2 driver overtook him quickly and carried on about its race. It reminded him of how quickly he'd gotten by Watson's driver. It was easy. Whoever the driver was, he was being too cautious and got caught.

Are both of Watson's other drivers not Bathurst 1000 winners?

Maybe I should tackle that race next, Ganesh thought.

The task of getting to the front of the field lay before him, despite what the team was wanting him to do.

He hadn't responded to them, and, truth be told, he didn't care to. His job was simple: drive faster and get to the front.

And with Watson's team now behind him, that task just become a whole lot easier.

* * *

"Ganesh, do you copy? We need you to back off."

The second attempt to reach Ganesh had come back fruitless.

Sitting next to the race engineer, Arthur listened to the silence that followed the latest radio call to his driver.

He's doing it again. He's shutting the world out and getting in his own head.

Arthur knew well and clear that Ganesh had struggles he continued to deal with. His family had essentially disowned him as they saw him as a failure. Although he'd talked with Ganesh about these struggles in great detail, Arthur wasn't entirely sure if his driver was just giving him lip service when he said that he had moved on from these issues. These thoughts, Arthur observed, seemed to come to the forefront whenever Ganesh was behind the wheel.

It was his fuel, he'd once told Arthur.

For the most part, Arthur seemed content to simply let Ganesh be as the results began to speak for themselves.

Indeed, this *fuel* seemed to give Ganesh a great deal of speed. Significantly more so than when he'd first started. Possibly more than that of Chad Watson. As Arthur soon discovered, however, there was also a price to be paid for this speed from Ganesh.

Although allowing Ganesh to get lost in his own thoughts had its benefits, it also made him unpredictable. He became difficult to control and as the team he'd hired to support their Daytona endeavors put it, "The guy just goes rogue."

This was a perfect example.

Any attempts to further reach out to Ganesh to save fuel would only cause him to become irate, which had the possibility of affecting his driving. Arthur had to put the team above Ganesh, and as much as it pained him, this often meant letting Ganesh do what he saw fit. The last thing he needed was another toxic environment such as when Chad was on the team. The hostility shown between him and Ganesh nearly tore his entire racing operation apart.

Ever since he'd let Chad go, a certain level of peace had been restored. As Arthur pondered, however, the memories of the last several months surfaced in his mind. The investments he'd made into driving coaches for Ganesh had certainly paid off. He'd even succeeded in getting faster lap times than Olivia. But as time went on, Arthur observed Ganesh as he seemed to slip back into his old ways. It wasn't enough for him to know he was the fastest on the team. Ganesh had to let everyone know he was the fastest and he did so on a regular basis.

It was such a tiring argument and one that someone like Olivia always declined to participate in.

That was one person Arthur had never been able to crack. He knew she also had a past. The struggle with her parents is what led Olivia to apply for the position Arthur had posted at the very beginning of this endeavor. Beyond that, however, Olivia was one who kept to herself. Despite the constant remarks from Ganesh, Olivia never seemed to rise to the bait. Indeed, Olivia seemed like she was done fighting against people. Her battles were fought on the track.

Regarding Chad, things weren't as black and white as they once seemed. The person Arthur now witnessed on a different team weathering storms, being a team player, speaking well in front of the camera, acquiring high-level sponsorship, all while outpacing the driver Arthur had hired as Chad's replacement was vastly different from the arrogant and egotistical driver who was once on his team.

His corporate investors and board members had once mentioned how embarrassing it would be if they sacked Chad, only to see him go to another team and bring the hurt to them. Arthur had initially doubted it. Chad was many things, but someone capable of dealing with the corporate world—the only place he'd be able to secure enough funding to go racing at this level—he was not.

Or so he'd thought.

Where did this new Chad come from? On top of his impressive skill behind the wheel, he seemed like a natural leader. He'd taken a once broken-down team on the verge of selling their entire shop and turned it into a factory-backed team that packed some serious firepower—all in a short amount of time.

Then there were his co-drivers.

Despite their apparent connection from Chad's dad, being able to recruit two Bathurst 1000 winners who—from what Arthur recalled after reading the stories of their past—hated each other, Chad had so far succeeded in keeping this team together while also gaining much in the way of outside support.

In spite of Arthur's original thoughts regarding his lack of corporate capabilities, Chad and his team were legitimately beginning to look like a threat.

Should Arthur become defeated on a global stage by Chad's team, his investors—who were against kicking Chad off the team—would undoubtedly call into question the future of this racing operation.

In short, Arthur needed a solution...and it was Ganesh who'd approached him with a possible answer.

The idea itself was simple: slip the story Ganesh had overheard Chad sharing with Olivia of his drug-induced karting crash to the press and let them do the dirty work. They would handle Chad and he would be none the wiser as to who filled them in. If everything worked out, Chad wouldn't be permitted to race and all could go back to normal.

Although Arthur begrudgingly agreed to it, what Ganesh ultimately did in that press conference was not only a betrayal of his trust but several steps too far past what he'd deemed morally right.

The wild imaginings on Arthur's mind seemed to pound their way to the forefront of his thoughts. Amidst the chaos of various pit crews running about and the chorus of engines screaming across the track for the past several hours, a doubt that had already taken root now seemed to be growing.

Have I made a mistake? Am I putting this entire endeavor, the reputation of my company and the millions of dollars I've invested at risk because I may have fired the wrong person from my team?

It was a moot point, Arthur knew, and he quickly shook his head free from the thought. He'd made his decision and stuck with it. That was what leaders did. Even if it was the wrong decision, what's done is done and he stood by his drivers. Glancing up at the timing and scoring screen, Arthur nodded as he saw his team in fifth in the overall GTD field while being third in class.

Even as he reassured himself that he'd made the right call, part of Arthur couldn't help but feel that his driver, who was now racing by the start/finish line, had somehow goaded him into the position he was now in.

43

A New Dawn

The hours pressed on as the 24 Hours of Daytona continued to race away. The light of the day had now been overtaken by the horizon as night enveloped the city of Daytona Beach. Despite the starless night, the various lights on and around the track made the speedway anything but dark.

The entire track surface was illuminated with an intensity similar to streetlights and the carnival-like Ferris wheel gave its passengers a unique vantage point of the night racing.

For Nick Lathan, however, these were nothing more than distractions. Able to get a few hours of sleep while Chad and Derek ran their stints, Nick hopped back into the car and began what was to be at least a double stint for him.

Before getting in the car, however, Nick observed its current position in the race. Currently fourth in class, sixth in the overall GTD standings, Nick was briefed by Jason on what had unfolded. Derek had lost a bit of ground after getting held up in traffic, losing a position to a Porsche in the struggle.

Content with what he'd heard and eager to get back in the car, Nick soon replaced Derek in the driver's seat and hit the corners once more.

With the field now thoroughly spread out, the energetic feeling he'd once had at the start of the race was now replaced with one of strategy and consistency.

Now several laps into his stint, Nick fixed his eyes farther up the road as a group of taillights became his next set of targets.

Nick worked through the infield section of the track just as two LMP3 cars appeared in his rearview mirror. Maintaining his line as he made the left onto NASCAR 1 & 2, the LMP3 cars were soon able to pass Nick, which worked to his advantage. Although faster than the GTD cars, the LMP3s were the least powerful of the prototypes. Nick was able to hang with them for some time while progressing down the backstraight.

After a few laps, the LMP3 cars had stretched away from Nick but, in turn, had caught the back of the pack he was in pursuit of.

He could only shake his head as the first of the two LMP3 drivers attempted a dive bomb down the inside of several GTD cars at *International Horseshoe*. Out-braking itself, the first LMP3 nearly went off into the grass as the driver threaded the needle of GTD cars while the second LMP3 driver went by. Although there was no contact, the entire incident further slowed up the sportscars as they waited for the LMP3 drivers to get themselves sorted.

This all worked to Nick's advantage, as he was now on the back bumper of a red and black Lamborghini at the rear of the pack.

Doubling down, it was almost as if there was blood in the water as Nick went on the attack. Powering through the corners, Nick used the draft to pull up alongside the Lamborghini and complete the pass while entering the bus stop. He was now directly behind the blue Porsche, which he'd previously learned had blitzed Derek.

This driver, however, seemed to be playing it calm and possibly saving fuel. One lap later, Nick noted that the driver was not defending while heading into *International Horseshoe*. As such, Nick was able to make a move down the inside and complete the pass for position.

With only one car left in the pack, which had finally been cleared by the LMP3 drivers, Nick was initially caught by surprise when a slight bump came from behind him. Racing out of NASCAR 2, the bump was essentially a push, which allowed Nick to gain a bit of speed on the yellow Corvette

C8.R, which had the GTD Pro badge on the rear.

Exiting the bus stop, Nick could only smile as the blue Porsche once again bumped him. Staying nearly locked onto the back bumper of Nick's McLaren, the Porsche driver proceeded to push Nick up to the back of the Corvette.

It would be several laps later, when Nick was nearing his pitstop, that the move would come. Entering Turn 5, Nick braked a bit later while entering the corner, which allowed the McLaren to pull along the right side of the Corvette.

Completing the pass, Nick checked his mirrors to see that the blue Porsche had followed him through as well. It was an impressive drive from the opposing Porsche driver, which didn't seem to fit the profile of the one who'd previously passed Derek.

"Who's driving that thing?" asked Nick as he entered NASCAR 1.

"Chad's crush, Olivia Calo" responded Jason over the radio; a touch of laughter in his voice, "But you didn't hear that from me."

Exiting NASCAR 4, the blue Porsche cut to the left and entered pit lane just as Jason sounded off.

"Give us one more clean lap and we'll bring you in. Good job saving fuel."

"Copy."

Nick's response to Jason was snappy as he entered Turn 1 with the Corvette just behind him.

"We've got a foot on the podium but let's see if we can improve," added Jason. "Class leaders are seven seconds up the road."

Before Nick had a chance to respond, the sound of thunderous eruptions filled the air as no small amount of fireworks were set off from the infield.

Nick could only shake his head and smile at the annual tradition.

"Americans."

Turning his attention back to the road ahead, the colors from the fireworks cast shades of orange, blue, red and green across the track as Nick progressed onward into the night.

* * *

Derek trudged down the dimly lit path, one foot in front of the other, his muscles protesting as they demanded more rest. Making his way down the paddock, he breathed in the cool air of the early Florida morning. The light of a new dawn was just cresting over the horizon as Derek observed the beauty, shutting out the world around him as he did.

Beneath the weariness, past the sleep deprivation and even deeper than the memory of him agreeing to swap final stints with Chad, there was a level of peace in him now and a resolve that gave him a renewed purpose and a drive to push on.

This is it, thought Derek. *My last walk through the paddock to enter a race car.*

He thought back to well over a decade ago when he had battled Bill Watson at Mount Panorama. He didn't know it at the time, but for Bill, those were to be his last laps in a race car.

Derek wondered how Bill felt during those final laps. Was there an unquenchable fire that propelled him forward or a quiet level of resolve that told him to treasure those last moments?

Judging from Bill's actions, Derek recalled, he leaned more towards the former.

The roaring of engines continued to fill the air as he made his way to his team's pit stall. The team had kept the car out of trouble, the pit stops had been good, the racing had more or less been clean, and thanks to Nick's efforts, the team was in position for a podium finish. Considering how quickly things had come together just to get the car on the grid, the fact that they were in contention for a possible podium was more than Derek could've hoped for. It was enough, he thought, to end his career on.

He was kicking himself for agreeing with Watson's request to finish things off, though.

This was Chad's endeavor, Derek knew. He was the one who brought everyone here. If he wanted to be the one to carry the team across the finish line, more power to him.

The team had worked out the math as they needed to stay within the limits of the driver rules. That was for the people with the hats and headphones to figure out, however. For Derek, he just got in the car when they told him it was go-time.

He glanced up in time to see the orange McLaren sprint across the line to begin another lap, and Derek readied his heart for what was to be his final act as a race car driver. Sliding his helmet over his head, he pictured the quiet spot he'd picked out near Hunter Valley in New South Wales, the place he'd be calling home if he played his cards right.

The pit crew, with bloodshot eyes and all, were lined up along the wall to make ready for the coming stop. Derek took his position as he gave one of the tire changers a pat on the shoulder. As the two locked eyes for a brief moment, Derek gave the young American a nod as the latter soon returned his gaze forward.

Taking a deep breath, Derek lowered his visor as his mind went through the checklist of everything his body would need to do to perform the upcoming driver swap.

In his heart, however, Derek knew this was it for him.

One last race; one final drive.

44

Never Quit

The alarm sounded, and my still-weary eyes fired open.

The symphony of engines continued its dull roar in the background, which told me things outside were still proceeding. Although it was daytime, the sun wasn't shining through as I pulled up the timing and scoring on my phone to see how we were holding up.

It took my eyes a bit to adjust enough to read the words and numbers on the screen. Being able to only grab a few hours of sleep between stints quickly began to take its toll as we entered the predawn hours. Although Nick, Derek and I had trained for this, the added stress of going through the motions during the actual event brought my anxiety to a new level.

Having been in and out of the car multiple times, I knew that everyone across the paddock who was still in the race was feeling it just as much as I was.

This race wasn't just a test of the machines or of individual skill, but of willpower as well.

Once my eyes finally adjusted to where I could actually read, I saw that we were still maintaining second position in class. After I'd finished my previous stint, Derek had jumped in, and before I could even get my fire suit off, he'd passed a BMW for position after it collided with an LMP2 car at Turn 1.

Although the BMW was able to continue (albeit at a greatly reduced speed) on its long road back to pit lane, the LMP2 car became stranded, which brought out the second full course caution of the race.

This was fortuitous in one sense because it allowed us to close the gap to the class leader, who was, at the time, several seconds in front of us. Under a full course caution, all of the cars on the field had to slow down to pace car speed, which meant that any gaps were effectively eradicated. But it also works both ways, as the lead we'd had on Arthur's car had vanished, and they were once again on our back bumper.

It was interesting to watch Derek and Olivia duel it out. Derek must've flipped that *kill switch* because he wasn't taking any prisoners on the restart. He wasn't able to catch the GTD leader in our class, but he left Olivia behind as he maintained the roughly two-second gap to our class leader.

There was just over three hours remaining. As I stood up—using my bed for balance—I slowly began to stretch my still-weary muscles. The task I was about to attempt landed firmly on my shoulders.

Call it egotistical, call it whatever. I just wanted to finish the race that I felt I'd started months before ever showing up to Daytona, and no one seemed to have a problem with it.

I was about to grab my gear when a sudden rumble caused me to stop in place and look around. My entire trailer shook. True, I was on the infield of a racetrack, but this wasn't the rumble of cars. I had a sudden sinking feeling.

Grabbing my cane, I stepped closer to window and moved the curtains aside to take a peek at the sky.

Storm clouds were moving in. I couldn't see any rain, but it was only a matter of time.

"Oh, Florida, how I *don't* love you."

Knowing I'd be needed by the team, I grabbed a quick bite to eat before getting my gear bag and heading out the door.

* * *

"It doesn't look like anything terrible. Well, not terrible for us here in the garage, I mean."

Jason flashed a grin at me, and I could automatically tell he was feeling the effects of sleep deprivation. The usual robotic-natured race engineer who was doubling as our crew chief wasn't one for humor, so this was a new side of him.

We both turned our gazes to the radar display, which showed the weather system that was continuing to develop over the Daytona Beach area. The blue and light green colors showed that the severity of the storm wasn't anything to worry about. That is, unless you were planning on driving a half-million-dollar race car at 180 mph on a wet road.

I still had thirty minutes left before Derek's final pit stop of the race. I made my way around the garage to chat with some of the pit crew. Although they were able to get some sleep between pit stops here in the garage, they had to be ready at a moment's notice in case something happened on track with the car.

As such, the folding chairs that were spread out over the garage were what the crew had called home for the past twenty-one hours. They were the heartbeat of this entire operation, and I made sure to thank each and every one of them for their efforts thus far.

With my gear on, I walked towards the entrance of our garage and turned my eyes upward. Where there were once clear blue skies, there were now dark and foreboding storm clouds.

If it rained, the race would continue unless it was a hazardous amount of water. Lightning, on the other hand, would cause the race to be red flagged. But that only meant the *racing* stopped, not the clock. The timer would continue until the twenty-four hours had elapsed, and we would potentially finish in our current position.

I said a silent prayer for the weather to clear. Wanting a battle to the very end, I wasn't content with where we were. Yes, we had a foot on the podium, and yes, we were in front of Arthur's team. But we were also in second. Having come this far with our small team, I knew we could make a push at the end if the odds swung in our favor. We just needed things to go smoothly between now and then.

We also needed a bit of luck...

The leader in the GTD class—a European team that had participated in the 24 nearly a dozen times—had so far been nearly untouchable. Their silver Mercedes was piloted by a team of four highly skilled drivers, and they'd demonstrated they were a force to be reckoned with.

A rumble of thunder caused me to shift my gaze skyward again.

It looked like I would be hopping into the car just as the weather was about to erupt.

Still, I figured, it wasn't like I hadn't weathered my share of storms before in life. Why should this be any different?

"You ready for this, Watson?"

Caught off guard, I turned to see Nick standing just behind me.

"Yeah, I think so," I replied. "Although the rain may have other plans."

Nick smiled as he stepped alongside me. We both stood for a moment as we watched the various cars race across the tri-oval.

"You're a damn fine driver, Chad," Nick added. "Before you jump in and finish this race up, I wanted to tell you that it's been an honor racing with you. Your old man would be proud."

Instantly, I could feel my eyes beginning to water.

"Shit, Nick," I tried to play it off. "What are you trying to do to me before I get in the car?"

Nick slapped me across the back as I braced with my cane.

"Just remember what I told you about driving in the wet. Stay off the racing line as much as you can. She'll get loose on you but you've been around the block enough to know how to wrestle it back under control."

I nodded in understanding.

"If I'm lucky, I won't have to..."

As if on cue, the skies opened up and the rain began to fall.

"You were saying?"

The smug look on Nick's face was quickly replaced as the pit crew behind us came alive in panic.

"Get ready! Wet tires!"

"Where is he? Where's Derek?" I shouted.

Jason kept his eyes fixed on his data display as he shouted back.

"He's coming out of NASCAR 4 now but he's going slow!"

"Watson!" I turned just as Nick handed me my helmet. I quickly donned my balaclava and slid the helmet over my head.

Due to my need of a cane, putting my helmet on wasn't something I could do while I moved, which caused me to panic. Knowing I was in trouble if I didn't get over to the pit wall as quickly as possible to replace Derek in the car, I was taken completely by surprise as I felt my feet suddenly leave the earth.

"I've got ya, mate!"

Scooping me up into his arms, Nick physically carried me from the garage to the pit stall as he ran while cradling me like a child.

I just *knew* that every camera in the Speedway saw me being carried this way. Still, I used this time to get my helmet firmly strapped on. Just as Nick had set me down by the wall, Derek was pulling up to the pit stall.

It was messy. Derek wasn't able to stop squarely in the stall. I watched as the car hydroplaned across the surface and slid about three feet into the next pit stall. The crew sprang into action and pushed the car back into our stall.

There was no time to think about the amount of time we lost in the ordeal as the crew went to work changing the tires and refueling the car. The door swung open as Derek stepped out of the McLaren just as I was making my way over the wall.

As I stepped in, Derek assisted with getting me strapped up.

"I guess this would be a bad time to thank you for changing stints with me!" he shouted. Not bothering to respond due to the panic in my mind, I attached all of the necessary connections and felt a slap on my chest as Derek finished helping me with the belts.

"You give 'em hell, Watson!"

Derek's shout was barely audible above the falling rain and the noise all around as the door slammed shut.

My heart was beating through my chest as I took a brief second to collect myself.

You've been here before. Just go through the motions.

I pressed the radio button on the steering wheel and confirmed comms with Jason. The crew were now on the left side of the car changing the tires when I heard what I determined to be an unusual amount of noise coming from the left rear.

Checking my driver side mirror, I noticed that the rear tire changer was frantically trying to get the wheel lug nut screwed on, but it looked like his air gun was having issues.

"Stand by, Chad!"

Jason's voice on the radio sounded more panicked than usual.

"Sonofabitch," I mumbled under my breath. Ahead, I saw the field of GTD cars already leaving their stalls as a fresh dose of anxiety landed on my shoulders.

Right before my eyes, I was physically watching our race get washed down the drain.

Slamming my palm against the steering wheel, I cursed.

"C'mon, dammit!"

Checking the mirror again, I watched as the tire changer from the front left of the car ran over with his air gun to assist. In a moment, the left rear tire was on, and the car dropped down to the ground.

"Go! Go! Go!"

I powered away down the wet pit lane, narrowly avoiding another car that was turning down to enter its own pit stall.

The pit lane speed limiter in the McLaren made the engine sputter as I maintained the maximum designated speed limit of 55 miles per hour. Passing the exit point, I disengaged the speed limiter to enter the track...as the rear of the car immediately fired sideways.

I didn't even have a chance to take a breath before my hands wrangled the McLaren back so it was pointing in the right direction.

Proceeding onward, I engaged the windscreen wipers as I tried to assess where we were and how much time we'd lost. Within a moment, however, I noticed the double yellow flags indicating a full course caution. This was followed by the sight of what I guessed were four cars; one GTP, two LMP2 and one GTD Aston Martin; all stuffed into the guardrail on the outside of Turn 5.

I followed the track while driving off the racing line to avoid the rubber that had built up over nearly twenty-two hours of racing. Water and rubber make for a slick surface. Before long, I'd caught up to the back of a black and green BMW, which I recalled being farther back on timing and scoring.

"Jason?" I called out on the radio. "Where are we at, bud? What's the damage?"

"We're assessing. Standby."

Waiting patiently, I was eager to hear the news, whether it be for good or for ill. I knew they were waiting to see how the grid shook out after they passed pit lane, and I wasn't disappointed.

"All right, Chad." The tone of Jason's voice was already less than ideal. "We're down."

Shit.

"We're back to eighth in class."

My eyes shot wide open at the revelation.

"From second to eighth?"

"I'm sorry, Chad. The air gun jam during the stop really killed us, but we've still got about two hours left on the clock. We may be down, but we're not out."

A memory suddenly surfaced.

"Never give up, Chad," Grandad once said to me as we watched Dad's battle at Bathurst against Derek Renshaw on TV; Grandad's fists clenched as he relived the moment. *"Never. Give. Up."*

As I looked ahead towards the storm I was about to face I decided then and there I would attack it head on. There would be no relenting. There would be no giving up. I knew firsthand that life had a strange way of throwing unique trials and circumstances at you. However, that didn't mean you needed to take it lying down.

As I progressed through the track while under caution, memories of my dad began to surface.

He was a fighter; a man who never let life's circumstances dictate his actions. Although many of his words had since been forgotten, there are some that will stay with me forever.

"*Always keep fighting and never quit,*" he'd once said to me. "*Even when you fall down and even when the odds are stacked against you. Fight to stand back up because you never know where you'll end up if you keep moving forward.*"

As his words filled my mind, I doubled down and gripped the steering wheel with eagerness and anticipation as the field made ready to resume the race.

For nearly all my life, I'd felt like I'd been pursued. Now I was the hunter.

"This one's for you, Dad."

45

Battle Lines

Being just a few laps away from finishing her final stint of the twenty-four-hour race, Olivia doubled down as she tried to catch up to the McLaren driver.

After the last restart following the full course caution, she'd initially managed to slip by the driver. By doing so, however, Olivia figured she tripped some sort of internal land mine within this guy. Whoever it was, the driver decided from that point on to choose violence.

Heading into Turn 5, Olivia had glanced in her mirror to see the McLaren behind her. When she looked again, it was gone.

She was completely caught off guard when she noticed the orange car barreling towards her right side as they entered the corner.

Surely he's going to back out of the move, she thought. *There's barely enough room to...*

Immediately proven wrong, the McLaren driver elbowed his way past Olivia to complete the pass upon the corner's exit. Although there was contact, it was purely cosmetic as she noticed a fresh tire mark along the left side of the McLaren, partially smearing the image of the fish that stared back at her.

Looking for a way to fight back, the sight of water droplets on the windscreen made Olivia lose her train of thought. She was just now progressing onto NASCAR 1 & 2 when the rain began to increase in intensity.

"It's raining! Are you guys seeing this?"

"We see it, Olivia," returned the weary voice of Arthur. "Pit this time. We're about to all get wet."

"Copy."

Coming out of the bus stop, Olivia initially lost all steering in the car as it hydroplaned straight towards the outside wall.

Just as the car got off the rubbered-in racing line, however, she found grip and was able to catch it, avoiding what would've been a race-ending disaster.

Engaging her wipers and greatly decreasing her speed, Olivia's heart was thundering in her chest as her breathing rate increased.

"Just get it to the pits," she said out loud. "Just get it home. C'mon, Livy. You've got this."

Reaching the entrance to pit lane, she found that it was a mess of cars, lights, pit crew and still more water. She knew it would be difficult to find her pit stall until a voice came over the radio.

"We see you. Stop in three, two, one..."

Seeing the pit stall at the last moment, Olivia was lucky enough to have a clear entrance as she brought the car in and stopped squarely in the box.

Ganesh stood by, ready to hop in.

Unstrapping her belts, Olivia grabbed ahold of the metal door bars and hoisted herself out of the car. One of her hands, however, slipped on the rain-slicked surface.

Frustrated by the loss of time, Ganesh decided to take matters into his own hands. Reaching into the car and grabbing the shoulder straps on Olivia's fire suit, Ganesh physically pulled her out and tossed her aside. As Ganesh entered, Olivia sprang back to her feet and headed over the pit wall.

Marching over to Arthur who was standing close to the pit wall with an umbrella in his hand, Olivia stood in the rain as she slid her helmet off her head.

"What the hell was that, Arthur?" she shouted. "I just raced my ass off for you, and this is how I'm treated? Do you even care anymore what Ganesh does?"

With a defeated expression, Arthur turned towards Olivia.

"I'll talk to him," he said flatly, the tone of his voice noticeable weary.

She stood there for a moment, just staring at him.

He won't do anything. What can he do?

Olivia turned to watch Ganesh drive off, freshly equipped with rain tires. Moments later, the unique sound of a V8 engine came to her ears as the orange McLaren rolled past her.

What were they doing behind us? They should've exited the pits long before us.

Noticing Chad's helmet, Olivia's world lit up as she suddenly found herself smiling in the rain.

Then a sudden realization hit her.

Chad would be on track with Ganesh.

Something inside told her it would come down to a duel between the two...

...and she knew exactly who she'd be cheering for.

* * *

Right away, I went on the attack.

As we crossed the line, I used the fears of those around me to my advantage. Many were driving cautiously in the wet weather conditions.

Some were driving *too* cautiously.

Picking the outside lane on Turn 1, I out-braked a red Ferrari in front of me and proceeded to stay off line as much as possible to complete the pass. Feeling the car slide under me, I applied a healthy amount of countersteer and wrestled it back under control.

The car in front of me was now a green Lamborghini who saw me coming as we headed towards *International Horseshoe*. The driver covered the inside line in what would normally be a defensive move.

This time, I didn't want the inside line.

Hanging my McLaren on the outside, I succeeded in finding enough grip to allow me to pull up along the left side. On exit, I initially found the drive I needed to make a clean getaway but soon felt the effects of an on-track slip 'n' slide. Driving over a rubbered-in patch, the McLaren got squirrely as the Lamborghini held the inside line at the exit of the corner. Now side by side, with me on the left, I held my breath as we headed towards the dog leg.

Going two-wide through there in normal conditions could be sketchy. Doing it in the wet was borderline madness.

"Ohhhh shit!"

At the last second, the opposing driver must've taken note that I wasn't going to back out. Had things gone bad, it was *his* car that would've taken a trip through the grass. Sure, I would've given him some room—or at least tried to—but he decided it would be better to fight another day.

Now clear and up to sixth in class, I sized up the field in front of me. Everyone was still stacked up pretty close together.

The leader in the silver Mercedes was struggling to find grip as the blue Porsche belonging to Arthur's team swerved about in a ridiculous attempt to get around him. The Porsche was going to end up in the fence if whoever was driving kept it up.

What it succeeded in doing, however, was keeping the field stacked together.

A large cloud of water mist sprayed up from the pack as we all raced out of NASCAR 2 and onto the backstretch. I soon found myself pulling up to the back of a Lexus and tried to send it in deep at the bus stop but the driver grabbed the ideal line and defended.

As the laps continued to tick by, I couldn't gain the position. These guys were definitely playing for keeps.

Up front, the same song and dance continued as the blue Porsche was making all kinds of kamikaze moves and dive bombs in an attempt to make a pass stick.

At one point, the driver actually pulled it off...only for the car to out-brake itself and slide slightly off the track while entering NASCAR 1. Able to recover, albeit down a position, the blue Porsche driver pressed on.

Finally, I couldn't take it anymore.

"Who's in the blue Porsche?"

A few moments later, my suspicions were correct.

"It's your old buddy Ganesh."

I didn't have time to think too much about it as I noticed several sets of headlights coming up fast in my mirrors. The overall GTP leaders—with their spaceship-like race cars—had come around to lap us and were ripping through the field.

One of them took a low line around the inside of Turn 1 and a few others followed closely behind. They stayed just behind the next GTD car in line until they reached *International Horseshoe*. Once there, they did the same thing to the Lexus driver who I'd so far been unable to pass. Seeing an opening at the tail end of the GTP pack, I put the McLaren in position to follow the GTP drivers around the slower-than-usual corner while the Lexus driver went wide.

Once out of the corner, I held it tight and stayed on the center of the track where there was a bit more grip. Squeezing the hand-throttle on my steering wheel, I succeeded in finally passing the Lexus and moving us back up to fifth.

"Nicely done," replied Jason over the radio.

With Ganesh just two cars in front of me, I had to fight to restrain myself. I felt like a caged lion. I wanted blood, but I knew patience was my greatest ally.

Considering we were already about halfway through this stint, I knew I couldn't afford to be *too* patient.

46

Water and Gasoline

Gripping the steering wheel tightly as he raced just off the back bumper of a black and orange Aston Martin, Ganesh could feel the heat on his face as he continued to press forward. Having lost a position just a few laps ago, he had forced...no...*willed* himself to calm down.

Staying calm under pressure wasn't one of his strengths. He preferred action and results over laying back and hoping something fortuitous landed on your lap.

Still, he knew from experience that his ability to press forward often landed him two steps back. At least, that's what his driving coaches would tell him.

Now, however, he decided to take it safe; play the long game and roll the dice when the opportunity was right.

That is, until he saw the orange McLaren creeping in his mirrors.

Finishing behind that car was not an option.

He could already hear the words his family would toss at him. They weighed him down and fogged his mind. He could feel their eyes watching from the other side of the world.

They would be laughing at his futile efforts to win.

No, thought Ganesh. *I'm in control. Not them.*

Sealing the deal, Ganesh moved to the left while heading down the backstraight and went hard on the brakes upon entry into the bus stop. He could feel the car sliding underneath him as the tires fought for traction.

Modulating the brake pedal, Ganesh was able to get his team's Porsche under control just as he turned the car into the left corner. The Aston Martin driver wisely backed off as a fight in these conditions and at these speeds while entering the bus stop would've been catastrophic. Now clear and back up to second, Ganesh powered onward.

He was surprised, however, when he noticed the McLaren still just one car behind him. Whoever was behind the wheel had done the exact same move and made up a spot. To top it all off, they looked to be getting a solid run out of NASCAR 3 & 4.

Braking hard again, Ganesh noticed the driver complete the pass for third while entering Turn 1. Whoever this driver was, they were on the move. For Ganesh, he also had no plans to stick around.

Putting his focus back onto the GTD leader, Ganesh made every attempt to stay smooth and precise through these slippery conditions.

Although the rain was still falling, the intensity of it had decreased but even so, there was more than enough water on the ground to take the situation seriously.

Playing offense and defense, Ganesh had one eye in front and the other in his mirrors. He needed to attack and get past the leader quickly.

The laps continued to tick by as the amount of fuel in his Porsche was surely running low. Soon, nearly everyone still left in the GTD field would be pitting. Frustrated by being unable to pass the skilled driver, Ganesh decided they were far enough into the race. It was time to roll the dice.

Heading out of the dog leg and into the Turn 5 Western Horseshoe, Ganesh sent his Porsche down the inside of the silver Mercedes. It was an ambitious move.

And as he soon found out, it was *too* ambitious.

Unable to get the car slowed enough, Ganesh did his best to find traction while the car pushed wide to the left side of the track...and into the silver Mercedes.

The two slammed into each other as Ganesh escorted the leader wide.

They were both fortunate to not end up beached in the grass, although the Mercedes did dip its two outside tires into it.

Ganesh knew he'd left himself open to an attack, so he wasn't surprised at all when it came.

What caught him off guard, however, was the insult to injury that came with it.

As Ganesh turned to see the McLaren pass by on the right, time seemed to stand still for a moment as he suddenly had the unmistakable view of a middle finger being held up from the driver's side window of the orange McLaren.

This could only mean one thing.

Chad Watson.

The cripple had passed him and made him look like a fool in doing so.

Getting back on the track, Ganesh could only watch as two other cars passed him for position before he could get back up to speed. Braking for Turn 6, he successfully defended against another pass before making the turn into NASCAR 1 & 2.

"We're gonna pit you this time around, Ganesh," said the voice over the radio. "Tires and fuel only. Last stop of the race."

Indeed.

One more stop. One more battle.

One last fight to the end.

* * *

The crew back in the garage exploded in cheers as they witnessed Chad overtake both of the cars in front of him and move the McLaren into the GTD class lead at Daytona.

Watching from the television monitor, Derek screamed as he put Nick into a bear hug and picked his fellow countryman off the ground in celebration.

"The kid's done it!" shouted Derek. "Holy shit balls, mate! We're leading the 24!"

Wrestling his way free, Nick seemed to be the only one in the garage reserving his celebration.

"There's still over an hour of racing left," responded Nick. "Don't crack the champagne open just yet."

Continuing to watch, Nick couldn't help but laugh as a memory surfaced in his mind.

Recalling the time when he was forced to sit by and watch the remainder of the Bathrust 1000 after breaking his wrist during a driver change, Nick distinctly remembered Chad—still in a wheelchair at the time—absolutely glued to the television as he watched his father go around the track.

Now, here he was again.

This time, however, he watched as that same kid was out there leading the 24 Hours of Daytona.

Wiping his eyes before anyone could see him, Nick could only shake his head as a smile worked its way onto his face.

"His old man would be so proud of him."

* * *

The call came over the radio shortly after I exited the bus stop and entered NASCAR 3.

"Pit this time, Chad. Fuel and tires to the end."

Acknowledging, I couldn't believe my ears.

We'd made it so far and we were only one pit stop away from finishing this race.

Not wanting to tempt fate, I risked a thought: *Can we actually hold on for the win?*

Coming out of NASCAR 4 while holding onto the lead in the GTD class, I turned the McLaren to the left towards the pit lane entrance. Minding my speed and remembering our stall was close to the entrance, I braked accordingly, engaged the pit lane speed limiter and made the short trip to our pit box, where I brought the car to a stop.

The crew were immediately over the wall as they went to work on refueling the car and changing its tires. Rain continued to drizzle on my windscreen but not nearly as much as earlier. Even so, it would take a braver man than me to go out there with slick tires.

I watched as the IMSA official walked around the car, monitoring our stop just as they did with everyone up and down pit lane.

Taking a deep breath, I suddenly became aware of just how tired I actually was. Before my mind could fully process the thought, however, I felt the car come back down from the air jacks, which meant the tire change was complete. Just waiting on fuel before...

Feeling the large fuel nozzle being removed from the car, Jason came alive shortly thereafter.

"Go! Go! Go!"

It was a clean stop and one that our boys should be proud of. Once I'd cleared the pit stall and was on my way down the long pit lane, I made sure they knew.

"Good job, fellas! Thanks for busting your asses all day."

Just before beginning the left turn that would take me out of pit lane, I glanced up in my mirrors to see a blue Porsche ducking into the line of cars behind me. The voice of Grandad was suddenly in my head once again.

"Head down, eyes forward!"

I led the pack of cars off the pit lane exit road and reentered the track to begin what would be my final stint of the race.

For the next several laps, everything was progressing well. I was maintaining the lead while also minding the gap to the car behind. I was amazed at how well the McLaren felt once it broke into clean air with no one in front of me.

In an instant, however, a call on the radio from Jason seemed to change everything.

"Chad, we're running the numbers, and it looks like we will need to stop again before the end of the race. We're gonna be a bit short on fuel."

Shit.

I wanted to be mad. Hell, I wanted to be furious. I was reminded, however, that if *we* were in this boat, that meant every other GTD driver who'd just pitted would be in this scenario as well. Words and anger wouldn't change that, so there really was no point in arguing about it.

"Copy that," I replied. "Is there any way I can make it without stopping?"

As I raced out of the bus stop, Jason finally replied.

"We're either gonna need a full course caution or an act of God."

That was it, then. If we ended up pitting and just one of the cars behind us didn't, we'd lose. If I laid off the throttle to save full, I could potentially save enough fuel to finish, but then the question would be: *Will I lose too much ground?*

Just then, I noticed Ganesh's blue Porsche make a wild pass up the inside as we crossed the line and braked for Turn 1. He was on the move again. He wanted nothing more than to take this lead from me.

So I did something potentially foolish. Something I hoped I wouldn't come to regret later on, and something I hoped I wouldn't be ridiculed for the rest of my life over.

Ganesh wanted the lead...

...so I gave it to him.

47

Elbows Out

It was a daring dive from as far back as he was while entering Turn 1. For Ganesh, however, it was time to get aggressive. This was it; the final stint in the twenty-four-hour race.

Ganesh had steadily climbed the ranks and now had Watson—and the lead of the race—in his sights.

With each passing moment, he was getting closer and closer to the McLaren. As the speed of Ganesh's Porsche began to increase, so too did his heartbeat as his adversary didn't even bother moving to defend. Braking for the bus stop, Ganesh tipped his Porsche into the corner and got back on the power to...

...watch Chad Watson's car lose grip?

Just like that, Chad Watson—the little golden boy that he was—seemed to make a critical mistake and got loose while coming out of the bus stop. Nearly sending his own car into the wall, he was fortunate to be able to continue on.

Ganesh cleared Watson with ease as he fixed his gaze down the track. In doing so, he saw only faster traffic and open road in front of him.

He'd done it.

He'd taken the lead of the 24 Hours of Daytona and was now mere laps away from taking home the win.

He hoped his family back home in India were watching. Racing into

NASCAR 4 and towards the line to lead his first lap of the race, he suddenly realized he'd been lying to himself all along. He *did* care what they thought of him.

"Ganesh."

The call on the radio was expected. His team would undoubtedly be congratulating him for his incredible drive.

"We're short on fuel," said the voice of the team's crew chief. "Expect a quick splash 'n' dash pit stop towards the end."

It had a whiplash effect on Ganesh: expecting to hear one message but hearing another instead.

As such, he was momentarily distracted and missed his braking point for Turn 1. Having to apply an ample amount of countersteer to keep the car on track, the mistake caused Ganesh to run wide and lose a considerable amount of time in the process.

Getting back on the racing line, the glance up into the mirror showed just how much time he had in fact lost.

There he is again; Chad Watson and that orange McLaren.

Given the radio call he'd just received, Ganesh knew he should lay back. There was always the chance he could save enough fuel to get the car home without stopping. But with Chad behind him, Ganesh knew that if he truly wanted to win this race, he wouldn't be able to give an inch. As much as he didn't care to admit it, the actions he'd seen up to this point had proven one thing:

Watson was here to win.

* * *

"What in the bloody hell is he doing?"

Derek couldn't believe his eyes as he watched Chad not only forfeit the lead but also nearly smash the car into the wall on the right side of the oval section while exiting the bus stop. He turned to his longtime rival and saw the same look of bewilderment on his face.

Derek stepped in behind Jason to see the wall of information on the numerous monitors in front of him.

"If he's short on fuel," asked Derek, "why don't we just pit him now, get him the fuel he needs and get him out of the traffic?"

It was a sound strategy, but Jason was quick to dismiss the idea.

"If we pit him now, we may lose the pack and the advantage it brings. Plus, Chad seems to thrive when he has a target to chase after, so I'm comfortable with letting him race."

Rolling his eyes, Derek took his leave and returned to stand beside Nick. Noticing his perplexed look, Derek spoke up.

"What is it?"

Turning towards Derek, Nick spoke softly as he indicated towards the monitor.

"He's up to something."

* * *

The slide coming out of the bus stop was a lot more dramatic than I'd intended it to be.

The ploy seemed to be paying off, however. Although I nearly lost another position in the process, I was now just behind Ganesh, saving fuel by following in his draft. On the NASCAR sections of the track, I could apply about 80 percent throttle and still keep up with him.

I could tell Ganesh knew he was in trouble. He came out of every corner a tad slower than he should have, so I turned the pressure up. I needed him to know I was ready to strike.

Coming out of the Turn 5 Western Horseshoe, I showed my nose as if I were about to pass while heading towards the left turn towards NASCAR 1. Ganesh covered down and kept his speed up through the high bankings and the eventual backstraight.

Making a move again while entering the bus stop, I needed to keep his head on a swivel and make him focus on me. That was the only way this was going to work. We exited the bus stop with my nose seemingly glued to his back bumper as I once again reduced the amount of throttle to save fuel.

This was a huge gamble, and I knew it. As we raced our way out of NASCAR 3 & 4, Jason's voice called out via the radio.

"Ten minutes left, Chad."

His voice suddenly sounded stressed as we crossed the line. Ten minutes left in a twenty-four-hour race, and I was rolling the dice. I thought about telling my plan to Jason, but I didn't think he'd approve.

As we entered *International Horseshoe*, I fed Ganesh a bit of rear bumper as he over-slowed for the corner. Something was different about his behavior, I noticed.

As much of an asshole as he was, he wasn't stupid; not all the time, at least. He had to know he was also short on fuel as his crew would be telling him as much. Ganesh's greatest weakness, however, was pride.

He never yielded, refused to show weakness and never stopped chasing the prize…even if the chase took him off the edge of a cliff.

Now, however, he seemed to be slowing up; probably to save fuel as well. Entering the short shoot towards the dog leg, Ganesh actually moved over to the left side of the track and slowed more.

He was trying to let me by.

"Not this time, asshole."

I stayed with him just as LMP3 traffic was catching up. Working their way through the GTD cars, the prototype drivers were in a fierce battle and were taking no prisoners. Slowing and yielding the racing line, I gave the LMP3 drivers the lane, which afforded them the best momentum through Turn 5. It also allowed me to stay directly behind Ganesh. This continued for the remainder of the lap.

The other GTD cars were playing similar games behind us in an effort to save fuel. Even if they were going to pit, the more fuel they saved now meant less fuel they'd have to put into the car. It was a game of time and every team seemed to have a chip in the game.

As the overall leaders in the GTP class came upon us again, they blitzed past Ganesh and me as we continued our own game of cat and mouse.

The laps dragged on as I continued to pressure Ganesh into maintaining his pace. In the meantime, the rain had decreased even further, from a drizzle to a light mist. The track was still wet, but a dry racing line was beginning to form. As such, I stayed off the line in an effort to keep my tires wet. Once wet weather tires dry out, they fade quickly.

Ganesh—refusing to yield the lead—maintained race pace through the infield.

I knew he was going to pit for fuel. He had to.

As we exited the bus stop, I continued to follow in Ganesh's shadow but when we approached the line, the call I'd been waiting for came over the radio.

"Two laps to go, Chad," commented Jason, his voice sounding more urgent than usual. "We're gonna pit you next time by."

"Is there still not enough to finish without pitting?" I asked.

Jason promptly responded.

"No, we've got enough fuel for one and a half laps and there are two laps left."

Racing towards the start/finish line to begin the penultimate lap of the race, I could already see a few of the GTD cars behind me ducking into the pits. I lifted off the throttle long before the entry into Turn 1, a last-ditch effort to save as much fuel as possible.

A frantic feeling entered my heart.

Am I about to make a mistake? Am I about to cast aside all of the efforts the entire team have put into this race?

Even as I lifted the hand-throttle on my steering early once again as Ganesh and I headed into *International Horseshoe*, the thoughts and memories of all the work leading up to this race surfaced in my mind.

Am I really about to throw it all away?

The faces of all the crew came to my mind. The thought of Reggie and Mama Fuller watching me on TV back home gave me peace but also anxiety.

They would all be watching: friends I'd grown up with, those I knew back in Australia, co-workers and an entire following of younger fans I'd acquired since beginning this adventure. Based on the messages I'd received, some of them saw me as an inspiration; an example of someone who kept going even when the odds were against them.

I could suddenly feel all of their eyes on me at once.

I must've been on autopilot for a few corners as I found myself braking hard for the bus stop and still on Ganesh's back bumper. Ganesh got a slightly better run than me out of the bus stop, but it soon wouldn't matter.

We rounded NASCAR 3, and then came the moment of truth—the moment I'd been waiting for—and truth be told, the moment I'd been dreading.

"Chad, the crew's ready," Jason said over the radio. "Pit this time. Splash and go."

My heart sank. My certainty over my plan was vanishing. As I approached the pit lane, my dad's words suddenly filled my mind. I recalled a journal entry he'd made about his decision to race at Bathurst.

"Sometimes you make a decision that makes sense to you but defies all logic and reason to everyone else," he'd written. *"When that happens, go with your gut."*

As I approached pit lane, I did just that.

Against all knowledge, against all wisdom and bypassing the instruction I'd received from Jason, I took a deep breath and said a silent prayer...as I passed the pit lane entrance and kept going.

Ahead of me on the flag stand, the white flag was waving.

One lap to go...and there was no turning back now.

* * *

"Pit this time, Ganesh. Do you copy?"

Too focused on what was going on in his rearview mirror as he continued to monitor Chad, Ganesh failed to respond to his crew chief, but he got the message. There would be one lap remaining once they crossed the line, and he had to pit to make it to the finish.

Behind him, Chad peeked the headlights of the McLaren in Ganesh's mirrors; just as he'd been doing for the last several laps since his mistake.

Either way, he knew that the win in the GTD class would come down to a battle on the pit road and then a one-lap sprint to the end. Ganesh knew that Chad would be fighting him until the bitter end.

Approaching the pit lane, Ganesh made ready as he turned his Porsche down to make the entrance on the left side of the track. Behind him, however, he saw the McLaren maintain its line and stay out.

"He's going for it."

Whether it was instinct, impulse, pride or arrogance, Ganesh wasn't sure. All he knew was that the entire GTD field behind him had pitted except for Watson...and now Ganesh.

Continuing on, the two took the white flag even as Ganesh's radio lit up with frustration.

"Ganesh! What the hell are you doing?!"

* * *

The sheer amount of expletives that flowed from Derek's mouth was breathtaking.

"That sonofabitch! What in the bloody hell is he doing?" Derek shouted. "He's throwing the whole damn race away!"

Squatting down and grabbing fists full of his hair with his hands, Nick felt a new level of defeat and betrayal as the race was now effectively over. All of the battling, all of the hours in the car...all for nothing.

Jason slumped back in his chair, resigning himself to the inevitable defeat. Turning towards the two other drivers behind him, all that Jason could do was shake his head.

"It's not enough to complete the lap," said Jason, exhaling the words more than actually speaking them. "He's not gonna make it."

Behind Derek and Nick, however, a face that everyone on the team recognized entered the garage.

48

Eyes of the World

The silence I heard over the radio was deafening.

And as Ganesh and I completed Turn 1, I couldn't help but feel like I'd just made a grave mistake.

I wasn't surprised when I noticed Ganesh stay out with me. Now, he was slow, and I stayed in his shadow as we navigated towards *International Horseshoe* for the final time. Feeling a pain in my hands, I became keenly aware of just how tightly I'd been gripping the steering wheel. My breathing was heavy but shallow as a sudden lightheaded feeling seemed to darken the world around me.

In that moment, I found myself praying aloud between shortened breaths. "Please, God. Help me, God."

This is madness. What am I even doing? My own thoughts betrayed me as they showed me potentially going down in history as the greatest fool in the history of motorsport.

I was throwing it all away, ignoring the people I'd come to trust and destroying all of their hard work in the process.

This was quite possibly the last lap of my professional racing career. No team would ever consider working with me again after this.

My eyes suddenly had difficulty focusing on one location for more than a second as they bounced from spot to spot. Reminded of how my dad had a near panic attack while racing in the rain at Bathurst, I realized I was on the verge of one myself.

Inside the car, I was alone, sealed off from the rest of the world. In a few moments' time, however, I knew this seal would be broken, and I would soon be forced to face the very team whose trust I was effectively betraying.

It was only a matter of time before the McLaren ran out of fuel. When it did, any hope of winning this race would sputter out of existence.

* * *

The chaos unfolding all around was a mix of sheer frustration and utter sadness. The eyes of the crew—watching helplessly as their driver disobeyed team orders—were bloodshot from remaining on near high-alert status for a whole twenty-four hours. Now, they witnessed their hard work seemingly washing away with the rain waters as their driver drove off into what would the untimely end to their race.

She stepped past the crew, nodding to a few along the way, and closer to Derek and Nick. Nobody seemed to care that a driver from an opposing team was walking through their garage. As she approached, they both met her eyes, shook their heads in disbelief and turned their attention back to the monitors in front of them. Seated at the center of monitors was a man now slumped over with his face buried in his hands.

She approached, placing a calming hand on his shoulder.

Turning up to see who it was, he recognized her instantly.

"Olivia Calo," said the man she remembered as Jason van der Berg. Slowly sitting up and sliding the headphones he wore off, he held them out towards her. "Any last words to Chad before he's crucified by his own team?"

"Actually," Olivia responded, "yes."

* * *

I had tunnel-vision as the full weight of what I'd done began to press down upon me. As I wheeled the car around *International Horseshoe*, I tried calming myself in an effort to see myself through to the end. If anything, I only succeeded in diving deeper into the anxiety attack I was experiencing.

What happened next, however, startled me as a calm and steady voice came over the radio.

"Chad, give me max fuel save. Lay back. Minus one hundred percent."

Olivia?

"Save as much as you can before you enter the oval section." Her voice was like a light I could follow home.

"Copy," I nervously replied. My voice was shaky and cracked. The weight of the world was on my shoulders, and I felt every overbearing pound of it.

Traversing the Turn 5 *Western Horseshoe* for the last time, Ganesh was still just ahead of me as I gave the car a slight push of throttle before entering the braking zone for Turn 6.

Making the left turn onto NASCAR 1 & 2, I was still in second place, and Ganesh and I entered the banked corners when Olivia came on the radio once again.

"Lay back, Chad. Stay with him, but don't give it one hundred percent."

I nodded my head as if Olivia could see me. Going as slow as I was, I began to wonder when the cars that had pitted behind us would be catching up. My saving grace was that the pit lane at Daytona was incredibly long. From the second they'd entered pit lane and engaged their 55 mph speed limiter, I was getting farther and farther away.

With enough fuel to get them to the end, however, they would be able to go full song on the throttle while I was running on vapor.

I followed Ganesh as we entered the backstraight and headed towards the bus stop, still not giving it full power and keeping the revs lower as I shifted gears early.

My heart sank once again as I noticed a change in Ganesh's car.

Just before reaching the bus stop, his car slowed greatly. So much so that even at my reduced speed, I managed to pass him before the bus stop.

Coasting through, I watched in my mirrors as Ganesh tried to roll his car through the corners in an effort to make it to the finish line, but he was losing momentum. I knew he was out. He was at a near crawl by the time he'd exited the corners.

I cleared the bus stop and had nothing but wide open road ahead of me. Olivia came on the radio once again.

"Now, Chad! Full throttle! Give it everything!"

I didn't waste a moment. I pushed the McLaren flat out through the gears and held the low line around NASCAR 3 & 4 as the car sang one last time.

Seconds later, the revs suddenly stopped their ascent as the engine sputtered.

"Clutch it! Roll it home! You've got this!"

Pulling the clutch lever on my steering wheel, the revs dropped to idle as the car began to coast. The only sound I heard was that of the air passing over and through the car.

I exhaled deeply. There was nothing more I could do. I'd given it my all, had done everything I knew to do and even ruffled a few feathers along the way. Now, with the wide open road in front of me and everyone behind chasing me, all I could do was sputter to the finish.

In the end, wasn't that just like life?

Time seemed to hang for an eternity as I felt the McLaren slowly decelerate. In the rearview mirror, I could no longer see Ganesh. What I could see, however, was an angry pack of GTD cars racing towards me at full speed.

In that moment, the memory of the words spoken to me by a man who'd just ran his last race surfaced in my mind.

These words had been replayed thousands of times throughout my life as I always searched for the deeper meaning in them.

Now, however, the meaning was plainly obvious.

"Always keep fighting and never quit," he'd said to me. "Even when you fall down and even when the odds are stacked against you. Fight to stand back up because you never know where you'll end up if you keep moving forward."

Like taking your first steps after learning to walk again, starting a new life after nearly ending it all or simply crawling to the finish line of the race you find yourself in, you keep moving forward.

It had been his words that inspired me...

...and her light that guided me.

As I approached the finish line, the pack of GTD cars was barreling down upon me at nearly three times the speed I was now doing but with the checkered flag waving in the air, I crossed the line just ahead of them.

I had done it. *We* had done it.

We'd won.

The radio erupted with cheers as the pack of cars behind tore past me. "You did it, Chad! You won!"

I had to wipe my eyes as I felt the sudden urge to scream. In the grandstands, the crowds were on their feet. I could hear their thundering cheers from inside the car.

Rolling the McLaren to a stop, I didn't even have enough fuel to complete the first corner. I stopped the car close to the NASCAR pit lane exit and simply sat for a moment.

I'd just won the biggest race of my life. I should've felt beyond happy and excited for all that the team and I had accomplished.

In that moment, however, I felt sad.

More than anything—more than race cars, more than the Rolex watch I was taking home for the win and more than the feeling of winning a race of this magnitude—I wanted my parents to be here.

I began to unbuckle my belts and swung the door of the McLaren open; the cheers of the crowd now a near-deafening roar. As I stepped out of the car, I leaned heavily upon the frame for balance as I gave my feet a few quick shakes.

Turning towards the crowd, I leaned forward onto the car and extended my right arm into the air in celebration.

"Chad!"

Above the noise of the crowd, I heard her calling my name. Turning around, I noticed our team's golf cart heading towards me carrying every member of the team. Hanging off the sides, sitting on each other's laps and even riding on the front nose of the cart, the team members were already screaming. Through all of them, however, one stood out.

Still wearing her team's racing suit, Olivia smiled widely as she hung off the side of the cart.

Removing my helmet, I placed it on top of the McLaren just as the team reached me. They promptly dismounted from the cart and barreled towards me, screaming.

Surprisingly, the first to reach me was Derek. He lifted me off the ground and screamed.

"You're the most foolish, reckless, inspiring and ballsy driver I've ever met, mate! I can't believe you pulled it off!"

Before I could even respond, the crew had picked me up and lifted me into the air for a moment before, thankfully, setting me back down.

Thanking each and every one of them for their efforts, Nick—the man who'd nearly driven to victory with my dad—stood stoically among the celebrations. Stepping towards me, he extended his arms and grabbed both of my shoulders.

"Your old man would be proud of you, Chad. You stuck with it, ran the course, took the chances and finished your race. As crazy as I think you are, you're a bloody inspiration to me."

I wanted to tell Nick how much just having him around was like having my dad around. It was almost as if a piece of him lived on whenever he would give me advice on racing. I never got the chance, however, as Derek wrapped his arms around both of us.

"Bring it in, boys! We just won Daytona!"

The crew around us erupted as I wrapped my arms around the two drivers. As a spot in the crowd cleared, however, I soon found my ally in the mess of what my whole plan had nearly become.

Olivia stood just behind my team, her smile causing my world to light up even more. As she approached, the crew must've taken note, as a path seemingly cleared before her.

"So how about that drink?" I said.

I heard whistling sounds zip through the air from the crew as Olivia reached me, wrapped her arms around me and planted her lips against mine.

The crowd seemed to erupt once more as I wrapped my arms around her.

This was a moment I truly wanted to live forever...

...and it was a kiss I never wanted to end.

Epilogue

It's an odd feeling to suddenly find yourself somewhere you'd never thought you'd be again. It can cause you to look back and realize that over the course of many years, life and its many happenings had been leading you back there all along. For me, it was where I was right now; standing on the top step of where it all began for my family.

Many long years ago, my grandad William Watson became a legend by taking a win here. This was followed years later by my father who came close to victory but still made a huge impact on not just the sport, but on the lives of those he'd touched along the way.

Now here I was, albeit at a slightly smaller event than the Bathurst 1000.

After receiving an opportunity to make the voyage overseas and race at Mount Panorama, we were all on the next flight out and soon found ourselves taking part in what's known as the Bathurst Motor Festival. Held annually during the Easter weekend, the event attracted well over 10,000 spectators, hundreds of participants and culminated in a race known as the Bathurst 6 Hour.

Sharing the bottle of champagne, Olivia and I celebrated a hard-fought victory after we'd both shared the driving duties during the race. Taking the overall victory, we were now circled by friends whom I considered part of my family. Although they were happy to celebrate the win with us, they'd come not just to watch us race but to congratulate us on another type of victory.

If my heart could smile, it would be doing it now as Olivia and I watched the ever-foreboding figure of Tubbs reach down and pick up the newest Watson to join our team.

"Look at this little fella!" smiled Tubbs.

I stepped forward to see the smile on my son's face.

"Tubbs, meet Miles Watson."

The large man chuckled.

"Miles, huh? Not Kilometers?"

"They don't do metric, Tubbs," said Derek Renshaw, who stood alongside his partner, Lola. She smiled as she leaned into Derek. "They still speak in cheeseburger over in the States."

"Well, he was a handful during your race so I think you'll have a chatty one for sure." It had been nearly two decades since I'd last seen her. Now married with two kids of her own, Abby and her husband were more than happy to take on a third child, albeit temporarily, while Olivia and I ran our race.

"We could hear the little fella over the cars!" added Tubbs. "Maybe he's got a future in the opera house."

"I think it runs in the family." Reggie still looked a bit jet-lagged from the long flight, but it hadn't dulled his wits or his snappy comebacks one bit. "Have you ever heard Chad sing? This guy used to belt it out on the way to work every morning. The notes he used while singing were...numerous."

Our small group erupted in laughter.

"Well, I hope little Miles here gets his looks from his mum," continued Tubbs. "No offense to present company, of course."

I shook my head.

"None taken, Tubbs."

Seeing the people who had essentially become my family over the years all together again here at Bathurst made my life feel whole. Hearing them banter brought a smile to my face, which made me happy to be alive.

Having Olivia beside me as I wrapped my arm around her made me feel complete.

"So, how's it feel, mate?" asked Nick Lathan, who stood alongside his sister, Abby. "You're both Bathurst winners now."

I let the question hang for a moment.

"I've gotta say, it feels pretty damn good."

"Yeah, but you need to aim bigger, Watson," blurted out Derek. "You wanna make some waves? Go for the Bathurst triple crown. Take wins in the 6 Hour, the 12 Hour and the 1000, and you'll be a living legend. Only a few people have ever done it, mate. After your win today, you're already a third of the way there!"

"Plus," added Nick, "you've already got the makings of a small racing team between the three of you."

At that, Olivia and I turned to look at each other in unison.

"Well," said Olivia, "it won't be just us three for very much longer."

As Olivia placed her hand over her stomach, our group erupted in cheers as drivers and bystanders who were milling around stopped to look.

"We just found out this morning," added Olivia. "Let's just say this will be my last race for a while."

"Congrats you two!" cheered Abby.

"Damn, son," replied Reggie, slightly chuckling under his breath. "You're not wasting *any* time."

"You're gonna have to win a few more big races if you keep popping out fresh mouths to feed," added Derek.

"Speaking of food," I added, more so to change the subject. "Who's hungry?"

Tubbs was the first to speak up.

"I'm bloody hungry."

"You're always hungry, Tubbs," added Nick.

"C'mon, let's go celebrate and then we'll head up the mountain for a view," replied Abby. "The sunsets around this time of the year are gorgeous."

* * *

Orange and pink hues filled the evening sky and caused the various clouds to look like the paint strokes of a master. It was a breathtaking view as all of us traversed the circuit on foot, which was little more than a public road when not used as a racetrack.

Reaching the top of Skyline, the surrounding scenery ingrained itself into my mind as I had a feeling of connection to what I considered sacred grounds. Standing on the same track that my grandfather, my dad and now I had raced at, I knew that Mount Panorama would always hold a special place in my heart.

Our family's legacy was born here. Perhaps it would continue on in the future.

As the group of us walked along the surface of the track, I stopped for a moment with Miles. He was awestruck at the display of colors that filled the sky. Breathing in deeply, I allowed a moment to think back on the events that had led me here.

In the years following my initial win at Daytona, Olivia and I continued to develop our relationship, but as I grew older, I hesitated to make any sort of commitment. Before doing so, I needed to make sure I was clear of a certain predisposed medical condition, the very condition that had claimed the lives of both my dad and grandmother.

After a long but successful treatment, I was eventually given the *all clear* from the doctors.

The day after being discharged from the hospital, I proposed to Olivia.

Even after marriage, we continued to race together, taking several wins and many more podiums across the world.

After the birth of our son Miles, however, I was given a shocking surprise by my dad's old business partner, Pat Henderson.

He revealed he was the trustee of a large sum of money my parents had set aside for me. Once I came of age, that sum was released to me. Additionally, I was also given possession of a very special 1968 Ford Mustang that had once belonged to my grandad.

I had taken many turns over the now twenty-nine years of my life. Some of them were the correct turns to take, while others were not. Even so, the various turns and roads I'd traveled on had connected and ultimately became the path that led me to this very point. It was a keen reminder that even when things seem like they're at their worst, there's always more road to travel on so long as we refuse to give up.

A few murmurs from Miles caused me to reach down and pick him up as I leaned up against the wall on the left side of the track.

"Chad," said Olivia as the others stopped to turn. "You coming?"

"You go on ahead," I replied. "I'll catch up."

Olivia smiled at me as she and the others turned and continued their trek across the mountain.

For a moment, it was just my son and me as the voices of the others eventually faded into the distance. Miles, still focusing his attention on the display of colors in the evening sky, was quiet as the two of us soaked in the moment.

"This is where it all began for us, Miles," I said softly to him. Miles looked up at me as I spoke. Turning him to face me, I continued.

"You know, my dad—your grandad—would be so happy to see this. I like to think that by simply being here, it somehow brings us closer to him. Your grandma would probably be telling me this is past your bedtime, but we'll make an exception this one time." I sighed as a few of the now distant memories I had with my dad at this track surfaced in my mind.

"One day," I added, "I'll tell you all about your grandad. Trust me when I tell you that you won't find these stories anywhere else."

Turning slightly, I pointed towards an area just down the grassy hill towards pit lane.

"Just down this hill is where my dad told me something that I'll never forget. Miles, whether you decide to get into racing or not, just remember to *always keep fighting and never quit*," I said, echoing the words of my father. "*Even when you fall down and even when the odds are stacked against you. Fight to stand back up. You never know where you'll end up if you keep moving forward.*"

Looking out towards the setting sun, I held Miles close to me.

"There's a long road ahead, Miles. What do you say we go and see what the world has in store for us."

Placing Miles back into his stroller, I grabbed the rear handles, and together we continued our trek around the circuit.

"C'mon, son," I said. "I'll race ya."

END OF BOOK TWO

About the Author

Paul Slavonik is an American author and award-winning filmmaker who has written for such publications as Motorsport.com, RACER.com and iRacing. A former U.S. Army combat photographer and video production specialist, Paul has a Bachelor's degree in Audio Production from Full Sail University and currently resides in Texas with his wife, Christina, and their three cats.

If you've enjoyed reading *Though I Fall*, please consider leaving the book an honest review on Amazon. Your contribution and feedback would be greatly appreciated.

Follow Paul on social media for the latest news on the *Legacy Drive* series and his other writing endeavors!

You can connect with me on:
- https://www.dmgunited.net
- https://www.facebook.com/PSlavonik
- https://www.youtube.com/c/PaulSlavonik
- https://www.instagram.com/paul_slavonik

Subscribe to my newsletter:

✉ https://www.tinyurl.com/pslavonikbooks

Also by Paul Slavonik

Legacy Drive: A Motorsport Story (Book 1)
Mount Panorama in Bathurst, Australia was the track that made his father a legend. Now, Bill Watson must overcome more than just his own fears as he and his family face adversity and sudden loss. A tale of rising again and again, this multi-generational story of heroism, love and loss takes readers on an edge of your seat journey into the world of auto racing, the family we meet along the way and the trials we must navigate…all while racing at 200mph.

Made in United States
Orlando, FL
24 October 2024

53060478R00255